JULIE C

WHERE THE TRUTH LIES

First published in Great Britain in 2010 by Hodder & Stoughton
An Hachette UK company

First published in paperback in 2011

3

A CIP catalogue record for this title is available from the British Library.

ISBN 978 0 340 91893 7

Typeset in Plantin Light by Palimpsest Book Production Limited,
Falkirk, Stirlingshire

Printed and bound by Clays Ltd, St Ives plc

Hodder & Stoughton policy is to use
recyclable products
and

Prologue

I didn't see it coming.

No black cats crossed my path. No clear-eyed crows cawed alarm from the trees. There was nothing to warn me about what was up ahead.

An invisible clock was ticking, each beat drawing my family closer to danger and I was oblivious. Busy with the normal, everyday things that make up a life, I didn't know about the threats or the blackmail, or about the brutal turn our lives were about to take. I didn't know that someone close to me was on course to devastate my family. I thought my home was a safe place, that danger kept its distance.

I thought wrong.

I

It's the first of June, Bea's fourth birthday. The party's over and the other mums have arrived to collect their children. I move between the kitchen and the back garden, handing juice to children, tea or coffee to mums, catching snippets of conversations and adding a sentence or two myself before going back inside. My stepmother, Wendy, is tidying up the remnants of wrapping and streamers that lie across the kitchen floor, squashing them into the recycling bin. I start to clear the table: plates of half-eaten sausage rolls and sandwiches; over a dozen pudding bowls, most of them scraped clean of chocolate ice cream and tangerine jelly.

'I can't believe she's four already,' Wendy says, as she arranges Bea's cards in front of the plates on the Welsh dresser. 'It seems like only yesterday she was learning to walk.'

'I know.' I look through the big picture window to where Bea and another child are hanging on to my husband, Julian, one on each arm. He's twirling them round. I lean my head against the window frame and smile, then laugh out loud as they drag him to the ground and start to pummel him with their small but persistent fists. They stop when he pretends to cry. Bea crouches beside him, trying to soothe, patting his hair until he jumps up and chases her and she screams with a kind of terrified ecstasy. When he catches her, he throws her up in the air and tickles her until her face is almost puce.

'It's such a pity Lisa can't be here,' Wendy continues, coming to stand beside me. 'Her scan results will be out tomorrow, won't they?'

I nod.

'Oh, Claire, I do hope it's good news.' She gives a small sigh. 'It would be lovely to see her well again.'

My heart squeezes. The last round of chemotherapy has left Lisa weak, emptied out, drained of almost everything that makes her my sister, and we're all praying it's been worth it.

'When I visit her tomorrow, I'll show her the party photos,' I say, putting my arm round Wendy's shoulder. 'And I'll take her some of the lovely birthday cake you made.'

'Give her a hug from me,' Wendy says, moving to one side as my friend Jem comes in from the garden, her arms loaded with a couple of discarded sweaters, a miniature cricket set and two Frisbees.

'Julian's going beyond the call of duty out there,' she says, dumping all the stuff on the table. 'They're running him ragged.'

'He's enjoying it,' I say, looking at my watch. 'He has to leave for Sofia in an hour. He can nap on the plane.'

'What's he going there for, then?' Jem asks.

'It's the case he's working on. He needs to double-check some details with the Bulgarian police.'

'He's prosecuting Pavel Georgiev,' Wendy says. 'You'll have heard of him, Jem. There's been a lot about him in the papers.'

'Yeah, I have.' Jem looks from Wendy to me. 'I didn't realise he was working on *that* case.'

'It's really very serious,' Wendy says, her voice hushed. 'Georgiev and the men who work for him . . .' She shakes her head at both of us. 'Shocking stuff. It's hard to believe that people can be so evil.'

'And that's not the half of it,' I say. 'There's a lot the press can't print because it could prejudice the trial.' I think of some of the things Julian has told me, details I've avoided discussing with friends and family: young girls trafficked and used for sex, men tortured and then killed because they refused to hand over a percentage of their earnings. I shiver. 'I'll be glad when the trial's over and he's locked up for good.'

Jem gives me a quick hug. 'You'll want some family time before Julian leaves.' She tilts her head in the direction of the garden. 'I'll get the ball rolling on the goodbyes.'

As good as her word, one mother and child after another come inside. A dozen children's voices fill the hallway. Shoes and sweaters are found, goodbyes are said, and Bea hands each of her friends a party bag. She takes this very seriously, peering into each bag before handing it over. 'That one's for you, Adam,' she says. 'It has the red water pistol.' She looks up at me. 'He likes water pistols.'

'OK, sweetheart.' I stroke my hand across her forehead, bringing wispy blonde hair away from her eyes and tucking it back under her Alice band. She's wearing a white party dress with a turquoise ribbon round the bodice. It exactly matches the colour of her eyes, still turned up towards mine.

'I'm four.' She touches the badges pinned to her chest, each one shouting out the same number.

'You are.' I kiss her pink cheeks. 'But you'll always be my baby.'

'I'm not a baby, Mummy!' She stares at me earnestly. 'I'm four now.'

'Well, still, you'll always be my precious baby girl.' I tickle her middle. 'That's just the way it is.'

The corners of her mouth twitch in a smile and then she hands out the next party bag. It's been a long day and I expected her to be over-wound by now, but she's taking all the attention in her stride. It makes me feel very proud of her and I can't help but give her another hug.

The front door opens and closes countless times, the late-afternoon sunshine warming the black-and-white chequered floor tiles in the porch. Almost everyone is gone when I leave Bea at the door with Wendy and find one of the mums a spare T-shirt for her daughter, Jessica, who has spilled juice down the front of hers. We talk in Bea's room for a few minutes, about nursery and about the ubiquitous road works that have sprung up at the end of the crescent, and by the time we get back downstairs, Bea has left her post and the last remaining party bag is lying on the floor. Thinking nothing of it, I give the bag to Jessica and say goodbye to them both with a promise to arrange a play date soon.

I walk back along the hallway to the kitchen and find Julian taking a glass from the shelf.

'That went well.' I cuddle into his back. 'Thank you for being chief entertainer. When the clown didn't turn up, I thought we were going to be in for trouble.'

He holds the glass under the running cold tap until it's full to the brim. 'Couldn't have done it without Charlie.'

'You're right. It's great having him home.' I look outside into the garden but can't see our elder son, Charlie, or his girlfriend, Amy. Wendy is the only one there, righting chairs and picking stray sweet papers off the grass. 'Being away at university has helped him grow up.'

'It has.' He swallows down the water, wipes the back of his hand across his mouth and then stretches out his spine. 'I'm getting too old for children's parties.'

'Fifty is the new forty, you know.'

'Tell that to my knees.' He collapses down on to a chair and eases off his shoes.

'There's grass all over you.' I brush it off his upper back, then let my hands slide round his neck and rest my elbows on his shoulders. I put my mouth next to his ear. 'Do you really have to go to Sofia today?'

'I do.' He pulls me round on to his lap. 'I have a meeting early tomorrow.'

'It's been so nice having you home on a weekday.' I rest my head close to his neck. 'I hope the trial's over before the summer ends. We could go to Dorset, take Lisa with us and have a family holiday, all of us together.'

I feel his body tense ever so slightly.

'We're not going to get a holiday?' I say.

He doesn't answer me. I sit back so that I can see his expression.

Almost twenty-five years of looking at his face and I've yet to
grow tired of it. He has good bone structure: high cheekbones
and a straight nose. His mouth is wide and made for smiling.
His eyes are the colour of rich mahogany; his hair is jet black
and curly with a smattering of grey at his temples. Not for the
first time I think that he's far too handsome to be a barrister.
But today the way he's looking at me, staring in fact, is puzzling.

'Are you OK?' I say.

The phone rings, high-pitched and intrusive. I reach behind
Julian and take it from its cradle on the dresser.

'Hi, Mum. It's me.'

'Jack!' I automatically smile at the sound of my younger son's
voice. 'Bea's had a great party. She loved the present you sent.
How's the revision going?' Jack is at boarding school and in the
throes of his GCSEs. 'You prepared for the last couple?'

'Getting there.'

In the background, I hear a voice shouting his name.

'I just called to wish Bea a happy birthday,' he says.

'OK. I'll pass you over to Dad while I find her.' Julian takes
the phone from me and I go to the bottom of the stairs. 'Bea!' I
call. 'Jack's on the phone.'

No answer. There's no way she'd want to miss out on a call
from him. Although separated in age from Jack and Charlie by
twelve and fifteen years, Bea loves both her brothers with a blind,
full-on passion. She must be listening to a story tape or else all
the excitement of the day has caught up with her and she's fallen
asleep somewhere.

I have a quick look in the sitting room – empty – then climb
the stairs to her bedroom, calling her name as I go. I push open
the door, but she isn't in there either. I check the master bedroom
– it wouldn't be the first time she's decided to raid my make-up
or try on my shoes. I go into our en suite bathroom. I even open
my wardrobe, but there's no sign of her.

The shower is running in the family bathroom and I can hear
Charlie singing quietly. Our house is on four floors and I go

quickly up to the top floor, where we have two spare rooms. I don't expect to find her here and I don't. Both rooms have an unlived-in feel.

'Jack's on the phone!' I call, going down the stairs again. 'Bea, if you're hiding, you have to come out now.'

I go all the way down to the basement level, where there's the utility room, Julian's study and Jack's bedroom. There's nobody here. The utility room leads straight out on to the garden at the back and I shout to Wendy, 'Bea's not out there with you, is she?'

'No. I last saw her in the sitting room.'

I climb the stairs again and am almost back in the kitchen when I remember. 'Wait!' I'm speaking to myself. I raise both my palms in the air in front of me, then turn back along the hallway, my sandals drumming a hectic beat on the tiles. Bea has a den under the stairs. She keeps her soft toys and a pile of cushions carefully arranged for optimum comfort. She can often be found there, playing with her animals or simply lying with her thumb in her mouth and a faraway look in her eyes. I pull aside the curtain that conceals the space. She isn't there. I take a deep breath, feel it catch in my throat. With all the comings and goings today she could easily have slipped out through the front door. Perhaps she followed one of her friends. But why would she do that? It's more likely that she's playing somewhere in the house, somewhere I haven't thought of.

I go back to the kitchen. 'I can't find her,' I say, fully expecting Julian to smile and remind me of some obvious place that I've forgotten to look.

He doesn't. His eyes hold mine for a split second and then he's out of his seat so quickly that I lurch back against the work surface. He slides his feet into his shoes and speaks curtly into the phone. 'Jack, we'll call you back.' He puts the handset on the table and looks at me. 'What do you mean you can't find her?'

'I've called her, but she isn't answering. I think I've looked everywhere.'

'She couldn't have gone off with one of the mothers?'

'No, of course not.' I shake my head. 'Nobody would take her without asking.' I look around helplessly. 'She must be in the house somewhere.'

He moves past me and goes to the stairs. 'Bea!' He calls her name several times, both up and down the stairwell, his voice so loud it's almost a roar.

'Julian!' The volume of sound is making me jump. 'That will frighten her.'

He ignores me and, taking the stairs two at a time, goes up to the first floor. 'Charlie!' He bangs on the bathroom door.

Charlie, looking bewildered, comes out into the landing, a towel round his waist and another in his right hand which he's using to rub his hair. 'What?'

'Have you seen Bea?'

'Amy's taken her to the park. Didn't she tell you?'

'No.'

'There we are, then.' I allow my shoulders to relax down from my ears. 'Whew! Panic over.'

But Julian isn't reassured. He goes into our bedroom, looking through the front window. We live in a terrace of white town-houses in a crescent in Brighton. The road curves round a grassy play area with three swings, a slide and a chunky wooden climbing frame. I follow Julian's eyes and see at once that Bea isn't there. The park is empty apart from Jem, who's pushing her son, Adam, on the swing. Without looking at me, Julian goes down the stairs again. I follow him.

'Julian?'

He's not listening. He's out the front door and crossing the road. He shouts to Jem, 'Have you seen Bea?'

She shakes her head and Julian starts to pace in front of the iron railings. I try to catch his arm, but he doesn't even register I'm there. His expression is strained, his pallor strangely grey considering the speed of his breathing and the heat of the after-noon sun. But worst of all is the frantic look in his eyes, as his gaze trawls from one end of the street to the other. I reach for

his arm again, but still he isn't seeing me, his attention gripped
by whatever has sparked his panic. This behaviour is so shocking,
so un-Julian-like that I'm stunned. It's as if I've woken up in a
parallel world where the sky is down and the ground is up. My
head fills with a heavy, stifling blackness and then a succession
of flashing lights blind me. I hold on to the railing next to me
and try to breathe. Blood booms against my eardrums with a
forced, almost manic intensity. And behind all of this, I have only
one coherent thought – for some inexplicable reason, Julian thinks
Bea is in danger.

As soon as my vision clears, I grab on to his shirt. 'Julian!' I
jerk him towards me. 'What's going on?'

His eyes when they finally look into mine are flooded with
apprehension and I flinch, draw back. 'What's the matter with
you?' I say. 'Why are you reacting like this?'

'Where are they?' His eyes scan the street again.

'I don't know, but surely . . .' I take a deep breath. 'Surely you
don't think Amy's going to harm Bea?'

'I don't know, Claire.' His lips, his face, his whole body is held
still, tight with tension. 'But think about it. What do we actually
know about this girl?'

'Well . . .' I pause. 'She's studying biological sciences. Charlie's
been going out with her for about nine months. Her parents used
to live in Manchester but now they live in Cyprus. She is—'

'Mostly unknown to us,' Julian says. Then he holds my shoulders and shakes me, not roughly, but enough to make my aching
head feel an increase in pressure. 'Where else could she have
taken her?'

'The corner shop. But—' He's gone before I can finish the
sentence. 'Bea normally only goes there with one of the boys,' I
say quietly to myself. The truth is that Bea isn't particularly fond
of Amy and has told me several times that she likes it better when
Charlie comes home on his own. I can't say that I've warmed to
Amy either, but not because she monopolises Charlie, more
because of her manner. She is abrasive, direct to the point of

being rude. Charlie told me this is one of the reasons he's attracted to her – she tells it like it is, unlike most of the girls his age, who say one thing and mean another.

I put my hands to my cheeks, close my eyes and allow myself to visualise Bea's face. If she were in danger, I would know. How could I not? She is my child. I spend most of every day with her and often the night too, when she climbs into our bed. Though no longer joined by a physical umbilical cord, there is an invisible rope that's just as strong, just as vital, that binds us together. I have a sixth sense for her well-being. I know her likes and dislikes. I anticipate her needs. I tell myself again, if she were in danger, I would know. Whatever is going on here, I think it has more to do with Julian's state of mind than it does with Amy's.

I open my eyes and search the pavement for signs of Amy and Bea but see only a couple of people walking purposefully in the direction of the main road.

'What's happening, Mum?' Charlie comes down the steps behind me. He's wearing shorts and flip-flops and a worried expression.

'Dad's . . . concerned,' I say, almost baulking over the under-statement. 'They aren't in the park and . . .' I shrug. 'Can you think of anywhere Amy might have taken Bea?'

'I dunno.' He shakes his head. 'But she'll be OK. Why's Dad panicking like this?'

I follow Charlie's gaze to the end of the street. Julian has come out of the corner shop and is running towards us. And he's running quickly. I don't remember ever seeing him move with such urgency.

'Your dad has been tense recently . . . what with the trial and everything.' I hear my voice saying this and I believe it, because it's the only explanation that makes sense. Before a trial begins, Julian is unusually preoccupied, his mind packed full of evidence and witness statements and arguments for the prosecution. This is the most high-profile case he has ever been involved in and it's a career-maker. He's bound to be more on edge than normal. I understand this. I was a lawyer myself; I know how pressured the job becomes. What's more, twice in the last fifteen years Julian has been involved in trying to bring Georgiev to justice and both times the case fell apart because of problems with witnesses – one mysteriously disappeared, and another retracted his statement at the eleventh hour. This time, though, the main witness is being protected by the Witness Anonymity Act and this is the best shot that Julian and his team at the Crown Prosecution Service will ever have at convicting Georgiev.

'The corner shop's empty and the girl serving hasn't seen them.' He stops in front of us, his hand reaching into his back pocket. 'I'm going to call the police.'

'Dad! What the hell?'

'Julian, shouldn't we wait a bit?' I hold on to his arm. 'She'll be fine.'

The look he gives me makes my stomach shrivel.

'I'll call Amy and find out where they are,' Charlie says.

'Good idea,' I nod.

'Quickly, then,' Julian says.

'Yeah. OK.' Charlie takes his mobile out of his pocket and presses two buttons. 'Chill.'

Seconds tick by.

'She's not answering?' Julian asks.

'Give her a chance.'

More seconds and Julian loses patience. He takes his own phone from his pocket. I watch his fingers move over the buttons.

'Look! Look!' Charlie shakes his father's arm. 'They're coming.'

He's right. Amy, Bea and Mary Percival, Bea's nursery teacher, are walking along the pavement towards us. Bea is skipping between the two women, holding on to their hands. Relief surges through me like a wave, washing me clean of the confusion of the last few minutes. I watch Julian walk towards them and swing Bea up into his arms. He says something to Amy. She gives a careless shrug and he turns away. My eyes meet his as he climbs the stairs. He looks as if he's been put through a wringer.

Amy is tall for a girl, around five feet nine, and has a loose-hipped walk, accentuated by the way she dresses: floaty skirts with leggings underneath and short, tight tops that force her larger than average breasts to spill out over the top. When she's within earshot, she shouts to me, 'What's with Julian?'

'He was worried. We didn't know where Bea was.'

'She asked me to take her out. She saw her teacher through the window.'

'It's my fault,' Miss Percival pipes up.

'It's OK.' I half smile at them both. 'But next time, Amy, if you could just tell me before you take her ou—'

'I did.' Her brow furrows with indignation. 'I called up the stairs. You were there with another mother.'

'I'm sorry – I didn't hear you.'

She gives another careless shrug. 'I thought you had.'

'Nothing happened, Mum,' Charlie says, his arms protectively encircling Amy's shoulders. Not that she needs it. She is, as ever, sure of her own ground. 'Dad seriously over-reacted.'

'Perhaps he did, Charlie,' I say, keeping my tone even, 'but nevertheless, next time' – I look at Amy – 'you need to make sure I've heard you before you go off with Bea.'

'There doesn't have to be a next time,' Amy says, making wide eyes at me, her head shaking from side to side. 'I was only trying to be helpful.'

I stop short of apologising again. Instead I hold my tongue very firmly between my teeth. Amy spends most of the university holidays and at least one night a week during term-time living in our home and eating our food. Not that I grudge her this. Nor do I expect any great thanks for it. But her persistent I'm-right-and-you're-wrong attitude grates on my nerves.

However, whether we like it or not, she's Charlie's girlfriend and I can already see that the incident is dividing his loyalties. He gives me an imploring look over her shoulder while drawing her still closer into his chest. I manage a smile and he smiles back, then leads Amy up the stairs and they both return indoors. I'm left with Miss Percival.

'All's well that ends' – she sees my face and hesitates – 'well.'

'Yes.' I take a deep breath. 'I suppose that's true, but you can imagine . . . It was alarming to find that Bea had disappeared from the house.'

'I completely understand,' she says, taking my hand, then dropping it almost at once as if shocked by her own temerity. Not much more than five feet tall, her brown hair is cut short, and she has unremarkable grey-blue eyes. She comes across as someone who is more comfortable with children than adults, and is usually either shy or overly formal when talking to me. But with the children she relaxes into another part of herself and is clearly great fun. Bea absolutely adores her, and I've no doubt that when she saw her through the window, she wanted to run outside and say hello.

'Bea just loves coming to nursery,' I say. 'She's very fond of you.'

'Well . . .' She blushes. 'She's a lovely little girl. She brings so much enthusiasm to the class. That's why we were at the end of the street – she wanted to show me where the men are building the new crossing. We've been talking about road safety at circle time.'

'I see.'

'I'm sorry to have caused you concern.' She blushes again. 'It's the last thing I would want to do.'

A taxi pulls up alongside us and the driver winds down his window. 'Taxi for Julian Miller.'

'He's inside,' I say. 'I'll tell him you're here.'

Miss Percival smiles her goodbye and I go indoors. Julian is on the phone in the kitchen.

'The taxi's here,' I tell him.

He holds up a hand. I tap my watch and give him a signific-ant look. I know that he's cutting it fine. He smiles distractedly and turns away from me, still talking into the phone, the fingers of his free hand drumming an impatient rhythm on the table. I can't hear what he's saying and I have no idea to whom he's talking. His suitcase, already packed, is in his study and I go downstairs to fetch it.

From here I see that Bea is in the garden with Wendy. They are looking down into the vegetable patch where spinach and rocket are growing like weeds.

'I get my water can, Grandma,' I hear Bea say, and she runs off towards the shed. She's still wearing her party dress but has swapped her sandals for her favourite *Finding Nemo* Wellington boots.

As I watch her, my heart expands with two distinct feelings: the first, a sweet relief that she's safe and happy; the second, a bitter rush of horror at the thought that she could have been missing for real and we could now be living every parent's worst nightmare.

The taxi beeps its horn from the front of the house and that sets me in motion again. I go upstairs with Julian's suitcase and leave it in the hall. Outside, I find the driver on the pavement, leaning against the side of the car. 'I'm sorry – could you wait just another minute or two? My husband's on the phone.'

He gives me a resigned look and lights up a cigarette as I return indoors.

Julian is coming along the hallway from the kitchen and I turn to meet him. 'Julian.' Suddenly I feel overwhelmed and throw my arms around him. He hugs me to him and I breathe in his smell, feel the familiar weight and tilt of his body as it leans in to mine. 'That was a bit scary, wasn't it?'

He nods. 'Claire, I—'

'I know neither of us particularly likes Amy,' I whisper, 'but—'

'I over-reacted.' He kisses me, makes it last, like he has all the time in the world. 'I'm sorry.'

'It's OK.' I rub his cheek. 'I know the trial is looming and that makes for a stressful time.'

He looks away, but not quickly enough and I see a dark shadow move across his face.

My spine straightens and I take a step back. 'What was that?' I say.

'What?'

'That look on your face.'

'What look?' He throws out his arms and smiles at me, innocence personified, but I'm not convinced.

'Julian?' I move in close again. 'Everything's all right, isn't it?'

'Listen—' His attention strays towards the front door as the driver sounds his horn again. 'I'll be back in no time.' He lifts his suitcase off the floor. 'I have my BlackBerry with me, but in case the signal is poor, I've left contact numbers on the pinboard.' He runs his hands up and then down my back. 'I love you, you know.'

'I know.' I hold his eyes for a moment, warmed by the sincerity in them, and then I let him go.

I stand on the step and watch him climb into the taxi. He waves and I do too. I watch the taxi drive away. I stay there until it turns on to the main road and disappears from sight.

2

I'm still standing on the step when Jem walks across from the park and shouts, 'Everything OK?'

'Yes.' I realise I'm holding my breath and I exhale with a loud sigh. 'Just a bit of a mix-up with Amy and Bea.'

'Oh . . . OK.' She looks at me uncertainly. 'Is Friday fine for me to finish off the room?'

My mind is still with Julian and for a moment I'm not sure what she's talking about.

'For Lisa,' she reminds me, taking Adam's hand before he steps out into the road. 'One last coat and we're there.'

'Of course. Sorry.' I shake my head. 'It's been a long day.' Jem is more than just a good friend. She runs her own painting and decorating business and has been helping me fix up a room for my sister, who's going to move in with us. 'Friday's ideal. Lisa should be coming out of hospital on Saturday.'

'How's she doing?'

'She's finished her second round of chemotherapy. We'll find out tomorrow whether it's done any good.'

'It's a cruel disease. Robbed me of my mum and dad just six months apart.' She gives my upper arm a squeeze. 'Fingers crossed it's good news. I know how close you two are.'

'I'm hoping the cancer will all be gone.' I lean against the railing and fold my arms. 'You read about these things in the papers, don't you? People who were given two months to live and five years later they're still going strong.'

'How's Wendy coping?'

'She's like me. Hoping for good news.'

'Look, Mum!' Adam has been climbing the railing and has managed to trap his feet in the spaces at the top where the horizontal and vertical bars meet. He is hanging upside down, swinging one arm and holding his T-shirt away from his face with the other. 'I'm a monkey.'

We both laugh. Then Jem extracts him from the bars and turns him upright again. 'Better get him home before he starts climbing the walls.' She sets off along the pavement, shouting back, 'See you Friday.'

'See you then.'

Back inside, Wendy is getting ready to leave. 'Bea's making a good job of the vegetable patch out there,' she says, gathering up her bag and nodding her head towards the window.

I glance out into the garden, where Bea is heaving the big rake backwards across a long strip of soil. She sees me watching her and waves up at me. I wave back and blow her a kiss. She pretends to try to catch it, reaching up so high that she falls backwards in a giggling heap.

'What was happening with you and Julian earlier?' Wendy says. 'I caught the tail end of Amy saying something to Charlie about neither of you trusting her.'

I explain about Amy taking Bea to the end of the street. 'She said she called up the stairs to me and she probably did, but I didn't hear her and—' I lower my voice. 'In all honesty, I haven't warmed to her. I know Charlie is bowled over by her, but' – I force some carrier bags into the bottom drawer, then push it shut with my foot – 'she's not the easiest girl to like.'

'I've always found her a little off.'

'With any luck Charlie will get a new girlfriend soon.'

'I wouldn't bank on that,' Wendy says. And then, 'She made quite a play for him, didn't she?'

'She did. He couldn't believe that a third-year with as many friends as she has would be interested in him.'

'She comes in a package that's hard to resist.'

'She has sex appeal and she isn't afraid to use it?' I say.

Wendy gives me a knowing look.

'You're absolutely right.' I sigh. 'Step into the body of a nineteen-year-old boy and she's practically irresistible.' I give Wendy a kiss on the cheek. 'Thank you for all your help today.'

'Always welcome. You know that.'

Next morning I wake up late. Without Julian in bed beside me, it took longer than usual for me to fall to sleep. I lay for hours mulling over the day. Bea's party was a success, but Julian's reaction afterwards cast a shadow over it. He must be under more stress than I thought. I wonder whether the evidence isn't stacking up quite as he'd hoped. The defence may well have thrown a spanner in the works, but what with Bea's party and everything that's been going on with Lisa, he can't have had a chance to tell me yet.

Lisa. I swing my legs over the edge of the bed and silently pray that her last chemotherapy treatment hasn't been for nothing. She is such an intrinsic part of my life, of the whole family's lives, and to have her well again would be the best news we could have.

I spend a few minutes in the bathroom, then pull on some underwear and a grey velour tracksuit, and go downstairs. It's already eight o'clock: breakfast time. I walk along the hallway and push open the kitchen door. Charlie is sitting on a high stool at the kitchen island with Bea on his knee. When she sees me, she slides off him and runs to me. She is wearing a pink corduroy pinafore with embroidered flowers round the hem, a white T-shirt, three strings of coloured beads and her *Finding Nemo* Wellingtons.

I lift her up to hug her. Her blonde hair is soft and wispy and smells of shampoo. 'Have you had a bath this morning?'

'She had chewing gum stuck in her hair,' Charlie says through a mouthful of cereal.

'What were you doing with chewing gum?' I say, tickling her

middle so that she giggles. 'Were you going through Charlie's bags again?'

'I looked for his washing.' She takes a big breath. 'Mummy, *you* say – you always say – "Charlie!"' She cups her hands around her mouth and shouts, '"Bring me your washing!"' She drops her hands and pulls on the beads. 'That's what you do.'

'So you were helping?' I say.

She nods. 'Because Charlie *always* comes home with washing. They don't have wash machines at the 'versity.'

'Or if they do, I haven't found them yet,' Charlie says, pretending to look sheepish.

Normally in student accommodation, Charlie's living at home during exam week. He is in his first year at the University of Sussex, studying ecology and conservation. As the university is based in Brighton, he often pops home between lectures and so, in some ways, it feels as if he hasn't really left. Perhaps I should have encouraged him to go further afield, but the course was perfect for him and I'm the first to admit that giving my children up is not something I'm good at. I want them to do well. I want them to be happy, to find partners and have children of their own, but I don't want them so far away that I don't see much of them. Sending Jack to boarding school was difficult enough, but then, as he had been offered a sports scholarship, I could hardly stand in his way. What's more, Julian went to boarding school himself and felt that the set-up would only improve Jack's grades and self-discipline. And for two years it did. Only recently has Jack's behaviour started to slide.

'What time did you get up, then, young lady?' I say to Bea.

'About half past six,' Charlie says.

'I'm sorry, love.' Bea's stool is already taken – her soft toy Bertie is perched on it – so I sit her down on the counter next to Charlie and kiss his cheek. 'You should have woken me.'

'You were out for the count,' he says. 'I didn't have the heart to disturb you.'

'Thank you for looking after her.'

'That's what big brothers are for,' he says, winking at her.

'And look, Mummy!' She holds up strands of her hair. A whole section is shorter than the rest. 'We had to cut it.'

'It was the only way,' Charlie says.

'The only way,' Bea echoes, nodding her head wisely.

'Well, never mind.' I walk behind her to put the kettle on. 'These things happen.'

'Why?'

'Why do these things happen?' I say.

She nods again.

'Because chewing gum is meant for mouths, not hair. And anyway, you're too young for it.'

She shakes her head. 'Jack eats chew gum.'

Charlie tickles her knees. 'Jack is sixteen and you're only four.'

'Next time I have a birthday, I'll be five.' She looks down at her fingers, then holds up two hands and six fingers. 'See?'

Charlie takes her hands in his and counts her fingers with her. His head is bent close to hers, his mop of curly black hair, grown long around his ears and neck, contrasting with her blonde one. As he speaks, she looks up at him with wide-open eyes. I lean against the worktop and watch them. I'm smiling; I can't help it. They are such opposites, an almost grown man and a small girl, and yet they have a deep connection. The age gap between them is over fifteen years but still they are devoted to one another.

I always wanted to have a large family and would have had half a dozen children if I could, but in spite of the fact that we never used contraception, I only fell pregnant three times. I had the two boys three years apart and then a twelve-year gap before Bea came along, a gift for the whole family and just at a time when we needed it most. My father had died unexpectedly of a heart attack and a year later Bea was born, a reason to celebrate and get back on with living. I feel proud to be their mother.

As if on cue, my mobile rings. It's Jack. My signal is weak in the kitchen, so I go out into the hallway.

'Morning, love. Sorry we didn't ring you back yesterday afternoon. Dad went off to the airport and then time ran away from us. Bea was so tired she was in bed by seven.'

'Dad sounded a bit weird when he hung up.'

'It was nothing,' I say. 'What are you up to today?'

'Revision. Sport . . . and stuff.'

He sounds subdued. He hasn't been particularly reliable lately and I wonder whether he's in trouble with his housemaster again or if it's something to do with a girl. I decide not to push for details. It will only cause bad feeling, and I know the school will be in touch if there's cause for concern. Still, I can't help myself saying, 'You are behaving, aren't you?'

'Yeah!' He gives a derisory snort. 'You always jump to the worst conclusions.'

'I wonder why,' I say, my tone as light-hearted as I can manage. 'Your last term report wasn't exactly glowing.'

'Yeah, yeah.' He doesn't even try to keep the boredom from his voice. 'I just called to wish Bea happy birthday for yesterday.'

'I'll get her for you.'

I call to Bea and she sits on the bottom stair, clutching my mobile to her ear, as she starts telling Jack all about her party. I go back into the kitchen, where Charlie is rinsing the breakfast dishes.

'Jack?' he asks me.

I nod.

'What's he up to?'

'Revising, I think . . . I hope.' I pour myself some coffee. 'I've a feeling there's more trouble on the horizon.'

'I was too easy,' Charlie says. 'Makes Jack seem worse than he is.'

'So it's normal for teenage boys to lie to their parents, get cautioned by the police for carrying false ID and get spectacularly drunk on the contents of their friend's parents' drinks cabinet?'

'You wait and see,' Charlie says, handing me the milk. 'By the time he's twenty, he'll be through with the dark side. He'll be wearing cardigans and reading *The Times*.'

I laugh. 'He doesn't need to go *that* far. He just—' I stop short of saying, *He just needs to be a bit more like you*, because I know it isn't a fair comment. Charlie has always been straightforward. He is Julian all over again. He has the same sense of fun and fair play and a solid core of common sense. He doesn't need to rebel. He has an easy relationship with the world around him.

And much as I find it hard to admit, Jack is like I was. A bit too impulsive. A bit too loud when he needs to be quiet, a bit too forceful when he needs to back off. I remember comparisons were always being made between Lisa and me: 'If only Claire could be more like her sister'; 'If only she was content to listen and accept instead of always arguing every point.' Comparisons between children are never fair and I, of all people, should know better.

'You're right,' I say to Charlie. 'He'll come round.'

'Second-child syndrome. They push harder against the boundaries. It's natural.'

'And how did you become so wise?'

He shrugs. 'Ask my mum and dad.'

I smile.

'Talking of Dad . . . is he OK now?'

'I think so. I haven't spoken to him since he left. I'll call him this evening. See how his meetings are going.'

'He really went off on one,' Charlie says. 'He's normally Mr Cool and he was acting like disaster had struck.'

'We all behave against type occasionally.'

'Yeah, but not Dad.'

'He's only human, Charlie,' I say. 'He has a lot going on with the case.'

'He'll get Georgiev this time, though, won't he?'

'The odds are definitely in the prosecution's favour, but Georgiev's crafty. I wouldn't be surprised if the defence have something up their sleeve.' I take a bite of a leftover crust of toast. 'Amy still asleep?'

'She'll be down in a minute. She's meeting one of her tutors in the library.'

Suddenly the kitchen door flies open and Bea comes running back in, a look of concentration on her face. She pulls the heavy fridge door open and stands on tiptoes to reach last night's leftover chicken. I expect her to put some in her mouth, but instead she crams pieces into the pocket in her pinafore.

'What are you doing, Bea?' Charlie and I say at the same time.

'Douglas likes chicken. Miss Percival says I can give him a treat if he sits nicely.'

'Ah!' Charlie hunkers down beside her. 'Miss Percival's little West Highland terrier?'

'He comes on Weds-days and we take him for a walk.'

'Why don't we put the chicken into a plastic bag?' I say.

'Miss Percival says plastic bags are bad for the 'vironment.' She gives me a you-should-know-better look. 'The birds are sick because it stays in their neck.' She makes a coughing noise and then puts her right hand over her throat. 'Like that.'

'Oh dear.' I retrieve a piece of chicken meat from her right Wellington boot and put it in the bin.

'Why do birds try to eat bags?' she says, the question creasing her forehead.

'They don't mean to. They're nosing around for food and they eat the bag by mistake.' I open a cupboard and find a small plastic box. 'Look!' I hold it out to her. 'We can put the chicken in this.'

Her face lights up. 'It can be Douglas's treat box!'

'Exactly.'

Charlie helps her transfer the chicken from her pocket into the box.

'Douglas is having puppies,' she tells him.

'I thought Douglas was a boy,' he says.

'He made friends with a lady dog and *she* is having puppies.' She looks up at me. 'Miss Percival says I can have one.'

'Does she now?'

'Well, she didn't *say*, but she says . . . she says . . .' she jumps in the air a couple of times as she thinks '. . . I'm good with animals.'

'And she's right – you are.' I kiss the top of her head. 'And we need to get going otherwise we'll be late.'

She follows me into the hallway. 'So can I have a puppy?'

'Let's ask Daddy when he comes home, shall we?' In fact Julian and I have already talked it through with each other and with Miss Percival and have decided that we will buy one of the pups. Although Bea isn't old enough to completely care for an animal, she is old enough to help and she has been asking for her own dog for as long as she's been able to talk.

I look through the window out on to the street. The morning began with a summer rain shower, but this is now long gone and the sun is warming the pavements, steam rising lazily upwards. 'Do you want to wear your sandals?'

She points down at her feet. 'My *Nemo* boots.'

'Are you sure?'

'I have to bring Bertie.' She runs back into the kitchen to get him. In recent months there are two things Bea won't be parted from: her boots and Bertie. She wears her boots everywhere and can only just be persuaded to take them off at night, when she puts them neatly by the bed ready to wear first thing in the morning. And then there's Bertie. Wherever Bea goes Bertie goes too. He is a brown, furry, bedraggled creature with one ear beginning to fray and the stitching at his foot coming away, but she won't let me fix him. He doesn't like needles, she told me. They make him cry.

I slide my feet into a pair of sturdy, comfortable sandals and open the door into the porch.

'Are you going out like that?' Amy has come down the stairs and is staring at me.

'Yes.' I glance down at myself. The velour tracksuit is a bit worn, the grey faded with frequent washing, but it's one of my favourites. 'I'm only walking to nursery.'

'Just looks a bit . . .' she hesitates as her eyes make a final critical appraisal '. . . tired.'

'Well, I suppose—'

'You should make more of yourself.' She walks past me and heads towards the kitchen. 'While you still have a figure.'

Charming. Perhaps I should be flattered that she thinks there's still hope for me, but, as is often the case when conversing with Amy, I'm left feeling that unless I'm willing to tackle her head on, I'm unlikely to get my point across.

I help Bea slide on her backpack, Bertie's head poking out of the top, and we set off down the steps. She skips along beside me, interested in everything around her, and we haven't even left the street when she veers off the pavement to peer at a dead frog in the gutter. The innards fan out from its squashed body like the trailing tentacles of a jellyfish.

She pokes it with the toe of her boot. 'Is it dead, Mummy?'

'Yes, it's dead.'

We are standing between parked cars and the one directly in front of us has two men inside. One is on his mobile and is looking through the side window towards the park. The other man is watching us and gives me a polite smile. I smile too and try to persuade Bea back on to the pavement. She is still soaking in the macabre sight of the frog: legs splayed, one eye popped from its socket on to the road and what was once a stomach now an empty sack.

'Poor frog.'

'Yes,' I say. 'Now let's get going. Douglas will be waiting.'

After a few more seconds she drags her eyes away and we walk to nursery. Miss Percival is standing at the door of the classroom waiting to welcome in the children. Bea and I are the first to arrive. Wednesday is a special day because it's the day Douglas comes along. When he sees Bea, his tail starts to wag and he strains on his lead to reach her. She runs to greet him, crouching down beside him to stroke his head.

'Look, Mummy!' She is giggling. 'His tail is polishing the floor.'

Douglas is sitting down, his tail swishing from side to side on the wooden floorboards.

'So it is!'

'He wants some chicken.' She stands up and swings her backpack off her shoulders.

'I hope you don't mind,' I say, looking at Miss Percival. 'She has a treat box for Douglas.'

'Not at all. But, Bea, perhaps you might fill up his water dish first? He's thirsty after the walk over here.'

'Yes, Miss Percival.' She wends her way across the floor, around tables and chairs until she gets to the big sink.

'Did your husband get away OK yesterday?' Miss Percival asks me.

'Yes, thank you.' I'm watching Bea as she climbs up on to a little wooden stool so that she can reach the taps.

'There's a lot going on for you and your family at the moment,' Miss Percival says, and then she clears her throat. 'Bea has mentioned the trial.'

'Has she?' I stare at her, surprised. 'In what context?'

'Children talk as they play. About their lives and what's going on at home.' She manages to make this sound both sinister and secretive, and then she adds, 'Parents don't always realise quite how much their children pick up on.'

'I'm sure.' In fact I'm well aware that Bea is in the habit of listening in on adults, absorbing snippets of information here and there. She often tells me about conversations she's overheard and I'm not surprised to know that some of it spills out when she's at nursery. But both Julian and I try hard to prevent her from hearing anything that might upset her, especially if it relates to his work or to Lisa's illness. 'What has she said?'

'That her daddy was putting a bad man in prison.'

I raise my eyebrows. 'That's the nub of it, I suppose.' I pick Bea's backpack up off the floor and hang it on her peg. 'But she didn't seem worried by it, did she?'

'Not exactly.'

'Not exactly?' I repeat. I'm frowning with concern and she blushes, looks down and moves back a step.

'I was just anxious about the effect her father's job and her aunt's illness might be having on her,' she says stiffly.

'That's kind,' I say, 'but I think we're managing to shield her from the worst of both those things.' I turn and look along the corridor, mindful that other mothers are arriving and are beginning to form a queue, waiting to hand their children over. 'But if you have any specific concerns, then please tell me.'

'Of course.'

She gives me a tight smile and turns away. I feel like a child who's been dismissed and I almost leave there and then, but Bea is walking towards me, her face solid with concentration. She has filled the water dish to the brim and is taking small steps to ensure it doesn't spill on to the floor. I give her a careful kiss goodbye, then turn to go. Miss Percival has already been cornered by another mother and I smile at her and at everyone in general, then walk towards the door.

My skin prickles. I know how much Bea loves coming to nursery. More than that, I know that Miss Percival is especially fond of Bea. In fact Adam told Jem that Bea was Miss Percival's favourite. Nevertheless, whenever I talk to Miss Percival, I'm often left feeling that there's a subtext I'm not tuning in to. This isn't helped by the fact that we haven't yet made it to first-name terms. She's younger than I am by a good ten years and several times I have asked her to call me Claire, but she persists in being formal with me. And yet I hear her call most of the other mums by their first names and they call her Mary. I've trawled my memory for a moment when I might have rubbed her up the wrong way, but I've never been able to come up with anything. It feels like she wants to keep her distance from me, but then she breaks this by asking me quite specific questions about Julian and Lisa. Only last week she was asking me about Lisa's treatment and whether she would soon be out of hospital. And the week before that she asked me how I'd met Julian and how long we'd been married. It's like she's on a seesaw, a push and pull of wanting to know my family and yet not.

I walk away shaking my head. I don't know what to make of her and I don't see any point in dwelling on it.

3

We moved to Brighton from London just over five years ago and it took me a while to appreciate the flavour of the city. Just as the Thames adds colour and history to London's identity, the sea brings a similar sense of power and timelessness to Brighton's. It looms large across the southern edge of the city. Devoid of curves and twists, the coastline stretches in one long, uninterrupted line, a clear delineation between land and sea. The beach isn't sandy; it's covered in pebbles large and small, and Bea and I have spent many a happy afternoon pottering along the shoreline collecting shells, then spreading a towel on the pebbles to eat a picnic and watch the boats go by. I was brought up further inland, so I'm not someone who was used to living by the sea, but the longer I live in Brighton, the more I enjoy it. Today, as I walk back from nursery, the sea is slate grey and calm, its glassy expanse spreading as far as the eye can see. I stand and watch the waves break gently on the shore. Sunlight glints off the fire-damaged remains of the west pier, gradually being eroded by weather and water. The closest section, already collapsed, is half submerged in the waves, the twisted metal all that's left of better times.

Leaving the prom behind, I walk home along Western Road, stopping at the wholefood shop to buy some provisions. For the last month I've employed a cook, a young Turkish woman called Sezen Serbest. I'm not used to having help in the house – not since the boys were young and I worked full-time – but Sezen has been a godsend. When Lisa was diagnosed with cancer, our lives changed. Just like Wendy, Lisa had been an almost daily visitor to our home, a much-welcomed aunt, sister and sister-in-law. But the last year has seen her spending more and more time in hospital, for chemotherapy treatment and for a series of complications that have led to weeks of in-patient care. It didn't take us long to realise that the hospital food was at best palatable and at worst downright inedible. Just at the time when she needed food that was as nutritious and health-affirming as possible, Lisa was eating the worst diet she had ever had. At first I cooked for her, taking food in at lunchtimes. This worked well for a while, but I soon realised that although I knew the principles of good nutrition, if Lisa was to be given the best possible chance of survival, I needed to up my game. After looking on the Internet, I found out about macrobiotics. At that point I knew nothing about this type of diet, apart from what I'd picked up in a few articles I'd read in glossy magazines that mentioned it was a favourite with the Hollywood A-listers. With an emphasis on whole grains and vegetables, macrobiotic cooking was shown not just to encourage good health but to have therapeutic benefits. That was enough for me. I found Sezen, an experienced macrobiotic cook, through an agency and she comes in for four hours every day. At first she prepared food solely for Lisa, but gradually she has been teaching me dishes to make for the whole family.

When I reach the house, I go straight through the hallway and into the kitchen. Sezen is standing at the island in the middle of the kitchen using a spatula to move biscuits from a baking tray on to a wire rack.

'You have been shopping!'

'Thought I might as well. Miso, bulgur wheat and I even managed to get a daikon.' I dump the bags on the kitchen table. 'I could murder a cup of tea. And those biscuits.' I breathe in the smell. 'Can I steal one?'

'Of course!' She laughs. She is small and neat with dark hair tied in a plait that hangs halfway down her back. 'They are sweetened with malt syrup.' She watches me while I bite into one.

'I thought you could take some to Lisa when you visit her at lunch, and I have made some soup.' She lifts the lid and I place my head over the rising steam.

'Wonderful!' I say appreciatively. 'It smells of cinnamon.'

'It is warming,' she says. 'And the biscuit?'

I savour the taste in my mouth. Raisins and oaty crunch. 'Delicious.' I switch the kettle on. 'Tea?'

'No, thank you.'

She never says yes, but I always ask her anyway. I know she takes working for me just as seriously as if she was employed in a hotel or somewhere similar where breaks were regulated.

'Charlie has gone out. He told me to let you know he will collect Bea at one o'clock.'

'Great.' I make a cup of tea for myself, take another biscuit and sit down on the sofa by the window. 'So it's the big day tomorrow, Sezen.'

'Our move down from London? Yes. Lara and I are both looking forward to living in Brighton. The air here is fresher. Being close to the sea will be a joy. And it will make coming to work so much easier. There are my hours for you and also I start maternity cover for a café in Hove next month.'

'Are you all packed?'

'Our suitcases are ready.'

'Do you have a lot of stuff?'

'Not so much. Lara wanted to bring absolutely everything, but I told her to select only her favourite things. The rest we have given away to some of the other children who live close by.'

'How are you travelling?'

'We will manage on the train.'

'On the train?' I can't hide my surprise. 'But Lara's only four and you will have all your belongings with you.'

'Yes.' Her amber eyes look into mine. 'We will need to move slowly, but we will manage.'

I shake my head. 'I can easily come to collect you. I'm sorry I didn't think to offer sooner.'

'No, no, no.' She shakes her right index finger at me. 'You must not do that.'

All her worldly goods, plus her young daughter, on a train? The mind boggles. 'Really, Sezen. I want to come for you. Please let me. Bea will be at nursery. I have the time.'

She pushes out her bottom lip, half thinking, half doubtful. I reassure her that it's the least I can do after all she has done for me. She gives in then, but I can see that she's still reluctant. 'It's absolutely no trouble.' I look at my watch, then stand up. 'I should get going to the hospital.'

'Here is Lisa's lunch.' Sezen hands me the bag she has prepared. 'I put some of Bea's birthday cake in there too. I know it is not macrobiotic, but treats every now and then do not do any harm.'

We arrange a time and place to meet tomorrow and I go out to my car. The hospital is only a ten-minute drive away, and while parking is never easy, I've sussed out a side street close by where there is invariably a space. The ward is particularly quiet today. Often there are nurses bustling in and out of Lisa's side room, but not at the moment. I stand at the door and watch her through the glass. She is fast asleep, her cheeks the colour of the bed sheets, in stark contrast to the blood that's running from a bag on a drip-stand into a vein in her left arm.

'She's washed out today.' One of the nurses has stopped beside me. 'Her haemoglobin is low – that's why she has the blood up.'

'And the rest of the test results?' I turn to face her, apprehension filling the space in my throat.

'The scans, well . . .' She looks behind her to where the ward sister has just come out of the treatment room. 'Lynn can give you the details.'

'Claire.' Lynn puts an arm round my shoulder and guides me into the relatives' room, closing the door behind her. My heart sinks. I know that if the news was good, she'd have told me in the corridor. They do that. Good news is worth sharing, spreading to others who might be listening, hoping their own relative will be spared. 'We have the results back now.'

'The cancer?' My mouth is dry. I try to work some saliva into it but fail. 'It isn't gone, is it?'

She shakes her head. 'Unfortunately not.'

'Right. I see.' I take a couple of steps backwards. I want to be sick. I feel disappointment, heavy as concrete, lodge in my chest. No miracles, then. The cancer is still in her liver, and could still be travelling in her bloodstream, making up its mind where to settle next. *The bowel or the bones? Eenie, meanie, miney, mo.* 'Does Lisa know?'

'Yes. Dr Doyle told her this afternoon.' Lynn comes towards me, as always maintaining eye contact, and it strikes me afresh how very good she is at this. Very good at being there for patients and relatives. It's the stuff of her working life, delivering bad news while showing herself willing to pick up the pieces.

'How did she take it?'

'She took it well.' Lynn strokes my hands. 'She was more worried about you.'

'Right.' At once I feel ashamed. My sister, age forty-seven, is facing the prospect of premature death and she is more concerned with my reaction than her own.

'All is not lost, Claire.'

I nod. I know she's right but I need time to come to terms with the worry and the fear. I look down at a patch of linoleum and allow my eyes to seek out each of the scratches. I want to cry but know that if I do, Lisa will notice the tell-tale signs – red eyes, blotchy cheeks – and then she will worry about me. So instead I grit my teeth and spend ten minutes with Lynn discussing taking Lisa home on Saturday and what community support staff will visit. When I go into Lisa's room, she is just beginning to wake, but she looks far from rested. She's painfully thin, her skeleton barely covered by anything more·than a layer of skin.

'How are you today?' I kiss her cheek. She feels cold, so I pull her blanket up over her shoulders.

'Hello, Claire.' She gives me a tired smile. 'This is a nuisance.'

She points to the line going into her arm. 'It's been stopping and starting all morning. They've changed the site twice already.'

I stroke her arm near where the cannula slides under her skin. Purple bruises bloom in three separate places on the soft skin of her inner forearm. 'The blood will perk you up a bit, though. Put some colour back in your cheeks.'

'For a little while,' she acknowledges.

'I spoke to Lynn about your results.'

She frowns. 'Let's not talk about that now. But tell me' – she widens her eyes – 'how was the birthday party?'

'Great fun.' I tell her about the clown not turning up and how Julian stepped in to organise party games. 'Charlie was a big help.'

'He's such a good brother.' She shifts her head on the pillow. 'Did Amy come too?'

'She did.' I busy myself at the end of the bed.

'Romance still happening there, then?'

'With bells on.'

She sighs. 'It was great being young and in love, wasn't it?'

'All that intensity, though!' I bring the soup, homemade spelt bread, biscuits and cake out of my bag. 'All that aching and wondering . . . Will he call? Does he fancy someone else? What if he thinks I'm boring or his parents hate me?'

Lisa gives a gentle smile.

'Am I sounding old and jaded?'

'Just a bit.'

We both laugh.

'Now here!' I hold out the flask. 'I have some butternut-squash soup to tempt you with.'

'How wonderful.' She starts to haul herself up into a sitting position and immediately I help her. Her arms feel like spindles; each vertebra in her back is a raised knuckle of bone. 'I'll start with half a cup.' I pour some out for her and she takes a sip, smiles. 'It's good. Tasty.'

'Sezen's recipe,' I say. 'Mealtimes have improved no end since she came to work for us.'

'I can't wait to meet her.'

'She's lovely.' I sit on the edge of Lisa's bed. 'She's a real find. And in just a few more days you can come home to us and experience her cooking first hand.'

'Do you think?' She throws a weak arm outward to take in the clutter of medical equipment, dressing packs and creams. 'I don't travel light any more.'

'I've already discussed it with Lynn. The nurse will come in to administer your drugs and check on your general state of health. The rest we can work out between us.'

'Are you sure?'

'Sure?' I give a short laugh. 'You're my sister. I want to look after you. And we're all set up for it. Jem's almost finished decorating the room. Wendy will come round every day to help out with Bea. Sezen will take care of the cooking. She'll make anything you fancy, but her expertise is macrobiotics.' I pause. 'This isn't the first time she's cooked for someone with cancer,' I add quietly.

'You've thought of everything.'

I doff an imaginary cap. 'I aim to please.'

'Then I accept.' She leans forward to hug me. 'I'm so tired of these four walls. I can't wait to come home with you.'

My heart lifts.

'I don't want any special concessions, though,' she says. 'No keeping the children quiet or worrying about them tiring me out.' She breathes in deeply and then places her hand over her ribs as she tries to hide a grimace of pain.

'Are you hurting? Shall I call someone?'

She waves aside my concern. 'Lively family is just what I need. I might not be able to join in, but I'd still love to be a part of it.' She takes hold of my hand. 'So did Julian get away OK?'

'Yes.' I hesitate as memories of yesterday's drama come flooding back. 'After a bit of a do.'

'What happened?'

I tell her about Jack phoning and me going to look for Bea and

Julian's reaction when I told him I couldn't find her. 'I've never seen him react so strongly. He went from perfectly normal to distraught.' I shake my head. 'We found out she was with Amy, but still . . . It was like he really believed Bea was in danger.'

'What do you mean?'

'Well . . . that Amy might somehow be a threat to Bea. I have no idea what was going on in his head.' I shiver as I remember those few interminable minutes when Julian was completely unlike himself, gripped by an irrational fear that made no sense to me. 'He was really freaked out.'

'I don't understand,' Lisa says.

'Neither do I.' I shrug. 'I mean, you know Amy isn't our favourite person?'

She nods.

'But Julian seemed to think that Amy might have disappeared with her or something.' I shrug again. 'It was completely irrational.'

'Julian's never irrational.'

'I know!' I laugh. 'Charlie was saying that too, but the only thing I can think of is that he's under a lot of stress. The trial date's approaching and—'

'Still,' Lisa interrupts, 'it's not like Julian to be alarmed without good reason.'

As she says this, I have a sudden, clear picture of the expression that crossed his face when we were in the hallway, just before he left. It was a shadowy look. A secretive look. A significant look. Shit. There is something wrong. I've been dismissing his panic as nothing more than a reaction to stress, but Julian's as steady as a rock. His feet are firmly planted in reality. He would never panic without good reason.

'You're right,' I say to Lisa, then stand up and walk a few paces, thinking. My heart begins to pound, and bubbles of anxiety spawn in the pit of my stomach. 'The taxi arrived before we had the chance to talk.' I rub my forehead and look across at my sister. 'What do you think I should do?'

'He calls every evening when he's away, doesn't he?'

I nod. 'He didn't call last night because he'd only just left, but he'll call this evening.'

'Talk to him about it.' She gives me a reassuring smile. 'There's probably a simple explanation.'

'Yes, probably.' I take a big breath. 'I'm sure it's fine.'

'Now, here.' She pats the space next to her. 'I was promised party photos.'

I take my digital camera out of my bag and plug the cable into Lisa's laptop. A happy hour passes as we look at the photographs, many of them viewed twice as Lisa exclaims over something Charlie or Bea is doing. Lisa has had several long-term relationships but never married nor had children of her own. She is a doting aunt who loves my children almost as much as I do. I can sing their praises without feeling like I'm overdoing it because, of course, I am completely biased. As far as I'm concerned, my children are extra special, the love I feel for them manifesting in a mixture of protection and pride and absolute loyalty.

When it's time for me to go, she walks with me as far as the main corridor, pushing her drip-stand ahead of her. As I hug her goodbye, I'm careful not to hold her for too long. Since she was diagnosed, I've promised myself that I won't be a burden to her, so although I feel a crushing disappointment over the scan results, I keep my grief to myself.

On the drive home, Lisa's words about Julian nag away at me. More so because she was only voicing what in my heart of hearts I already knew – Julian would never go off at the deep end without good reason. Pre-trial stress makes him quieter and often short-tempered; it doesn't make him over-react. He believed Bea was in danger. He believed it.

I shift in my seat and force my hands to relax their grip on the steering wheel, hoping to dissolve the bubbles of anxiety that have clumped together and are now lodged like a fist in the hollow of my stomach. I drive home faster than I should, parking haphazardly outside the house, running up the steps and bursting in through the front door. Holding my breath, I stop at the bottom of the stairs and listen. I hear Bea's laughter coming from her room, Wendy and Charlie's voices as they talk to her. All is well. I gulp in some air and call up the stairs, 'I'm home!'

'Come and see me, Mummy!' Bea shouts, and then Wendy appears on the landing above me.

'How's Lisa?' She comes down the stairs towards me. 'And her scan results?'

I tell her the news and watch tears gather at the corners of her eyes. I hug her to me and we stand like that for a moment until she pulls away and becomes her practical self again. We talk for a bit about arrangements and then she heads off home.

Bea calls for me again, but first I go into the kitchen and use the house phone. I'm itching to speak to Julian. I don't want to wait until this evening, so I call his mobile number. It rings twice, then goes through to the answering service. I don't leave a message. Instead, I stand in front of the pinboard. Whenever he goes abroad, he leaves the hotel address and telephone number here for me to find, should I need it. My eyes scan the board, seeing take-away menus, school and university phone numbers, postcards and more, but no sign of where Julian's staying. I search next to the telephone, go through the piles of papers on the Welsh dresser, but don't find the details there either. I even look under the table and behind the cushions on the window seat. Nothing. And yet just before he left, he made a point of reminding me that the contact numbers were on the board. And they're not. If they'd fallen off, they'd be on the floor and they're not there either.

I go upstairs and find Charlie reading a story to Bea. 'Where's Amy?' I say.

'In my room, finishing off an essay.'

'Did either of you see Dad's hotel details? He usually puts them on the pinboard in the kitchen.'

'I haven't seen them,' Charlie says. 'I'll ask Amy.'

He goes next door and Bea slithers off the bed. 'Look, Mummy, I have all my toys here.' She points to the floor, where she's arranged her birthday presents in a straight line against the wall.

She holds up the soft toy Jack gave her. 'I'm going to call him Douglas because he's the same as Miss Percival's dog.'

'He is,' I say, sitting down on the bed. 'He's a little West Highland terrier just like the real Douglas.' Charlie comes back. I look up at him. 'Has Amy seen the details?'

'No.' He shakes his head. 'Is there a problem?'

'Not really. Dad will call soon anyway.'

'Feel his fur, Mummy!' Bea has climbed on to my knee and is holding the dog against my cheek. 'It's soft.'

'It is,' I say. 'Softer than a cushion.'

'But I still love Bertie best.' To prove it, she reaches under the duvet, pulls Bertie out and hugs him tight.

'Charlie!' Amy's voice shouts from the bedroom and he goes at once, pulled by an invisible thread.

'She wants him again,' Bea says with a sigh. 'She always wants him.'

I hide my smile – Bea isn't happy with Amy's power over Charlie.

'I had a good party,' Bea says, settling herself on my knee. 'Daddy made everyone laugh.'

'Yes, he did.' I smile as I think about Julian playing musical chairs and balloon football with over a dozen three- and four-year-olds. 'We didn't need the entertainer after all.'

'Has Daddy gone on the plane now?'

'Yes. He arrived yesterday. One sleep has passed and then another sleep will pass and then he'll be home.'

The thumb of her left hand goes in her mouth, while her right hand reaches up, seeking the ends of my hair. She moves the strands through her fingertips and then sucks harder on her thumb. We stay like this for a couple of minutes, me enjoying the feeling of having her close, while Bea grows ever more relaxed, her body leaning heavily into mine.

I look down at her blonde head. 'Are you hungry?'

She takes her thumb out of her mouth. 'Grandma Wendy gave me food.' She pats her tummy. 'We had eggs and strawberries.'

'That's a funny combination!' I tickle her cheeks and she grins up at me. 'Well, let me know if you get hungry.' I kiss her forehead. 'I'm going downstairs.'

Before I have the chance to slide her off my knee, she sits up straight and looks at me wide-eyed because she's just thought of something. 'Is Daddy going to see the man?'

'What man is that?'

'The man what sends the emails.'

'What emails are those, sweetheart?'

'On Daddy's 'puter.' She looks at me and shakes her head so that her hair falls into her eyes. 'I didn't go on Daddy's 'puter. It was Daddy.' She frowns and shakes her head again. 'Daddy doesn't like the email man.'

'I see,' I say, not really seeing at all. I think of Miss Percival's comment this morning about the things children pick up on. Bea is in the habit of squirrelling herself under tables or in the corner of rooms and she often does this in Julian's study. Sometimes he forgets that she's there and it's not unusual for her to report back to me snippets of what she's heard. I think, in this case, that she must be talking about Georgiev. But Georgiev is in prison, having been denied bail. It seems unlikely that he would be sending Julian emails. And if he was, then surely Julian would have mentioned it to me.

'Megan doesn't like the man,' Bea continues. 'She said to Daddy he has to be careful.'

The anxiety-lump in my stomach shifts, releasing a tremor that ripples through my body, raising the hairs on my arms. Megan is one of the instructing solicitors with the CPS. She and Julian have spent hundreds of hours working on the Georgiev case. If she is urging Julian to be careful, then it's because there's something wrong.

'I'm sure Daddy will sort it all out,' I say lightly, easing Bea off my knee. 'I'm just going downstairs for a bit. Why don't you make a bed for Douglas?'

'I can put him in beside Bertie.' She pushes her hair out of her eyes, then runs to the corner of the room where Bertie has a real dog bed, small in size but complete with a cosy sheepskin and an extra blanket. 'Bertie will look after him.' She hops from one happy foot to the other. 'Bertie knows about puppies.'

I leave her to it and go downstairs. The inside of my skull feels as if it's expanding. I stand in the living room and look through the window. Mary Percival is walking the real, live Douglas in the park opposite our house. The sky is beginning to darken above their heads as clouds gather for a burst of summer rain, but Douglas isn't in a hurry. Every bush and tree trunk is given a comprehensive sniff before he's willing to move on. Mary looks up at the window, sees me and gives an acknowledging wave. I wave back. My eyes are looking at her, but my thoughts are elsewhere.

I go through to the kitchen and have one last search of the pinboard. I'm not imagining it. The details aren't there. OK. There are other ways for me to find out where he's staying. I scroll through the numbers on my mobile phone and stop when I get to Megan Jennings. She hasn't gone with Julian on this trip, but she'll know the name of the hotel. And judging by what Bea might have heard, she'll know quite a bit more than that. I call her number. She answers almost immediately.

'It's Claire Miller,' I say.

'Claire, hi! Everything OK?'

'Fine, thank you. I'm wondering whether you have the number for Julian's hotel . . .'

'Did he get away OK?'

'Yes. It's just' – I take a breath – 'he left the number for me but I can't find it and I thought you might be able to help me out.'

'Of course. I have the details on my computer. I'm not in the office at the moment, but I'll be back there in a few hours and will call you then.'

'That's OK,' I say quickly. 'Why don't you stop by here on your way home?' Like Julian, Megan commutes from London to

Brighton. She lives in a small flat round the corner from us, the proximity a mixed blessing, as work often stretches into the weekend. 'I can even rustle up some supper for you. It will save you cooking when you get in.'

'Sure.' A slight pause. I can almost hear the gear change in her brain. 'I'll be with you just after eight thirty. Is that OK?'

'Perfect.' Time to put Bea to bed. 'I'll see you then.'

Megan has eaten with us before but always when she's been working with Julian in his study and has happened to be here over a mealtime. I know she'll be wondering why I'm asking her to come round when she can easily give me the details over the phone. She is every inch the professional and won't want to breach confidentiality, but as whatever is going on seems to have seeped into family life, I don't intend to let her leave without her shedding some light on Julian's mood. I want to know whether she can make sense of what Bea's just told me and whether it's linked to the way Julian reacted yesterday afternoon.

And then it occurs to me – why wait for Megan when I can check for emails myself? Julian isn't here, but his laptop is. I can log on and see whether there are any suspicious emails in his inbox.

I go down to his study and switch on his laptop. The system begins to load and then I click the icon to log on to his server at work. Almost at once a box appears asking me to type in the password. I'm confident I know this. Less than two months ago, Julian was in Durham when he called and asked me to log on to the server at his chambers. His password alternated between numbers and letters – J1A9C9K4 – Jack and the year he was born.

I type it in. In less than a second 'Incorrect password' comes up on the screen.

Damn. He must have changed it.

I try the same pattern with Bea and Charlie and their birth years. It doesn't work. I try with Julian's and mine. Nothing.

I stand up and take a couple of deep breaths. Slow down.

Think. Be logical. When Julian changes his password, he keeps it personal. Not as obvious as a single name – hence the alternate numbers and letters – but obvious enough to him and surely, therefore, to me. I pace up and down a few times, running names and numbers through my head, then sit back down and try other obvious combinations: our wedding anniversary, the date he took silk, the date we moved to Brighton.

The door to Julian's study opens. I look up. It's Amy. She starts back in surprise. 'I didn't realise you were in here.'

'Well, I am.' I try for a smile. 'Did you want something?'

'I came down to make Charlie and me some tea.'

I point to the ceiling. 'The kitchen's upstairs.'

'Yes, but I heard a noise down here and thought that maybe Jack was home and I could offer him a drink or something.'

'Jack won't be home until late next week.'

'Well, can I get you anything?'

'No, thank you.' I give her a distracted smile, then look back at the screen.

'Are you on Julian's laptop?'

'Yes.'

'Something wrong with yours?'

'Why?'

'Nothing.' Her hair is long and wavy and is a luxurious copper colour. Normally she makes nothing of it, preferring to tie it up under a thick multicoloured hairband, but today it falls over her right shoulder and she is holding the end of it, swinging it from side to side. 'It's just that I'm pretty good at diagnosing problems.'

As she reaches my side of the desk, I minimise the window. She's looking at the screen but the only thing she can see is Julian's desktop photograph of Bea and the boys taken at Easter.

'Oh! You're not doing anything much, then?'

I turn my head to look up at her. 'What I'm doing is private.'

'Sorry.' She gives a stifled giggle, like an embarrassed schoolgirl, something I'm sure she never was. 'I'll leave you to it, then, shall I?'

'Yes, please.'

She is wearing patchouli, a strong, heavy scent that I remember from my own student days and didn't much like the smell of then. It lingers in the room after she's gone. She heard a noise? She heard me typing *from the top of the stairs*? Not possible. So what's she playing at? Was she snooping? I don't know what to make of it, so I decide that I'll think about it later.

I stare back at the screen. The interruption has allowed time for guilt to creep from the back of my mind to the front. I don't feel comfortable going behind Julian's back. This is his work email. I shouldn't be doing this. I should wait until I have the chance to speak to him. I trust him. When there's something I need to know, he tells me.

I take my hands away from the keyboard and rest them on my lap. I have to approach this one step at a time. Megan will be here soon. I'll tell her about what happened yesterday afternoon, see what she says. And Julian will be back at his hotel in a couple of hours. I'll be able to talk to him. There's no need for me to resort to hacking into his email.

And then, just as my mind's made up to go back to the kitchen, it comes to me – Lisa – the sixth member of our family. I decide to check, just to see whether I'm right. My fingers move over the keys and I don't stop them. L1I9S6A3. At once the system fires up. I'm torn between looking and not looking, realise that I am literally sweating and wipe my forehead with a tissue. As soon as the desktop is loaded, I let curiosity get the better of me and click on the icon that opens Julian's email. There are already half a dozen unopened messages in his inbox, but all the senders are either solicitors at the CPS or other barristers in chambers. I scroll down through his inbox but can't see anything suspicious. He is methodical at record-keeping and has lists of folders down to one side, most of them case names. I click on 'Georgiev'. There are over two hundred emails, but once again all the addresses are from other solicitors. I don't see how there can be anything to worry about there.

I start clicking on the folders titled with numbers and letters.
The first three folders contain admin and account emails. The
fourth has eight emails in it, all from the same address. What's
unusual is that none of them have been replied to. I open the
first one.

'Mum!' The study door opens again. It's Charlie this time. His
hair is dishevelled and he's grinning. I hear Amy laughing behind
him. 'Do we have any Worcester sauce?'

'Look in the pantry.'

The first email is on the screen. I glance at it and see the
phrase 'extreme lengths'.

'Everything OK, Mum?' Charlie's watching me from the door.

'Fine.' I smile. 'I'll be upstairs soon. Megan's popping round.'

'OK.'

He closes the door and I hear them both jostle and tease each
other back up the stairs. I read the first email and know at once
that I've found what I'm looking for:

*I'll be blunt. You have information I want and I'm willing to go
to extreme lengths to get it. The witness in the Georgiev trial – I
want his name and his whereabouts.*

I sit back in my seat. Apart from the low hum coming from
the laptop, the room is completely quiet. A lone blackbird sits on
a branch of buddleia, just visible in the garden, beyond Julian's
window. Its orange beak points skywards as it sings a summer
song. I'm no longer sweating. My body is relaxed and I feel
strangely clear-headed. Julian's over-reaction and Bea's comment
about emails – could both events be linked? There are seven
more emails in the folder. I don't take time to read them. I don't
take time to think about how frightening this could become. I
decide the best thing is to print them out and take them upstairs
where I'm less likely to be disturbed. The cursor whirls as the
printer receives the information and churns out eight sheets. I
shut down Julian's laptop, collect the sheets from the printer tray

and fold them in half. I climb the stairs and tiptoe past Bea's bedroom. She has always been good at occupying herself and is quietly talking to her soft toys. I opt for guaranteed privacy, walk through my bedroom and shut myself in the en suite bathroom. I lay the pages out on the floor.

Then I read them.

4

I kneel on the bathroom tiles and line up the emails in the order they were sent. The first one is dated Monday, 24 May, nine days ago. I read it for the second time.

I'll be blunt. You have information I want and I'm willing to go to extreme lengths to get it. The witness in the Georgiev trial – I want his name and his whereabouts.

There isn't a name at the end of the message, but it's clear that whoever's written it, Georgiev is behind it. He wants to silence the main witness. He's done this in the past and that's exactly why the judge granted Julian an anonymity order in the first place.

I move on to the second email. It arrived a day later and, like the first, it gets straight to the point:

There are two ways for me to come by this information. At the pre-trial hearing, you support the defence counsel's request to lift the anonymity order. Or you tell me who and where the witness is. Simple.

Julian has already mentioned to me that the pre-trial hearing is scheduled for this Monday, 7 June, five days from now. It's unimaginable that, as prosecuting counsel, he would ever agree to lifting the anonymity order. His case has been built around this man's evidence and without it a conviction is unlikely.

The third email arrived at midday exactly a week ago:

Leaking the name and the whereabouts of the witness will be
easy – by letter, email, phone call or text. You choose. We can
arrange it.
   I'm sure you'll make the right choice.
   For Bea.

My blood slows and cools. I sit back on my heels. I think about
Julian's reaction yesterday afternoon and know at once what the
emailer is building up to. I feel as if my heart has stopped beating.
My body is completely still, spellbound. Only my eyes are moving,
flicking silently around the everyday mess in the bathroom. We
have double sinks set back into the alcove. Julian's shaving stuff
is in a disorderly heap next to his sink; assorted creams and oils
are crammed into the space next to mine. The laundry basket is
in the corner. Several of Julian's socks haven't made it that far
and lie on the floor next to it. Bea likes to bathe in here because
we have a corner bath. She has a family of yellow ducks that
squirt water out of their mouths and a selection of boats, all of
which sit in and around the tub. The towels aren't straight on
the rails, and the rubber seal is beginning to come away from
the lower edge of the shower door so that water leaks on to the
mat on the floor. It's all completely normal, familiar and
grounding.

I look back at the emails. The fourth is dated 27 May, last
Thursday:

I watched Bea and Claire this afternoon as they walked back
from nursery. Bea was wearing a pink dress with a white
flower pattern on the hem and pale green sandals with two
buckles across each foot. She was carrying her stuffed dog,
Bertie. They stopped at the Italian delicatessen on Western
Road. Claire bought mozzarella cheese, Parma ham and a
chocolate treat for Bea. She told Bea they were going to make
pizza for dinner.

I think back. I see Bea and me walking along the road. She was skipping, telling me about one of the girls at nursery who has three dogs and a cat. She was asking me why we didn't have any pets and then we turned into the deli and she was distracted by the chocolate lollipops on the counter. We chose cheese and meat from the chilled cabinet and Bea was allowed a lollipop for later.

The email is accurate, down to the colour of Bea's dress and the food we bought.

We were being followed.

I think this without a trace of emotion. I wait for my heart to respond, my blood to race, the rush of adrenaline to spike in my bloodstream. Nothing. Someone was watching us, listening to us. The walk back home is almost a mile and not once did I suspect we had a stalker. No hairs rose on the back of my neck, no gut feeling that something was amiss.

My eyes shift to the fifth email:

This morning Bea played in the sandpit. She was told she had to wear her sunhat. She doesn't like the elastic under her chin, so she wore a boy's cap instead.

I could have taken her then. I could take her still. And you'd never see her again.

I imagine a stranger's hand reach out to catch hold of my daughter's shoulder and I wonder why I'm not screaming. The blackmailer is creeping forward, low in the grass, like a lion after a zebra, and I'm fixed in an emotional limbo, my heart struck almost dumb by the enormity of this.

The sixth email came on Monday, just two days ago:

How will Claire react, I wonder, when she finds out you're sacrificing your own daughter in order to protect the witness, a criminal out to save his own skin?

This isn't a straightforward case of good versus evil. But then again, Julian, is it ever?

Julian. For the past nine days, he has been reading these, and Bea has already told me that Megan knew about them. He told her, but he didn't tell me. Bea is my daughter and yet he has kept me in the dark about this. I feel the merest swell of anger rise up through my ribcage. I don't grab hold of it. Not yet. I let the feeling trickle away and then I read the seventh email:

You doubt me?

Have I mentioned that I've killed before? Mostly I favour the knife – a five-inch blade with a serrated edge. Last time, I pushed it in just below the fifth rib. It sliced through the muscle in her heart.

She died quickly.

Sometimes I enjoy making it slow.

I sit back on my heels again. I try to take a deep breath . . . fail. I feel like something or someone heavy is sitting on my chest. I notice a small tremor in my hands and press them firmly down on my knees. I wait a moment and in that space of time my mind hauls me back to before I had Bea, when I was employed as a solicitor with the CPS and I saw, first hand, the damage a knife can do. The last case I worked on was a young woman called Kerry Smith, murdered by her ex-partner, the father of her two children. She had been stabbed in the chest. I had known her when she was alive and I saw her body when she was dead. Her face, without blood to liven it and personality to shape her smile, was a grey-blue colour, inert as moulded clay.

I force myself to finish what I have started. I read on. Email number eight:

Let me refer you to a couple of unsolved crimes: Carlo Brunetti, Rome, 2006, and Boleslav Hlutev, Sofia, 2008.

That's it. Short but not sweet. I read it several times, memorising the names, places and dates. Then I collect the emails into a pile, go into the walk-in wardrobe and slide them under a row of sweaters.

I move silently from my room along the carpeted hallway. I can hear Charlie and Amy laughing in his bedroom. I stop at the entrance to Bea's room and watch her from the doorway. She's changed from her pinafore into a pair of mismatched pyjamas: pale blue trousers bottoms and a pink top with a faded picture of Barbie on the front. She's lying on her side on the floor, feet close to the door. Her right arm is stretched out and she's leaning her head on it, her face turned towards her left hand, holding Douglas. She makes him run across the carpet and jump on top of Bertie. She does this a few times and then she sits up and takes the squashed Bertie out of his basket and cuddles him.

I almost walk into the room to hold her, but stop myself because I know that I won't be able to speak. The magnitude of what I've just read is sinking in and my impulse is to grab Bea, pack our bags and drive away. Drive and keep driving until we are beyond the blackmailer's reach. But I know that this situation is too critical for me to act on impulse. I have to talk to Julian. I have to find out how seriously he is taking these threats and whether or not he has a plan. Has he spoken to the police? Has Georgiev been questioned? Are the emails traceable?

I go downstairs to the kitchen and take a bottle of wine from the fridge. I pour myself a glass, then sit at the table and face the back garden, where shadows lengthen as the sun slips lower in the sky. I sip the wine and think about the tone of the emails, the fact that we were followed and that the blackmailer watched Bea at nursery. The emails said that Bea was playing in the sandpit, and that's positioned close to the four-feet-high fence, bordering a pathway. I know that Miss Percival and her two helpers are always outside with the children, so if the blackmailer stopped for any length of time on the path to watch her playing and hear the exchange about the sunhat, he would surely have drawn attention to himself. He has to be someone who blends in or is pretending to blend in. A policeman or a janitor, lollypop man or postman.

'I've got grumbles in my tummy.' Bea comes running into the kitchen, her hand over her middle.

'I'm sorry, poppet!' I jump to my feet. 'Let's make dinner together, shall we?' I scoop her up into my arms, kiss her cheek and hug her tight.

'You're squeezing me, Mummy!'

I want to keep her close to me for ever, but I make myself set her down on the work surface, between the sink and the hob. 'Let's have some of this lovely soup Sezen made.'

She peers into the pot. 'I like fish fingers.'

'We'll have fish fingers too, then.' I turn on the gas under the soup and take a packet of fish fingers out of the freezer. I lay several under the grill.

'Your hands are shaking, Mummy!' She points to my hands and then stares up at me. 'You have a sad face.'

Her expression is so earnest, so kind that I feel a rush of tears at the back of my eyes. It takes all my inner strength to stop them spilling on to my cheeks. I give a forced laugh. 'Mummy's just feeling a bit sorry for herself.' I put my hands on my hips and say brightly, 'Shall we do some fish fingers for Charlie and Amy?'

'They're not hungry.' Bea screws up her face. 'They're doing kissing again.'

'Ah.'

'Amy says I have to *knock*.'

'Well, that's probably a good idea.'

'But Charlie likes playing with me.' She slumps down, her back rounded, her hands in her lap. 'He's *my* brother, not *Amy's*.'

'Where's Bertie?' I tickle her feet. 'Is he looking after Douglas?'

'He's very tired. He had to go to bed because Douglas was climbing all over him all the time.' She tells me the whole saga, her eyes widening or narrowing depending on the ups and downs of the story.

When the food is ready, she eats four fish fingers dipped in tomato ketchup and in between I spoon soup into her mouth. Afterwards we go upstairs and I help her with washing and brushing her teeth, read her a story and sit on her bed. It takes next to no time for her breathing to settle into the rhythm of sleep, but still I sit there, stroking her hair, soaking up the essence of her. I move from one of her features to the other: the curve of each eyelash, the rosy blush of her cheeks, the slightness of her arms wrapped tightly round Bertie, who, not unlike Bea herself, rarely manages to spend the night in his own bed.

I sit beside her until I hear the doorbell. Leaving the bedroom door slightly ajar, I go downstairs to let Megan in. She's about five eight, slim, dark hair pulled back in a tight ponytail. She's someone who is neither pretty nor plain. She's dressed in a tailored black trouser suit and a white blouse. On some women this would look sexy, but on Megan it just looks smart. But she's not someone to be underestimated. She has a sharp, incisive intelligence. She was top of her class at her girls' school and achieved a double first from Balliol College, Oxford. She is an ambitious solicitor and is out to impress – not that I hold that against her. I was a solicitor myself once. I know that it takes focus and a healthy dose of ambition to make the grade, and for all her brisk efficiency, she always takes the time to chat to me and the children.

'Come on through,' I say.

She follows me along the hallway into the kitchen and sits down on the window seat. 'It's been a fabulous day.' She crosses her ankles and smiles at me. 'Did Bea enjoy her party yesterday?'

'Very much.' I offer her some wine, which she refuses, and then I gesture towards the pot on the hob. 'I know that it's more salad weather, but this soup is really very good.' I give it a stir. 'Butternut squash. Sezen made it.'

'How's she working out?' She picks up a magazine and starts flicking through it.

'Great. She cooks all sorts, but she specialises in macrobiotic food.'

'This is a wonderful resort.' She holds up the magazine so that I can see the photograph of wooden chalets nestling in the snowy hillside. 'I spent my gap year working in the Alps.' She smiles. 'Absolutely loved it.'

She continues reading the article as I place some bread, cheese and tomatoes on the table, and then I sit down and we both eat. Megan asks me how Lisa is doing and I tell her, keeping it short because I want to steer the conversation elsewhere.

'So this business of the emails,' I say.

She gives me a wary look.

'I know you already know about them.'

She tilts her head. 'So Julian told you?'

'You're not being threatened too, are you?'

'No, I'm not.' Her eyes cloud with sympathy. 'But then I don't have children.'

I tear off a piece of bread and chew it slowly. Megan's right. For the purposes of blackmail, children are the perfect leverage. Most adults are willing to risk their own lives for something they really believe in, but risking their children's lives? That's not an option.

'How worried should I be?' I say.

She shrugs one shoulder. 'It could simply be Georgiev's men posturing.'

'Posturing?'

She purses her lips.

'You think the threats are meaningless?'

'It's not for me to say. Julian is taking them seriously and so are the police.'

'The police?'

'Didn't Julian mention that the police were involved?'

'We haven't had much of a chance to discuss it.'

'They're trying to trace the emails.' She cuts a slice of Cheddar and transfers it to her plate. 'Not easy as the emailer is using a proxy server. You know how it is.'

I nod. 'Georgiev hasn't become this powerful without being one step ahead.'

'Well, he's no longer powerful. He's in prison, pending trial.

A trial that will be won by the prosecution. Of that there is no doubt.' She says this with an uncompromising straightening of her back. 'As long as we have the witness, Georgiev doesn't have a hope of being acquitted.'

I think she means to reassure me, but it has the reverse effect. If the witness is so crucial, then Georgiev won't stop until he has the name. In prison or not, he still has clout among his criminal gang, who will work hard to ensure his release.

'The trial will go on, of course,' Megan continues. 'It's just unfortunate that Julian has had to resign' – her fingers move through the air, putting quotation marks round 'resign' – 'when he's worked so hard on the case.'

Julian has resigned? I try not to show that this is news to me. I take a spoonful of soup and move it around in my mouth before forcing it down my throat. 'Yes,' I hear my voice saying. 'It's been difficult for him.' So difficult that I didn't notice. And so concerned was he that he didn't feel the need to tell me he has resigned from a case he's spent almost a full year working on. Two hulking great secrets that for nine whole days he's successfully kept to himself. I would never have believed it.

'He's a fantastic barrister and a great teacher,' Megan continues. 'I've learned such a lot working with him.'

The undisguised hero-worship in her voice is both touching and hurtful. Megan knew about both the emails and his resignation. So why didn't I? My head scrolls through a thousand different reasons, but the only one that fits is that he feels closer to Megan than he does to me, that somewhere along the line she became his confidante. And yet this is about our family. This is about Bea. I can't believe that he would keep this from me. It feels like the worst sort of betrayal.

'So what's the plan?' I say.

'Well, clearly there's a conflict of interest for Julian and so he's been obliged to step back from the case. Gordon Lightman is now lead counsel.' She raises her eyebrows. 'Nominally. Everyone knows this is really Julian's case.'

'I don't mean with the case. Bea's safety is what concerns me.'

'Hasn't Julian told you himself?'

'He had to go off in the taxi. It was one of those conversations that was cut short.'

'Well, why don't I find you his hotel details?' She stands up to fetch her laptop bag. 'I have the address and phone number in here.' She sits down, takes out her laptop and switches it on. 'Won't take a moment.'

'I understand that he needs to resign,' I say. 'His position is compromised. I see that. So why, then, has he gone to Sofia?'

'Officially Julian is off the case, but he's taken Gordon with him for a handover. He wants to make sure Gordon is completely up to speed.'

'Twice before in fifteen years Julian has tried to bring Georgiev to justice and failed.'

'Exactly. And this is our best shot yet. Julian wanted to introduce Gordon to Iliev, the chief of police out there, so that they could review the evidence together.' She takes some paper and a pen from the side pocket of her laptop bag and writes. 'Here.' She holds the paper out to me. 'Address and phone number.'

'Thank you.' I take it and put it in my pocket.

'The soup was delicious.' She stands up again. 'I need to head off.'

'Date?'

'I wish.' She rolls her eyes. 'Bundles to check through. Should keep me up till midnight.'

I walk with her to the door.

'Nothing will happen until after the pre-trial hearing on Monday,' she says, setting off down the steps. 'There's still time to find out who's sending them. It doesn't have to turn nasty.'

'Turn nasty?' My feet follow her down on to the pavement. I catch hold of her arm and another question occurs to me. 'Those two cases that the blackmailer quotes, Brunetti and Hlutev . . . what happened with them?'

'I don't know,' she says quickly. Too quickly. She puts her arms round me and gives me a brief, awkward hug. 'I'm sorry this is happening, Claire. Truly I am.' She pulls away. 'Call Julian. He has more information than me.'

I go inside and lean my back against the closed door. My head spins with a jumble of half-questions and incomplete answers. And then, in the midst of it all, I see Bea's face: smiling, uncomplicated, safe. My hands start shaking again. I push the palms together to make them stop. I try to think my way forwards. I need information and I need a plan. I take the piece of paper from my pocket and go into the kitchen. When I'm a few steps away from the phone, it starts to ring. I lift it and press the green button.

'Claire?'

The relief at hearing his voice sets up an ache inside me: part fear of what's to come and part hope that simply lying in his arms would make it all go away.

'I was just about to call you,' I say.

'How were Lisa's results?'

'Not good . . . but listen.' I sit on the window seat and lean my forehead against the glass. 'Julian, what's going on?'

'I've been meeting with Iliev, the chief of poli—'

'I don't mean that. I mean I know there's something you should be telling me.'

A couple of seconds pass before he replies. 'Why don't we talk when I get home?'

'I know about the emails.'

Silence.

'I know about the emails and I know about the fact that you've resigned and I feel scared and I feel hurt.' My voice cracks. I try to take a breath, but I feel as if I have a lump the size of a walnut in my throat. 'And I can't for the life of me come up with a good reason why you wouldn't have told me that our daughter's life was being threatened.'

More silence.

'Aren't you going to say anything?'

His voice when it comes sounds more distant that mere miles could account for. 'Who told you about the emails?'

'Bea told me.' Anger flares in my stomach. 'Because for some reason you were unable to.'

'Bea? How did she—'

'She listens. She picks up snippets of conversations. You know that.'

'I'm sorry.'

'And Megan told me you resigned.'

Across the distance I hear him sigh.

'Why didn't you tell me?' I hear the puzzled tone in my voice and try for a firmer one. 'Julian, I'm your *wife*. You should not have kept either of these things from me.'

'Sweetheart' – he takes a quick breath – 'let me explain everything face to face. I'll be home by four tomorrow. Can we leave it until then?'

'Bea and I have been *followed*. Someone has been watching her at nursery. Doesn't that bother you?'

'Of course it bothers me. It hasn't been easy keeping this from you.'

'Then why did you?'

'Because we thought we had a lead on the blackmailer and I thought it could all be resolved without worrying you and without bringing it into our home.'

'Yet you had no difficulty telling Megan, and in front of Bea.'

'I had no idea that Bea was listening.'

'So that makes it OK?'

'Claire . . . please. Trust me on this. Will you?'

I don't answer. I keep my jaw clamped shut. I want to shout at him. You told Megan? *Megan?* And yet you didn't tell me?

'Nothing will happen before the pre-trial hearing on Monday.'

'But yesterday you clearly thought Bea had been taken.'

'Yes, I did. And as I said yesterday, I over-reacted.'

'So what are the police doing? Have they traced the emails?'

'Not yet. But I think you'll be reassured to know that Andrew MacPherson's running it.'

The name vibrates in my ears and travels up the neural pathways into my brain. I hope I've heard wrong. I clear my throat. 'Who?'

'Andrew MacPherson. You worked with him, didn't you?'

I'm not breathing.

'He's with Serious and Organised Crimes. Has recently had a promotion to DI. Everyone calls him Mac.'

I know what everyone calls him.

'He'll come to the house and talk to all of us after the pre-trial hearing on Monday.'

My mind is reeling. As if the threat to my daughter's life isn't enough for me to cope with, now Mac has been thrown into the mix. There must be a dozen senior policemen who could have been assigned this case and it ends up being him. I drop my head into my hands.

'Claire? Are you still there?'

'I'm thinking,' I say.

'You had a lot of respect for Mac, didn't you?'

'He's a good policeman,' I say flatly. 'Efficient, patient, intelligent.' *Dangerous.* 'He's as good as they get.'

'I feel that too. I think we're in good hands with him.'

'Mm.'

'I'll be home by four tomorrow. Sweetheart, we'll get through this.'

'I know,' I tell him. 'I'll see you soon.'

'I love you, Claire.'

I hesitate for a second and then say with complete conviction, 'And I love you.' I end the call and stand up. Today is Wednesday. I have no intention of waiting until Monday before I speak to the police. To Mac.

Mac. Jesus. I sit back down on the window seat and rest my elbows on my knees. I never expected to have contact with him again. It's been five years since we've been in each other's company, since I deleted his mobile number from my list of contacts and erased all thoughts of him from my mind. But half a dozen times in the last five years he has texted me. The last time only a month ago and I'm sure I've yet to delete it. I take my mobile from my handbag on the dresser and scroll through the messages until I find it: *You ever coming back to work or what?*

I don't know why he's kept up these intermittent communications with me. Guilt? Friendship? Or something more? I don't know, and I've never given it serious thought. Neither have I ever replied to his texts, but now I access his number and call it. It rings twice and then he answers.

'Claire?'

'Yes.'

'How are you?'

'How do you think?'

'Has Julian told you?'

'I found out.'

'How?'

'That doesn't matter.' I take a breath. 'I understand you're running the case.'

'That's right. I know what's happening is awful, but we will do everything we can to keep you all safe.' He sounds exactly the same, his Scottish accent a melodic, comforting lilt. It almost makes me smile. 'I know you must have loads of ques—'

'I do. I want to talk to you. Do you have any free time tomorrow?'

'Sure. What suits you?'

'Anytime.' I've already decided not to send Bea to nursery. I'm not taking any chances. And then I remember – Sezen is moving from London down to Brighton and I offered to help her with the move. 'No. Sorry. In the morning I'm driving up to Tooting. I could meet you there . . . although I'll have Bea with me, so that isn't ideal. Shit.' I press my free hand against my forehead.

'I can come down to Brighton.'

'No. Wait. Taking Bea all the way to London in the car isn't ideal.' I think. 'I'll ask Wendy to babysit. I could meet you at about ten?'

'Can do.' He names a café in Tooting, on the High Street.

'See you then.'

At once I make another call. It's already almost eleven, but I know that Wendy turns in late. I tell her that Bea isn't going to nursery tomorrow and would she mind looking after her for me. She agrees at once and suggests that Bea and she bake some cakes. I wish her a goodnight, then tidy the bowls and leftovers off the table. When I'm finished, I go down to the basement and make sure that every window and door is locked. I do the same on the ground floor, coming into the sitting room last. The sky is navy blue and starless; streetlamps shed light on what little activity there is outside. And it's under the closest streetlight that I see two men standing on the pavement talking to one another. One is smoking; the other is drinking from a metallic flask. They are dressed in suits, and the smoker is leaning on a Ford Mondeo. I recognise them. When Bea stepped off the pavement to examine the dead frog, these men were the ones sitting in the car. Surely they haven't been here all day? They look innocuous enough, but this is a residential area and it's unusual for people to loiter. They could simply be waiting for someone, but then why the flask? I won't be able to sleep knowing they're there, so I go through to the kitchen to get my mobile. I'll ask Mac to send a local policeman round to find out who they are and, if necessary, move them on. But by the time I come back into the living room, they're nowhere to be seen. I look through the side panes of the bay window to either end of the street, but there is no sign of them and no sign of their car.

I close the curtains and go into the porch to set the burglar alarm. I know that until the blackmailer is caught, this is the way it will be. I'll be suspicious of every stranger, every unknown car or curious passer-by. Someone is watching us and until I know who that someone is I'll have to be vigilant.

I climb the stairs to bed. The house is quiet. Bea is asleep, and

Charlie and Amy are watching a film in his room. I go into the en suite, drink a glass of water and get ready for bed. I feel simultaneously dog-tired and wide awake. My heart aches with worry; my mind sparks off in different directions. It flashes to a picture of Bea, talking to her soft toys, watering the garden or skipping along to nursery, not a care in the world. The thought of someone taking her, hurting her, makes me feel immediately and overwhelmingly sick. Images flash through my mind: sick, unpleasant images from news stories. Some of the water I've just swallowed comes back into my mouth. I go into her room. She's lying on her side almost completely submerged by the duvet. I pull it back and see that she still has her arms round Bertie. Being careful not to wake her, I lift her slowly from her bed and take her into mine. Her eyes half open and then close again at once. She snuggles down into the middle of the bed without complaint. I slide into bed beside her and turn off the light, only to lie awake staring at the ceiling. I have never felt more afraid.

5

I wake up early the next morning with my arms round Bea. Like a new mother with her first baby, throughout the night I found myself reaching out to make sure she was safe. And whenever I did drift towards sleep, the words from the emails haunted me – *Have I mentioned that I've killed before? Mostly I favour the knife* – razor-sharp phrases that jerk me awake, my heart racing.

I slide out of bed quietly, leaving Bea asleep, and go into the shower. The water is warm and invigorating, stinging my skin into life. I think about the day ahead. I'm meeting Mac at ten and don't have to collect Sezen from her flat in Tooting until around twelve o'clock, so that gives Mac and me a good hour and a half to talk. I want to know everything: every detail, every suspect, every lead they've had so far.

Mac. I don't relish the thought of seeing him again, his very existence bound up with a period in my life that I'd rather forget. Five years ago he was a colleague. I was a solicitor with the CPS, and Mac was a detective. We were thrown together on several of the same cases. The last case we worked on prompted my decision to re-evaluate my life, to stop work altogether and concentrate on being a wife and mother. It was the murder of a young woman named Kerry Smith. She was a good person who had, as a teenager, got in with the wrong crowd. She wasn't well spoken, her education had been intermittent, but she was trying to better herself and make a future for her kids. Becoming a mother had changed her. The only mistake she made was to become involved with the wrong man – Abe – a harmless-sounding name for such a violent criminal. The father of her children, he was wanted for aggravated assault, burglary and drug-dealing. Kerry had experienced the brunt of his temper, and she'd also witnessed the damage he inflicted on other people. She was prepared to give evidence against him, not because she hated him or wanted to get her own back, but because she had children now and she wanted men like Abe off the streets. She was given accommodation in a safe house. All was fine for a week and then Abe found her. When she was coming home from the corner shop, he knifed her nine times in the chest.

Mac and I tormented ourselves with the realisation that we should have better protected her. We operated within the law, but we knew that perhaps we should have, could have found a safer safe house. Had we pulled out all the stops? Had we?

We both knew we hadn't.

To try to make up for it, we put all our energies into catching Abe, breaking down his alibi and convicting him. At the backs of our minds we knew it was too little too late. Her two young daughters were motherless, their grandparents out of their depth. And this made us push harder. We skated a fine line between what was lawful and what was not, but there was no way either of us could let him walk free.

And then there was Kerry's funeral.

I turn off the shower and start to dry myself, knowing full well that I'm going to have to remember what happened at the funeral sooner or later. Just not right now.

'Mummy!' Bea shouts through from the bedroom. 'Look at me!'

I open the bathroom door and call out, 'I'll be there in a minute.' I finish drying myself and dress in three-quarter-length trousers, a baggy T-shirt and flip-flops, then stop when I catch sight of myself in the mirror. I don't look my best. I don't look my worst. I look like someone who hasn't the time, or maybe the interest, to make the most of herself. I think about Amy's scathing comments yesterday and decide that if I'm going to see Mac for the first time in five years, I need to make more of an effort. I go into the walk-in wardrobe and change into a pair of fitted jeans and a red crossover top that flatters my figure. The shoes I wear with it are wedge sandals that I bought only four weeks ago. Comfortable and stylish, they give me an extra few inches, and as I'm only five feet three, I immediately feel more confident. I usually let my blonde hair dry on its own, but I blast it quickly with the hairdryer, flicking out the ends and running some wax through it to help it hold its shape. Then I go into my bedroom and sit down at my dressing table.

'I can do tumble-overs,' Bea says.

She is bouncing on the bed, and with Bertie under her arm, she throws herself into a perfect forward roll.

'Hooray!' I clap. 'That's very good, Bea.'

'I can do lots of them.'

'No nursery today,' I say. 'Grandma Wendy is coming to look after you while I collect Sezen.'

'Is it the weekend?'

'Not yet, poppet, but it's a good day to stay at home and Grandma will do baking with you.'

'And I can show her my birthday toys because she hasn't seen them all yet.' She does another forward roll, then slithers off the bed and comes to stand beside me. 'And Daddy comes home today because one more sleep has passed.'

'That's right.'

'Looks nice.' She watches me closely as I brush blusher on my cheeks. 'I can have pink cheeks too.'

'OK.' I smile at her. She stands perfectly still as I brush the dusky rose powder over her cheekbones. 'Now look in the mirror,' I say.

She moves in close to the mirror and turns her face from side to side. 'Dust sparkles like fairies have.' She points to the palette of colours. 'I need eye stuff now.'

'Just a little, then.' I apply some to my own eyelids and then some to Bea's.

'Amy has lip gloss,' she tells me. 'It tastes like strawberries.'

'This one doesn't taste of anything, I don't think.' I smear some gloss on her lips and at once her tongue comes out to taste it.

'Broccoli,' she says, screwing up her nose.

'No, it doesn't.' I laugh. 'Have a look at yourself now.'

'I look pretty.' She hops a couple of times in front of the mirror. 'Grandma might not recognise me.'

'Let's get you dressed and breakfasted before she gets here.'

By the time Wendy arrives, Bea is wearing her favourite shorts and T-shirt and has eaten a huge bowl of cereal.

'Hello, you,' Wendy says, when Bea opens the door to greet her. 'Have you been raiding Mummy's make-up box?'

'Mummy made my eyelids blue. Look, Grandma.' She moves in close to Wendy, closes her eyes, then quickly opens them again. 'Sparkles.'

'And very pretty you look,' Wendy says. 'Just like Mummy.' She kisses me on the cheek. 'You look lovely too, Claire.'

'Thought I'd make the effort.'

I glance beyond Wendy and am shocked to see that the same two men are back in the street. One is stretching his legs; the other is leaning up against the side of the car talking on his mobile. Talking on his mobile and looking straight at me. His glance is purposeful, directed, so much so that I have the distinct impression that as he watches me, he is talking about me to whoever is on the other end of the phone. Goosebumps prickle my arms and legs. I slam the door shut. Wendy and Bea go into the house while I hang back in the porch. Could these be Georgiev's men? A heavy coldness sweeps through me and for a moment I'm numb. I stare straight ahead, seeing and hearing nothing, and then I look at the wall to one side of me. The burglar alarm. And not just any old alarm, a state-of-the-art one that has CCTV cameras on the front and rear doors. I'm reminded of a conversation I had with Julian a couple of months ago, when we were having it installed. The conversation went along the lines of 'You can't be too careful.' He was quite specific, twitchy even, about us making the house more secure, checking the locks on the windows and doors, priming the boys on personal safety. Did he know then that Georgiev was likely to threaten our family?

'Surely not,' I say out loud, disappointment and frustration flooding through me. 'Bloody, bloody hell.' I come in from the porch and close the inside door behind me.

'I'm going to get my dogs, Grandma!' Bea is running up the stairs, tripping over her feet in her haste.

Wendy gives me an uncertain smile. 'Everything all right, Claire?'

'Fine.' I try to smile back.

'So is nursery closed today, or . . . ?'

'No. I just thought Bea could do with some downtime. She's had a busy couple of days.' I kiss Wendy on the cheek. 'I really appreciate you dropping everything to come and look after her.'

'No trouble.'

'Really, Wendy.' I hold her shoulders and look directly into her eyes. 'I don't know how I'd cope without you.'

'Goodness me! What on earth's brought this on?' she says, looking both pleased and puzzled at my sudden rush to compliment her.

'I'm just—' I stop. I want to pour it all out and then I want to be held and reassured that everything is, and will be, fine. But I know that, in this case, a problem shared is not a problem halved. 'I just want you to know you're appreciated.'

'Thank you. I'm delighted to be part of this family. I'm only sorry your dad's no longer alive to be part of it too.' She takes hold of my hand. 'He'd be very proud of you, you know?'

'I know.'

'Bea's so like you when you were little. You loved your stuffed animals and all your little games.' She lets go of my hand and walks towards the kitchen. 'I thought that while the cakes are in the oven, we might pop out for a bit.'

'I don't want you to take Bea out,' I say abruptly, and she turns to me, surprised.

'Why ever not? We won't go far. Just across to the park.'

'I'd rather you didn't,' I say again.

'Has something happened?' She looks at me closely. 'Is everything all right?'

'I'm feeling . . .' I consider being almost truthful but realise that I don't know enough to answer her questions fully. I will only succeed in spreading some of my own fear and uncertainty, and that feels neither wise nor kind. I look her squarely in the eye. 'Do you trust me?'

'What sort of a question is that?' She shakes her head at me. 'Of course I trust you!'

'Then, please' – I think about the men outside – 'I'd feel happier if Bea didn't go further than the back garden.'

Her grey eyes stare back at me, firstly confused and then accepting. 'No problem.' She nods her head. 'We have lots to do in the vegetable plot. I know Bea's looking forward to planting some late potatoes. Ones that will be ready for Christmas dinner.'

'Thank you.' I start off along the hallway. 'I'll just get myself organised. Charlie and Amy are still asleep.'

'I won't disturb them.'

I go downstairs to quickly log in to Julian's email account. I need to see whether another email has arrived. Within minutes I see that there's nothing new. I've already put into my handbag the ones I printed out last night. I want to discuss them with Mac. I want to hear his theories and put forward some of my own.

As I'm leaving, Bea is halfway down the stairs with most of the animals from her toy chest.

'I'm bringing them for tea and cakes,' she tells me.

'You be a good girl.' I hug her tight.

'You're squashing Bertie, Mummy!'

'I'll be back soon.'

'You go and collect Sezen,' Wendy says. 'And take your time.' She gives me a gentle nudge. 'We'll be fine here.'

I come outside on to the pavement and stop in front of my car. The two men are still there. Still looking at the house. Still looking at me. I make a snap decision and, ignoring the possibility of danger, walk towards them, smiling as warmly as I can. 'Do I know you?'

'Mrs Miller.' The older one slides his mobile into his back pocket and holds out his hand. 'DS Baker, and this is DC Faraway.'

His handshake is solid and warm. 'Policemen?' I say.

'Indeed.'

DS Baker takes his wallet from his trouser pocket and shows me his ID. I should have guessed. And now that I know, I see that they have 'plainclothes policemen' written all over them, from the make of their car to the lazy turn of their heads, belying sharp glances and cynical appraisal of everything around them.

'When I saw you outside, I wasn't sure what to think.' I shrug. 'Thought you might be with Georgiev.'

'Just the opposite.' He inclines his head. 'Your safety is our priority.'

'Are you going to be here all day?'

'We are.'

'I'm going out now.' I fold my arms across my chest and look down at my feet. 'I'm not sending my daughter to nursery this morning.' I look at Baker, then Faraway. 'She won't be leaving the house unless myself or my husband is with her.'

They both nod.

'Understood,' Baker says. 'Hear you're meeting up with the boss.'

'Yes.' I try to smile. 'I need to get a handle on what's going on.'

'Rest assured we're doing our best this end.' His expression is sympathetic. 'Our very best.'

'Thank you. I really appreciate your presence here.' I shake their hands again. 'Can I get you a coffee? Something to eat?'

They both shake their heads and I reiterate my thanks, then walk back to my car. On the one hand I feel reassured that the police are already mobilised to protect us, and on the other my heart sinks further. The threat is real. The danger is not imagined or exaggerated. This will get worse before it gets better. And once again Julian has kept me out of the loop. I would have noticed if the men had been here all week. This must have been the result of the call Julian made before he went to the airport.

I climb into my car and set off. The traffic is light and it's not long before I'm heading up the A23 towards London. I turn on the radio and try to get lost in the inane chatter. At any rate, it keeps my mind occupied, and so when I arrive in Tooting and find the café, I've yet to think about how to approach this meeting with Mac. I'm fifteen minutes early. I sit in a quiet corner near the back of the room, order a coffee and wait.

The waitress can't be more than sixteen. She has a nose-ring and lank brown hair that reaches her collar. Her eyes are bright, interested, older than her years. She looks me up and down. 'Nice sandals, those,' she says.

'Thank you.' My legs are crossed and I rotate my raised foot in the air. 'Haven't had them long.'

The table is wooden and has one leg slightly shorter than the other three, so when she puts the coffee down, some spills over the lip of the mug.

'Sorry.' She uses the cloth hanging from her belt to wipe it up. 'Sure you don't want anything else?'

'No, thank you.'

'You waiting for someone?'

I nod.

'It's not a date, is it?'

'No.' I almost laugh. 'Far from it.'

'You've got that look about you,' she says, walking back to the counter. 'Nervous but excited too.'

I can't believe I look excited. Tense, scared, anxious – definitely. After all, my daughter's life is being threatened and the man who's in charge of helping us prevent such a thing is Mac. And I don't know whether that makes it better or worse. We haven't been alone in each other's company since after Kerry's funeral, when we gathered at her parents' semi in Gravesend. They were both wide-eyed and bewildered. Every now and then the gravity of the situation seemed to dawn on her mother and she'd gasp, clutch a hand to her chest, then turn towards the family gallery on the wall and calm herself, reassured by the smiling ten-year-old Kerry in the photographs.

That morning, the morning of her funeral, my breakfast had been a muesli bar on the Underground and I hadn't eaten any lunch, so two quick, large whiskies and the alcohol ran through me, leaking into my bloodstream, into my limbs and my head until I drifted into a numb, cocoon-like state. I climbed the stairs to the bathroom. When I came out, Mac was standing in the hallway and I lurched into him. He had his jacket off, his tie was loose, and his shirt was coming untucked. He was attractive; everyone thought so. And he was completely unaware of it. A fact that made it all the more potent.

Before Kerry's burial, we had spent two long weeks together building the case against Abe. We worked all hours sifting through the evidence, living on coffee and muffins and the odd takeaway. Our thoughts were in synch, our ideas mutually appreciated. Our closeness was professional. It didn't feel sexual, but it did feel meaningful. I liked and respected him. I recognised that he was attractive, but I wasn't aware that I wanted him until the moment outside the bathroom.

I was drunk and I was exhausted and I should have kept on walking, but I didn't. I went back over that moment a hundred times, trying to work out why I did what I did. All I could come up with was that I'd drifted too far away from the person I really was: a wife and mother who valued her husband and children above all else. At that moment my family were in a parallel world, cared for by another me. Mac, on the other hand, was slap bang in front of me. He looked both familiar and foreign and overwhelmingly desirable. He held my hand. I examined his fingers and then kissed them. He walked us into the bathroom. I locked the door behind us. He undid my blouse. I undid his trousers. He wrapped his arms round my waist. I leaned in to him. He kissed me slowly, teasingly. I pulled back to look into his eyes. He smiled at me. I smiled back. He sat on the edge of the bath. I pushed his head into my breasts. He pulled me on to his knee. He slid a hand up my skirt.

We didn't speak. We held eye contact throughout. It felt like the most uncluttered sexual experience of my life. It was a perfectly erotic, electric episode. At first the rhythm was quick, and then he slowed us down – held me away for a moment while we looked at and into each other – and then we moved quickly again. I came almost at once and so did he. I rested my head on his shoulder. My limbs were soft; my insides felt profoundly relaxed. We stayed like this for several long seconds before somebody tried the door handle. It rattled, swung to the right and then to the left.

'I'll be a minute,' Mac said.

I stood up, gasped – sudden emptiness; my legs were unsteady. He buttoned his trousers. I pulled down my skirt and buttoned my blouse. He straightened his tie. I tried to unlock the door. My fingers weren't working together. He covered my hands with his, unlocked the door, turned me towards him and hugged me. I shut my eyes. He stroked my hair.

'We should go back down now,' he said. He opened the door. The hallway was clear. 'You first.'

He pushed me gently forwards. I went downstairs. My whole body was zinging with energy. I felt more vital than I had in years. I ate four sandwiches one after the other and then I had a cup of coffee. I was just finishing up when Mac came back into the room. We had travelled here together, but I already knew that he was driving back to Scotland Yard, while I had accepted the offer of a lift to the station and then home. I watched as he said his goodbyes to Kerry's parents, held Mrs Smith while she cried into his shirt. He promised to ensure that Abe was locked up for as long as possible. Then he moved around the room, saying a quick goodbye to the rest of us. He gave me a casual hug, as he usually did, and then he left.

Mac didn't call me; I didn't call him. I saw him at work and there was nothing in his face to suggest that he knew me any better than he had before. I didn't know what to think. I didn't know what to feel. Neither my feelings nor my thoughts could settle on one course of action. Like a deck of cards thrown up in the air, the pieces of me were all muddled up. I knew I didn't want him – not really, not the way I wanted Julian – but still there was something about him that made me feel both ashamed and exhilarated. Some clever, insidious charm that once under my skin, was hard to shift.

I finish the last of my coffee and know that the waitress is right. In a small, dark corner of myself I feel a flicker of excitement at the thought of seeing him again. And when, at just after ten, the door to the café opens, that flicker becomes a flame.

6

Mac sees me at once. He walks towards me and I stand up. Unlike Julian, he's not conventionally handsome. He is tall and broad as a rugby player and has a receding hairline, a nose that's too large for his face and brown eyes that are slightly too close together. What makes him attractive is the powerful charisma he exudes. Wendy would call it animal magnetism.

We kiss cheeks. He hugs me. He feels warm and solid. He smells of peanuts. And so, after not having seen each other for five years, it's the first thing I say: 'Have you been eating peanuts?'

He brings a half-empty bag out of his pocket. 'I missed breakfast. You want some?'

We both sit down. I take a handful of nuts and put some of them in my mouth and the rest down on a paper napkin in front of me.

'So . . .' He smiles. It's not just about his mouth or his eyes. It comes from deeper than that. And I remember that he uses his smiles sparingly. Must be why they're so effective. 'Long time no see.'

I nod.

'You look well,' he says.

'Do I?' I half smile, ignoring the way my spirits lifted as soon as I saw him and lift further still with his compliment, because this isn't about me. It's about Bea. 'What I feel is afraid.' I breathe deeply. 'I have a lot of questions.'

'Fire away.'

'Why were you assigned this case?'

'Someone had to be.'

'Did you request it?'

He steals a quick glance at me. 'No.'

'Shouldn't you have turned it down?'

He frowns. 'Why?'

'We know each other.'

'Claire!' He throws his arms out in mock surrender. 'I don't see any conflict of interest here.'

'Really?'

'Really.' He holds my eyes as he says this. It's a look that's both serious and compassionate. 'I will do my absolute best to ensure we get a good result. You know I will.'

There's no doubting his sincerity. The sceptic in me takes a step back. Maybe the fact that we know each other will be to my advantage. I can approach him directly. I don't have to observe male protocol and go through my husband.

'It was just a bit of a shock.' I shrug. 'Of all the policemen in London . . .'

'There are three teams working this aspect of serious crimes. Makes it a one-in-three chance of it being me.'

'I heard you're a DI now.' For the first time I smile fully. 'Congratulations.'

'I have a good team to work with.'

'I'm glad to hear it.' I lean towards him. 'Is there a chance the blackmailer could be bluffing?'

'I don't think so. Georgiev is known for this sort of intimidation. Sofia and Rome are proof of that.'

I'm reminded of the cases mentioned in the emails – *Carlo Brunetti, Rome, 2006, and Boleslav Hlutev, Sofia, 2008*. 'What happened with those two cases?'

'Both of them involved blackmail.'

'And?'

'And family members ended up paying the price,' he says quietly.

'Georgiev had them killed?'

'Yes.'

I swallow quickly. 'Did either of them involve children?'

'The Italian one. A little boy.'

'Was he—' I stop abruptly, thinking about the blackmailer spying on Bea as she played in the sandpit. *I could have taken her then. I could take her still. And you'd never see her again.* 'Was the little boy—' I stop again. 'Was he kidnapped?'

Mac nods. 'I believe so. We don't have all the details at the moment.'

'Will you show me the details when they come through?'

'Claire—'

'Crime-scene photos. All of it. Whatever you have, I want to see it.'

He sits back and looks down at his hands. He's in two minds. I'm not having any of it.

'Whose idea was it to keep me out of the loop, yours or Julian's?'

'It wasn't like that.'

'Like what?'

'It wasn't a case of keeping you out.' He shakes his head at me. 'It was more about not worrying you unnecessarily.'

'Was it your decision or Julian's?'

He sighs. 'It was Julian's.'

'And you just went along with it?' My mouth trembles. I didn't expect this, but as I ask the question, I realise that Mac's silence has hurt me too – not nearly as much as Julian's – but it still feels like a betrayal.

'I have to accept that he knows you better than I do.'

'Forewarned is forearmed.'

'He's only trying to protect you, Claire. And anyway, there really was nothing to be gained by you knowing earlier.'

'Because the threat will only be realised after the pre-trial hearing?'

'Exactly.'

'And yet after Bea's birthday party, when Julian thought she had been taken, two policemen appeared in the street.'

'Getting a feel for the place. Taking note of the comings and goings.'

'They aren't exactly subtle, you know.'

'They're not meant to be.'

Anger simmers inside me, against both these men who have made decisions that affect Bea's safety and yet have neglected to include me. I look away from him and across at the counter. The young waitress is putting glasses on a shelf, her mind only half on the job as she catches my eye and gives me a thumbs-up. I rub my forehead and then look back at Mac. 'Did I ever strike you as the sort of woman who needs to be protected from the truth?'

'Yes . . . and no.'

'I've coped with worse than this.'

'Yes, you have. But this isn't work. This is your family. That makes it different.'

'I want to know everything you know.'

He gives me a prolonged look as if checking to see how much I mean this. I hold myself steady. I feel like I'm treading close to the edges of my own strength and that at any moment I might break down, run home and lock Bea up so that no one can reach her.

'All right,' he says at last. 'But some of it makes for uncomfortable listening.'

'I understand that.' I reach down to the floor and bring my handbag up on to the table. 'I've brought copies of the emails with me.' I lay the pages out in front of him. 'I'd like to go through them. Hear your thoughts.'

'So Julian showed you these?'

'He doesn't know I have them.'

He cocks his head on one side. 'Who gave you them?'

'No one. I logged on to his email. I didn't feel good doing it,' I acknowledge, 'but when I'd worked out there was a problem, I couldn't just sit on my hands until he came home.'

'OK.' He weighs this up, then tips the last of the nuts into his mouth, managing to chew and speak at the same time. 'Firstly, I want you to know that we're giving this top priority.' He tells me about the manpower and resources that are being thrown our way. He has carte blanche with the budget. This case is important to the government and to the police force. It shows they're fighting crime and winning, that they aren't afraid to target the big boys. I listen to everything he has to say, hearing words like 'imperative' and 'risk assessment' and 'profilers'. My brain hasn't felt this engaged since I gave up being a solicitor and I realise that the person I thought I left behind was just waiting for the chance to show her face again.

'And are you having any luck tracing the emails?' I say.

'Not yet. The messages have been coming through several IP addresses that were hacked into. Tracing them back to source is nigh on impossible.' He widens his eyes. 'But what we are doing is bringing in for questioning all known criminals and informants who work or have worked with Georgiev.'

'And at one point you thought you had a lead?'

'Turned out to be a dead end.' He stands up, takes off his jacket and puts it over the back of the chair. 'I need something to drink. You want another coffee?'

'Please.' I watch him as he goes up to the counter, the waitress tripping over herself to serve him, smiling for all she's worth. He comes back with two coffees and a packet of biscuits. Over his shoulder, I see her giving me another thumbs-up.

'So I hear Charlie's at university now. And Jack's what – year eleven?'

I nod. 'Charlie's doing well. Jack's sixteen. He's had a bit of a rocky year at school – in with the wrong crowd – but so far his GCSEs have gone without a hitch.'

He breaks open the packet of biscuits. 'And then there's Bea.'

'Bea.' Precious Bea with her funny little ways. My baby girl. 'She's very sweet and happy. She's brought so much to our family.' And somebody intends to harm her. A wave of fear passes through me, so intense that I hold on to the table to stop myself tipping over. I feel Mac watching me. I dredge up a polite smile. 'And how's life been treating you?'

'Much the same.' He offers me a biscuit. I shake my head. 'Got married a couple of years back.'

'You're married?' I feel a pang of something like envy. It's brief because it's immediately extinguished by the thought that follows – Mac's a lot of things, including intelligent and sexy, but he's not a man to marry. He's a man's man through and through, and they don't make the best husbands. 'You didn't mention that in the texts you sent me.'

'Didn't I?'

'No, you didn't.' I drink some coffee. It's too hot and my mouth burns. 'What's she like?'

'She's . . . nice.'

'Nice? *Nice?*' I roll my eyes. 'I think you need to try a bit harder than that.'

'She's pretty. Interesting. She has long legs.' He thinks for a bit. 'She has long legs,' he confirms, 'and she has a liking for—'

'Wrapping them round you?'

He laughs. 'She has a liking for tiger prawns and holidays in Crete.' He dunks a biscuit in his coffee. 'And country walks.'

I smile. The Mac I knew was always exercise-resistant unless it involved a football. I rest my hand on the copies of the emails. 'Do you think the blackmailer will leave us alone because Julian has resigned from the case?'

'We're hoping.'

'But it doesn't alter the fact that Julian knows who the witness is, does it?'

'No.'

'Isn't Georgiev able to work out who it is?'

'It's harder than you might think. He's had a lot of criminal associates over the years, most of whom would rather slit their own throats than give evidence against him. But this man, the witness, is . . .' He shrugs. 'He's got balls.'

'The blackmailer also says he wants to know his whereabouts. Julian knows this too?'

Mac nods.

'Who else knows the details?'

'In this country, there's myself, Julian, James Alexander at Crown Prosecution and a couple of others.'

I know James Alexander. He is single-mindedly devoted to his job, a public servant in the truest sense.

'And in Bulgaria, there's Iliev, who is Sofia's chief of police, and a couple of his men. They've been tracking Georgiev's movements for over twenty years now.'

'And are any of them being threatened?'

'No.'

'They don't have children?'

'No, they don't.'

'One of the emails' – I find the one I'm looking for and read it out – 'dated 31 May, says, "How will Claire react, I wonder, when she finds out you're sacrificing your own daughter in order to protect the witness, a criminal out to save his own skin?"' I look at Mac. 'Is that true?'

'They're guessing.'

'Yes, but is it true?'

'He's not squeaky clean, no. But he's no monster either.'

'So somewhere in between?'

'Closer to good than to bad. He came forward of his own accord.'

I can tell that Mac admires his bravery and in other circumstances I might too. Now, though, I want Bea's safety to be worth more than his.

'Claire.' He leans towards me. 'Georgiev is worse than the worst of them. The man is an experienced killer and torturer. He has destroyed more lives than you and I could count. Earlier this year he had a fourteen-year-old girl raped and murdered because she refused to have sex with one of his men. As long as we have the witness, the case against Georgiev is rock solid. He needs to be put away for life.'

'I'm sure. But give it a few months and some other scum will rise to the surface to take his place.'

'And we'll get him too. That's the job.'

'Well, Julian's job has now crossed over into our lives. I have to be able to protect my children. I'm their *mother*.'

His eyes acknowledge this. 'I'll help you every way I can. I hope you know that.'

I lean back and sigh. It's not that I don't believe him, but his priorities are different from mine. 'Has Georgiev been questioned? He's obviously pulling the strings.'

'He's been questioned numerous times. His cell has been searched. His post is checked. His visitors are screened. He's refusing to admit he's playing any part in this.'

'Why can't you make him cooperate?' Even as I say it, I know it's ridiculous. The law is reasonable, controlled, non-reactionary. It doesn't resort to torture or manipulation. Marvellous for protecting the innocent, but not so great when hardened criminals use our own civility against us.

'He's not a man who is ever going to cooperate with the British judicial system.'

I use my chin to gesture towards the pages of emails. 'So what did you think of these?'

'Profilers have been casting their beady eyes over them.'

'And have they come up with anything?'

'So far just what you might expect – that the English is flawless, the pace controlled. They think the most likely perpetrator is not one of Georgiev's heavies but someone more sophisticated.'

'Maybe.' I have been considering this myself. 'But profilers don't always get it right.'

'They don't, but the two guys we have at the moment are shit hot.'

I have the feeling he's saying this to reassure me. 'But what do *you* think?' I say. 'Do you have any idea who might be writing them?'

'Georgiev has an extensive network of criminals working for him from accountants through to delivery drivers, but his closest people are usually relations: cousins, nephews, in-laws.' He taps the pages. 'This approach is subtle for him. Often he favours the heavies turning up with their Kalashnikovs. I think they're very deliberately going for the gradual build-up of fear in the hope that Julian will crack.'

'And will he?'

He stares at me for a few seconds, trying to gauge the reason I've asked him such a question. 'No, I don't think he will. Do you?'

'He's not easily intimidated.'

'Would you like him to give in?'

'Yes.' I nod. 'If you can't find this emailer within the next couple of days, then I would.'

'Claire—'

'I know all the arguments. But these people are talking about kidnapping my child.' I press my chest. 'My four-year-old daughter, Mac. The world's population is what – almost seven billion? And I have given birth to three of them. How can I not be biased? How can I not put their welfare ahead of other people's?'

'Every person is someone's child.'

'For sure, and I know about the girls who're trafficked and I know their lives are hell and I do care. I do. But when it comes to making a choice, I will put my own children first.' I sit back in my seat and take a few deep breaths.

He holds up the packet. 'Do you want this last biscuit?'

I shake my head.

'Are you sure?'

'Yes.' I push the peanuts on the napkin towards him. 'Have those too.' And then I can't resist. 'Doesn't your wife feed you?'

'She's modern. She expects me to muck in.'

'No packed lunches?'

'Should I be asking for those?' He narrows his eyes. 'She's good with a gun.'

'She's a policewoman?'

'She teaches yoga, but her family hunt, shoot, fish – all that good stuff.'

I start back. 'You married a posh girl?'

'Yes.' He tips the peanuts into his mouth. 'And no.'

'You're nothing if not cryptic.' I stop talking and put my head in my hands. This whole meeting feels surreal: the flux from deadly serious to casual teasing. 'I can't believe I'm having this conversation.' I lift my head, shake it and then keep going. 'I thought I was done with this world. You are the company you keep, you know? And for the past five years I've been having a quiet time at home with my family. I don't see criminals round every corner. I don't presume people are lying. That's not my world any more.' I take a deep breath. 'Or it wasn't until now. Fucking hell.' I make a face. 'That's another thing – I haven't said "fuck" since I worked with policemen.'

'You're softer now.'

'Yes.' I look at him sideways, but he seems to mean it.

'Not in the head,' he adds. 'Obviously.'

I smile. 'Well, I can feel the old me coming back. I'm toughening up again.' I look down at the emails and then say what's been slowly crystallising since I first read them. 'I think there's a good chance that whoever's writing these is a woman.'

His eyes widen.

'The detail about Bea's shoes and dress,' I say. 'The shopping we bought.'

'You think a man can't notice these things?'

'I think it's less likely. But what really strikes me is this.' I lift the page and read from the fourth email. '"She was carrying her stuffed dog, Bertie."'

Mac sits back in his chair, his arms folded. 'You think that the fact Bea's toy is named makes it more likely to be a woman?'

'Yes, I do, and more than that, I think it's someone who knows us and I think Julian thinks that too, otherwise he wouldn't have been so afraid when Bea was with Amy.' I also sit back in my seat, feeling not exactly triumphant but sure that I have added insight to the investigation. 'He told you about that, didn't he?' I say. 'Isn't that why the policemen appeared in the street?'

He nods. 'We're not ruling out the possibility that someone close to you could be the blackmailer.'

'But you think it's unlikely?'

'As I said, Georgiev uses people he knows, mostly fellow Bulgarians. Do you have any friends who're Bulgarian?'

'No.'

'Do any of your friends have criminal records or criminal links of any kind?'

'Not that I know of.'

'Were you with a friend when you and Bea walked home last Thursday?'

'When we went to the deli, you mean?'

'Yes.'

I shake my head.

'Did you talk to anyone? See someone you knew across the street?'

'No.'

'Did you feel like you were being followed?'

'No.' My optimism that we might be getting somewhere is beginning to deflate. 'But—'

'Are you suspicious of anyone you know?'

'No. Not exactly!' I throw out my hands. 'But still . . .'

'The truth is, the information in these emails could be got in a twenty-second observation from a passer-by.'

'But think about it, Mac. If Bea has been watched at nursery, if we have been followed, it has to be easier for a woman than some beefy guy with a gold chain and tattoos. And I think the language of the emails backs this up.'

'I'm not ruling out your idea and I will speak to the profilers about it,' he says, his tone placatory, 'but I think we have to keep an open mind, otherwise we could set off in one direction and be taken unawares when the threat comes from an unexpected source.'

'OK, OK,' I concede. 'But the bottom line is the pre-trial hearing's five days away and we have no definite leads?'

'Nothing definite, no.'

'Well, I've been thinking. If the witness protection order is not overturned at the hearing, then I'm going to take the children away – all three of them – because if I only take Bea away, then the spotlight could fall on Charlie or Jack. I'll take them to France or America, I don't know where, but I'm not letting them stick around here when they could be in danger.' I hold my hands up to stop him from butting in. 'I appreciate that you have a job to do and that putting this man away is important to the country – I understand that – but it makes sense for the children and me to—' And then I remember Lisa. 'I can't take Lisa abroad.' Even somewhere in the UK would be difficult. She needs continuity of medical care. She needs speedy access to an oncologist, and she needs a community nurse to administer intramuscular medication and check her vital signs. 'Shit, shit, shit.'

'I have a solution to that,' Mac says. 'Julian has already told me about your sister. We can arrange specialist nursing in the UK.' He looks uncomfortable suddenly. 'I have suggested to Julian that on Tuesday you all move to a safe house.'

'A safe house?' Dread seeps into my mouth. It tastes of metal, of blood. 'No,' I say tersely. 'Absolutely not.'

'We're making one ready.'

'No.'

'The best option is to get right away from where they expect to find you.'

'You're forgetting that the last time I had anything to do with a safe house, Kerry Smith ended up dead.'

'That was different, Claire.'

'Was it?' I fold my arms. 'Why?'

'It was more of a women's refuge than a safe house.'

'Well, she thought – in fact we *promised* – that she and her children would be safe and yet she was knifed to death in front of them.'

'Will you please consider the safe-house option?'

I don't answer.

'Are you worried that Lisa won't move into it with you?'

'No.' My fists are clenched on my knees under the table. 'I'm sure she would come.' The room is growing airless. I feel like I have a tight band round my throat, but when I touch my neck, there's nothing there. Lisa. She needs stability. Good food. Peace. Quiet. Not a tense, fearful few weeks or months when we will be staying in an unfamiliar place, all of us cooped up and waiting for something to go wrong.

'I understand your reservations about a safe house.'

'Do you?' I frown at him. 'How do you think Abe found out where Kerry was?'

'We never established that. You know we didn't.'

'Do you think it was a member of the police force, social services, or was it just chance that he found her?'

'Claire, I know how badly that case affected you.' He cradles his coffee mug in his hands. 'But you didn't make a mistake.' He leans across and takes my hand, a comforting gesture. 'It wasn't your fault.'

'Well, it wasn't not my fault,' I say quietly. 'And if I'd been totally focused, I would have pushed for her to be moved to another house when I came into work on the Monday and saw where she was.'

'I was as much to blame.'

I bring my hands on to my knees. 'It's on my conscience, Mac. I felt uneasy, but I ignored the feeling when I should have acted on it. There's no excuse for that.' And there's nothing I can do about what followed either – our no-holds-barred investigation to get Abe convicted and then my once-in-a-marriage slip-up with the man opposite me. I look at him. There's the merest flicker of acknowledgement that one event followed another: Kerry's death, Abe's conviction and then our coming together in the bathroom.

'You're not that sort of woman,' he says.

'What sort of woman?'

'The sort of woman who has affairs.' His face is without expression. 'So that's one less thing to feel guilty about.'

'Maybe.'

'Definitely.' His eyes grow serious. 'You're the last person who needs to beat herself up for extra-marital shenanigans. You were known for playing it straight.'

'Thanks.' In truth, I hope Julian has forgiven me. We haven't talked about it for years and I hardly think about it any more, but the sight of Mac, in the flesh and up close, has brought it all back to me. I betrayed Julian's trust, and the very fact that I'm talking to Mac now means that I'm betraying him again. 'Julian knows that I had sex with someone,' I say quietly. 'He just doesn't know who. I think he assumed it was another solicitor.'

'I guessed as much. He showed no reaction when I met him.' He pauses and looks at me sideways. 'You're not going to be tempted to tell him, are you?'

'No.' We lock eyes. 'Are you?'

'Why would I?'

'I remember you telling Jim Peterson that you'd been with his wife.'

'Aw, come on!' He throws out his arms. 'Peterson was a wanker. There was a grudge behind that.'

'So you had sex with his wife?'

'I'm not proud of it!' He pretends to think back. 'I was probably drunk when I told him.'

'You were completely sober. It was ten o'clock in the morning. He missed your face and punched a hole in the wall.'

'The walls were plasterboard.'

'Please, Mac.' I grip the edges of the table, watch his eyes clock that fact, before moving back to my face. 'The focus has to be on keeping my family safe. We have to get this right.'

'And we will. I promise you.'

'It has to be watertight.' I allow my scared eyes to meet the sincerity in his. 'I can't risk my child being hurt.'

'She won't be.' He shakes his head. 'It won't happen.' He leans in closer. 'Claire. Listen. You can trust me. I know you and—'

'Don't!' I pull away, wary of the power he so easily exerts.

He's a good listener. He has a wide and generous heart. But I, more than anyone, know that what feels like comfort can so quickly flip into something altogether more dangerous.

'I was only going to say that I've missed you.' He smiles. 'Is that so bad? You never came back to work. It seemed like one day you were there, the next you weren't.'

'I don't want to be a solicitor any more. I'm happy with my life. I love being at home. You might shake your head, but really, who needs it? Who needs work with all its hassles and responsibilities?'

'You're missed, Claire.'

'After all these years? I doubt it.'

'You have a huge likeability factor, which, let's face it, can't be said for most of your lot.'

'Is that why you texted me?'

'Yeah.' He clicks his tongue against the roof of his mouth. 'And I guess you haven't missed me or you would have answered them.'

'I crossed a line with you. I don't want to cross it again.'

'You think this is me seducing you?' He gives a short, mirthless laugh. 'A bitter coffee and some custard creams?'

'No.' I frown. 'Of course not. I just want to keep things . . . simple. If past stuff gets in the way, if Julian finds out . . .'

'No distractions. I get it.' His face hardens. 'I take my job seriously. My priority is your family's safety. End of.' He stands up. 'I have to get back to the station. I'll be coming to see you all on Monday after the pre-trial hearing. Better not say anything to anyone before then.'

We walk to the door together. 'What about my stepmother, Wendy?'

'In terms of the safe house?'

I nod.

'We've included her in the plan.' He holds the door and I walk out on to the pavement. 'Julian wasn't sure but he thought you might want her along for support.'

'Yes,' I say, wondering how she'll cope, wondering how we'll all cope, Jack separated from his friends, Charlie from Amy. There are the logistics of packing and of caring for Lisa. 'And then there's Sezen.'

'She cooks for you?'

'Yes.' I realise that Julian will have told him our family set-up. He will already know about everyone who goes in and out of our house.

'Can you do without her?'

'I'd rather not. I haven't employed her for me, or for the family. She's with us for Lisa. She has the sort of expertise I don't have.'

'The more people involved, the more likely there is to be a leak.' He looks regretful. 'She has a child. Always complicates things.'

It's true, and anyway, how could I expect her to be cooped up with us, unable to get in touch with friends or even take her daughter to the shops without looking over her shoulder?

'Where are you parked?'

I point along the street. 'That way.'

'I'm the other way.' He holds me to him, hugs me tight. 'It's been good seeing you again. You take care.' He crosses over the road and shouts back, 'I'll be in touch.'

7

Leaving Tooting High Street behind, I walk to my car, climb inside, close my eyes and let my head flop back against the headrest. In the space of twenty-four hours, life as I know it has hurtled into a dark and ominous place. I feel emotionally exhausted. It's every parent's worst fear that harm could come to their child and this is what's happening to us. Right here. Right now. Bea's safety is under threat, and every time I think of someone hurting her, fear creeps through me, deep into every muscle, every organ and every bone. I can't even begin to imagine how any of us would cope without her. Our whole family would be destroyed. Julian, Charlie, Jack, Wendy, Lisa – our lives would be for ever altered. And I for one doubt whether I could hold on to my sanity.

The only silver lining in this otherwise threatening cloud is that the blackmailer is giving us time to react. Bea hasn't been taken out of the blue and she won't be taken at all if we either hand over the witness details or keep her out of harm's reach. I've yet to speak to Julian, but I suspect that handing over the details would be a last resort. And the best Mac can offer is for us all to be incarcerated in a safe house. Although this is an outwardly sensible option, it fills me with yet more dread. We will, most probably, be living miles from home, where we won't know anyone. We will be powerless, utterly dependent on the integrity of the police. While I trust individuals within the law and the police service, I don't trust the system. I know that sometimes, no matter how much manpower and money you throw at a problem, the outcome still isn't good. And I don't trust that everyone involved will keep their mouths shut. Georgiev has long fingers that stretch into other people's pockets. Some he takes money from, in payment for drugs, prostitution and guns; others he pays for information. And I would bet my life on the fact that some of those people will be in the police service.

Of course, there is a third option. Today is Thursday and the pre-trial hearing is on Monday. Time enough to catch the black-mailer, either by tracing the emails or by working out who she might be. Because the more I think about it, the more convinced I am that the threat is coming from a woman. It makes sense. All of us imagine women to be more trustworthy than men – especially around children. This may not always be accurate, but it is the perceived wisdom. So if this woman is out there, spying on us, following us, then I am in the best position to work out who she might be. A newly appointed nursery teacher or shop assistant? Someone who has suddenly made efforts to befriend our family? A brand-new neighbour?

I rack my brains, but nothing and nobody springs to mind. Whoever she is, she's keeping herself well hidden. But from now on I will watch and listen and report anyone even remotely suspicious to Mac.

Mac. He's another reason I'm feeling emotionally drained. Seeing him again has not been easy. I am treading a fine line and I need to concentrate on keeping my balance. Sure, the fact that I know him has an upside. We have professional respect for each other and that will make it easier for me to be kept informed. I can talk straight with him. I know the way he thinks. This whole case revolves round Bea, and as her mother, I want to be part of the decision-making process. I am confident that Mac under-stands this.

The downside is that because of our previous intimacy, the waters could grow muddy. I'm not sure I entirely believed him when he agreed to no distractions. It would be natural for us to fall back into an easy familiarity and further breach the trust Julian has placed in me. I don't want it and I don't need it. All I want is for this to be over as soon as possible, for my family to be safe and for me to be able to go back to concentrating on helping Lisa become well again.

I open my eyes and type Sezen's address into the sat nav. The meeting with Mac has taken slightly longer than I thought and she will be waiting, excited at the prospect of coming to live in Brighton. I know the flat she lives in is close by, but I'm not sure exactly where. I watch the route pan out on the display before me and am about to start the engine when my mobile rings. The screen tells me it's an unknown number. I answer it anyway, knowing it could well be Julian, and it is. He's ringing from the airport in Sofia.

'I called the house just now. Wendy told me you're up in Tooting collecting Sezen.'

'I offered to help her with her move to Brighton.'

'And Wendy's looking after Bea?'

'I kept her out of nursery.'

'I understand. It doesn't do any harm to play completely safe.' I hear apology in his voice. 'Claire, I'm sure you're not very happy with me.'

'An understatement if ever there was one,' I say, under my breath.

'I didn't catch that.'

'It doesn't matter,' I say, unwilling to enter into the futility of another long-distance disagreement.

'Let's make time tonight for us to talk about what's been happening and what the police are doing.'

It's my chance to say that I logged on to his computer and printed off the emails and that I've just spent the last hour and a half with the policeman in charge. If Mac is to be trusted, and I'm ninety-nine per cent sure that he is, then I'm as up to date with the details of the case as Julian is.

But I don't tell him this. We talk about the children and about arrangements and then say our goodbyes. I wish him a safe journey before tossing my phone on to the passenger seat. Then I sit

completely still, staring through the windscreen at the rows of
cars lined up in front and to the side of me, sunlight reflecting
off glass and metal. I feel bleak. Talking to Julian, the man I love
and cherish, should make me feel better, but it hasn't. It's made
me feel worse. Normally, I'm not someone who holds back. I
don't keep secrets from Julian. I never lie to him. Before today,
I would have bet my life on the fact that our marriage is as honest
as they get, and that our love and commitment to each other and
our children keep our actions transparent. But now secrecy has
its foot in the door, wedging it open, allowing doubt and duplicity
to creep inside. Why didn't he tell me about the blackmail? Could
it be as simple as him not wanting to worry me, or is it something more? This question nags at me and now here I am, doing
the same. I am holding back on my meeting with Mac. The same
man I have history with. The same man on whom Julian and I
must now rely.

Ironic, when five years ago it was sex with Mac that almost
cost us our marriage. It's a time I will never forget. For two whole
weeks after Kerry's wake I lived with my infidelity, my stomach
in knots, my heart heavy with shame. I hadn't told Julian about
what I'd done, partly because I was afraid of his reaction – what
if he was so hurt that he left me? Took the boys? – and partly
because it felt unreal, as if I'd dreamed it. I didn't do that sort
of thing. I had never so much as looked twice at another man,
let alone had sex with one.

And yet I just had. I'd behaved completely out of character.
Sex and death, not an unusual combination, my behaviour in
keeping with the sort of criminals I was mixing with. Fast lives
and premature deaths, living on the edge, living for the moment,
taking comfort where you can get it, never thinking about
tomorrow. A life can easily slide out of control, and that's what
had happened to mine.

Over those two weeks I realised that my job was incompatible
with my life. It was time to reassess. I was married to a man I
loved. We had two children together. At that point Charlie was

fourteen and Jack was eleven. Our lives needed an overhaul. Julian and I were both working too hard. While we were professionally linked and often shared lunch, at home we passed each other on the stairs and in the bathroom, hardly came together in the bedroom. Any energy we had left we gave to the boys at the weekend. It was one of those moments of clarity when I knew that if I didn't put my marriage and my family first, pretty soon I wasn't going to have a marriage or a family.

And cheating ruins lives. My father cheated on my stepmother, Wendy, more than once and I knew I never wanted to be that person or have it done to me. Julian deserved the truth and so I sat him down when the boys were in bed and I confessed. I told him I'd had sex with another man, that it had only happened once and would never happen again. Before I had the chance to tell him how much I loved him, he stood up and left the room. When I followed him, he held me at a distance with one arm, packed a case and left. For over a week he stayed away and in that time I was consumed with guilt and remorse. I could barely sleep, barely breathe, terrified that he might have left me for good.

On the ninth evening he came back. I'd told the boys he was away on a case. They were delighted to see him and we spent an almost normal evening eating and chatting. When the boys were in bed, he started to talk.

'I don't want to know his name. I don't want any details,' he said. 'But I do want to know whether you love him.'

'No.' I shook my head. 'I don't. It was ten minutes of madness. I can't explain it. I don't know what possessed me to do it. But what I do know' – I dropped on to my knees in front of him – 'is that as long as I live, I will never do anything like that again.' Perversely, having sex with Mac had made me realise just how much I loved Julian and my family. 'I love you, Julian. I love you more than I can express.'

'Do you see us growing old together?'

'Yes.' I took his hand. 'I can't imagine my life without you.

I see us age eighty or ninety or a hundred even! Helping one another, laughing, sharing everything.'

He looked at me for a long time and then agreed that we could put it behind us. On one condition. 'You have to promise never to see him again.'

'Absolutely.'

I promised and then asked him how he felt about me giving up work to become a full-time mother and wife. We could move to Brighton. My father, Wendy and my sister were all living there. We could spend more time as a family. At first he was sceptical – didn't I love living in London? How would I cope without the buzz of taking criminals to trial? – but when we talked further, he could see that as a family we needed a change and so we shed the bulk of our mortgage and moved to the coast. The boys settled easily. They loved the open spaces and the sea, and they made new friends at once. Julian managed the commute by reading through documents on the train, and I quickly settled into life as a stay-at-home mum. A choice I have never regretted. And until today I've kept my promise to Julian and never been in touch with Mac.

But now the parameters have shifted. Bea's life is under threat and Mac is back in both our lives. Somehow Julian and I have to negotiate a way through this without losing our trust in each other.

I already feel like it's a big ask.

Sezen and her daughter, Lara, live in a flat, one of three unimaginative blocks of grey, each about ten storeys high. The balconies are a dirty blue colour, the paint chipped and worn. What little green there is around the buildings is trampled on and strewn with litter. Sezen is waiting for me outside, and as soon as my car pulls up, she comes across to meet me. She looks distracted; her normally serene amber eyes are troubled.

'Everything OK?' I ask.

'Yes. We can be quick.' She glances around as if expecting to see someone lurking behind a lamppost. 'This is not a good place for you to come. I have packed all our belongings. Lara is upstairs.'

I follow her into the tower block, relieved not to have Bea with me. The glass in the door has been smashed and, despite the summer morning outside, there is a vicious draft blowing up through the stairwell. Squashed cans, cigarette packets and plastic bags swirl round in a circle, but at least the fresh air dilutes the smell of urine and stale beer. There is a sign on the lift that screams, 'Fuckin' out of order again!' Sezen looks embarrassed, as if she is personally responsible for all of this, and I realise too late that she didn't want me to see exactly where she lived. Then it strikes me that in the time it takes to gather everything together my car could be broken into. So much for me thinking my brain was back in streetwise-solicitor mode. I look behind me to where it is parked by the kerb, a lone vehicle, much shinier and grander than its surroundings.

'We can be gone in minutes,' Sezen says, and starts to climb the stairs two at a time. I follow, glad that my sandals are functional as well as fashionable.

When I worked for the CPS, I spent time interviewing witnesses, often in their own homes, so I'm no stranger to the run-down places some people are forced to live in, but there is a pervasive feeling of tension in this building and I want to get away as soon as possible.

Lara is on the third floor, sitting on top of a black bin bag just inside the front door of one of the flats. She stands up as soon as she sees us coming. She is seven months older than Bea but about six inches shorter. She is petite, with thick black hair that falls in ringlets past her cheeks. Her eyes are amber, like her mother's. She is clutching a child's pull-along case, both her hands tight round the handle.

'Hello.' I squat down in front of her. 'I'm Claire. You and Mummy are coming to live close by.'

Her eyes are solemn. She extracts her right hand from the handle and offers it to me. 'I am happy to meet you,' she says.

Sezen gives her a brief, pleased smile.

'And I am happy to meet you.' I give her a welcome hug and then I look around. Apart from the bin bag and Lara's small case, there is one other suitcase tied in the middle with a scuffed leather belt. 'Is there anything else?'

'No.' Sezen is whispering. 'We share the room and already the others are sleeping. They work night duty. We have all our belongings here.'

I know from her references that her last position was a well-paid one, so I wonder why they've been living in such run-down, cramped circumstances, but I don't ask. I want to get home. I want to take Bea in my arms and never let her go.

I pick up the suitcase and start down the stairs. We're in the car and on the road in minutes. Lara is in Bea's car seat, and Sezen is next to me. On the drive back to Brighton, Lara falls asleep.

Sezen talks about the preparations she has made for Lisa. 'I have been researching,' she says. 'We must use food's healing properties. That will be important for your sister. A ginger compress is effective for removing poisons from the blood. A kudzu drink strengthens digestion.'

She reels off some more remedies, ticking ingredients and their potential for healing off on her fingers. I join in with the conversation, ignoring the fact that all of Sezen's plans could come to nothing. She has brought skill and enthusiasm to my kitchen and revitalised Lisa's appetite and I don't want to give her up. Until the safe house becomes our only reality, I'm determined to employ her as usual.

'This is the street.' Sezen points to the left. 'Number seventeen is about halfway along.'

We're back in Brighton now, close to where Sezen and Lara will be living. I indicate left and pull into the nearest spot.

Sezen turns to Lara, who is just waking up. 'Lara! This will be our new home.'

Lara looks out of the window, taking in the houses but making no comment.

The three of us climb out and go to the front door. The house looks tired – the external walls are stained, and the woodwork around the windows could do with being rubbed down – but the windows themselves are clean, and the curtains inside are hanging neatly. The garden at the front has been gravelled and a car sits to one side of the two-car parking space.

Sezen rings the bell and within a minute the door opens. The man standing there looks about sixty. His moustache is a silver-grey colour, his eyes and skin a deep caramel.

'Mr Patel?' Sezen says.

'I am he.'

'I am Sezen Serbest.' She holds out her hand and he shakes it. 'This is my daughter, Lara, and my employer' – there's a split-second hesitation – 'and friend Mrs Claire Miller.'

'I am enchanted to meet you all.' Mr Patel bows his head at each of us in turn.

'I spoke to your son about renting the small apartment on the top floor. I have my belongings in the car.'

'I see.' He nods. 'But we have very little space. I was expecting you to bring your belongings with you when you move in.'

'Yes.' Sezen smiles uncertainly. 'And that is today. After one o'clock.'

'We are not expecting you this week. Mrs Patel and I are expecting you in almost three weeks.' He stresses the last two words by nodding his head from side to side. 'Twenty days, to be exact. When our tenant Mr Archibald has moved out.'

Sezen looks at me and then back to Mr Patel. 'But we arranged for me to move in on 3 June. I spoke to your son and—'

'I am afraid you are mistaken. My son would not say such a thing. Mr Archibald has not left and therefore you cannot move in.'

'I do not understand.'

'I am so sorry. There is nothing to be done.'

Sezen clutches her chest and turns to look at me, disappointment darkening her eyes.

I take her hand. 'Don't worry,' I say. 'There has been a mix-up, but we can fix it.' I look at Mr Patel. 'So Sezen definitely has a place when?'

'She most definitely has a place on 23 June, when Mr Archibald is leaving for Sheffield.'

'Thank you.' I hold out my hand. 'We will return then.'

'I am a man of my word.' His handshake is warm and firm. 'And I am most sorry for the misunderstanding.'

When he closes the door, Sezen is still looking confused. 'I am sure he said 3 June. I am sure he did. I gave his son my deposit.'

'You have a receipt for that and a tenancy agreement?'

'Yes.' She digs around in her pocket. 'Here.'

She hands me the paperwork. I read it. Everything looks above board, and what's more the date of entry into the apartment is 23 June, just as Mr Patel said. I point this out to Sezen and she shrinks back into her jacket, then murmurs something under her breath. 'I am so stupid.' Her face is flushed, and she pushes back a small tear that has escaped from her right eye on to her cheek. 'I am so sorry this has inconvenienced you.'

'These things happen.' I manage to smile. This whole time Lara has been standing silently. So different from Bea, she barely makes her presence felt. I lift her into the back seat of the car and strap her in. 'It's nobody's fault.'

'You went out of your way to come for me and help me with my things.'

I feel for her and on almost any other day of any other week I would immediately offer her a place to stay, but I hold my tongue. While Sezen seems a lovely person, hardworking and considerate, I'm disinclined to extend that to a live-in position. There's enough going on in my life as it is.

'Your journey has been wasted and now we will have to go back to London.' She is pacing the pavement, her fists clenched by her side. 'I will talk to someone in . . . I may be allowed back.' Her face betrays her doubt. 'And if not, the neighbour was . . . may be willing . . .'

She goes in and out of my earshot as she strides back and forth along the pavement. Lara is watching her pace. Her eyes are large and liquid, her breathing shallow. Although she doesn't say much, I can see that she misses nothing and her mother's distress is worrying her. I recognise the signs. My childhood wasn't always a bundle of laughs. After my mother died, when I was just four, and for the two years before Wendy came along, Lisa and I were often left to fend for ourselves while my father drank himself into a stupor. I don't know much about the particulars of Sezen and Lara's background, but I do know something about the weight of uncertainty, and I see it fill Lara's small frame until she begins to tremble.

'You can't go back to Tooting,' I say, remembering the smell in the stairwell, the broken windows and lift, and picture this vulnerable child living among it, as out of place as a blind man in a war zone. 'Apart from anything else, it isn't safe.' I make a quick decision. It's not their fault the timing is off. I can't just leave them here and I don't want to drive them back to Tooting either. 'We have a room in the top of our house you can stay in for a couple of days. Until you sort out some interim accommodation.'

'No.' Sezen pulls her back straight. 'You have already been very kind.'

'Sezen—'

'I will find somewhere temporary in Brighton.'

'Well, in the meantime you can come and stay with us. Just for a couple of days.' I close the door to the back of the car and open the front one, gesturing for her to go inside. 'We have the space. It's really no trouble.'

I watch her do battle with herself. I know that she is independent. Accepting help is difficult for her. In the back seat, Lara is sitting quietly, her fine features as delicate as bone china. 'For Lara,' I say. 'It's the least disruptive solution for her.'

Sezen glances quickly at her daughter and reluctantly agrees. We set off again, round the corner and into my street. Lara spots the park opposite our house and points and shouts, 'Look, Mummy! Swings!'

'Yes.' Sezen turns round to address her. 'Later, Lara. You can go on the swings later.'

In the rear-view mirror I watch Lara deflate back into her seat. 'We can go now,' I say, my eyes seeking out Baker and Faraway and finding them exactly where I left them this morning. 'I'll get Bea from the house and come and join you. It'll be a good place for the girls to meet each other.'

'Should we unload the car first?'

'We can do it afterwards.'

Sezen and Lara cross the road to the park and I go inside. The house is completely quiet. I walk through to the kitchen and look down into the garden. Bea is playing outside, hopping first on her left foot and then her right, round and round in circles until she grows dizzy and has to hold on to the handlebars of her bike.

I hear the flush of the downstairs toilet and Wendy comes out. 'Oh! You're back!'

'Sorry I took so long.' I hang my car keys up on the hook. 'And thank you for looking after Bea.'

'No problem at all. You know how much I enjoy her company. How's Sezen? Is she pleased with her new rooms?'

'There was a mix-up.'

'What sort of a mix-up?'

I summarise our conversation with Mr Patel.

'Oh, no! That poor girl! As if life hasn't been hard enough on her.' Wendy likes Sezen. She liked her instantly and is convinced that although she has said very little about her past, she has been put upon, exploited even – not least by Lara's absent father.

'So she and Lara will be staying with us for the next couple of days. They're in the park. Do you want to join us?'

'Perhaps next time.' She looks at her watch. 'I'll pop along and visit Lisa. Take her a late lunch.' She lifts her bag off the kitchen table. 'Oh, and Mary Percival called from the nursery.'

'I should have let her know Bea wasn't coming in.'

'Wasn't a problem. I said I wasn't sure about tomorrow and that you'd be in touch.'

'Are Charlie and Amy home?'

'They're upstairs.'

I open the patio door to shout to Bea, who comes running in to give Wendy a goodbye-grandma hug. Bea and I follow her to the front door to wave goodbye and then, before Bea shakes off her boots, I tell her that we are going to the park to play with Lara.

'Who?'

'Sezen's daughter. She told you about her. Remember?'

She thinks. 'Why is she here?'

'Because she's coming to live in Brighton.' I kneel down in front of her. 'In fact, for a couple of days she's coming to stay with us.'

'Why?'

'Because her house isn't ready yet.'

'Why?'

I can just about see her blue eyes regarding me with confusion, through strands of her hair, which is still as soft as when she was a baby and has slid out of the two grips on either side of her head.

'You'll like her.' I pin back her hair and she winces as the grips rub against her scalp. 'She loves to play outside, just like you do, and she likes animal tea parties.'

'How do you know?'

'I asked her.'

'Can she talk?'

'Of course!' I laugh. 'She's a little bit older than you.'

She thinks some more. 'Does she not have a house to live in?'

'No, darling.'

'Then I'll let her play with Bertie because he knows about these things. Grandma says Bertie is a wise old dog.'

'That's very kind, Bea.' I kiss her forehead. 'I'm sure she'll appreciate you sharing your toys.'

'He's not a toy. He's a dog.' As if to prove it, she pulls Bertie out from underneath her arm, looks into his lopsided face and makes a woofing sound.

I laugh. 'You are a funny Bea!' I hug her hard enough to make her squeal.

'Mummy!'

'I can't help it.' I let her go. 'Sometimes I love you so much I want to cuddle you and never stop.' We move out on to the front step. 'Look! There's Lara.' I point ahead to where Lara is climbing the ladder on the slide. When she gets to the top, she sits down carefully and then lets go, her face frozen in an ecstatic smile all the way to the bottom. Bea holds my hand while we cross the road, then runs off to join her. They find common ground instantly and play together for some time. Sezen and I sit down on a bench and chat. Out of the corner of my eye, I notice that the two policemen are watching us, their presence reassuring.

When the girls have had enough, we unpack the car and go inside. Bea takes Lara to her den under the stairs, while I show Sezen around the house. Although she's been coming here for a month, it occurs to me that she hasn't been beyond the ground floor. The level of the front street is higher than the back garden, which is accessed either from the basement level, where there is the utility room, Jack's bedroom and Julian's study, or from the patio doors in the kitchen and down a series of steps. As well as the kitchen and sitting room, the ground floor has a bedroom and en suite, where Lisa will sleep. On the very top floor are the spare rooms: two bedrooms and a bathroom. When I show Sezen where she and Lara will sleep, she exclaims with delight at the view. It stretches over the rooftops and out to the sea, which is two hundred metres or so in the distance.

'I grew up on the coast,' she says. 'I love to be close to the sea.' She wanders into the bathroom next door. 'This is lovely, Claire,' she says. 'Much more than I expected.'

'Mummy!' Bea is shouting up the stairs. 'Come and see what we've done.'

We join the girls downstairs and they show us the tea party they've set up for the dogs: miniature cups, saucers and plates spread out on a blanket. Sezen offers to prepare dinner and I accept, knowing that I couldn't concentrate on making a meal. My thoughts are a powerful tide that drag me elsewhere, preoccupying me to the point of obsession. I look at my watch. Just under an hour until Julian gets home. I think about all the things we have to say to one another. We don't often argue, and it's been years since I lost my temper, but anger has been simmering inside me since I found out he was keeping the emails from me. I want an explanation. I want reassurance, and I want him to prioritise Bea's safety over everything else.

A text arrives. I take my phone from my pocket and read the message. Julian's on his way back from the airport. I go down to the basement level and check his email – nothing new from the blackmailer. I wander next door to busy myself with laundry, moving clothes from one pile to the next, building mounds of dirty and clean clothes. As I stand there, I hear steps in the corridor. I expect whoever it is to be heading for the garden and to walk through the room I'm in, but they don't. The door to Julian's study opens and closes. I wait for a couple of seconds and then it occurs me that it will be Bea, sneaking Lara into Julian's study so that she can have a turn on Julian's swivel chair and show her the wig Julian wears when he's in court.

I leave the laundry and open the study door. 'Now, young lady—' I stop short. It isn't Bea; it's Amy. She has her bag slung over her shoulder and is standing by the built-in unit in the corner rummaging through a drawer. 'Amy?'

'Yeah?'

'What are you doing?'

'Looking for some plain paper. I thought I'd do some drawing with Bea and Lara.'

'The paper is over there.' I wave my arm towards the substantial printer that rests on the corner of Julian's desk. Next to it there is a stack of paper. An obvious place. A visible place.

'Oh.' She raises a languid eyebrow. 'So it is.'

'So what were you really looking for?'

'Excuse me?' Her stare is bold.

'You said you were looking for paper, but it's sitting on the desk, as large as life.' I give a short laugh. 'Instead, I catch you going through a drawer.'

'I wasn't looking at anything private!' She snorts. 'If that's what you're implying.'

'Amy—'

'It's not a problem.' Her tone isn't aggressive; it's perplexed. Her fingers trail along the spines of some books as she walks across to stand in front of me. 'Is it?'

'You know, Amy. Yes . . . I think it is.' I hold her gaze. Her eyes are the navy blue of stormy seawater. She blinks twice in quick succession. 'I'm sorry but it's not acceptable for you to come into Julian's study like this. He has confidential files stored here.'

She snorts again and her bag swings forwards on her shoulder. There's a piece of paper sticking out of the top and something is written on it. I do a double-take. It's Julian's handwriting. Even from a few feet away I recognise his neat, legible script.

'The paper on top of your bag, would you pass it to me, please?'

'What?' She looks down at the bag, then back at me. 'Why?'

'Because I don't think it belongs to you.'

My tone is growing colder, but it doesn't bother her. With what seems like deliberate nonchalance, she takes it out of her bag and looks at it. 'It's scrap paper. I found it in the kitchen.'

'Let me see it, please.'

She sighs, rolls her eyes, then passes it to me. At the same time Charlie comes into the room and I glance at him briefly before reading it. On one side Amy has scrawled an address, and on the other are the details I was looking for – the name and phone number of Julian's hotel in Sofia.

'This piece of paper was on the pinboard,' I say quietly. 'Julian left it for me, and Charlie specifically asked you whether you'd seen it.'

'I didn't know he was talking about *that* piece.'

'Airhead.' Charlie gives her an affectionate slap on the backside.

'I wrote Bug's address on it,' she tells Charlie, 'but your mum thinks I'm up to no good.' She says the last four words with wide, mock-scary eyes and a humorous tone. Charlie laughs.

'Charlie, I need to have a word with you,' I say tersely. 'A private word.'

'Well . . . OK, yeah.'

I turn away as they kiss each other and then Amy saunters upstairs.

'Charlie.' I twist my hands in front of me. 'I don't know quite how to put this.' I hesitate. 'I'm not sure I trust Amy.'

'Eh?'

'This is the second time I've caught her coming into your dad's study. None of your other friends has ever done this.'

'Well.' He looks sheepish, shifts from one foot to the other. 'She probably doesn't realise it's private. I'll ask her not to.'

I remember Mac's question earlier – *Are you suspicious of anyone you know?* Am I suspicious of Amy, or is it just that I haven't warmed to her? I don't know. And under normal circumstances I would give her a second chance, but having her to stay while all this is going on with Bea doesn't feel right. I need to have people around me I can trust, not people who undermine me.

I move across the room and pull open the drawer that she was rummaging through. Julian is in the habit of tidying anything that's lying around into one of the half-dozen drawers. It's stuffed full of bits and pieces: batteries, golf tees, screws, a spare calculator, numerous wires and stray sockets for headphones and radios, a couple of broken mobile phones, an old necklace and a stash of keys. None of it's important; in fact most of it needs binning. I can't see anything in here that Amy would have wanted, or indeed taken. But still.

I turn back to Charlie. He's staring at me expectantly. 'Is Amy going to be staying much longer?'

He shakes his head at me. 'What do you mean?'

I think of an angle. Amy, like most students, is chronically hard up. The reason she's spending her third year in halls and not a shared flat is because she needs to save money. 'She has her room back in university accommodation, doesn't she?'

'Yeah, but . . .' He shrugs. 'We like being together.'

'I thought the deal for her cut-price room was that she was there as a mentor for the first-years?'

'It's June already. They don't need their hands held.'

'Still. She has been staying here for four nights.'

'What are you getting at, Mum?' His eyes cloud over. 'Isn't she welcome here?'

'No.' The word is out of my mouth before I can stop myself.

'Mum!' Charlie starts back, confusion and hurt battling it out on his face. 'She's my girlfriend.'

'I know and I'm sorry I'm saying this, but—'

'That drawer doesn't having anything important in it!'

'I know, but that's not the point.' He's looking at me with such naked hurt that for a moment I falter. Then I think about what we're facing as a family and know that I can't leave any room for doubt. 'I'm so sorry, Charlie, but I really would like Amy to leave.'

'But she—'

'Not for ever.' I hold my hands up and go to place them on his shoulders, but he moves backwards. 'Just until . . . life is more settled.'

'What's that supposed to mean?'

'Well . . .' I give myself a couple of seconds to think. Mac said it would be better to keep this quiet until Monday, when he comes to talk to the family, but Charlie is nineteen and I think that keeping him completely in the dark is unfair. 'We have to be careful of security because of Dad's trial.'

'Eh?' His neck cranes forward in disbelief. 'You think Amy's a security risk?'

'Not exactly. But she doesn't behave the way most people would if they were in someone else's house.'

He throws out his arms. 'She's a free spirit!'

'Actually, Charlie, she's—'

'And she's not afraid of you, Mum. Is that what you don't like?'

I bite my lip. 'Please, love. I know this is hard—'

'Bollocks to this.'

'Charlie!'

He stomps past me to the bottom of the stairs. 'Am *I* welcome here, then?' he shouts back.

'Of course you are!'

'Or should I go as well?'

He takes the stairs two at a time. I call after him, but he ignores me. I lean my head against the wall and shut my eyes. I didn't handle that at all well. It might have been better to wait until Julian arrived home. Charlie would have taken it better from him. I contemplate going upstairs to them both, but I'm not about to change my mind. Much as it upsets Charlie, I really don't want Amy here. I find it at best astonishing and at worst suspicious that I ended up discovering her in Julian's study again. Despite Mac's scepticism, I feel in my gut that the blackmailer is a woman. A woman who knows our family. And as Julian pointed out, what do we really know about Amy? Sezen has come into our home with cast-iron references, but the boys' friends and girlfriends are invited in on trust. I know that Amy made a play for Charlie. I also know that it was just around the time Julian was asked to represent the Crown against Georgiev. A coincidence? Most probably. But it's not a risk I'm willing to take.

8

I stay in the laundry room until ten minutes before Julian is due to arrive home. Charlie and Amy have left the house, the door slamming loudly behind them. I figure I'll give Charlie a cooling-off period, then call him on his mobile. I ask Sezen to keep the girls busy in the kitchen so that I can have some time alone with Julian. The taxi pulls up outside the house and I open the door as he's paying the driver. He comes up the steps, drops his suitcase in the porch and holds out his arms. I am always taken aback by how happy I am to see him. Even after twenty-odd years together, and with all that's going on, I still feel a rush of excitement and then a quieter feeling of a shared life and sense of belonging with each other.

'How was Sofia?'

'Hot and sticky.'

'Cup of tea?' I ask without thinking, and immediately hope he says no. If we go into the kitchen, Bea will monopolise him until bedtime.

'I'll have a shower first, I think. All that waiting around in airports has left me feeling grubby.'

I follow him up the stairs. I feel I should give him a couple of minutes to acclimatise before we start to talk about the emails. When we reach our en suite, he says, 'How's Lisa bearing up?'

'The same. You know how stoic she is. Results weren't good and now . . .' I shrug. 'It's a case of waiting and seeing . . . and hoping.'

'I'm sorry, love.' He leans towards me, gives me a kiss, leaves his hand on my hair. 'I know this is difficult for you.'

'I want to have everything sorted for her when she comes out of hospital. Jem's coming round tomorrow to finish off painting the room.' I hold his eyes, wait for him to mention the safe house, but he doesn't. He looks strained. I know he will be as worried about the blackmail as I am. I don't want arguments. I want us to be a united front, but we're not going to get there unless Julian understands how hard the last twenty-four hours have been, learning about the blackmail and about his resignation.

'Are you ready to talk?' I say.

'Let me have a quick shower first?'

A question rather than a statement. I nod and go back through to our bedroom, sit down on the bed and wait for him. I count the seconds – all three and a half minutes of them – and then he's standing in front of me drying himself.

'Where's Bea?'

'In the kitchen with Sezen and Lara, her little girl.'

'How are they getting along?'

'Bea and Lara?'

He nods.

'Really well. Bea even let her play with Bertie.'

He raises an eyebrow at this. 'She must like her.' He drops the towel on the bed and takes boxers and a T-shirt from the chest of drawers.

'Sezen's made a macrobiotic dinner for tonight.'

'I look forward to eating it.' He finds a pair of jeans in the wardrobe and pulls them on top of the boxers. 'You must almost be able to cook that way yourself now.'

'Not even close,' I say quietly. 'Which is a pity because what with everything that's going on, it doesn't look like we're going to be able to keep Sezen, does it?'

He sits down on the bed beside me and takes my left hand, staring at my wedding and engagement rings as if it's the first time he's ever seen them. 'I'm sorry, Claire.'

'Sorry for what?'

'Sorry for all of it.'

'You should have told me.'

'I know.'

'From now on will you talk to me?' He tries to pull me into his chest. I hold my back straight and lean away from him. 'Let me know what's going on?' He looks into my eyes. 'Will you?'

'Yes.'

'Good.' I take a breath. My chest feels tight and I have to force in air. 'When I found out about the emails, I was shocked and confused and afraid for Bea. And then I invited Megan round and she told me you'd resigned and . . .' I feel my lips trembling and tense my jaw.

'Claire—'

'Do you know how that made me feel?'

He rubs his hand across his forehead.

'Really. You should think about it,' I say. 'I had to ask your instructing solicitor for details that affect our family's safety.'

He keeps his eyes averted.

'Two months ago, when you had the burglar alarm installed, was it because you thought something like this might happen?'

'Yes.'

Anger swells inside me like a balloon filling with air. 'Why didn't you tell me *then*?'

'At that point I hadn't received any emails. I did it as a precaution.'

'But you must have had a suspicion?'

'I knew that Georgiev had threatened people before.'

'So why not tell me that? Forewarn me?'

'I felt you had enough on your plate with Lisa. I didn't want to add to your worries when there was a chance that nothing would come of it.'

'Don't make this about my sister,' I warn him. 'You should have told me.' My cheeks are burning up. I go to the bedroom window, open it and let the sea air cool my face. 'How do you see me, Julian?' I frown back at him. 'As some sort of flaky, weak-willed woman who can't cope with reality?'

'Of course not.' He comes and stands beside me. 'I know how strong you are. I was trying to protect you.'

'Protect me?' Anger spikes again. 'You went off to Sofia without a word of warning!'

'There are two policemen ou—'

'Yes, I know,' I snap. 'Two plainclothes policemen in a beat-up Ford Mondeo, parked in our street, sticking out like tarts in a nunnery.'

'Claire—'

'Big bloody deal,' I shout. 'Fat lot of use they'd have been if a couple of gunmen turned up at the front door and me none the fucking wiser.'

He flinches at the F-word.

'I'm sorry, Julian.' I widen my eyes and lean towards him. 'Are you offended by that?'

'Sarcasm will not—'

'Will not *what*? Will not change the fact that you left your wife and children in danger?' I pace across the floor. 'How dare you? How fucking dare you waltz off to Sofia and leave me and the children with no knowledge of what was going on?'

'Will you please calm down.' He tries to take my hands.

'Do. Not. Touch. Me.'

He steps backwards. 'I was trying to protect all of you.'

'By keeping us in the dark?'

'I didn't feel . . . *We* didn't feel there was any point in worrying you before it was absolutely justified.'

'*We?* Who's "we" exactly?'

'The police. Andrew MacPherson. He's taking this extremely seriously.'

Another moment to confess that I printed out the emails, that I met up with Mac this morning and that, in doing so, broke the promise I made to Julian five years ago. But I don't say any of these things. Instead, I say, 'Have you considered giving in to the blackmailer's demands?'

'Claire' – he gives me a puzzled look – 'you must know that isn't an option.'

'Of course it's an option,' I say. 'Are you willing to consider it?'

'Apart from the fact that giving in to someone like Georgiev goes against everything I believe in, I would be disbarred and imprisoned.'

'So we spend months living in fear?'

'Our witness will be called to give evidence first.'

'And if the defence manages to think of reasons to delay?'

'They have no more options open to them.'

'You can't possibly know that! They could have anything up their sleeves.' I feel agitated. I pace backwards and forwards, five steps in one direction, five steps in the other. 'If we make it impossible for the blackmailer to get close to Bea, she will be forced to go after one of the boys. We can't let Charlie go back to university or Jack to school.'

'She?' He starts back. 'Why did you say "she"?'

'I think the blackmailer's a woman.'

'But you haven't read the emails.' He pauses. 'Have you?'

'This is *me* you're talking to, Julian.' I bang my fist against my chest. 'After the way you reacted when Bea was missing with Amy . . .' I look down at the floor and then back into his eyes. 'You honestly think I was just going to trot off to bed when I knew you were receiving threatening emails?'

'You logged on to my laptop?'

'What option did I have?'

'And have you read them?'

'I have. And I printed them out.'

He gives a slight shake of his head.

'If you had been honest with me,' I say quietly, 'I wouldn't have had to do that.'

'I know,' he acknowledges. 'Perhaps, in your shoes, I would have done the same.'

'You would never have been in my shoes,' I say, keeping my voice low. 'I wouldn't have kept this from you. And another thing.' I fill my lungs with air. 'I called Andrew MacPherson this morning and met him in a café.'

'I see.' He purses his lips and turns away from me.

'I would rather we had been together but' – I shrug – 'you weren't here and I didn't want to wait.'

He sits down on the edge of the bed.

'What's the matter?' I bend low so that I can see his expression. 'Shouldn't I have done that?'

'You know . . . Claire.' He looks weary, his eyelids dropping low over his eyes. 'I'm not the enemy here.'

'I know.' I'm not enjoying this. We rarely fall out. I'm not trying to take the upper hand. I'm simply trying to make him understand how hard it is being excluded. 'But it's like the train is already moving and I'm running alongside, trying to catch hold of your hand. I feel hurt, Julian.' I kneel down at his feet. 'I feel let down.'

The kitchen door slams. Next thing, Bea lets out a delighted shout. I know she'll have seen Julian's case by the front door. Within seconds she's in our bedroom, launching herself at him. She screams with delight as he first throws her up in the air and then tosses her on to our bed and tickles her breathless. I love seeing them together, but right now my insides are churned up like a ploughed field and only Julian and I working together will fix that. I leave the room. I help finish setting the table, hoping that Sezen's calm demeanour will rub off on me, but it doesn't, and when Julian joins us, carrying Bea, my heart is still sore. He says hello to Sezen and then she introduces him to Lara.

'Bea tells me you like to play on the swings, Lara,' he says.

She blushes and looks down at her feet.

'She is shy of men,' Sezen says.

'That's no bad thing,' Julian says, smiling.

Sezen speaks to her daughter in Turkish and Lara looks up at Julian.

'Thank you for my room,' she says.

'And I would also like to thank you,' Sezen says. 'It is very kind of you to offer us a home.'

Julian looks across at me.

'Sezen's accommodation in Brighton isn't ready yet. I invited her to stay with us for a couple of days until she can organise somewhere else.'

He nods and smiles at me, with his mouth but not with his eyes. Then he looks at Sezen and says, 'Glad we could help.'

We all take our places at the table – apart from Sezen, who insists she be the one to serve. Bea won't sit in her own chair and there's no point trying to make her. She will start to cry and then wail and we will all end up with fraught nerves and indigestion. She stays on Julian's knee, cosying in towards his chest, one thumb lodged in her mouth while the other hand twirls her hair round her index finger.

'We are going to start with miso soup,' Sezen says. 'It is very refreshing on the palate.'

'Charlie not around?' Julian says.

'We had a bit of an argument.'

'Over what?'

'Amy.' Bea has slithered off Julian's knee to fetch Bertie, and I check that Sezen is out of earshot at the hob. 'I told Charlie she had to leave.'

'Why?'

'I don't trust her. I couldn't find your hotel details. She had taken the paper from the pinboard and written something on the back of it, and yet when Charlie asked her whether she'd seen it, she said no.'

'She is a bit scatty.'

'Maybe. But I found her in your study – twice.'

'What?'

'Nosing around.'

'In my desk?'

'She was standing by the corner shelves, looking through one of the drawers. She said she was looking for printer paper.' I throw my hands out. 'I just didn't buy it.'

'How long do you think she was down there?'

'No longer than thirty seconds.'

'Do you think she could have taken anything?'

'She had a bag with her, but I don't think so.' I breathe in. 'I think it's extremely unlikely she has anything to do with Georgiev, but I don't want to take any chances.'

'Fair enough.' He leans back to allow Bea to climb on to his knee again. 'Is Charlie angry?'

'Yes.' I sigh. 'He may not talk to me for a while.'

Sezen brings full bowls over to the table. Small pieces of spring onion and cubes of tofu float on the surface of the pale brown soup. We start to eat.

'This is really tasty,' I say. 'Don't you want to try some, Bea?' I hold the spoon towards her, but she shakes her head.

The doorbell rings and I get up to answer it.

'It'll probably be Megan,' Julian shouts after me.

It is Megan. She is standing on the step clutching bundles of documents to her chest. I know that even although it's already six o'clock in the evening, she will be keen to catch up with the latest developments. We kiss each other on both cheeks and then I say, 'Would you like to join us for supper?'

'I don't want to interrupt a family meal.'

'You're not.'

I hold the bundles while she takes off her jacket and hangs it up in the porch.

I'm just about to lead the way to the kitchen when she takes hold of my arm. 'Claire?'

'Yes?' I force a smile.

'I'm sorry if I was a bit off with you last night.' She smooths back her hair. 'I don't want to step on any toes, but I don't want you to think I'm not supportive.'

'It's fine, Megan.' I shrug. 'I understand your position.'

Julian introduces Megan to Sezen and she helps herself to soup. I say nothing for the rest of the meal, preferring instead to order my thoughts. I want to go through the emails some more, and I want to check whether another one has arrived. I feel there might be clues none of us are seeing and if we pore over them for long enough, the answer will come. But now Julian will be taken up with Megan. I'll have to wait until she leaves, and that probably won't be for a couple of hours at least. When everyone's finished pudding, Julian excuses them both and they go down to his study, Bea still with him, to bring Megan up to date with what's happened in Sofia.

I hang back in the kitchen with Sezen, tidying up and planning food for tomorrow, and when she takes Lara upstairs to bed, I go into the sitting room and switch on the television, half an ear listening out for Megan leaving. I pick up a novel that I'm partway through and then put it down again when the phone rings. It's Jack's housemaster.

'Unfortunate incident this evening, Mrs Miller.' Without preamble, he goes on to tell me that Jack and three other year elevens stole some whisky from the staff common room and are 'suspended herewith. Obviously this is a serious offence and one that ordinarily results in expulsion, but with GCSEs still to be completed we're going down the road of suspension.'

My initial thought is a desperate *Can't anything go right?* Why does Jack have to pick this moment to get himself suspended? 'I'm so sorry, Mr Schreiber,' I say out loud, while inside my heart grows heavy with disappointment. 'I'll come for him now, shall I?'

'Excellent. The boys are packing for home as we speak.'

I go downstairs and open the door to Julian's study. Bea is fast asleep on his knee. Megan is on the chair opposite, reading aloud from a document in the bundles. 'I'm going to school to fetch Jack,' I say. 'He's being sent home.'

'What's he done?'

'He and some others stole some whisky.'

'Did they drink it?'

'I expect so. I'm not sure.'

Julian sighs heavily, then shifts Bea across one arm and attempts to stand up without waking her. 'I'll go, Claire.'

'No, no.' I wave him down again. 'You've been travelling all day.' I kiss his cheek, say goodbye to Megan and head off feeling dismayed that several more hours will pass without another opportunity for Julian and me to talk.

The school is over an hour's drive north, along country lanes, motorway and more lanes. The driveway is long and curves round several slow bends, past playing fields, the cricket pavilion and staff housing until I arrive in front of the main reception, a tall, imposing brick building with long symmetrical windows, a clock tower at one end and chapel at the other. Jack's house is through the entrance hall and behind the chapel. I follow the polished wooden floors through the sixth-form area, where young adults are milling about, talking on their mobiles, drinking coke from cans and generally making enough noise to wake sleeping lions. I smile and say hello to the ones I know, before finally arriving at Jack's house, where the four boys are waiting on chairs in the corridor, surrounded by their belongings. I don't speak, suddenly realising that I can't, without unleashing a barrel-load of anger and frustration, not all of which should be directed at Jack. When he sees me, he sighs, stands up and balances his bags over his shoulders and arms. He has more stuff for one term than Sezen owns for herself and her daughter.

Mr Schreiber comes out of his flat and fills me in on the details. Not only did they take the alcohol and drink it, they used a permanent marker to graffiti the French teacher's workspace. I make repeated apologies, promise punishment and urge Jack ahead of me out of the school. A small crowd has gathered at the exit and Jack grins at some of them. I grab his arm and propel him to the car.

'I am ashamed of you,' I say sharply. 'You have let yourself down. And Mr Schreiber. And your family.'

We put his bags in the back, then climb into the car. He reaches for the radio, changes the station and ups the volume.

'Feet off the dashboard and I'm not listening to that music all the way home. Change it back, please.'

He does so and I then proceed to give him a lecture on respect. Halfway through he slumps down into his jacket and surreptitiously tries to put his iPod earphones into his ears.

'Don't even think about it,' I warn him. 'And sulking won't help you. You need to write a letter of apology to Mr Schreiber and the French teacher, and you need to work for the money to replace the alcohol you took, and—'

'Jeez, give it a rest, will you?'

'And,' I say, raising my voice several notches, 'you need to stop being influenced by Oliver Traynor because he is not the sort of boy who will do well.' I look across at him. 'Or there will be no rugby tour later in the year.'

He gives a sarcastic laugh. 'I knew that was coming.'

'I mean it, Jack. I absolutely mean it.' I take the turning on to the motorway. 'Do you have nothing to say for yourself?'

'It was just half a bottle of whisky. Schreiber loves to make a fuss.'

'*Mr* Schreiber.'

'I didn't even do the graffiti.'

'Well, you were with the boy who did. You have to pick your friends more carefully.'

'So you've said.'

'I have yet to hear an apology.'

'Sorry,' he mumbles into his collar. 'Is Dad home?'

'Yes.' I look at the clock, my heart sinking as I realise that no matter how quickly I drive I'm unlikely to get home before Julian is in bed. Normally, when he's working on a case, he stays up well past midnight, but tonight I know he will be too tired. 'He'll most likely be asleep by the time we get back.'

'Well, that'll stop him having a go.'

'Do you ever think about anyone other than yourself?' I snap. 'Your dad is tired.'

'Cry me a river.'

'Enough!' I accelerate into the outside lane. 'I am *so* disappointed in you. Not one more word.'

Stalemate. We drive without speaking for over thirty minutes and my mind slides back to what happened this evening. I wish I hadn't argued quite so strenuously with Julian. I know I have to move past the point where I feel let down and just accept that he genuinely had my best interests at heart. It's difficult, but I remind myself that he's my husband and the father of my children. He's my best friend and, mostly, usually, my confidant. This is no easier for him than it is for me. I know he loves Bea and the boys as much as I do. I know that the fact his job is putting us in danger will not sit easily with him. I have to make it up with him. I can't afford to let this wound fester.

It's gone eleven o'clock when we get home. I pull into a space in front of the house. Jack gets out straight away and goes inside. Three spaces behind me, two policemen are sitting in their car. The interior light is on and one is reading something aloud to the other. They're not the same men as are here during the daytime. This must be the night crew.

I go inside. There's no sign of Sezen or Lara, and I'm relieved to see that Charlie's shoes are by the front door. Thank heavens he came home. I was worried that he might stay away to punish me. And for all Jack's teenage cheek I'm glad to have him home too. I set the alarm and go upstairs. Bea is fast asleep in her bed. I tuck in her covers, kiss her forehead and go through to my bedroom. The bedside lamp is on. Julian is lying fully clothed on the bed, dozing. I go into the en suite and get ready for bed.

When I come back, Julian is still asleep. I stand next to the bed, looking down at him. I feel an acute, almost painful love for him. All I want is for us to be in this together.

I bend down and kiss his cheek. At once his eyes open. They focus on mine and stay there. I see inside him as if seeing inside myself: love, anger, level-headedness and a burgeoning, visceral fear. We are no different. He swings his legs over the side of the bed and hugs me to him. I soften at once. His arms are too tight round me, but I don't complain. I hold my breath and kiss the top of his head, wait until the shaking has gone from his body, then pull back a little.

He looks up at me. 'We will get through this.' His tone is urgent and I stroke his hair.

'I know.' I kiss his lips and smile. 'Now get undressed.'

He starts pulling off his clothes and then my nightdress and then we make love. It becomes electric, both of us naked, his hands and mouth warm, expert. It feels healing, like we are fixing each other, restoring blood and oxygen, honesty and love to each other's hearts.

Afterwards we lie together, arms and legs entwined. I feel as light as candyfloss, young and carefree, until I remember we are up against a greater crisis than we've ever faced before. I lean up on my elbow, propping my head on my hand. Julian is lying with his eyes shut. His jaw is relaxing open. I watch him for a few seconds – not thinking, just feeling.

Suddenly he opens his eyes and says, 'Did you collect Jack OK?'

'Yes.' I fill him in on the details.

'Is he sorry?'

'Not particularly.' I nuzzle my face into his neck. 'I think we need to have a serious talk with him.'

'We can do that over the weekend.' He closes his eyes and relaxes his head back on the pillow again. I close my eyes too and allow myself to wallow in the warm waters of post-coital bliss. This works for about ten minutes and then slowly a thought starts to intrude. At first I ignore it and then it grows louder until I speak the words: 'Did another email come today?'

Julian's body jerks as my voice breaks into the stillness. 'Yes. It came a couple of hours ago.' His right hand feels around my neck and rests on the crest of my collarbone. 'Do you want to read it?'

'Please.'

'I printed out a copy. It's on the chest of drawers.'

I climb out of bed to get it and don't look at it until I am back under the covers. Like all the others, there is no preamble. I read it aloud:

Bea's birthday party didn't go to plan, did it? How did you feel when you realised she was gone?

I think it's time we copied Claire in on these emails, don't you?

'Jesus!' I stare at Julian. 'So it has to have been someone who was at Bea's party.'

'It looks that way.' His eyes are wide open now and he pulls himself up into the sitting position. 'But I've just run it by Mac and he agrees that it's hard to imagine it could be any of the people there.'

'Amy?' I say. 'Now that I've asked her to leave, she could be throwing caution to the wind.'

'But do you really believe Amy could be working for Georgiev?'

'Maybe she isn't directly working for him. Maybe she's just earning a bit of extra money and feeding information to a person who is part of his organisation.'

'Still. The blackmailer could just as easily have got the information about the party second hand.'

'From whom? I mean' – I come up on to my knees – 'the blackmailer doesn't have to be a killer. She only has to be in a position of trust in our family. Her only role apart from feeding information could be to open the front door. Crime is about access and opportunity.' My mind immediately thinks of Sezen. Earlier this afternoon I invited her to stay with us. And as she's been coming for a month, she already knows the code for the alarm. But how can Sezen be involved in this? She didn't seek me out. I employed her through an agency, a reputable one. I checked her references. They were genuine. 'And she wasn't at the party,' I say out loud.

'Who wasn't?'

'Sezen. And all Bea's friends' mums had left by then. So if it isn't Amy, it has to be Jem or Miss Percival.' I shake my head. 'And it can't be Jem. We've been friends since Bea and Adam were born. I'd trust her with my life. I'd trust her with Bea's life.'

Julian makes a face. 'Miss Percival doesn't strike me as a valid suspect.'

'Me neither, but then she could be playing the part of a shy, slightly awkward nursery teacher. And she's often quite strange with me.'

'Strange how?'

'When I collect Bea, I have the feeling she's staring at me, trying to listen to what I'm saying to the other mothers.'

'That hardly makes her our emailer.'

'And there's the business of Bea being watched when she was playing in the sandpit.'

He still looks dubious. For the moment, I let it drop. 'So did Mac have anything else to say?'

'Just that he holds you in high regard.' He reaches across, takes my hand and kisses my fingers below my knuckles. 'I'm sorry I didn't tell you about the emails straight away.' He shakes his head. 'It was wrong of me.'

'I see the logic in it.' I smile, glad that we're finally getting somewhere. 'And I know I've been preoccupied with Lisa. I don't blame you for thinking it might all be too much for me.'

'Mac also mentioned your reluctance over the safe house.'

I can't help but stiffen. He feels it and slides down until his face is level with mine. 'It is the best option.'

'I'm not so sure.'

'I know what happened with Kerry Smith preyed on your mind, but this is different.'

'Is it? Her ex-partner, her killer, found her, either because she was spotted or because someone in the police service gave away her location. Exactly the same thing could happen to us.'

'Apart from ourselves only three people will know where we are: Mac, the specialist nurse for Lisa and the armed police-woman who will live with us.'

'Mac's not going to notify the local police?'

'Not about us, no. But where we're going is normally the home of a senior member of the Foreign Office. If the alarm does go off, the police response time is less than two minutes.'

'A lot can happen in two minutes.'

'The house has a state-of-the-art home security system, cameras front and back, and all the windows and doors are laser-protected.'

'We have that here,' I say.

He nods. 'We are well protected here, but with an increased threat it makes sense to move somewhere else.'

'Is the house in London?'

'No. Further north. I'm not sure exactly where.'

It all sounds perfectly sensible, but my gut isn't convinced. 'Let's just see how the next few days go,' I say. 'With any luck the police will have a breakthrough. Maybe that last email will help.' I put out the light, relax on to Julian's chest and close my eyes.

He falls asleep immediately. I don't. I lie awake for several hours thinking about what little information we have and trying to make connections. I know there's a danger I'll see what I want to see, be suspicious of women who don't deserve it, but I don't have the luxury of blind trust, not with Bea's safety at stake. Amy has already left the house and I don't intend to send Bea back to nursery, so Miss Percival will also be out of our lives. It sounds like the blackmailer intends to copy me in on the next email. That alone will narrow the field because I'm not a regular emailer.

I don't belong to social networking sites; I rarely shop on the Internet. Very few people know my email address.

Finally my limbs grow heavy and I fall asleep. I dream about car chases along badly lit streets and Bea, always ahead of me, being taken away into the darkness.

9

Friday morning and I wake just before seven. The curtains haven't been pulled completely shut and a shaft of bright light cuts its way across the carpet. Outside, seagulls squawk over the rooftops and I'm reminded why so many Brighton residents complain of lost sleep during the summer months. Julian's side of the bed is empty. The smell of freshly brewed coffee and burnt toast drifts up the stairs. I grab my dressing gown and pop my head round Bea's door. She's still fast asleep. I go down to the kitchen, keen to see Julian, stopping short when I spot Megan sitting at the table. She's dressed in a different suit this morning, trousers and, as ever, an immaculate white blouse. She has spread papers out across the table, and when I come in, she immediately shuffles them together as if I'm about to read them over her shoulder. I'm not. I make a beeline for Julian, who is taking the final bite of a piece of toast.

'Claire.' He gives me a wide smile and kisses me.

I look over at Megan. 'Do you mind if I just borrow my husband for a minute?'

She shakes her head and her ponytail swings across her shoulder. 'Of course not.'

I take Julian's elbow and he doesn't resist as I pull him out into the hallway. 'I hoped you'd be in bed when I woke up.'

'You looked so peaceful.' He slides his hands under my dressing gown. 'I didn't have the heart to wake you.'

'A replay of last night would have been nice.'

'Can you hold that thought until this evening?'

'Definitely.'

'What are your plans for today?'

'Nothing much. I'll visit Lisa over lunch, but otherwise I'll stay at home. Will you call me if you hear from Mac?'

He nods.

'I'll be checking my emails every five minutes to see whether she copies me in, like she said she would.'

'Don't let it dictate your day, Claire. I promise I'll be in touch if another one arrives.'

Megan comes out from the kitchen and Julian pulls his hands away from me, his eyes lingering on my face as we say our good-byes. I watch from the sitting room window as they begin their walk up the hill to the station. The after-effects of making love still resonate, a sweet liquid in my limbs and heart. But seeing him walk away makes me feel vulnerable and twice I whisper his name. It's not until I turn round that I realise Sezen is behind me and I jump.

'I didn't hear you come down,' I say. 'Did you sleep well?'

'Yes.' Her eyes are large in her face. 'Is everything OK?'

'Of course.' I'm biting my nails. I stop at once and thrust my hands into my pockets. 'I'm just . . . Julian's off to work. So' – I manage a smile – 'on with the day.'

'I hear the girls,' she says. 'I will make them some breakfast.'

I get dressed and potter about. Bea and Lara play under the stairs – a teddy bears' picnic this time – and Sezen goes shopping. Wendy calls to remind me that she and Sezen have arranged to cook together today and is that still OK? I tell her it is and try to get on with some vacuuming. Twice I pull the emails from their hiding place in my wardrobe and pore over them, not coming up with anything new, and over a dozen times I press the refresh button on my email inbox, but nothing has arrived. It still seems likely from the last email that the blackmailer witnessed the after-math of Bea's party, and that sheds suspicion on Amy and Mary Percival. Neither is an obvious suspect, but I know from my work as a lawyer that it's not always the obvious ones who end up being guilty.

By eleven thirty I've yet to see signs of either Jack or Charlie. I hesitate outside Charlie's bedroom door, listening for movement, but hear none. I wonder whether I can somehow make it up to him but realise I have no idea how to go about this, so decide to leave him be and go down to Jack's room at the bottom of the house. I knock and say his name. No answer. I go in. He's dumped his bags behind the door and I have to push hard to open it. His room is sparsely furnished: a bed, a wardrobe, a desk with a computer, a television and games console. Last night he must have started to unpack the bags. Clothes and textbooks are spread all over the carpet. He is still fast asleep, lying on his front, one arm and leg hanging over the edge of the mattress, the covers pushed down to his waist. For almost a minute I stand watching him. A residual bubble of anger at his behaviour is lodged beneath my sternum. As I watch him sleep, peaceful as a nine-year-old, the bubble dissolves.

'Jack?' I shake him gently. 'It's after eleven. You need to wake up.'

'What?' He shifts position. 'Why?'

'I need you to watch out for Bea.'

'Why?'

'Sezen's here and Grandma Wendy's coming round, but they'll be cooking and I'm going to visit Auntie Lisa.' I rub my forehead. 'It would be really helpful if you could take care of the girls.'

'Does that mean I won't be grounded?'

'It means you'll go some way towards redeeming yourself if you look after your sister. But don't go outside with her.'

'Why not?'

'Because I'd prefer you not to.'

'She'll want me to take her to the corner shop.'

'Well, don't. Play with her in the house or in the back garden. Watch *Finding Nemo*.'

'For the thousandth time.'

'Just do it!'

'OK, OK!' He rolls over. 'No need to shout.' He sighs. 'I'll get up in a minute.'

'Good.' I stroke my fingers across the top of his hair. It feels stiff with hair gel. 'And have a shower.'

'Yeah, yeah.'

I go upstairs. There's still no sign of Charlie, but Wendy has arrived and is in the kitchen with Sezen. I take the food parcel that Sezen has prepared for Lisa and go off to the hospital. Lisa is on good form and we spend a happy couple of hours together. It's on the tip of my tongue to tell her what's going on in my life, but I don't. She'll find out soon enough and then my problems will become her problems. There's no way to save her from that.

When I return home, Jem is standing in the porch, having turned up earlier to finish painting the room. Although she is the neatest of workers – nothing is ever spilled, no paint marks end up on the skirting or around the light switches – her dungarees and shoes are spotted with paint, standing testament to what she does for a living.

'I'm just nipping out for a roll-up.' She walks past me and sits on the step. 'Finished the room.' She opens her silver cigarette box and rolls the tobacco with an expert hand, which is as rough as sandpaper and stained with paint. Then she sees my face and thinks that I'm judging her habit. 'I know – I'm a slave. An hour goes by and – ping! – it's like an alarm goes off in my head. I start to itch. I crave it. Nicotine. I'm an addict.' She lights it quickly and takes a grateful puff. 'It's too late for me. Cancer, here I come.' Then she realises what she's just said. 'Shit, I'm sorry, Claire.' She stands up. 'Me and my big mouth.'

I shake my head. 'Lisa's cancer had nothing to do with smoking. And anyway, we all have our vices.'

'And yours would be?'

'A glass or two of wine, a big piece of chocolate and some trashy TV?'

'I'm sorry, hon, that's more comfort than a vice.'

I think harder. 'Many moons ago, when I was at university, the person I was *then*,' I stress. 'She liked to have a joint or two. Three even. At one time it was quite a habit.'

She gives my shoulder a friendly nudge. 'That's more like it.' And then her face becomes serious as she asks me, 'How was Lisa today?'

'Good. The thought of leaving hospital has perked her up no end.'

'Talking of which . . .' She takes a last drag of her cigarette, stamps it out underfoot, then puts the stub in her pocket. 'Do you want to see the room?'

I follow her inside and we stand for a moment admiring her work. Under the picture rail, the walls are now as yellow as the yolk of a corn-fed chicken's egg, while above the rail the colour is creamy, like country butter, freshly churned. She's put the curtain pole and pale blue velvet curtains back up, the ends just skimming the floor.

'It's perfect, Jem,' I tell her. 'It's just as I hoped – sunny, fresh and upbeat.'

'The paint smell will be gone by the morning.' She picks some dustsheets up off the floor. 'What time's she coming home?'

'I'll probably collect her around eleven.' I drag my eyes away from the black-and-white photograph of my mother that's on the cabinet beside the bed. It's the only one we have of her. She is standing on Brighton Pier, her hand shielding her eyes from the sun. 'Thank you for all your hard work.'

'And Julian's home, I see?'

'He came back yesterday afternoon.'

'All geared up for the trial?'

'Yes . . . and no.' I want to say more but know that I shouldn't. Jem is a good friend, but she doesn't need to be involved in this.

'There's something else I want to show you.' She takes me back out on to the step. 'Don't make it obvious, but behind you, about thirty yards away, this side of the pavement, there are two men sitting in a Ford Mondeo. I noticed them when I was passing by yesterday too.'

I look along the street and see Baker and Faraway parked in what's becoming their usual spot.

'You're making it obvious,' Jem says, swinging me back round to face her. 'Weird, eh?'

'Yeah.' I nod.

'You know what I think?' says Jem. 'I think they're policemen.'

'What makes you say that?'

'They give off a certain aroma.'

'You speaking from experience?'

'Not really.' She shrugs, her face turned away from me. 'Misspent youth. You know how it is.'

'You don't have cause to worry, Jem.' I smile. 'The car isn't expensive enough for them to be from the Inland Revenue.'

She gives me a weak smile and we go back inside. Bea and Lara come rushing up from the basement. They are both in pink dresses with angel wings on the back. They are flushed and screaming. The sound is high-pitched and shrill. Jack is chasing them, holding a battered wooden sword and wearing a pirate hat that is far too small for him and is attached to his hair with paperclips.

'Mummy! Mummy!' Bea hangs on to my leg and jumps up and down at the same time. 'Jack is a bad sparrow and he wants to kill us.'

'Woops!' I say, trying to hold her still. 'Careful with your wings! They have a jagged edge poking out.'

Too late – as she swings round to try and look behind her, the lower edge catches on the hem of my skirt. Before I can stop her, she pulls hard and the thread stretches the hem, then breaks. She frowns and catches hold of the hem, which is now hanging down at one side. 'Look, Mummy! Look what happened.'

Lara bends her head to have a look too. 'You can sew it,' she says. 'My mummy will sew it for you.'

I smile and put a hand on their heads. 'Not to worry. Have you girls eaten yet?'

Before either of them can answer, the kitchen door opens and Wendy comes out. 'What's all the commotion? I thought you girls were washing your hands for tea.' She shoos them towards the bathroom, then glances at me. 'How was Lisa?'

'Good.' I nod vigorously. 'She's having a good day.'

'Jack has been doing a sterling job,' Wendy says, smiling in his direction. 'How anyone at that school can ever complain about him I really don't know.'

Jack treats us all to one of his butter-wouldn't-melt grins. 'Can I go off duty now?' He gives a dramatic sigh. 'I'm exhausted.'

'Tea first, my dear.' Wendy unclips the pirate's hat from his hair. 'You're a growing boy. You don't want to skimp on meals. We've cooked you some spicy chicken.' She looks at Jem. 'I hope you're staying too, Jem. There's plenty of food. Sezen and I have been swapping recipes and cooking up a storm.'

'Well, I should be going.' She points her thumb in the direction of the door. 'Pete will have something at home for me.'

'Lucky you, having a man who cooks,' Wendy says. 'But still, take some goodies away with you! We can make you up a doggy bag.' She marches off towards the kitchen. 'Follow me.'

Jem gives me an apologetic smile and mouths, 'Is it OK?'

'Of course.' I check on the girls in the bathroom. They're both standing on the stool, leaning forwards into the sink to reach the taps. They're talking and giggling and I soak up the merriment. When their hands are washed, I hand them the towel and then they rush ahead of me into the kitchen.

Sezen and Wendy have prepared more food than we could eat in a week. There are at least a hundred jam tarts with decorated pastry tops, coconut creams, chocolate-chip cookies, star-shaped lemon biscuits, two fruit cakes and a treacle tart, not to mention the savoury dishes.

'Once we got started, we just couldn't stop!' Wendy says, wiping her hands on her apron. 'I know we went a bit over the top, but most of it can go in the freezer.'

'And I have not forgotten macrobiotic treats,' Sezen says,

pointing to one of the trays, where over two dozen small chocolate-coloured balls are lined up in neat, glistening rows. 'These are made with carob and amazake, brown rice syrup.' She takes an audible breath. 'I hope Lisa will enjoy them, and if there's anything else . . .' She trails off and I realise she is waiting for my approval.

'It all looks fantastic.' I'm holding Bea too tightly. She wriggles out of my arms. 'A veritable feast!' I say loudly. 'Is it all right if I try something?'

'Of course.'

I choose one of the macrobiotic sweets and bite into it. The taste is unusual but not unpleasant. It's neither particularly sweet nor particularly savoury. It tastes homely and comforting, like creamy porridge or rice pudding. 'It's good,' I say, putting the last piece in my mouth. 'Lisa's going to be so impressed. I can't wait to bring her home.'

Sezen's smile is wide and I feel a pang of sympathy for her and how difficult her life must be sometimes: no home to call her own, no father for Lara, her livelihood depending upon whatever work she can find. I watch her as she persuades Bea out of her angel's wings so that she can sit at the table. Then she helps her into her seat, kissing the top of her head as she pushes her chair in towards the food.

The doorbell rings and I go to answer it. It's Miss Percival.

'Good evening, Mrs Miller. I'm sorry to disturb you, but Bea left this at nursery on Wednesday. And as she didn't come yesterday or today . . .' She trails off and hands me a small knitted gnome with pointed hat and bushy beard. 'I didn't want her to miss him over the weekend.'

'That's kind,' I say, knowing full well that the only toy Bea is ever likely to miss is Bertie and I'm sure Miss Percival knows this too.

'Is everything OK with Bea?'

'She's just been tired, that's all,' I say. 'Come in and join us. We're having a bit of a tea party.' I throw the door wide, acting with a bonhomie that I don't feel, but there's something about her that doesn't add up and I wonder whether, if we spend more time in each other's company, I'll be able to put my finger on it. 'Wendy and Sezen have been cooking.'

Her face passes through a range of emotions: discomfort, anxiety and then a tentative hope. 'I don't want to interrupt . . .'

'The more the merrier,' I say. If she's acting, then she's making a convincing job of it. 'There's enough food in there to feed an army and Bea would love to see you.'

'And your sister.' She bites her bottom lip. 'How is Lisa?'

'Soldiering on,' I say, hanging her light summer jacket on a peg by the door. 'She's coming home to stay with us tomorrow.'

'The chemotherapy was a success?'

'Not really, no.'

'I'm so sorry.' Her eyes fill up and I wonder who she's thinking of, whether she's been through something similar herself or watched it happen to someone she loves. As far as I'm aware, she lives alone. She's never mentioned children or a husband, but there is a shadow that hangs around her – grief, loneliness, regret, I'm not sure.

We go into the kitchen and everyone says hello. Miss Percival sits between a delighted Bea and Lara, and then Jack comes up from the basement and we gather around the table. Wendy has called up the stairs to Charlie, but he's yet to appear.

Jem is trying the tempura: pieces of vegetables and fish covered in a light batter and then deep-fried. Small bowls of tamari and Japanese sweet-chilli sauce are placed on the table. She dips some tempura into it, then puts it in her mouth. 'Wow!' She smacks her lips. 'If this is macrobiotic food, then I'm sold.'

'Fried food is reserved for special occasions,' Sezen says. 'Macrobiotic cooking originated in Japan, so some of the ingredients are common to both cuisines.'

We're all quiet for a few minutes as we sample the dishes. The batter is crispy and melts in the mouth, the vegetables are crunchy, and the sauce is savoury and packs a punch.

Bea clutches her nose and giggles. 'It tingles,' she says.

'It's the chilli,' I tell her. 'Jack, aren't you having any?'

'In a minute,' he calls through from the pantry.

'Wendy and Sezen have cooked chicken especially for you.'

'Here you are!' Wendy says as Charlie walks into the kitchen. 'Amy not with you?'

Charlie helps himself to two pieces of tempura. 'A certain person asked her to leave.' He throws a sullen look my way.

'Oh.' Wendy pats his hand. 'Well, never mind. A couple of days apart won't do you any harm. Now, why don't you try some of this chilli sauce?'

'But is it only a couple of days?' He glares at me across the table.

'Let's talk about this later, love, shall we?' I say.

'Why not now?' He throws his fork down. It lands with a loud clatter on his plate.

'Because we're eating now.' I smile. 'Please, Charlie, I know you're upset, but—'

'Oh, do you?' He pushes his chair back and stands up. 'Do you know I'm upset?'

'What's going on?' Jack has finally arrived at the table carrying a jar of peanut butter and some pickles.

'Mum has thrown Amy out,' he shouts, so loudly that Lara and Bea both look round at the adults, their small faces fearful.

'Charlie, please.' I move to the other side of the table and take his elbow. He allows me to pull him into the hallway.

'You can't stop me seeing her.'

'Charlie, stop shouting,' I say as quietly as I can, mindful that in the kitchen behind us you could hear a pin drop.

'I'm nineteen.' He presses his chest. 'You can't control me. You can't tell me what to do.'

'I'm not saying you shouldn't see her.'

'I'll go behind your back.'

'I'm asking you to trust me.'

'Trust you how? Trust you why?' He takes several steps away

from me, quickly, on his toes, then walks towards me again. 'Amy means a lot to me.' I see tears well up in his eyes.

'I know.' He allows me to touch his shoulder. 'And I'm not saying she isn't welcome back.' He relaxes a little. 'Her room in halls isn't so bad, is it?'

'Surrounded by first-years?'

I don't mention the obvious – he's a first-year and Amy seems content to have him all over her. 'Anyway, she's going to stay with her parents in Cyprus soon, isn't she?'

'Next week.'

'Maybe she could go a bit earlier.'

'And change her ticket?' He glares at me as if I'm an idiot. 'It's way too expensi .'

'I'm sorry. I didn't think of that.'

'Yeah, well, welcome to the real world.'

'In the real world—' *your sister's life is being threatened.*

'What? What?' His head shakes from side to side and he throws his arms out. 'What?'

'Somebody is sending threatening emails to your dad.'

'Eh?' He gives a perfunctory laugh.

'It's serious, Charlie.'

'What sort of emails?'

'Nasty ones.'

'And you think it's Amy?'

'I think we have to consider every possibility, no matter how unlikely.'

'Jesus! What is this?' He takes a few more steps backwards and then forwards, rocking on the balls of his feet. 'Have you completely lost it?'

'You started going out with her soon after Dad accepted the case against Georgiev.'

'You base throwing her out on *that*?'

'I've caught her in Dad's study twice now.'

'Oh, let that go, will you? It wasn't the way it looked.'

'She's two years older than you and you said yourself that she was the one who made a play for you.'

'She can't have just fancied me, then?' He gives a bitter laugh. 'Gee, thanks, Mum.' He turns away and heads towards the stairs.

'Charlie!' I stand at the bottom and shout up after him, 'When Dad comes home, we'll all have a chat, OK?'

No answer.

I return to the kitchen and find the mood is subdued. Miss Percival is telling Bea and Lara a story. She has her arms round their backs and they are looking up into her face with rapt expressions. Sezen, head down, is busy clearing plates. Jack is spreading peanut butter on to bread, while Wendy tries to tempt him with something more substantial. Jem is staring into the distance, her thoughts miles away.

'I'm so sorry about that,' I say. 'Charlie and I had a disagreement earlier and it's been festering a bit.'

'What about? Is Amy gone, then? Did you ask her to leave?' Jack fires these questions in between bites of bread.

'Should I go and have a word with Charlie?' Wendy gives me a rueful smile.

'Would you, Wendy?'

'Of course.' She stands up and goes out of the room. Wendy has a way with all of my children. I hope she'll be able to win him round.

Jack is leaning back on his chair. 'Well, you certainly pissed Charlie off.' He doesn't say it with any degree of accusation, more with a sense of awe. 'Don't you like Amy, then?'

'Don't use that word in front of the little girls,' I say.

'What word?'

'You know what word!'

'Glass of wine, Claire?' Jem is in the fridge and holds out the bottle of white towards me. 'Knock the edge off things?'

I nod and she pours me some. I excuse myself and take my wine into the sitting room, silently wishing that I'd just kept my mouth shut. Bloody hell. That's twice I've handled Charlie

badly. It will be much easier after Mac visits on Monday, but I
don't know whether we'll make it that far without Charlie storming
out.

I finish the glass of wine, stand by the window and look out
across the park. Half a dozen children are playing tag, some of
them shouting and laughing their way across the grass, others
deadly serious as they sprint from one spot to another.

Jem comes in, refills my glass and then stands beside me.

'Sorry about that,' I say. 'You not having any?'

'Not much of a drinker.'

'No, of course not. I always forget that you don't drink.' I
watch a boy of about eight fall down on the grass and laugh as
his friend lands on top of him. 'It's so easy when they're young,'
I say. 'Teenage boys are such a challenge.'

'Charlie will come round.'

'I hope so.'

'You have a lot on your plate with Lisa being so ill.' She nods
in the direction of the street. 'And that one.' Megan and Julian
have just walked down from the station and are approaching the
bottom of the steps leading up to our house.

'What do you mean?' I say.

'I'm sure it can't be easy when Julian spends so much time
with another woman.'

I don't know whether it's the rush of wine affecting my percep-
tion or whether she's driving at something. 'I'm not with you.'

She shrugs. 'It's that thing, isn't it?'

'What thing?'

'Attractive woman, working together . . .' She trails off.

I start back. 'You think Julian's having an affair?'

'Well, no, but . . . I saw you watching them and I thought . . .
Well, isn't that what you were thinking?'

'I wasn't watching them!' I spin round to face her. 'I was
watching the children in the park.'

'Shit.' She shakes her head. 'Pete warns me about this.' She gives
me one of her perfunctory hugs. 'Please, Claire. I meant nothing

by it. It was the expression on your face. I thought you were looking at Julian and Megan and thinking they were closer than they should be.'

'I wasn't,' I say. 'I was watching the little boys in the park and thinking about Jack and Charlie at that age.'

Her face flushes. 'I need to keep my big mouth shut.' She looks genuinely remorseful, her eyes dipped, her head to one side. 'Shoot me now.'

'Apology accepted.' I lean my head against her shoulder. 'But really, Jem, Julian and Megan are colleagues, nothing more.'

'Of course.' Her smile is relieved. 'And now I'm going to love you and leave you.'

Before I have the chance to reply she's off. I hear the door slam and watch her say a quick hello to Megan and Julian, before she climbs into her van and drives away. I expect Julian to come straight inside, but he doesn't. Megan is still talking to him. He listens, every now and then making a comment himself. This goes on for almost five minutes. And after what Jem has just said, I find myself looking at Megan with new eyes. I've always seen her as a woman with no obvious sex appeal. Yes, she's tall and slim and has an easy smile, but she doesn't draw a second glance. Or at least I've never thought so. But now I'm watching her and Julian, searching for signs that they are intimate. Their bodies are close but not quite touching, and neither are their hands. There is no awkwardness between them, but nor is there any sign of the familiarity that exists between lovers: no lingering eye contact, no leaning against each other or hanging on to every word.

I can't say that it has never before occurred to me that Julian might have an affair. It's perfectly possible that he could be attracted to another woman – someone more like the woman I was – but I would never expect him to act on that attraction. I didn't marry a man like my father – that was a very conscious choice. My father was a great socialiser. Always the last man to leave a party, he liked to have an audience, and as a talented storyteller, he kept his audience amused. If the opportunity for infidelity presented itself, he was hard pushed to say no.

Julian is a quieter man, not boring, not introverted, but quieter, hardworking and very much a family man. Nothing like my father. But still . . . I feel concerned. When Julian and I both worked in London, we were together far more regularly than we are now. I saw him during the day two or three times a week, sometimes by design, but often we just bumped into each other. Now I only experience that world from a distance. And it worries me to recall seeing first hand how marriages are eroded when common ground is lost. My one-off with Mac is always there to remind me how easy it is for even the happily married to lose sight of what's important.

Ironically, the move to Brighton, me being free to be a wife and mother, was supposed to make our marriage stronger, but I know that not only does Julian miss the me who existed when we were pursuing parallel careers, but the last few years have been hard on us. First my father died, and now Lisa is sick.

Finally Julian climbs the first step and Megan raises her head, says something that makes him laugh. The look that passes between them is one between good friends: frank, honest, uninhibited, not lustful or sexually knowing, but there is a sense of sharing and commonality between them that sets off alarm bells. It reminds me of myself and Mac, and I know that although they haven't slept together yet, they may not be far off. She is Julian's work companion. She knew about the emails from the start; she knew about his resignation. I'm sure she even knows where the witness is being kept. Julian has shared his concerns with her. Not me. I haven't been his confidante, not for some time.

The realisation is a painful one. I hold the wine glass tight in my hand, so tight that the stem snaps and I cry out as wine spills and mixes with the warm blood that trickles from my palm.

10

I go back into the kitchen and grab some paper towels to wrap round my hand. The girls and Jack have gone to their rooms. Sezen and Miss Percival are tidying up. They both hover around me as I apply pressure to the wound. It takes three minutes before it stops bleeding.

'It looks deep,' Miss Percival says, concerned. 'Do you think you should visit the hospital? It might need stitching.'

'It is quite deep,' I acknowledge, frustrated that Julian hasn't come inside yet. What can he and Megan possibly still have to say to one another? They spend hours together as it is. 'But I don't think it needs stitching. A tight dressing will be good enough.'

I try to use my elbows to open a kitchen cupboard and Sezen steps forward to do it for me. She looks pale and her hands are shaking.

'Are you OK?' I ask.

'I do not like the sight of blood,' she says through gritted teeth.

The paper towel is now sodden with blood, the white colour darkened to a deep scarlet.

'Let me help,' Miss Percival says. She puts a dressing and then a bandage over the cut, while Sezen stands back, her eyes averted.

I look at them both. 'I'm sorry about Charlie's behaviour at the table. Life is complicated at the moment.'

Miss Percival looks up briefly from the bandaging to murmur a reassuring 'Think nothing of it.'

Sezen gives me a quick, distracted smile.

'Wendy's very good with Charlie.' Tears prick the back of my eyes and I'm glad I have the excuse of a painful cut.

'I'm sure he'll come round,' Miss Percival says.

I hear the click of the front door closing and Julian's footsteps along the hallway. He comes straight into the kitchen and takes in the work surfaces laden with food. 'Wow! There's been some cooking going on in here today.'

Sezen immediately steps forward to offer him something to eat, and Miss Percival finishes clearing the dirty dishes from the table. My hand is throbbing, so I don't go to help. Instead I find myself watching her. She moves unobtrusively, but not in the graceful, natural way that Sezen does. Her movements are more stooped, her back rounded, like someone who's trying to make herself insignificant, invisible even.

'Glad to be close to the end of another term, Miss Percival?' Julian asks her.

'Yes.' She looks down at her hand as she draws together crumbs with a wet cloth.

'Going anywhere for the summer?'

'No, I . . . em . . .' She finds my eyes. 'I must be heading off. Thank you so much for tea.'

'I'll see you to the door,' I say.

She's out of the kitchen before I've even finished replying. Julian raises his eyebrows at me as I walk past him and says quietly, 'Was it something I said?'

'I told you,' I whisper. 'She's odd.'

I find her at the front door taking her jacket off the peg. I decide to probe a bit to see whether I can find out anything more about her. 'Do you live alone?' I say.

'Yes. I do. I am.' She hurries into her jacket, her fingers shaking as she does up the buttons. 'I have for some time now.'

'Do you have family?'

'Yes . . . well, no. Not really.' She reaches for the door handle. 'Thank you for inviting me in.'

'Wait!' I place my hand on her shoulder. 'Bea will want to say goodbye to you.' I call up the stairs. Lara comes to the top and looks down at me. 'Is Bea up there?'

She nods.

I climb the stairs and call Bea's name again.

'I'm in here,' she says, her voice coming from the bathroom. I try the door, but it's locked. 'Do you need any help?' I say.

'No, Mummy. I'm four now.'

'OK.' I smile at Lara, who's waiting patiently outside the door. 'You all right, Lara?'

She nods and looks down shyly, her black curls falling over her cheeks.

I bend down to her height and whisper, 'Would you like to go and see the fish tomorrow? In the aquarium?'

She smiles. 'Bea likes fish.' She takes a big breath. 'She likes the Nemo fish.'

'She does.' I stand up and give her a quick hug. 'You girls will have a great time together.' I go back down the stairs and find Miss Percival still in the porch. 'Bea is on the loo. She may be a while.'

'He's not a man to be messed with.' She has a magazine in her hand and I look over her shoulder to see to whom she's referring. I recognise the picture; I recognise the article. It's one of the Sunday supplements from about a month ago. The story is about organised crime in Europe. The picture shows Georgiev and a couple of his heavies standing bare-chested, covered in tattoos. It was taken back in the 1980s, before he came to London and he was still peddling his criminality in Bulgaria.

For a moment I don't know what to say. My mouth is hanging open. I hear my father's voice: *You'll catch flies standing like that.* I snap my jaw shut.

'A monster by all accounts,' Miss Percival says.

'What do you mean by that?'

Her head jerks up from the page. 'Nothing.'

'Nothing?'

She steps back towards the wall, startled at my tone. 'I was just making conversation.'

'So you don't know this man?'

'Of course not.'

'Call me paranoid' – I fold my arms – 'but Pavel Georgiev features large in our lives at the moment and it seems an unlikely coincidence that you've brought this magazine to my house.'

'I didn't bring it in!' She drops it down on the table. 'It was lying here. Open at this page.'

'No, it wasn't.' I shake my head. 'There was some unopened junk mail on this table and nothing else.'

Colour spills across her cheeks like red wine across a table-cloth. 'I assure you I did not bring this magazine into your home.'

I stare her down. It doesn't take much – just my eyes looking into hers and she capitulates almost at once, turns on her heel and is through the door before I can say anything more.

I rejoin Julian, who is on his own in the kitchen, finishing off the rice. I show him the magazine. 'Did you bring this home?'

He glances at it and shakes his head.

'It was on the hall table. I just accused Miss Percival of bringing it here, but she denied it. Went scuttling off.' I open the fridge. 'Glass of wine?'

'Love one.'

I pour us both some wine and sit down opposite him. 'So who left it there, do you think?'

'Parting shot from Amy?' he says.

'She's been gone for twenty-four hours. I would have noticed if it had been there that long.' I think. 'Could Charlie have put it there to wind me up?'

'Would he do something like that?'

'Well, who else could it have been? He really is in a mood with me.'

'Is he upstairs?'

'Wendy's talking to him. He caused a bit of a scene while we were all eating. I really think we should tell him properly about the threat before Monday. He's very het up about Amy having to go.'

Julian weighs this up, his head tilting from one side to the other.

'We don't want him just disappearing off to be with Amy,' I say, leaning in closer to Julian. 'If the blackmailer can't get to Bea, do you think there's a risk that one of the boys might be taken?'

'It's much harder to kidnap someone adult-sized, and anyway' – he takes a sip of wine – 'after Monday's pre-trial hearing we'll be moving to a safe house.' He pauses. 'Won't we?'

'I hope not.' I clear away his empty plate. I'm not discussing this again. It's as if both Mac and Julian have accepted that we won't find the blackmailer and we're on an inevitable trajectory towards a safe house. I rinse the plate, being careful not to wet the bandage, then turn back to Julian. 'No more emails today?'

'Not so far.' He spots the bandage. 'What happened to your hand?'

'I broke a wine glass.' When I was watching you and Megan. 'Silly, really. And poor Sezen. She hates the sight of blood. She went really pale. Looked like she was about to pass out.'

He holds my fingers, turns the palm up. 'The blood's beginning to soak through. Are you sure you don't need it checked?'

'No. I can't face hanging around in casualty. I spend enough time in that hospital as it is.'

He looks at his watch. 'Why don't I get out of my suit and take you? We can spend a few extra minutes with Lisa before visiting time ends and then you can have your hand seen to.'

I shake my head. 'Lisa's coming back here tomorrow. If my hand's still bleeding, I can have it checked when I go to collect her.' I remember the way Megan was looking at him. And he at her. 'I think it's more important that we talk.'

'OK.' He finishes the last of his wine and stands up. 'I haven't seen Jack since I came home from Sofia. Shall I speak to him while you put Bea to bed?'

We agree on the way forward for Jack, and I go to persuade Bea into bed. Sezen is already organising Lara, so she comes willingly enough, after extracting a promise from Julian that he will take her to the Sealife Centre so Lara can see the Nemo fish.

Fortunately, she's so tired that before I've even finished *Charlie and Lola* – 'Mummy, why didn't you call *me* Lola?' – she has fallen asleep, her thumb in her mouth, Bertie lodged by her side. When I've settled Bea, I come out to find a note from Wendy saying that Charlie's accompanying her round to her house to help her move some furniture and that he'll be back later this evening. I smile. Good for Wendy. Keeping Charlie gainfully employed and no doubt slipping him a much-needed twenty-pound note in the process.

I find Julian in Jack's room, just as Jack is agreeing to write a letter of apology to Mr Schreiber and to the French teacher. What's more, he promises to begin sixth form with a better attitude.

'Does that mean I'm not grounded?'

'In a week you can go back to school and finish your GCSEs. After that you can meet up with your friends. Until then you can study and make yourself useful here.'

He thinks about this, less inclined to argue with Julian than with me. 'OK, then.' He throws himself back on to his bed. 'Could be worse, I suppose.' He sighs. 'But don't blame me if I die from boredom.'

'We could always confiscate your mobile phone,' Julian says, standing up to join me by the door. 'And the computer. A week without Internet games and Facebook – how does that grab you?'

'Fine.' He kicks off his shoes. 'I get the message.'

'And show me the letters before you seal the envelopes,' Julian says. 'No half-hearted attempts. You need to mean it.'

'Yeah, yeah. Pile on the pain, why don't you.'

We close the door on his grumblings and go upstairs to our room. Julian is about to put the main light on when he notices that Bea is in our bed, the muted light from the bedside lamp casting a golden glow over her sleeping form. 'Wouldn't she settle in her own bed?'

'I think she should sleep with us now. Just in case.' I bend down and kiss the top of her head. 'If she stays close to one of us, she'll be safe.'

He stands beside me and puts one hand on Bea's head and the other round my waist. 'No one will take her, Claire. I would never let that happen.'

He holds my eyes. I watch his thoughts as he watches mine. He takes my hand and leads me into the en suite bathroom. He puts on the light and closes the door behind us. 'I mean it. We can do this. No one will take her.'

He leans against me and I feel some of the weight he's been carrying seep into my bones. 'We need to check for another email.' I stroke his hair off his forehead. 'I'll go.'

Sezen is reading in the sitting room. She doesn't look up as I pass. I log on to my own laptop this time and feel my blood freeze when I see the now familiar address in my inbox. I connect my laptop to the printer and print it off without reading it.

Back in the en suite, Julian is now undressed and in the shower. There's another door from the en suite that leads into our carpeted walk-in wardrobe. I put the light on and sit down with my back against the wall. I take a deep breath, then read the latest email.

Let me tell you what you're thinking. You're thinking that everything will be fine when you move to the safe house.

Wrong.

You're thinking that even the worst sort of criminals don't kill children.

Wrong again.

And, Claire, it took a while for him to tell you, didn't it? And yet you think you can leave all this to the police and to Julian to fix.

Think again.

There's not much time left. I'm ready. Are you?

I put the sheet of paper down on the carpet. So now she's in the business of telling us what we think. I'm interested, almost heartened, to see that she's got me completely wrong. I don't think the safe house is a good option. I know there are people out there who kill children. And there's no way I would ever leave Mac and Julian to decide what happens next.

Julian comes through and stands behind me, drying himself. 'Another one came?'

I nod.

'What does it say?'

I read it out to him while he gets dressed. He sits down on the floor beside me. 'So what do you think?' I say.

'I think he—'

'Or she.' Mac hasn't got back to me yet on the profilers' opinion regarding the sex of the emailer, but my intuition tells me I'm right on this.

'Or she,' Julian acknowledges, 'is trying to influence your thinking. He wants you to lose confidence in the plans we're making.' He shrugs. 'He wants you to lose confidence in me.'

'What gets me is the information she has.' I sit forward. 'For example, how did she know that you didn't tell me about the emails straight away?'

'Because it would have affected your behaviour. It was only yesterday that you kept Bea home from nursery.'

'And how did she know about the safe house?'

'Standard police procedure,' he says. 'It's pretty obvious, isn't it?'

A beeping sound starts up in Julian's trouser pocket. His clothes are in a pile not far from my right hand and I reach forward to bring his BlackBerry out. As I pass it to him, I see Megan's name flashing on the screen. He presses the 'silence' button.

'Don't you want to take it?' I say.

'She'll leave a message.'

'A message about what?'

He gives me a look that says he's registered my curt tone but has no idea what I mean by it. 'I don't know.'

'Don't you want to listen to it?'

He puts the phone down on the floor beside his leg. 'It can wait.'

It's not entirely rational, but I feel like he's being evasive and a swell of irritation rises in my chest. 'So who else knows about the emails?'

'Only those who need to.'

'The clerks at Chambers? The other barristers?'

'Edward knows. As head clerk, I run developments by him.'

'And of course Megan knows.'

'Yes.'

'Did she know from the beginning?'

'Not quite.'

'Do you unburden yourself to her?'

He frowns. 'It's not a case of un-bur-den-ing.' He stresses each of the four syllables. 'She's my instructing solicitor and I have had to resign.'

'I'm a solicitor.' I bring my fist into my chest. 'And I'm your wife and Bea's mother. Plus I'm mentioned by name in the emails. I would have thought that gave me a vested interest that at the very least equals Megan's.'

He sighs. 'I thought we'd moved past this.'

'I think that because I'm no longer part of that world, you've shut me out.'

'That isn't true.'

'Isn't it? Once upon a time I was your best friend, your confidante.'

He takes my hands. 'And you still are.'

I give a short laugh. 'Are you denying that when I worked full-time, you talked about your work more?'

'Yes, I did, but it's only natural that now you're no longer practising law I talk about it less. We knew a lot of the same people then. You had a reference point for the cases and people I talked about.' He releases my hands and rubs his own across his face. 'You know perfectly well that most of my work is mundane: going through witness statements, advising on evidence, preparing cross-examination. Do you really want chapter and verse on that?'

'It's become a habit for us not to talk about your work,' I say.

'You share your thoughts and ideas with . . .' I pause '. . . other people.'

'I'm not sure what we're arguing about here.' I watch his body tense and the good feeling between us begins to evaporate into air that's rapidly losing its oxygen. He stands up and takes a sweater from the cupboard. 'I've apologised several times for not telling you about the emails sooner. 'Or' – he pulls the sweater over his head and glares down at me – 'is this about Megan?'

'You spend a lot of time together.'

'Working.'

I stand up too. 'Late evenings, weekends.'

'You're making something out of nothing.'

I rub my sore palm and think about the way they looked at each other when they were outside. 'Am I? She clearly has a crush on you.'

'A crush? That's for teenage girls. She's almost thirty. Here.' He picks up his phone and hands it to me. 'You check the message.'

I do. Megan's voice says, 'Gordon is happy with the handover. Speak to you on Monday.' I pass the phone back to him.

'So is that it, then, or am I about to be accused of full-blown adultery?'

'Well, now you mention it.' I make an effort to say it lightly. 'Have you had sex with Megan?'

'No.'

'But you've thought about it?'

'Not really.'

My stomach tips sideways and I stifle a gasp. 'So you have, then?'

'About three months ago she started coming on to me. Nothing too strong, just hints here and there.'

My arms fold over the bitter jealousy that's swirling in my stomach. 'And did you take her up on those hints?'

'Claire!' He looks at me as if he thinks I'm being deliberately obtuse. 'After the way we made love last night, I can't believe you're even giving it a passing thought, never mind voicing it.'

'I watched you from the window. It's the reason I cut my hand.'

He shakes his head. 'I don't follow.'

'You looked at each other with . . .' I can't think of the right word and settle for 'fondness.'

'Fondness?' He laughs. 'If I never saw Megan again, it wouldn't matter to me. That's the truth.'

'Couldn't you have asked for another solicitor?'

'Why?'

'To eliminate temptation.'

'There was no real temptation.' His expression is closed. 'Most adults can work with members of the opposite sex without sleeping with them.'

The implication is clear and it hurts so intensely that when I breathe in, my chest aches.

'I am happily married. I love you. It was nothing.' He takes hold of my elbows and I look up into his face. 'I'm committed to you and to our family. I would never jeopardise that for a cheap affair.'

Put like that, my fear seems ridiculous, but my heart is slow to catch up with my head. I briefly rest my lips against his chest. 'I'm sorry.' I bend down and pick up the email, pushing it in beside the others underneath a pile of sweaters.

'Let's go through to bed.' He takes my hand. 'We're both exhausted.'

I let him lead me into the bedroom. Bea is still fast asleep, her head almost completely covered by the duvet. 'I'm going to get a drink of water,' I say. 'Do you want anything?'

'Not for me.'

I go out on to the landing. I feel sad, ashamed, achy inside. I've always known that Julian is a better person than me. He has enough integrity and honour for ten men. He didn't have to spell it out for me to know that he found my suspicions about him and Megan insulting. I was judging him by my standards rather than his. I feel thoroughly put in my place and I'm reminded again of why he's so successful in court.

When I'm at the top of the stairs, I hear the front door close. Sezen comes in from the porch and goes into the sitting room. I'm not wearing anything on my feet. I make hardly any sound as I go down the carpeted stairs and she doesn't realise that I am behind her. When I reach the entrance to the sitting room, she is standing in front of the bay window, staring at a man's retreating back as he walks along the street. She leans right into the glass, her palms flat against the pane, so that she can catch the last sight of him as the pavement curves round the corner. Then she stands back and sighs, closes her eyes and turns her face up to the ceiling.

I don't want her to find me watching her like this, so I tiptoe along the hallway to the kitchen. Jack is taking some leftovers out of the fridge. He holds up a cold chicken leg. 'Is it OK if I eat this?'

I nod. 'Do you know who that was at the door?'

He shrugs. 'Some friend of Sezen's.'

'Did you speak to him?'

'Not much. I answered the door and he asked if Sezen was here and I said I'd get her.' He uses his teeth to tear off some meat. 'That was it.'

'Did he speak English with an accent?'

'Yeah.'

'What did he look like?'

'Unshaven. Serious fish.'

'Meaning?'

'He didn't smile.'

'Did Sezen bring him in?'

'They stood outside.'

'For how long?'

'A minute or two.'

'What did they talk about?'

'I dunno!' He looks exasperated. 'What's with the twenty questions?'

'I'm interested.'

'Then ask her yourself. Maybe he's her boyfriend.'

'Is Charlie back from Wendy's yet?'

'He's in his room listening to music. He told me to F off.'

I pour some water into a glass.

'I think he feels bad about what he said to you,' Jack says. He comes and stands beside me, claps a heavy hand on my shoulder. 'Don't worry, Mum.'

'I feel bad about it too.' I kiss his cheek. 'Don't you stay up too late, now. You need your beauty sleep.'

He gives me an affectionate smile and returns to tearing into the chicken leg. I take my glass of water and head to bed. My foot is on the bottom stair when I decide to have a word with Sezen. She's still in the sitting room, her book unopened on her lap.

'Was that someone at the door?' I say lightly.

'It was just a man.'

'A friend of yours?'

'No.'

'Oh!' I take a sip of water. 'Jack thought you knew him.'

'I met him before.'

'And you gave him this address?'

She stands up, walks towards me and stops a couple of feet away. Her expression is sombre, but her eyes are bright. 'He will not come here again.'

'It's not that I mind you having friends aroun—'

'I am an honest person.' Her tone is firmer. 'He will not come here again.' And then she adds, 'He is nothing to me.'

I don't believe her, but I can't read the expression in her eyes, cloaked as it is by a fierce self-control. I take a step backwards. 'I'm off to bed,' I say, half turning my body towards the door. 'I'll see you in the morning.'

'Sleep well.' She smiles. It's automatic and has none of her usual warmth.

I leave the room. I feel an impulse to apologise – but for what? Her words don't ring true. Why stand at the window as if hungry for further contact? Why stare so intently after a man who is nothing to you?

Julian has turned out the light. Bea is on my side of the bed. I climb over her and lie down between them both. 'There's just been a man at the door for Sezen.'

'Did she invite him in?'

'No. She denied he was her friend.' I shift my position, try to relax into Julian's side, but his earlier words are still stinging. 'And yet she stood right up close to the window and watched him all the way to the end of the street, like she couldn't get enough of him.'

'A secret lover?'

'Not one she's willing to admit to. Maybe he's someone from her past. Lara's father even.' I come up on to one elbow and look into Julian's face. There's just enough light for me to make out his features. 'Julian?'

'Mm?'

'Under what circumstances would you consider giving up the witness's name and whereabouts?' I say it lightly, but my heart is hammering in my chest. That's the simplest way to end all this, isn't it? For Julian to just give the blackmailer the witness. As she said in one of her emails, leaking the name and the whereabouts of the witness will be easy.

'You know I can't consider doing that.' He takes my hand and brings it up to his lips. 'We can't bend to this sort of intimidation.'

'But, Julian . . .' I can't say the words. I can't say 'Bea' and 'dead' in the same sentence. 'If the worst comes to the worst, you would put our family first, wouldn't you?'

'It's not going to happen.'

'But if it did,' I persist. 'Would you put Bea's safety before the interests of this case?'

'Claire, I will do everything in my power to protect our family.' He turns towards me in the bed and puts his arms round me. 'I'm surprised you even have to ask me that.'

I believe him. I trust him. He is always there for me and for the children. He's my husband, solid and true – he has never let me down.

So why am I not reassured?

11

Saturday and I wake early. Julian and Bea are still asleep. I climb over Bea, go into the walk-in wardrobe, take all the emails out from underneath my sweaters and sit down on the floor to read them again. By the time I get to the final one, I feel the intensity of the threat tightening, like a snake coiling round a human body. I am almost certain that if all these emails had been addressed to me, I would have given in by now. Not so Julian. I know that his resolve is stronger than mine. His belief in the criminal justice system runs deeper than mine. He trusts the system and he trusts others to do their best. I don't. I know that the system is only as strong as the people who are running it. I know that most people are weak. They respond to the offer of money. The blackmailer could be gleaning information from several sources, some of them within the police service, some of them people much closer to our family. From a professional viewpoint, I know that giving in to this sort of intimidation is not an option. The system stands and falls by its principles. But as a human being, I can't help seeing this as a simple case of knowing when to give in. Like the bully in the playground who wants your pocket money – after sustained intimidation, you just give it to him. Move school. Move on. Don't wait for the adults to sort it out.

But the fact that she has copied me in on the emails should make it easier for me to track her down. Few people know my email address. Miss Percival is one of them. As Bea's nursery teacher, she does on occasion send round nursery details. And the more I think about it, the more suspicious she seems. I see far more of her than I should, considering she doesn't live close by. She's often walking Douglas in the park opposite my house and yet there is a larger, far more dog-friendly park nearby. I'm going to mention her to Mac. See whether he will bring her in for questioning.

I put the emails away and have a shower. The cut on my hand has stopped bleeding, the edges of the wound pulling together nicely. I stand under the water, directing the flow on to my shoulders, where tension has tightened them into knots. My mind loops back to last night. Sezen. What was that all about? Even if I wasn't worried about the blackmailer, I would find her behaviour odd. I think about her sincerity, the look on her face when she said, 'I am an honest person.' I want to believe her. I asked her to work for me. Her references were exemplary. But how could she not know the man, when he found out where she lives, and asked for her by name? I wonder what she's hiding. Bad debts, maybe? Judging by her accommodation in Tooting, she has been living from hand to mouth.

By nine o'clock everyone apart from Jack and Charlie are up and dressed and at the breakfast table.

'How is your hand?' Sezen says to me.

'Feels much better.' I show her my palm and the smaller plaster now covering it. 'It'll be healed in a couple of days.'

Bea has reminded Julian of his promise to take her to the Sealife Centre. We have season tickets. It's her favourite place to visit. She is fascinated with fish and crustaceans and anything that lives in the sea. Julian has offered to take Lara too. 'There is the eagle fish and the dog fish,' Bea is saying to Lara, 'and the fish that nobody loves because he is very, very ugly.'

The way Bea says it, it sounds like 'velly, velly uggerley'.

'Uggerley?' Lara says.

'And at Christmas I saw Santa,' she adds. 'Because the Santa in the shopping centre wasn't the real Santa.' She shakes her head vigorously and her hair falls into her cereal bowl. I lean across to tuck it behind her ears. She takes a spoonful of cereal and says in hushed tones, 'The Sealife Centre had the real Santa. Didn't it, Mummy?'

'I don't think Nemo would settle for anything less.'

'See.' She looks round at Lara. 'He had a *real* beard and was fat with a proper tummy, not a cushion.'

I stand up. 'I have to go now. You girls have fun!' I kiss the tops of their heads and then Julian's cheek. 'I'm off to get Lisa.'

'Need a hand?'

'No, we'll be fine.' I kiss him again. 'Would you mind having a word with Charlie before you go out?'

'Will do.'

'What would you like me to do this morning?' Sezen asks.

'It's Saturday,' I say. 'Take some time off. It'll give you a chance to look for somewhere to stay between now and moving into Mr Patel's place.'

'But would you like me to help you with Lisa? I can make some food for when you return.'

I tell her it isn't necessary. There's enough food left over from yesterday's cooking session. She follows me into the hallway. 'But Julian is taking Lara,' she says. 'I would like to give those hours back.'

'Really, it's fine.' I smile at her. 'Take some time for yourself.'

'Claire.' She has followed me into the porch. 'About last night.'

'Yes?'

'I hope you did not find me rude.' She stops, thinks. I can see she's choosing her words carefully. 'I am very appreciative of this job.'

'You know that you can talk to me, don't you?' I see a moment of uncertainty flit across her face. 'Sezen, I hope we're friends. I hope you trust me.' I smile. 'I'm fairly unshockable, you know. If there's anything you need to tell me . . . something from the pas—'

'No!' she interrupts me, quite forcefully, and at once I know there is something in her past.

'The man who came last night?'

'I will not see him again.' The shake of her head is emphatic. 'He is not good for me.'

'Sezen.' I reach for her hand. She lets me take it. 'I'm a good listener.'

Her expression softens. Her eyes fill with tears. 'You are a good person, Claire.' She hugs me quickly and then backs away.

'You will talk to me?' I say.

'Yes.' She smiles her thanks. 'I will.'

She closes the door after me and, feeling like I might have made some progress, I'm about to climb into my car when Jem calls me on her mobile.

'Only me,' she says. 'I didn't leave my Stanley knife in Lisa's room, did I? I woke up this morning with a horrible feeling I had. I don't want Bea to get hold of it and hurt herself.'

'Hang on.' I go back in the house and look around the room. 'Can't see it anywhere.'

'Oh well, must be in the van somewhere. How's things?'

I tell her about Julian taking the girls out to give me space to collect Lisa, walking into the sitting room as I talk. I look through the window and spot Mary Percival heading towards me through the park opposite. There's a light summer rain falling and she has her umbrella up, but I can see her face just below the rim. Douglas is trotting along beside her, head up, beady black eyes fixing on passers-by. When she reaches the pavement at the edge of the park, she crosses over to my side of the street. She looks up at the house and I automatically pull myself back and to the side a bit so that she won't be able to see me at the window. She stands at the bottom of the steps, looks at her watch, then back at the house. She climbs three of the steps and stops. Douglas climbs the steps with her. He is watching her. She is watching the front door. I can just make out the expression on her face. She looks nervous, scared even. She is biting her lip. She climbs one step higher and then abruptly changes her mind, does an about-turn and ends up back on the pavement.

'Are you listening?' Jem's voice is suddenly loud in my ear.

'Do you ever find Mary Percival a bit strange?' I say.

'How did we get on to talking about her?'

I summarise what I've just seen. 'Odd, don't you think?'

'Maybe she wanted to invite you to a party: Tupperware, Jamie at Home, Ann Summers?'

'Then why not just ring the bell?'

'She's quite shy. Bit lonely maybe. Let's face it' – I hear her take a puff of a cigarette – 'she doesn't have the best social skills, but she's great with the kids. Adam's come on in leaps and bounds since he started there. She has a knack of bringing out the best in him.'

'She remembers absolutely everything I've ever told her,' I say, thinking about details I've given her about Lisa's illness and how she can repeat them back to me, word for word. 'Spookily so.'

'Maybe she has perfect recall.'

'There are eighteen children in her class and almost every mother talks to her at the beginning or the end of the morning and yet last week she actually remembered Lisa's blood count. I mean, you're my friend and you don't remember the details.'

'No, but I don't have that sort of brain.'

'And almost half the time I look out of my window she's out there with Douglas . . .'

'Maybe he has a weak bladder?'

'I kid you not, Jem, she's practically always outside my house.'

'I know!' She gives a dirty laugh. 'She fancies you.'

I roll my eyes. 'That must be it.'

'Have you found out what those two men are up to yet?'

It's on the tip of my tongue to tell her that they're policemen, but I don't because Mary Percival is still over the road, hanging around. It's too much. 'I've got to go, Jem,' I say. 'Talk to you soon?'

'Yup. Have a good day.'

I run out through the front door and across the road. Miss Percival looks up as I approach and smiles tentatively. The rain has eased off and she collapses her umbrella. Without pause for thought I say, 'Every time I look out of the window, you're there.'

She steps back, startled. 'I'm sorry. I—' She stops, tries again. 'I want to . . .'

'You want to what? What's going on with you?'

Her cheeks flush and her eyes fill up. My clipped tone is wounding her, but I can't back off. She is in prime position to harm my child. She's made a teacher's pet of Bea. She has Bea's trust. I remember one of the emails – *This morning Bea played in the sandpit . . . I could have taken her then. I could take her still. And you'd never see her again* – and I know I can't let her off the hook.

'Why are you so strange with me? You've made a favourite of Bea and yet you can barely look me in the eye.' I try to soften my tone. 'If you have something to say, then you should say it.'

'I do have something to say. I do have something to tell you. I haven't been able to up till now. I never intended to tell you, but then Bea came to the nursery and I made the connection and—'

'What connection?'

My arms are folded; I'm tapping my foot. Not conducive to her coming clean with me and I'm not surprised when she says, 'When you're less . . . busy.' She's clutching the dog's lead with both hands as if he's about to run off. 'I won't bother you now.'

'No.' I hold her upper arm. She makes no attempt to shrug me off. 'We need to clear this up here and now. Or else I will have to give your name to the police.'

'*What?* Why?'

'The magazine article you were reading. The one about Pavel Georgiev. Do you know him?'

'Of course not.'

'Are you involved in something that you no longer want to be part of? Something that's got out of hand?'

She stares at me, incredulous.

'Do you know what's going on in my family at the moment?'

I drop my voice to almost a whisper and lean in close to her. 'My husband is being blackmailed by someone who intends to kidnap Bea unless he gives her the information she wants.'

'My God, I'm so sorry.' I'm taken aback as I watch her face collapse with horror. Her jaw hangs open and tears slide from her eyes. 'So very sorry. If there's anything I can do . . .'

'Yes. There is. You can eliminate yourself from the enquiries. Because someone in my life, and in Bea's life, is feeding information to this blackmailer and I need to be sure it isn't you.'

The sun chooses that moment to come out from behind a cloud and shine down upon us both as if we have been singled out for extra light and warmth. I hold my hand up to shield my eyes so that I can see Miss Percival's expression. She looks completely crushed. She appears to have diminished in size: her shoulders wilting, her spine shrinking, her limbs pulled in tight towards her body. I search for signs of deception, but all I see is a woman who is devastated. It doesn't make sense. Most people, whether guilty or innocent, would have come back at me by now with 'How dare you!' or 'What makes you think you can talk to me this way?'

'Miss Percival, Mary,' I say, more gently now, 'this is clearly upsetting you. Will you please tell me what's going on?'

She glances down at Douglas. He has lain down on a patch of grass and rolled on to his side. His eyes are shut and he looks a picture of contentment. She unclips the lead from his collar and walks over to a bench, positioned in the shade under an oak tree. I follow her and sit down beside her, both of us facing one another at an angle.

'The timing for this can never be right,' she begins. 'I don't want to upset anyone or to change the view you have of your father.'

'My father?' I almost laugh. 'What does he have to do with this?'

She takes a huge breath. 'I am an only child. I was brought up near Brighton by my mum and dad – or at least for thirty years I believed he was my dad. But then, six years ago, in May, my mum told me that in fact she'd fallen pregnant to someone else. I got in touch with this man – your dad. I took a DNA test and the result was positive. He was very kind to me, but I was confused and angry that I'd been lied to all my life and I left Brighton for a while. I came back a couple of years ago, made up with my parents but discovered your dad, my biological father, had passed away.'

She says all of this in a deadpan tone as if she has stepped out of her body and her mouth is repeating these words by rote. I, on the other hand, feel as if I've landed slap bang in the middle of an episode of *The Jeremy Kyle Show* and I'm shaking my head so quickly that I can feel blood swish in my ears. 'You're telling me you're my *half-sister*?'

'Yes.'

'You've been Bea's teacher since *September* and you never said a word!'

'I know. It took me a while to get my head around it. I knew that you and Lisa existed – your father was very proud of you both – but we were a couple of weeks into the term before I put two and two together and realised we were related.'

'So why not tell me then? October? November? Christmas?'

'Because Lisa had been diagnosed with cancer and I didn't think it was the right time.'

I stare at her, still shaking my head. My mind is reeling. My father had another daughter. *My father had another daughter?* I find it impossible to comprehend, like squeezing an elephant into a phone box – I don't have the space to contain such enormous news.

'You're right – I have been strange towards you,' she continues. 'I've tried to be normal, but I just couldn't keep it up. I kept thinking that you were my sister and—'

'Why didn't my dad say something?'

'I asked him not to and, as I said, when I returned to Brighton, he'd passed away.'

'I'm sorry,' I say. 'I'm supposed to believe all of this. You've spent nine months looking after my daughter, your *niece* by the way, and not once did you bring this up.'

'I wasn't sure how to approach you. You're so . . .'

'I'm so what?' I realise I'm glaring at her and then I realise something else. This could all be part of an elaborate deception, a way to push further into Bea's life. 'I'm sorry, *Mary* – I suppose I'm allowed to call you that now? – but I don't believe you. You bear no resemblance to my father, or me, or Lisa.'

'I take after my mother.' She digs around in her bag. 'This is a letter your dad sent to me.'

'That you just happen to have with you?'

'It's the only thing I have of him.' She holds it out. 'I always carry it with me.'

I don't touch it, but still I can see that it's been repeatedly read. The paper is fraying at the edges and the two pages are heavily creased. And it is my dad's handwriting. No mistaking the long strokes on the 'f's and the 't's and the flourishes at the end of each sentence. It begins with 'My dear Mary, I was so delighted to meet you . . .' I have a sudden sense of him standing in front of me, smiling with that hundred-watt, winning enthusiasm that always made me feel special. Yes, he had his faults – not least his infidelity to Wendy – but he was my dad and I loved him with the same passion and trust that Bea feels for Julian.

'I don't want to read it.' I hold my hands up and back away from her. 'I can't deal with this now.'

'I understand.' She composes her face. 'You need time to think about it.'

'I have to go.' I walk away from her. My ears are ringing and I feel nauseous. When I reach the car, I sit in the driving seat and hold my breath while a powerful shake flows through my body, beginning in my stomach and ending in my toes and finger-tips. *What the hell just happened?* I can't believe it. I have another sister. A younger sister. I'm already calculating that Mary would have been born a couple of years after my dad married Wendy.

Wendy, who, two years after my mother's death, defied all step-mother stereotypes and came into our lives, bringing generosity and caring for two small girls and a grieving man. I wonder whether she knows that my father had another child. And should I tell her? Should I tell Lisa? I'm someone who values family above all else, so this should be good news, shouldn't it?

I don't know what to think or feel. I don't know what to do. On top of everything else that's going on, this is one more thing to squash into my already very full brain. It takes me only a second to decide that I'll do nothing. I won't tell anyone. I'll pretend that it hasn't happened. I've known Mary Percival for nine months without her giving me so much as an inkling of her relationship to us. This is something that doesn't have to be dealt with now. Another few days or weeks are not going to make any difference.

I take a few deep breaths, start the engine and head to the hospital. Lisa is sitting in an easy chair, her belongings in several bags arranged around her feet. When she sees me coming, she smiles wider than I've seen her smile in weeks.

'My rescuer!' she shouts, then leans in for a hug. 'Who needs a knight in shining armour when I have you?'

Lynn comes into the room to brief me on Lisa's medication regime. She has it all written up on a chart – some need to be taken with meals, others an hour before or after food.

'As if I'm not perfectly capable of working it out for myself,' Lisa chimes in.

'Little sister's in charge,' Lynn says, playfully nudging Lisa's shoulder before turning back to me. 'The community nurse will call on Tuesday, but if you need her before that, here's the number.' She points to it on the chart. 'And if Lisa gives you any trouble, Claire, you bring her straight back.'

'Not in a month of Sundays.' Lisa stands up. 'Much as I love you all, I have no intention of coming back.'

'Good on you, love.' Lynn hugs Lisa tight and gestures to me over her shoulder – her thumb to her ear, little finger to her lips. 'Phone me,' she mouths.

When we're outside, Lisa takes a huge breath of air. 'What happened to summer?'

'What's a bit of drizzle?' I say. 'We've had far worse in June.'

'You're right.' She throws her arms up above her head and then lets them fall back down to her sides. 'It's great to be outdoors again.'

My heart skips a happy beat.

'I can sit in the shade and watch Bea playing and you can bring me jam sandwiches and homemade lemonade.'

I smile. The food of our childhood. Wendy would make us up a tray and we'd take it to the bottom of the garden and lie on our backs munching on squares of sandwich while sticky lemonade dribbled down our chins.

'Happiness is all about small moments and simple pleasures,' Lisa says, climbing into the car.

'My sister the guru.' I climb in beside her and reach across to help her with her seatbelt.

'You mark my words.' She waves her finger at me. 'Those are the things we remember in the end. Do you remember Dad used to always say' – she deepens her voice and raises up her shoulders, pushing out her chest – '"You have to live life to the full, girls. No regrets."'

Dad. My eyes slide away from Lisa. Do we really have another sister? If so, when she came to see him six years ago, why on earth didn't he tell us?

'He was all about seizing the day.'

'From what I remember, the rest of us had to accommodate his seizing of the day,' I say, negotiating my way out of the hospital grounds and on to the main road. 'All those affairs. I mean, honestly! Who does that?'

'He never had an affair while Mum was alive.'

'It was Wendy who copped the brunt of it.' I shake my head. 'And why didn't he comfort us when Mum died? He acted like she'd never existed.'

'Some people don't do well with loss. They can't cope with the grief.'

'I suppose.'

'Nowadays there's grief counselling, but in those days you were expected just to get on with it.'

'That's true,' I say. 'But we were only kids, Lisa. You were six, and I was four – Bea's age. We were practically babies.'

'We had each other, Claire. Dad must have felt very alone. We had all our little games and imaginings and that made it easier.'

Our mother is a subject Lisa and I haven't spoken about for a while. Lisa is able to accept her death, but for me, it's always felt like unfinished business. She died of a brain haemorrhage. One sunny September day she dropped down in front of us, passing from life to death in the space of one ordinary moment. An extreme, abrupt ending that my child's mind found impossible to absorb. Every morning I woke up expecting her to have come back to us, but every morning the house was cold, breakfast unmade, our clothes lying where we'd dropped them. My dad put everything that was left of her in the wardrobe in their room. Piece by piece, crawling commando style, Lisa and I sneaked some of Mum's belongings out of her old room and into ours. Our dad never noticed and, in retrospect, I think the subterfuge was unnecessary. He seemed to have forgotten all about her. Lisa and I treated these objects with reverence, as if they were magical and would somehow bring her back. We kept a box under Lisa's bed. Inside were a silk scarf, some sling-back shoes, a bottle of perfume and a pair of earrings: small pearls set in silver. We had one photograph of her. We took turns placing it underneath our pillow. For years we believed that she would come home. We lived in a kind of limbo and said things to each other like 'When Mum comes back, we'll ask her if we can have riding lessons' or 'When Mum finds out we haven't been cleaning our teeth for three minutes, she'll tell us off' or 'We should eat an apple every day because Mum always said that keeps the doctor away.'

I must have been twelve before it really hit me that, of course, she wasn't coming back. She was dead, for God's sake! I cried then, for her and for myself.

'The secret with grief is, don't fight it, don't run from it,' Lisa says. 'Let it wash over you. And when the next wave comes, bend your back and take that too.'

I know that she's partly talking about our parents and about herself and coming to terms with her illness. And I know, too, that she's partly talking to me, helping me see a way through it. Lisa knows I struggle with grief and with acceptance. I have an inbuilt, visceral fear of losing members of my family. Death is so final, so utterly irrevocable. I think back to the way I behaved after Kerry Smith's death – having quick, escapist sex with Mac. Perhaps I am more like my father than I know. It's not a pleasant thought and I automatically turn the radio on, hoping to shut out the voices in my head.

The sound of a man singing fills the car. Lisa reaches over to turn the volume down and then she squeezes my knee. 'Did you hear me?'

'I heard you.' I look sideways to give her a quick smile.

'Do you mind if we stop by my flat on the way back to yours? I want to pick up some bits and pieces.'

'Course.'

Before she was diagnosed with cancer, Lisa taught biology in a girls' school in Brighton. Her flat is between my house and the hospital. Parking is a nightmare, so I risk stopping in one of the disabled bays close to the entrance to her flat. It's on the first floor. We go inside. She stops halfway up the stairs and leans the top half of her body on the banister while she catches her breath.

'This weakness is just so irritating.'

'Take your time,' I say. 'There's no rush.'

'I don't want you getting a ticket.' She sets off up the last half a dozen steps. 'You know what the traffic wardens are like around here.'

'I'll sit at the window and watch out for them.' I unlock her front door, pick up the letters on the mat inside and hand them to her. 'If necessary, I'll drive round the block a few times.'

She lives on a busy corner, almost on top of a small roundabout where seven roads branch out: to the station, to the seafront, others inland. I sit at the window to watch for wardens. It's a hectic Saturday morning and the whole world and his dog seem to be converging in this small space. There's a grocer's on the corner and five teenage girls come out. They are giggling and hanging on to each other. One of them is texting and the others peer over her shoulder, breaking into fits of laughter as they watch the words come up on the screen. It makes me smile.

I've been sitting for five minutes when I notice a man approaching the roundabout. He has a distinctive style of walking, leaning over to one side, not quite a limp, but there is a definite tilt to his gait. Exactly like the man who came to see Sezen yesterday evening. My heart ups its rhythm. I lean into the window, but I still can't isolate his features.

I go through to Lisa's bedroom. She is emptying the contents of her bedside drawer into a bag. 'Do you have any binoculars?'

'What for?'

'I want to spy on the neighbours.'

'Really?'

'No.' I shift my feet. 'Have you got any?'

'In the living-room bureau. They're Dad's old ones.'

I find them at once. The casing is scratched and heavy, the leather strap frayed and torn, but there's nothing wrong with the lenses. I lift them up to my eyes and turn the knob until the street is in focus. I home in on the man. He is as Jack described: swarthy and unsmiling. He waits on the corner, his heels on the kerb, his toes suspended above the gutter, rocking backwards and forwards. His eyes dart anxiously down towards the right – Monkton Terrace – the street a person would walk up if they were coming from my house.

He sees her just before I do and I watch a slow smile spread across his face. I move the binoculars to the right, following his gaze along the street. It's what I expect but still my hands shake as I focus on Sezen walking towards him. When she spots him, her feet quicken, almost to a run, and then she stops, straightens her spine, brings her feet back to a walking rhythm.

My vision blurs. I am flooded with disappointment. I remember her even tone, her unblinking expression as she said to me, 'He is nothing to me.' She stops a few feet away from him. Neither of them speaks. Her body sways towards him and then her jaw tightens and she pulls back. The third time she does this something inside her lets go and she clasps him to her like someone lost and now found.

'And this is a man who is nothing to you?' I hear myself say out loud.

The feeling between them is electric and I see passers-by drawn to watch them. One girl stands next to the post box and openly stares as Sezen and the man embrace, then step back and hold hands, their eyes fixed on each other. Nobody else exists. They stand like this for more than twenty seconds and then he says something. She smiles and replies. I try to lip-read, but I can't isolate any words, and anyway, I doubt that they're speaking English. She hands him a piece of paper and he reads it, asks her questions. She points to the page and explains the content to him. His hand goes into his trouser pocket and he pulls something out. I move and refocus the binoculars. It's a wad of cash, several notes rolled up into a bundle, held together with an elastic band.

My heart lurches as if I've just driven quickly over a speed bump. I'm witnessing an exchange. Payment for information or services rendered. It's too much. This woman has access to my house. I've trusted her with Bea. Everything she's told me I have believed. And yet here she is meeting a man she said she would never see again and giving him information for money.

I call Julian. No answer, so I leave a message. 'Julian, whatever you do, don't let Bea go anywhere with Sezen. I think she may have something to do with all this.'

12

I put my mobile back in my pocket and lift up the binoculars again. They're still standing there, talking and smiling.

'What are you up to?' Lisa has come up behind me.

'I'm watching Sezen.'

'Your cook?'

I nod and hand her the binoculars. She holds them up to her eyes, her slender wrists trembling under the weight. She steadies them on the cross-frame of the sash window.

'She's with someone she loves by the looks of it. Have you met him?'

'He came to the house last night. She told me he meant nothing to her.'

'Perhaps she's in denial. Sometimes it's hard for people to admit they're in love, especially if they've been let down in the past.' She puts the binoculars on the windowsill and searches my face. 'Why do you look so worried?'

'Because she lied to me. Why did she tell me he wasn't her friend?'

'Maybe she doesn't see him as a friend. And anyway, you're her employer, not her priest. She's entitled to her privacy, isn't she?'

'Yes, but . . .' I shake my head. I'm trying to add it all up. Sezen knows my email address because we ordered some macrobiotic ingredients on the Internet. She wasn't at Bea's party, but then she could have found out about it from Wendy. They talk all the time and I'm sure Wendy will have mentioned it.

'Isn't she?'

Lisa's waiting for me to say something else. 'It's complicated.'
'In what way?'

I briefly consider not telling her, but what's the point in prevaricating? It hasn't worked with Charlie and I feel even less inclined to lie to my sister. 'Julian has been receiving emails. We're being threatened,' I say flatly. 'By someone who works for Pavel Georgiev.'

'What?' She steps back and sits down hard on the arm of the couch. 'Why? Who?' Her head is shaking. 'What do you mean?'

'It's the case he's working on.'

'The Bulgarian gangster?'

'That's right.'

'What are they threatening him with?'

'The children's safety: most specifically Bea's.'

I fill her in on the details. She looks increasingly worried as I talk and then, when she can bear it no more, she bursts out, 'This is awful!' She grabs hold of both my hands. 'Claire, you should take the children and leave the country. Get right away from the danger.' She gives a sharp intake of breath. 'You're not still in this country because of me, are you?'

I glance back out of the window, trying to focus on Sezen and the man, but they're too far away for me to make out their expressions. I lift the binoculars. Lisa stops my hand.

'Claire.' She swings me round to face her. 'Look me in the eye and tell me that you're not still in the country because of me.'

I look her in the eye. 'It has nothing to do with you,' I say.

Her face flushes. 'I could always tell when you were lying. You're no better at it now than you were when you were five and you ate the Curly Wurly I kept underneath my pillow.' She shakes me. 'You mustn't put me before your children's safety.'

'I'm not.' I hug her to me, feel her ribs jutting out, curved sticks beneath her skin. I stroke her hair. She didn't lose it with the chemo, but it lacks lustre and feels coarse under my hand. 'I admit it was my first impulse to take them away, but then, when I had time to think about it, I realised it was a bad idea.'

'Are you sure?'

'Lisa, Georgiev is powerful. His reach extends further than England. Being in another country, waiting for that knock at the door or disturbance in the middle of the night would be far more stressful than staying here. I don't want you and I to be apart, and I don't want Julian and I to be apart. This is a time for us all to stick together. Safety in numbers. The thing is' – I take a breath – 'the police are organising a safe house. If we have to go, you will come with us, won't you?'

'Of course!' She doesn't hesitate. 'Of course I'll come with you all.'

'They're arranging a live-in nurse.'

'Is that OK?'

'Absolutely. It's the easiest way to not draw attention to ourselves. We'll have to live very quietly, stay completely below the radar.'

'Will Wendy come?'

'I hope so. She doesn't know about it yet, but on Monday the police will come to the house to brief us on what happens next.'

'This is really serious.' She looks beyond me, through the window, but her eyes are focusing inwards. 'How will the boys cope?'

'I think when they understand it's about keeping us all safe, they'll be fine.'

'What does Julian think?'

'He goes along with the police.'

'Julian's judgement is always pretty sound. He wouldn't expose any of you to danger.'

'I know that, but then . . . Well' – I breathe in – 'he hasn't exactly been keeping me in the loop.'

She frowns. 'What do you mean?'

'He kept the emails a secret for over a week, and when I found out, it wasn't through him.'

'How, then?'

'Bea.' I tell her about Bea letting slip about the emails. 'Julian said he was going to tell me, but' – I blow air out through my mouth – 'he didn't.'

'Why not?'

'Because he didn't want to worry me. And I do believe him. But I can't help thinking that before I stopped work and we moved to Brighton, he couldn't have helped but tell me. We talked all the time.'

'But, sweetheart, since you came to live here, Dad died and Bea was born and then there's been me . . .'

'Logically, I acknowledge all of that.' I pause. 'He told Megan, though.'

'His assistant?'

'The instructing solicitor who works for the CPS.' I think of Megan with her privileged background and top-of-the-class ambition. 'The more modern, up-scaled version of me.'

She catches my tone, which I know sounds sullen and not just a little bit sour. 'Are you regretting giving up your work?'

'No, but I'm regretting the effect it seems to have had on my marriage. I thought we were close, but now I just don't know. He spends more time talking and being with Megan than he does with me.'

'Claire, it's the nature of his work. When this trial is over, they'll go their separate ways.'

'Maybe . . . but at the moment it feels like he's closer to her than he is to me.'

She recoils back a step. 'You're not saying . . . ?'

'That he's having an affair?' I shrug. 'I asked him and he said no.'

'Claire!'

'And I believe him, but I just . . .' I try to find the right words to explain the unease I feel. 'For nine days he very successfully kept the emails a secret from me, so it's not a great leap to wonder whether he might be keeping something else under wraps.'

'Look, Claire, you've just had the most awful shock. You've found out your family is under threat and that's frightening. In fact it's beyond frightening. But Julian is your husband and your greatest ally.'

I want to believe her, but . . . 'Do you remember the policeman Andrew MacPherson? Mac?'

'Of course.' Apart from Julian, Lisa is the only person I told about my extra-marital sex. And, unlike Julian, she knew it was Mac. 'He was the reason you moved to Brighton, wasn't he?'

'He wasn't so much the reason as the catalyst, the final straw.'

'OK.' She inclines her head. 'If you say so.'

I let that go. 'Julian and Megan.' I think back to yesterday evening. 'I was at the window last night when they had walked down from the station and they were looking at each other with the kind of intimacy that people get when they work together: shared purpose, second-guessing, knowing what the other person's thinking.'

'And you're worried that means he's sleeping with her?' She shakes her head. 'Come on! Apart from the fact that Julian is devoted to you and the children, he's just not the type. He's someone who has integrity.'

I can't let that go. 'And I don't?' I say sharply. 'I, of all people, know how easy it is to slip up.'

'You had sex with Mac once.' Her tone slides from hectoring to reassuring. 'There was that whole business with Kerry Smith. The circumstances were extreme.'

'These circumstances are even more extreme,' I remind her. 'I'm his wife and he has kept this from me for nine whole days. The first email came on 24 May. And that's not all. He's also resigned from the case. He didn't tell me that either. You can't say that's not underhand.'

'I don't think it's underhand, but I can see why it would be hurtful. I really can. Nevertheless I don't think you should be jumping to conclusions about his relationship with Megan on the basis of him keeping the emails from you.'

She's right, of course, and when I tackled Julian about it, he was completely honest with me. I remind myself that he is not my father. There is no reason for me to suspect he's having an affair. None. I rub my hands across my eyes. 'I'm sorry. I know I'm rambling. I didn't sleep very well last night. This is all so sudden. It feels like a lot to cope with.'

'It *is* a lot to cope with. Bloody hell.' Her face creases and she takes a few quick breaths.

'I'm so sorry.' I hunker down beside her knees and take her hand. 'I didn't want to have to tell you.'

'Well, I'm glad you did.'

'I know, but you have enough—'

'Since when did *you* start to protect *me*?' She looks at me sternly. 'So what exactly are the police doing about these threats?'

In for a penny . . . 'Well, there's the thing,' I say quietly. 'Mac's been promoted since I knew him last. He's running this.'

'Mac?' Her eyes fix on mine. 'And have you seen him?'

'We hadn't spoken for years, but I met him just after I found out about the emails.'

'You met him with Julian?'

'No. I met him on my own.'

She raises an eyebrow.

'Because of the way Julian reacted after Bea's party. And doesn't that now make sense?'

'Yes, it does.'

'So I printed off the emails and arranged to meet Mac.'

'Without Julian knowing?'

'He was in Sofia and I was at home with enough information to scare me but not enough to feel like there was a way through it.'

'And then you met up with Mac?'

'Yes. We discussed the case.'

'And does Julian know?'

'That I met him?'

She nods.

'Yes.'

'And does he know that Mac was the man you slept with?'

'No.'

'This is dangerous, Claire.' She gives me her big-sister-knows-best look: head to one side, eyebrows raised. 'You have history with this man and if Julian finds out—'

'He won't find out. Our past involvement – brief as it was – will not get in the way of the case. I won't let it.'

'Do you still have feelings for him?'

'Sexually? No! Of course not.'

She lets my words hang in the air and grow heavy. The muscles on my face begin to stiffen and I remind myself that I'm telling the truth. There's no reason for me to feel guilty. This is about Bea and keeping her safe. It's not about Mac.

'He's a good policeman and I'm glad he's on the case. I feel like he's on my side.'

'*Julian* is on your side.' Her voice is firm.

'I know.'

'So why didn't you include him in the meeting?'

'Because he was still in Sofia! And I didn't want to wait. And because I was hurt and angry, and he'd been keeping a hefty great secret from me for long enough.'

'Evening up the score?' She looks washed out suddenly. 'Claire, tell me you're better than that?'

Her look says it all and at once I feel guilty: small-minded and cheap.

'This is not about me and Mac. And it's not about me and Julian.' I try to regain some ground. 'It's about protecting my family. And Mac will do the best for us. I know he will.'

'Good.' She turns away. 'I'm going to get the rest of my stuff together.'

I watch her slowly make her way back to her bedroom. I know she's disappointed in me and it hurts. Shit. I go back to the window and lift the binoculars in time to catch Sezen and the man coming out of the café on the corner. They part on the pavement after he kisses her, on the mouth, confidently, like he knows she wants it.

'Lovers, then,' I say out loud. 'And we all know what lovers are willing to do for each other. Look at Myra Hindley.'

'You really think she might have something to do with this?' Lisa is back. She is holding a couple of bags and a lamp.

'Let me carry those.' I put the binoculars down and she passes the bags to me. 'Yes, I really think she might. Details in the emails prove that the blackmailer either is or knows someone who has access to our family.' We head for the door. I wave the lamp at her as I walk. 'There's already a lamp in your new room.'

'I'm bringing it for Bea. She likes the lampshade.'

Out on the street, I can't see any sign of Sezen or the man. I look out for them as I drive home, but they must have gone in another direction. When we arrive back at the house, only Jack is home. He comes forward to give Lisa a hug and lifts her off her feet.

'We have another man in the house!' she says.

He flexes his muscles and rolls up the sleeves of his T-shirt so that she can see. 'I've been working out.'

'Haven't you just!' She hugs him again.

They are both grinning like mad and I realise afresh that bringing Lisa home will be a good thing for her and also for the children, who love her dearly. Jack helps bring Lisa's stuff in from the car and I go into the kitchen to put the kettle on. Sezen has left a tray of food, beautifully prepared, and alongside it are pale pink tulips in a vase. All this before she went off to meet the man who means nothing to her.

I hear the front door open and Bea shouts, 'Mummy!'

'In the kitchen!' I shout back.

She comes running in and throws her arms round my legs. 'I won a twirly thing and Daddy lifted me and Lara up high and we saw the men juggling.' She pushes her stomach out, leans back on her heels and puckers her lips. 'The juggling man looked like that. And he had plates on the end of a stick and he let me hold one.'

'Did he, now? Lucky you.' I hunker down to her height and hug her tight. 'But guess who's come to stay?'

'Who?'

'Auntie Lisa.' Her eyes light up. I give her a gentle nudge. 'Go and tell her all about the good time you had.'

She's off again, knocking into Julian on the way.

'The girls had fun, then,' I say.

'Great time.' He unzips his jacket. 'They had special events on, so Nemo wasn't the main attraction.'

'Where's Lara?'

'Sezen called me earlier. She met us down on the pier. They've gone off to see friends. She won't be back this evening.'

'Was she alone?'

'Who?'

'Sezen.'

He nods and puts his jacket over the back of a chair.

'Did she say where she was going to spend the night?'

'No. Why?'

'Did you get my message?'

'No.' He takes his BlackBerry out of his pocket. 'There is one from you. Sorry. Left it in the car.'

'I saw her with the man who came to the door last night. At the roundabout by Lisa's flat.'

'Did you?'

'She told me he meant nothing to her and yet they were hugging like long-lost lovers.'

Julian looks unperturbed.

'Are you listening?'

'Yes.'

'Don't you think that's a problem?'

'In what way?' He walks into the pantry and I follow him.

'The emails.'

He moves aside a jar of pickles, some tuna fish and a tin of peaches. 'Why would Sezen have anything to do with the emails?'

'She might be feeding Georgiev's men information. It would be a good way to infiltrate our family, wouldn't it?'

'But you employed her, didn't you? You approached her? Her references checked out?'

'Yes, but you know how clever people can be.' I think back to my time as a solicitor with the CPS. Even the most unlikely people can be deceitful. 'It's not beyond the realms of possibility that she could manoeuvre herself into a position close to us.'

'No, that's true,' he concedes. 'But Sezen's Turkish and she's a mother and just the other day you were telling me how trustworthy she was and that she'd become your friend.'

'I know, but . . .'

'I thought you were someone who trusted your gut feeling?'

'Normally I do, but I'm also someone who's willing to concede that I'm not always right.' My voice drops to a whisper. 'In some ways, her being so perfect is too good to be true, don't you think?'

He laughs. 'Well, not any more by the sounds of it. Is it the fact that she hasn't shared the details of her relationship with this man that's bothering you?'

This irritates me, but still I stay calm. 'No. It's the fact that she *lied*. I think that's cause for concern.'

'Do we have any teabags?'

I grab them from the shelf behind me and slap them into his hand. 'Under ordinary circumstances,' I continue, 'of course I wouldn't be suspicious of her, but these circumstances are hardly ordinary.'

'And that's why a cool head is important.'

'Fucking hell, Julian! I do have a cool head.'

He raises his eyebrows and then starts to smile. I feel the corners of my own mouth twitch in response, but I can't joke about this. It isn't funny. Not to me.

'I do have a cool head. I'm impatient, yes, I admit that, but I can still think straight. I just need the people around me to be honest. Look at the facts. For the last twelve days you, and now we, have been receiving threatening emails. We're worried about someone kidnapping our child. An unknown man turns up at our house. Sezen talks to him, lingers by the window to watch him, denies he means anything to her and yet next day I see her kissing him. And she gave him a piece of paper while he passed her a wad of cash. How can that be fine?'

He rolls his head from side to side. 'Put like that, it sounds like you have a point.'

I follow him back into the kitchen. 'Sounds like?'

'The two events are not necessarily linked. So she has a secret? It doesn't make her Georgiev's accomplice.' I go to protest and he holds up a hand. 'But you're right. Why risk it? We should ask her to leave.' He pours water into the kettle and switches it on. 'But it was only yesterday that you felt it couldn't possibly be Sezen. Mary Percival was definitely in the running, though.'

'Don't talk to me about her.' I put my hands over my face. 'It's not her . . . I don't think.'

'How do you know?'

'I had it out with her in the park earlier and . . .' I shake my head. I don't even consider telling him. The thought of forming the words on my tongue – *she's my sister* – feels too alien. 'It's not her.'

'OK. So Sezen is now prime suspect?'

'Julian. Please.' His face is still sceptical. 'I feel in my bones that there's more going on here. If you had seen her at the round-about, then I'm sure you'd feel the same.'

'Well, why don't we ask her when she gets back?'

I can't leave it at that. She won't be back until tomorrow and that's a long way off. Something inside me wants to get to the root of this now. Next thing I know I'm on the top floor, pushing open the door into Sezen's bedroom. I stand in the middle of the room and look around me. The space is neat and tidy. Both beds are made. Lara's bed has two of Bea's soft toys perched on top of the pillow. There is no spare change or used tickets on the chest of drawers, no clothes on the floor or empty glasses on the bedside cabinet. There's nothing lying around that gives me any sense of who Sezen is or where she has come from.

As I stand there, I think about what I'm going to do next. My fingers want to start poking and prying through her stuff; my head tells me it's an invasion of her privacy. I should wait. Ask her when she comes back. I'm flying off on a tangent again, determined to force the issue – just like I did with Mary Percival. And look at how that worked out.

On the other hand, this is my home and I am entitled to ensure my child's safety. I don't have the luxury of waiting to see what's behind Sezen's secrecy. We have two days to try to find the black-mailer. That's all. If suspicions arise and I can expedite that process, then I need to do so.

A compromise is reached between my conscience and my instinct. I decide that I won't go through everything. I won't look at photographs or read letters or diaries. All I will do is see whether there is anything obvious that might give me a clue as to why she's been lying to me.

I open the drawers one by one, carefully moving folded blouses and underwear to look underneath. I don't really know what I expect to find, but I keep on looking anyway. The bottom drawer is heavy and stiff. I pull hard and see that she has stored papers and books in this one. I make a point of not reading through them, but a casual glance reminds me that most of what's written is not in English. Right at the back there is a pouch containing passports – three of them. I bring them out. One is made out to Lara, one to Sezen and the third to a Sylvia Cyrilova, a Bulgarian national. I look at the photo. I look again more closely. I stare at it. I compare one with the other. Her hair is shorter and she's two or three years younger, but it's definitely Sezen.

I put the passports down on the carpet and sit back on my heels. Unease spreads through me like electricity, the sensation beginning in my stomach and filtering outwards through my body to the roots of my hair. Sezen is not the sweet single mother she seems. She has two identities. She is Turkish and she is Bulgarian. Or perhaps she is just Bulgarian. Like Georgiev. Of course, that's hardly enough to convict her, but taken together with the fact that she concealed it and that she has lied to me about the man she met at the roundabout, I think we have a problem.

'Should you be snooping in here?' It's Julian. He's standing at the door watching me.

Wordlessly, I hold out the passports.

'You've found something?' He steps into the room and takes them from me. I watch his face register two different names, two different nationalities, same woman. He looks back at me and I see fear creep into his eyes. 'I'll call Mac.'

13

I stand to one side and listen as Julian calls Mac. He explains that we've found the passports, indicating that Sezen is far from what she seems. Mac tells Julian he should call him as soon as Sezen comes back tomorrow and that she will be taken in for questioning. In the meantime, he would like to come and see us this evening. He has the case files for the two murders quoted in the email – *Carlo Brunetti, Rome, 2006, and Boleslav Hlutev, Sofia, 2008.* We arrange for him to come round at eight thirty and I spend the rest of the afternoon and evening with the family, trying to be normal while every twenty minutes or so I run to check my emails only to find that nothing else has arrived.

By eight o'clock Lisa is tired. I help her shower and then we go through the routine that Lynn has taught me. I have everything I need laid out on the low shelf in the bathroom. Lisa has an infected sore on her right hip. Fortunately, the infection isn't caused by a super-bug and is healing slowly with the help of oral antibiotics. Still, I take the precaution of wearing gloves and gently clean the wound, making sure I place the used swabs in a plastic bag. Every now and then Lisa winces, but for the most part I manage to do it without causing her discomfort. I organise all the medicines for the next day in a dosette box and put it on top of the cabinet. Then I stand in front of Lisa with a glass of water and half a dozen coloured pills.

'Who knew?' she says between swallows.

'Who knew what?'

'That you could be such a good little nurse.'

'Be thankful I haven't starched the sheets.' I take her elbow and we go through to the bedroom. I help her swing her legs round into the bed, where Bea, washed and pyjamaed, is lying with her head on one of the pillows, the covers tucked under her arms so that her hands are free. She's holding the switch for the bedside lamp that Lisa brought with her from the flat. The shade is patterned with stars of all different sizes, and when the bulb is illuminated, the stars make patterns on the walls and ceiling. Bea switches the light off and then three seconds later on again so that she can see afresh the shining stars. When she's done this half a dozen times or more, I ask her to stop.

'Auntie Lisa likes it.'

'Either on or off, one or the other.'

She pretends she hasn't heard me. She puts it on, then off again.

'Bea!' I go to take it from her, but she pulls her hand under the covers and smiles up at me.

'Sweet,' Lisa says.

'It's her most appealing face,' I say.

'More,' Bea pleads. She holds up four fingers of her left hand. 'Seven!'

Lisa laughs.

'That's only four fingers,' I say. 'Four more goes and then you stop.' I turn back to Lisa. 'Are you sure you're OK with her in your bed? She might kick you in her sleep.'

'I really don't mind,' Lisa says. 'I've missed her.'

'Well, if she gets pesky, just walkie-talkie me.' I pass her a handset. 'These used to be Jack's. It'll save you shouting up the stairs.'

She laughs. 'Don't you just think of everything?'

'I was going to plug in the baby monitor, but I thought that might be pushing it.'

'Did you hear that, Bea?' She settles her pillow close to Bea's. 'Your mum thinks we're babies.'

Bea switches off the light again. 'You have to be really quiet,

Auntie Lisa,' she whispers, 'and make a wish for the stars to come.'

Lisa shuts her eyes, her lips moving in a silent wish. I kiss them both on the forehead, close the door and look at my watch. Mac should be here any minute. I pour myself a glass of wine and go to wait in the sitting room. Breathing space. Time to think and reflect. For tonight, the family is settled. Jack is watching television in his room, still complaining about being grounded. Julian had a word with Charlie. I'm not sure what was said, but although he's still not talking to me, he isn't avoiding me any more, so I think a truce is in sight. Lisa already knows about the emails, and the boys and Wendy will find out the details on Monday. Yes, there's a chance that the judge will overturn the order and the blackmailer will be able to get the witness's name without Julian's help, but that chance is so slim that it's not worth factoring in to the equation. What's bothering me is the thought of a safe house – not just the logistics of packing for all of us but the whole idea of moving somewhere else at a time when home is where I want to be. Like most people, I feel safest in my own home with my own things around me. Going somewhere new, to an unknown neighbourhood, where every creak of the floorboard and every barking dog makes for a panicky moment is not a cheering thought.

A few minutes before nine the doorbell sounds. I open the outside door and Mac comes into the porch. 'Sorry I'm late,' he says. 'Managed to lose my car keys.'

'You're still doing that?'

'At least once a week.'

I usher him into the hallway. 'Give me your jacket.' He shrugs it off his shoulders and I hang it on a peg. 'Julian's downstairs in his study.'

'I phoned him just now.' He stamps both his feet. 'He knows I'm on my way.'

'Oh . . . right.' I walk backwards into the hallway. 'Do you want

to wait in here?' I gesture towards the sitting room. 'I'll just go
down and tell him you've arrived.'

He gives me a small smile and walks past me into the room.
I try not to feel awkward. This is my home. The familiarity I feel
for him is at odds with my role as a wife and mother. He's from
a separate world, one I left behind.

I go downstairs and pop my head round the door of Julian's
study. 'Mac's here,' I say.

Julian is already on his feet and we go upstairs together. In the
sitting room, Mac and Julian shake hands.

'Take a seat.' Julian gestures towards one of the easy chairs
and Mac looks at me first before sitting down.

'Something to drink?'

'Coffee would be great,' Mac says.

'Have you eaten? We have leftovers from supper.'

He smiles. 'I stopped off at home for a bit,' he says. 'Was in
time for some curry.'

'And you, Julian?'

'A whisky, Claire. Please.'

I make coffee, pour Julian a whisky and a glass of Merlot for
myself. My mind is whirring. Mac is here. He has information
on the two cases. I can't help but feel this might be the turning
point. From here we could start to make progress. The safe house
may not be necessary after all. Catch the blackmailer and we can
go back to normal. I can care for Lisa the way I want to, the
boys won't be restricted, and we can all be a family again.

I give out the drinks and sit down on the sofa next to Julian.
I hold my wine glass in one hand and place my other hand down
on the couch next to his. I take his hand. He smiles at me. I want
Julian to acknowledge that we're in this together, and I want to
show Mac that we are a solid couple.

'So.' Mac takes a breath. 'I came tonight to talk about Sezen
but also to give you both an update on the two cases: Brunetti
and Hlutev. It's taken a bit of piecing together, but we think the
blackmailer is giving us a clue to the pattern of events.'

'How so?' I ask.

'In both cases, in Rome and in Sofia, the blackmailer infiltrated the family.' He looks at Julian then back at me. 'The blackmailer in these two cases was a woman. Our profilers feel that there's a good chance the same MO is happening here. As was your hunch all along, Claire.'

'OK.' I try not to feel pleased that at least I've been right about something. Perhaps it will help Julian to take me seriously. I look at him. He's contemplating the ceiling. 'Did you already know about these two cases?' I ask him.

'I knew about Georgiev's links to them and that intimidation was involved but not much more than that.'

'Was that the reason you had the burglar alarm installed?'

He nods.

I bite my lip and pull my hand away from his. Anger is never far away. It crackles through my chest like an electric sky before the storm fully breaks. I do my best to ignore it and say to Mac, 'Do you know this woman's name?'

'There were two women. The similarities lie in the way Georgiev gained access to the victims. Both times it was through a trusted young woman.'

'Was either of them caught?'

'One was. She's in prison in Italy. She was Georgiev's girl-friend. He's had a few over the years.' Mac looks at Julian. 'Your witness has spoken about the hold Georgiev has over some women.'

'He's charismatic,' I say.

'He is. In all the wrong sorts of ways. But some women . . .' He shrugs. 'They're attracted by the power.' He brings a sheaf of photographs out of the folder, then gives us both a sober look. 'These don't make for comfortable viewing.'

Julian nods.

'I understand,' I say.

He lays the photographs out on the coffee table, dividing them into two sections. They are from crime scenes. There are full-colour close-ups of the injuries sustained. There's blood. Lots of it. Mac's index finger rests on the group of photos to his right. 'This murder was committed two years ago in the Alexander Nevski Cathedral in Sofia. The man was a priest. His brother repeatedly spoke out against Georgiev's crime syndicate.'

I examine one of the photographs. The man is young, no more than forty. He is lying flat on his back on a patterned rug. His throat has been cut in one uninterrupted line about four inches across. Spattered blood patterns the wall behind him. His eyes have a glassy stare. His fair hair is stained a brownish-red colour. His build is stocky; he must have been strong. No easy target, then. 'Was there any sign of a struggle?'

'None. It seems she caught him completely unawares.'

'How did the police know it was a woman?' Julian says.

'The priest had an appointment that morning. Every week for three months a woman who called herself Lucia Ivanova had been coming to him for spiritual guidance. She was described as around five feet six, slim, regular features. In this case she had blonde hair and blue eyes, but' – he shrugs – 'doesn't count for a lot. She's never been caught.'

He turns to the other set of photographs. They show a child, a boy not much older than Bea. His hair is black and curly; his dark lashes lie on cheeks that are the colour of alabaster, unnaturally pale and waxen. They would feel cold to the touch. I shrink back from the sight of him. 'Shit.' I grip the edges of the sofa.

'Sweetheart,' Julian says. 'If you'd rather not see this, Mac and I can—'

'No. No,' I say forcefully. 'I need to know what's happening. I'm fine.' My blouse feels as if it's constricting my throat. I try to undo the top button but find it's already undone. 'I can do this.'

'The boy was five. He was murdered four years ago,' Mac says flatly. 'His father was an Italian businessman, funding an organisation that tracked and rescued girls who'd been trafficked. Again the killer was a woman. She had been hired as an au pair and had been working there for almost a year. Her references had been checked and double-checked and they were genuine.'

'And she's in prison now?'

'Yes.'

'Has she spoken about how she came to be recruited by Georgiev?' Julian asks.

'She met him in Paris. She was an au pair for a couple he did business with. Legitimate business. A cover for his more lucrative illegal ones. Georgiev was charming company and seduced her. I expect he recognised something in her that he could use to his advantage.'

'Sezen worked in Paris,' I say. 'In the embassy.'

Mac nods.

'And was this woman willing to testify against Georgiev?' I ask.

'Not even close. She insisted the whole thing was her idea.'

'She was completely under his spell,' I say.

'He enjoys manipulating people,' Julian says, looking at me. 'In fact he not only enjoys it; he's a master of it. He's being held in Belmarsh pending his trial and already one of the guards is convinced that the police are fitting him up.'

Mac looks at Julian. 'Your witness has told us that Georgiev has several people working for him who have infiltrated government organisations.'

'Like the police service?' I say.

Mac nods. 'They gain people's trust. They're patient. They plan for months, sometimes even years.'

I look back at the photographs. 'Who kills a child?' I say, feeling heartsick at the suffering his parents must have gone through. 'It goes against everything in human nature to take a child's life.'

'It does,' Mac agrees.

I think of the email that describes Bea and me walking back from nursery. 'So some woman has infiltrated our lives.' I start to tremble. 'Bloody hell.'

'Take a couple of deep breaths,' Julian instructs me.

His words sting. They feel patronising. 'This just keeps on getting worse.' I stand up and look down at him. 'We're lucky she hasn't been snatched already.'

'The emails are warnings, Claire,' Mac says, standing up too. 'The blackmailer is letting us know that she can get close to you. That's why we need to look again at everyone who's in your life at the moment.' He takes a sheet of paper from his file. 'Julian already gave us some names. They've all been checked out and there are no direct links to Georgiev or any organised criminal, but there might be something we've missed, especially with Sezen.'

'I only found the passports because I went looking,' I say. 'She hadn't been telling me the truth. A man came to our front door last night, and when I asked her who he was, she wouldn't give me his name. She said he was nothing to her, but then I saw them together at the roundabout today. They were kissing. He handed her a wad of cash.'

'Did you take a photo of him?'

'No. I didn't have a camera, just my dad's old binoculars.'

'Would you recognise him again?'

'Yes.'

'We have photos of a number of Georgiev's men on file. If there is a link between Sezen and the blackmailer, then that might be the way to prove it. Will you come along to the station and look at them there?'

'Of course.'

'It's unlikely to be Sezen,' Julian says. 'She has a child.' He looks up at me. 'And you told me she's afraid of the sight of blood.'

'She could be a good actress.'

'You told me her face was pale when you cut your hand,' he replies, standing up alongside me. 'You can't act a pale face.'

'Then she could be giving the blackmailer information.' I look at Mac. 'That's a possibility, isn't it?'

He nods.

'Sezen might simply be doing it for the money. She has a child to bring up and no dad around.'

'Was she pushing for you to hire her?' Mac asks.

'No. I got her through an agency. Her references were excellent. But still. And apart from the man at the roundabout, there was something else not right. She's been working for years, in well-paid jobs, and yet she was living in such a run-down place, as if she had no money to pay rent.'

'What's your gut feeling?' Mac asks me.

I think for a moment. 'My gut says she's honest, but my head tells me there's a chance that she's so skilled at deception she can look me in the eye and make me believe she's innocent.'

'As soon as she arrives back tomorrow, call me and I'll send someone to pick her up.' He sits back down and reads another name on his list. 'Mary Percival.'

I shake my head. 'It's not her.'

'I thought she was behaving strangely around you?' Julian says, also retaking his seat.

'She was and then I saw her outside and I went out to speak to her and . . . Anyway' – I let out a big breath – 'I now have an explanation for her strangeness.'

There's a silence. I'm looking down at my feet.

'Claire?'

'What?'

'What's the reason?' Mac says.

'Well, apparently . . .' I start to laugh. I know it's completely inappropriate and I try to squash it down underneath my ribcage, but it won't stay there. It rumbles up into my throat and erupts from my mouth. I keep this up for about thirty seconds, aware that both men are staring at me as if I've lost it. 'Apparently . . .' I dig my fingernails into the palm of my hand, where the cut is still tender. The pain is enough for me to be able to hold my face straight. 'She's my sister.'

Neither of them says anything. They are both frowning as if they're in the process of translating what I've just said.

'On my father's side.' I widen my eyes. 'Obviously.'

'What?' Julian throws his head back, his expression incredulous. 'How has this come about?'

'Well, you know what my father was like.'

'I don't mean that. Why did she tell you this now?'

'I all but forced it out of her. I still think it's possible she's making it up, but then' – I sigh as the post-hysterical low hits me – 'she had a letter my dad had written to her.'

'What did it say?' Mac asks.

'I don't know. I didn't read it. It was all a bit surreal. I was taken aback.'

'You've always wanted more family,' Julian says.

I give him a weak smile. It's true. I've always envied Julian his raft of siblings and cousins and second cousins once removed, on and on, a horizon filled with family, while my family tree was little more than a branch.

'When are you planning to have her meet everyone?'

'She's already met everyone.'

'But not as one of the family.'

'Julian, apart from the fact that I haven't even begun to get my head around it, how can you possibly imagine we can invite her here with this going on?' I pretend to open a door. '"Welcome to our happy family! In three days we'll be moving to a safe house. Don't open the door to men with guns, will you?"'

Julian's face stiffens.

Mac clears his throat and says, 'I'm sure it took a great deal of courage for her to tell you.'

'Have you told Lisa about her?' Julian asks.

'No.'

'But you will tell her?'

'At the moment all I am able to think about is getting through this crisis,' I say sharply, gesturing towards the emails. 'So could we please stop talking about this now?'

Julian sits back. I can see that he wants to say more but won't. Not in front of Mac.

'I think it needs to be handled carefully and now is not a good time to do that,' Mac says.

'Exactly,' I say. 'Apart from anything else, there're Wendy's feelings to consider. Mary is my father's infidelity made flesh.'

Julian shakes his head at this. I know he thinks I'm being overly dramatic, and there's a part of me that agrees with him. He's about to say something else, then changes his mind and pats the space on the sofa beside him.

'I'm better standing.' I feel like I'm about to cry. Out of nowhere, I want my dad. I want to be seven. I want him to lift me up. I want to be carried, cosseted and cuddled like a baby. I grab my wine glass and tip what's left into my mouth. My hand shakes and two drops land on my blouse. 'Shit.' Mac and Julian are both staring up at me. 'What?' I snap.

Mac clears his throat and looks back at his list. 'Amy Barker.'

'She's gone back to her university accommodation.'

'Did you ask her to leave?'

'She was snooping around in Julian's office and . . .' I shrug. 'I don't know whether it's just that I don't much like her or whether she's a possible threat.'

'Well, let's keep her out of your home in the meantime,' Mac says. 'Is Charlie on board with that?'

'He's not happy about it,' I say, 'but I don't think he would sneak her back in.'

'I had a word with him,' Julian says. 'He understands the need to keep everything simple around here.'

'OK.' Mac gives us both an encouraging smile. 'Jem Ravens. She also comes in and out of your house a lot?'

'She's a friend,' I say. 'And she's done a lot of work for us too, but she's mostly a friend.'

'She has a police record.'

'Does she?' I frown. 'What did she do?'

'She spent five months in prison for grievous bodily harm.'

'What?' I start back. I was imagining possession of marijuana or episodes of teenage shoplifting. 'Was it her first offence?'

'It was.'

'What did she do?'

'The victim's head was stoved in with a golf club. I think she would have been given a longer sentence if he hadn't fully recovered. That and the fact that two bystanders gave evidence to support her assertion that she was provoked.'

'That's unbelievable!' I start pacing again. 'How could I not have known about this?'

'It's not exactly something you would advertise,' Julian says drily.

I think of all the coffees Jem and I have had, the lunches, shared childcare. And she's spent weeks at a time working around here. She built the patio, painted the hallway and tiled the family bathroom. 'When was this?'

'It was back in 2002.'

Eight years ago. She has been with Pete for seven of those years. He works for the council. He's a burly, good-natured bloke. Everybody's mate. I suppose he must know about this. And I suppose too that Julian is right – GBH is not something to advertise. Especially around mothers with small children. But only days ago she told me she'd never been in any serious trouble with the police.

'She knows almost everything about me,' I say. 'Apart from Lisa there's no one I confide in more.'

'She could have met anyone when she was in prison,' Mac says. 'You know what it's like for making contacts.'

'A contact from eight years ago? Seems unlikely, and anyway, I just can't believe she would have anything to do with this.' I look at Julian. I want him to back me up. I want him to say that it couldn't possibly be Jem. I want him to go further and say that in fact he's had a light-bulb moment and now he knows exactly who the blackmailer is. I want him to make this all disappear before it gets any worse.

'I'll have a chat with her,' Mac says. 'Just in case.' He stands up and puts a comforting hand on my shoulder. 'I know this is hard, Claire. You're doing really well.'

I give him a tight smile.

'We will catch this woman.'

'The Bulgarian police never caught the killer, and the Italians caught her too late.' I shrug. 'What chance do we have?'

'A good chance.' He nods to let me know his thoughts have travelled this way too. 'Systems grow better all the time. Exchange of information. Forensic evidence. And sheer, dogged, old-fashioned police work. We will get this right.'

I nod my thanks, but inside I feel desolate. I think of Bea asleep in the room along the hall, Lisa on one side, Bertie on the other. I see her hand still clutching the switch for the light. I imagine her dreams full of Douglas and the park and summertime. Her life thus far has been about love and laughter. She was born at a time when my dad had recently died and having a child, especially a daughter, could not have been more of a gift. She completely trusts her parents and her brothers to protect her. My mind flashes to an image of her standing in a room, rigid with fear, experiencing emotions she's never felt before, asking for me, for her daddy, being ignored, being told to shut up, being denied a drink or a blanket. Being tortured.

I walk across to the window, biting down hard on my lip.

'And your neighbours, Claire,' Mac says. 'Julian told me—'

'Our neighbours on the right are about a hundred and five,' I say flatly. 'Their groceries are delivered. They are a quiet, self-contained unit. They don't go any further than their back garden. And the ones on the left work for a children's charity. They've been living in Brazil for the past nine months. They haven't rented their place out.'

'No one else has shown an unusual interest in your family?'

'No.'

'It's more likely there's a leak within the police or the CPS,' Julian says. 'I think there's something else, someone else we're not seeing.'

Mac sits down opposite him again and they go through a long list of thirty or so names of everyone who's involved in the case.

Most of them are like Megan with spotless, all-English back-grounds, but a few take longer to discuss, as links with Eastern Europe show up in their private lives. I watch them talk: one my husband, the other a former colleague. I have been a friend and a lover to both of them and yet I trust neither of them to put Bea first. Julian believes in our legal system – he is determined to play this straight – and Mac has his career to think of. Sure, he wants a positive outcome. He's a good man. He doesn't want a dead child on his conscience. But, bottom line, I am the only person who has Bea at the top of the list. They are juggling the professional and the personal, whereas for me it's a hundred per cent personal. I don't care about my legal career – or for that matter Julian's. Ideally, I want Georgiev and all his henchmen banged up in prison for ever, but legal justice isn't always human justice and I won't sacrifice my daughter for the greater good.

And then, as I watch them both try to work this whole thing out, I have a moment of complete clarity. I won't allow either of these men to render me powerless. They know who the witness is and where he is being kept. I need to know that too. I can't trust Julian or Mac to get this right. I can't trust Sezen, or Mary Percival, or Amy. And now, it turns out, I can't even trust Jem. Lisa doesn't have the strength to help me and I don't want to put Wendy into a position where we may have to do something illegal. Same with Charlie and Jack. And in some ways having no one to help me makes it easier. I know my own motivations and my own strengths. I don't have to worry about someone else not playing their part. This is up to me. And so I'll do what I have to. I'll get the information. I'll find out who the witness is and where he is being kept and then, after the pre-trial on Monday, I'll email the blackmailer. She'll have what she wants and she'll back off. Bea will be mine again. She'll be safe.

'Claire?' Julian says.

I smile at him. 'Yes?'

'Is there anything else you wanted to ask?'

'No.' They both stand up and I step forward so that I'm between them. 'Thank you for everything you're doing, Mac,' I say, holding out my hand. 'It's much appreciated.'

There is a questioning expression in his eyes when he says, 'You're clear about the best way forward?'

'Perfectly,' I say. I walk ahead of him to the door. 'Let's stay in touch.'

14

Sunday. Lisa is tired today and decides to spend the morning in bed. The rest of us have a late breakfast together: porridge with Hunza apricots, pancakes with blueberries or maple syrup and scrambled eggs. It's only ten o'clock but already I'm on tenterhooks anticipating Sezen's arrival back in the house. Charlie has stopped being frosty with me. He sits down next to me and I put my hand on his. 'I'm sorry,' I say.

'Me too, Mum.'

'I'm sure it won't be long before you and Amy can be together again.'

'Yeah. I've told her we just have to be extra careful until Dad's trial is over. I think she gets it.' He points down into his bowl. 'Really good porridge.'

I smile my thanks and look over at Julian, who is at the hob cracking eggs into the pan, talking to Jack about rugby. I watch him, amazed that he can be so utterly unfazed by what's happening to our family. We have a very real threat hanging over us and yet he is talking and laughing as if nothing is amiss. I had no idea he was so good at disassociating himself from reality.

When he joins us at the table, he starts to talk about repairing the summerhouse – a grand name for the dilapidated shed that sits at the bottom of our garden. 'The roof is collapsing inwards,' he says. 'We need to think about fixing it up.'

We all look out of the window. The garden is about forty metres long. Most of it is laid over to grass, apart from the wild-flower borders and Bea's vegetable patch. There are three elderflower trees at the bottom of the garden next to the summer-house, which desperately needs a facelift.

'What do you think, Mum?' Jack is saying.

'Well . . . I'll mention it to Jem.'

Jem, who twenty-four hours ago, was a good and trusted friend. The idea that she could be anything other than honest was ludicrous. She was the epitome of what you see is what you get. But now I don't know what to think.

The front door slams. 'That's Lara,' Bea says, her eyes lighting up as she pushes her chair back from the table and runs out of the room.

I'm about to follow, but Julian, already on his feet, beats me to it. I hear him chatting to Sezen and they both come into the kitchen. Her cheeks are glowing; her eyes are sparkling. She looks like she's been lit up from the inside. There's no doubt in my mind that she spent last night making love. And I would bet my life it was with the man she met at the roundabout. Whether she's willing to admit it or not, she has feelings for him, and how far will people go for those they love?

The rest of the family drift off to their rooms and Julian urges Sezen to share the last of the breakfast with us. She says yes to coffee but no to food and goes to the sink to wash her hands. I give Julian what I think is a questioning look. Does he want to talk to her, or is he leaving it to me? Should I call Mac now? What?

His face is non-committal.

Sezen dries her hands, then goes to the fridge and brings some ingredients back with her to the table. 'This evening I will make a special dish with tofu,' she says to me. 'It should be marinated for a few hours first.' She begins shredding ginger into a bowl. I stop her hand with mine.

'We need to talk.'

She stares at me, puzzled by my tone.

'I can make something different if you like.'

'It's not about that,' I say. 'Please sit down.'

'OK.' She pulls out a chair.

'I have some concerns.'

'About my work?'

'No, no, no.' I shake my head. 'Your work is faultless.'

'Good.' She smiles again, open, clear. I feel like I'm about to break her in two, but I can't let this go on any longer. Julian sits down beside her and passes her a mug of coffee. She smiles her thanks.

'Sezen, we need to know more about you.'

She's frowning, trying to work out what I'm getting at.

'We need to be able to trust you.'

She tips back. 'You feel you cannot trust me?' Her surprise seems absolutely genuine. 'I do not understand.'

'I'm not saying that you can't have your own life and your own interests, but yes, at the moment I . . .' I look at Julian. 'We don't feel like we can trust you.'

She turns to Julian for help.

'Tell me again why you came to live in Brighton,' he says.

'Because London is busy and crowded.' She shrugs. 'For Lara and for myself. I have this job here with you, and another one starting in July. I love to be beside the sea.'

'You were brought up in Turkey. The Dardanelles?'

'Yes, that is right. My father was a fisherman. My brothers are still there, but I came to northern Europe for work and . . . to live.' She falters. 'Is that a problem?'

'No.' He shakes his head and smiles. He has a way of smiling that seems to be non-threatening. He does it when he's cross-examining a witness. He encourages them with a nudge here and a gentle prod there to paint themselves into a corner. 'I'm interested,' he says. 'In where you come from and where you've settled. I know what it feels like to have feet in two cultures. My father was a diplomat. I was brought up in West Africa. Sent back to boarding school when I was nine.'

She makes a sympathetic face.

'It wasn't so bad. It did make me feel like I wasn't quite sure where I belonged, though.' He looks regretful. 'I was English, but when I was in England many of the customs were strange: wearing shoes, eating tasteless food, endless rules about the right way to behave. Africa felt more like home.'

'And yet at the same time?'

'It didn't,' he admits, and she nods at their shared experience. 'I was never quite one of the boys.'

'I have a similar feeling,' she says. 'I am here and I know I am a foreigner, but when I go home, I also feel like I am foreign.' She gives a wry laugh. 'I have changed and now I do not belong here or there.'

'Your family must miss you?'

'Yes, but I am keeping the language alive with Lara and I hope to take her home soon for a visit.'

'To Bulgaria?'

'Yes, I have—' She realises her mistake and stops. Apprehension ruptures her steady gaze.

'Not Turkey,' Julian says. He is smiling, a perfectly relaxed and interested host. Sezen, on the other hand, is neither relaxed nor smiling. Her jaw is tight and she is staring fixedly down into her coffee, as if the answers are in there.

'Turkey and Bulgaria share a border,' she says at last.

It's a poor defence, but Julian lets it go, coming back instead with further evidence. 'Your name is Sylvia Cyrilova,' he says.

She lifts her cup to her mouth and tries to drink, but her hand is trembling. She puts it back down on the table and looks at me. Her eyes are pleading.

'It's a Bulgarian name, isn't it?' I say.

Moments pass and finally she turns her eyes to Julian's. 'Serbest,' she says. 'My name is Sezen Serbest.'

'And yet you have a passport that says your name is Sylvia Cyrilova.'

'It is not who I am.'

He brings the two passports out of his pocket and places them on the table. Then he stands up and leaves the kitchen. As he does, I see him press buttons on his BlackBerry.

'You went into my room?' she says to me.

The hurt in her eyes seems real and for a second my resolve wavers. I break eye contact, and when I look back at her, I say firmly, 'The man who came here on Friday night. You told me you didn't know him.'

'That is . . .' She shrugs. 'I . . .'

'I saw you with him,' I say. 'At the roundabout. I watched you embrace.'

She lets out a cry. 'You are following me?'

'No. Lisa's flat is there and I was looking out for traffic wardens. But I saw you, Sezen. I saw you. It was the same man.'

Her hand is over her mouth.

'I need an explanation. You told me you are an honest person.'

'With respect, Claire' – she takes an audible breath – 'this does not concern you.'

She shows all the signs of being genuinely shocked, but I won't be swayed. 'We have a situation here,' I say. 'The case Julian is working on, there are complications. We need to be absolutely sure that our children are safe.'

'You think I will make your children unsafe?'

'Because you haven't told me the truth, I don't know what to think.'

'You asked me to come here and now you are accusing me of wanting to harm your children?'

'You live in my home. This man you said was nothing to you came to our front door.' I lean towards her. 'You have two passports, one of them Bulgarian. You know that Julian is prosecuting a Bulgarian criminal.'

She bites her lip.

'I don't mind you having a relationship. What I mind is the fact that you have lied to me. That makes me suspicious and it makes me afraid.'

She is looking down at her feet.

'Are you in trouble, Sezen? Is someone asking you to do something dishonest?'

Her eyes flash towards me.

'Sezen.' I lean across the table some more. 'I saw him give you money.'

Her cheeks flush and the muscles in her jaw tighten. She looks down at the floor again. Her hair swings across to cover her face. I wait. Her fingers pick at the hem of her cardigan. A minute passes and then she looks back at me. 'I will leave.' She is composed again, her expression blank. She stands up. 'I am sorry.'

'Before you go' – I stand up too and fold my arms – 'the police want to speak with you.'

She gives a small gasp, the fear in her eyes so acute that I flinch.

'You would be wise to tell them the truth.'

'I am not your enemy.' She shakes her head emphatically. 'I am not.'

'I hope not,' I say.

'The police are coming here?'

'Yes.'

'Then I will wait.'

She sits back down again, crosses her ankles and settles her hands on her lap, perfectly serene and composed. I join Julian in the hallway.

'Mac is sending a couple of officers over,' he says. 'They'll take her to the station for questioning.'

I know at once that she'll be worried about Lara. While Sezen is clearly involved in something illegal, that doesn't detract from the fact that she's a good mother.

I go back into the kitchen. 'Sezen, the police officers will want you to return to the station with them. We are happy to look after Lara.'

She says nothing. She is staring straight ahead at the wall, her lips moving slowly as if she's reading something.

'I'm sure that if you're able to give the police an explanation, you'll be back in no time.'

Still nothing. I glance over my shoulder at the sound of the doorbell.

'Sezen?' I say.

She turns her face up. She looks hurt and puzzled, but mostly she just looks resigned. 'I thought you were different.'

'And I thought you were truthful,' I say, angry now. 'I believed you when you told me you were an honest person. I believed you when you said you felt nothing for that man. I believed you when you said you were Turkish.' I take a breath. 'It cuts both ways, Sezen.'

'Thank you for looking after Lara.' Her expression is blank again. It's a look she summons up at will. It makes me want to shake her. 'I will come for her as soon as I can.'

There are two officers: one male, one female. They come into the kitchen with Julian. While they talk Sezen through what happens next, I go upstairs to Bea's room and ask Lara to come and say goodbye to her mum.

'Why?' Bea says.

'Sezen has to go out for a bit,' I say.

Both girls come to the front hall with me. Sezen bends down and speaks to Lara in what I always presumed to be Turkish but now I'm wondering whether it could be Bulgarian. Lara nods. As ever tranquil and self-possessed, she doesn't make a fuss. She stands on the front step and waves to Sezen, who goes with the officers to the car.

'That was awful,' I say to Julian when the door is closed and the girls have gone back to their game.

'Mm.' He stands with his hands in his pockets and leans against the wall. 'She's not a practised liar. I expect that what she's hiding has nothing to do with this.'

I think it's far too early to make such a statement, but I don't tell him that. Instead I put my arms round him and rest my head on his shoulder. 'I'll be so glad when this is all over.'

He pulls me in to him and comforts me with words and with his hands, stroking my hair and my back. It feels good, but my intention is not so much to be comforted as to make this a prelude for later, because if Sezen isn't the blackmailer, then I need to

get the witness's name and whereabouts out of Julian and I'm
not going to get it through argument. The best chance is through
closeness. I need us to make love, let him see that we're both on
the same side. And then I think he'll tell me. And when I know
the details, I can finish this. Bea will be safe. That's all I care
about.

'How's Lisa this morning?' he asks me.

'Not great,' I say. 'It's the tiredness. Hopefully she'll be able to
get up later this afternoon.'

'I'm sorry, Claire. You know that, don't you?'

I lift my head off his shoulder to look at him.

'I'm sorry about Lisa and I'm sorry about all this. It's bad
enough that both events are happening at all, but happening
together . . .'

'It's not your fault,' I say. I kiss his cheek. 'It's no one's fault.
We just have to get on with it as best we can.'

His phone rings. 'Megan.' He looks apologetic. 'She wants to
come round. Is that OK?'

Normally I might grumble – *On a Sunday?* – but I'm working
hard to strengthen the good feeling between us and I won't jeopardise that. 'No problem. I know you need to be prepared for
tomorrow. Although because you've officially resigned, I would
have thought it's Gordon Lightman she should be meeting.'

'Yes, but—'

'You're still pulling the strings?'

'No one knows this case better than me. It's taken fifteen years
to get to this moment. I don't want anything to go wrong.'

'I understand.' I kiss him, on the lips this time. 'I think I might
go for a jog. Work off some of the tension.'

'It's not such great weather out there.' He looks out through
the window. 'There's a cold wind blowing in off the sea.'

'I don't mind.'

Before I leave I have a word with Charlie and Jack and they
agree to be in charge of the girls. I make a quick sweep of the
kitchen, tidying the dishes into the dishwasher, then put on my

running shoes and stand on the top step to do warm-up exercises. The cool air on my face makes me feel energised. I really do need to get out. The waiting is crippling. It'll be some time before we hear whether Sezen has anything to say that sheds light on the blackmailer's identity and another twenty-four hours before the judge will make his ruling at the pre-trial hearing. In the meantime I have to keep my head. My impulse is to demand that Julian gives me the witness's name so that I can protect our daughter, but I know that he won't respond to demands. The softly-softly approach will be far more effective, and while I'm not entirely comfortable with being this calculating, I don't see any other way to get the witness information.

I stretch out my hamstrings on the front step, my eye automatically drawn to where the policemen are parked. They are both out on the pavement in conversation with a woman – Megan. Looks like she's stopped to talk to them on the way to see Julian. She's flirting with them both, flicking her hair, leaning in towards them and laughing at everything they say. I'm surprised to see her like this. It makes a change from her usual strictly professional manner. But then I remember what Julian told me – three months ago she made a play for him. She doesn't look like she's had any trouble moving on. The older, and probably married, policeman, Baker, is giving her a wary eye, but poor Faraway doesn't stand a chance. When she sees me watching her, she waves like we're best friends and I wave back.

I set off in the other direction, making my way down the hill until I reach the prom. With the sea on one side, and the wind behind me, I find my stride and start to enjoy the feeling: one foot after the other, a steady rhythm of feet and pavement and pulse. I meet the odd jogger or cyclist, but this end of the prom is quiet, the crowds tending to gather at the easterly end by the pier.

The sky is moody. Heavy grey clouds hover just above my head and feel almost close enough to touch. The sea is choppy, restless, a prelude to rain, but I might just make it home before the clouds break.

I run for over a mile before I have to start dodging people: a couple up ahead of me are eating chips from a paper bag; some boys are meandering along slowly, hands in pockets, five abreast on the pavement; dads are out in force with their children while mums have a couple of hours off. I run as far as the pier and then stop, resting my hands on my knees for a minute or so.

And that's when I see Amy. She's standing close to the fast food stall, energetically snogging a young man in blue jeans and a hoodie. Initially I have a sinking feeling that it's Charlie, having snuck out to meet her, but the boy in question has lighter hair and is shorter than Charlie. I walk towards them.

'Amy?'

She turns round, slowly wiping the back of her hand across her mouth. She looks neither guilty nor apologetic. 'It's you,' she says. 'Everything running smoothly in the Miller household now that you've got rid of me?'

'Well, you don't seem to be suffering for it.'

'I'm a survivor. I move on.'

I think about Charlie and the look in his eyes when he tackled me in the hallway. And at breakfast this morning – he thinks they're still going out. He feels like he's in love with this girl. 'Does Charlie know you've moved on?'

She looks momentarily thoughtful. 'He'll get the message.'

'Amy.' I shake my head in disbelief, feeling hurt for Charlie. 'You've been going out with him for nine months. Don't you think he deserves better than this?' I gesture towards the boy she's been kissing. He's looking off across the sea, bored. 'How do you think he would feel if he knew you'd already hooked up with someone else?'

'Well, he should have taken my side, shouldn't he?'

'Over what?'

'Being thrown out!' She pauses for effect. 'There was a reason I was in Julian's precious study.'

'And the reason was?'

'I lost an earring in there last week and I thought Julian might have tidied it into one of the drawers.'

'Really?' I fold my arms. 'So you were standing in Julian's study and suddenly your earring fell out?'

'Are you dense or what?' She gives me a withering look. 'We had sex down there.'

I can't help but step back.

'Yes, your perfect boy shagged me on the rug.'

I look down at my feet while I collect myself, realise that I can't, look back at her and say, with venom, 'Go to hell, Amy.' I turn and start making my way through the crowd.

'Do yourself a favour,' she shouts after me. 'Go get fucked.'

My jog towards home is more of a run, anger fuelling my pace. I feel angry at Amy for her careless, selfish attitude, and I feel hurt on Charlie's behalf. Teenage heartbreak is hard to bear and it seems that Amy has no intention of sparing his feelings. As far as the sex goes, I'm not annoyed with Charlie. I'm surprised that he did it in Julian's study – it's not the sort of behaviour I would expect from him – but I'm sure it was Amy's idea rather than his. And I can understand why he didn't want to tell me. He doesn't like to let me down and he would have been wary of my reaction.

A fine rain is just beginning to fall and this seems to further agitate an already choppy sea. No longer just a collection of water molecules that could trickle through the spaces between my fingers, it takes on an animalistic quality, rolling and heaving, coiling back on itself like a snake readying to raise its head and bite.

I look straight ahead and jog faster, but within seconds my anger evaporates and an intense paranoia creeps over me. My back prickles with discomfort. I have the impression of eyes boring into me. I stop running and abruptly turn round. The pavement is teeming with people. I try to pick out a likely suspect, but most people have their heads down and are walking purposefully, carrier bags in each hand. I scan faces, but no one is looking my way. I start to run again, but the feeling doesn't lift. It grows. I feel like someone, somewhere is picking on me, that I have been singled out for attention. I stop again and look around me. Still there is no one who seems suspicious. I stare up at the sky, and as if waiting for just such a moment, the cloud above me rumbles. It's a low sound, like heavy furniture being dragged across a floor. Then it empties a stream of water down on to my face. It feels personal. Worse than that, it feels like it's all part of the greater assault. I clench my fists and shout upwards, 'You took my mother. You took my father. You're in the process of taking my sister and now my daughter is in danger too? Bastard!'

'Oi! Mind your language!'

There's a man behind me. He is red-faced and miserable-looking. He has two little girls with him, one either side. They both look under-dressed. Their heads are bare; their faces are pinched with the unseasonably cold weather. 'Not in front of the kids.'

'I'm sorry.' I hold up my hand. 'I'm having a bad day.'

'Well, we don't care about your bad day,' he says.

'I'm sorry,' I say again, looking at the children this time. 'I hope you have a lovely day out.'

'You need to watch your mouth.' He is pointing a finger at me now. He comes closer and waves it in my face. 'This is a public place.'

He's right up close. He smells like he needs a wash and I move back a step. I'm beginning to wish I hadn't apologised. 'I've said I'm sorry and now I'm heading off.'

'I'll be watching out for you.' The finger waves in my face again. 'You keep it clean next time.'

'Go fuck yourself.' I say it under my breath, but like the best of busybodies his hearing is extra sharp.

'What did you say?' His face is a snarl; his shoulders are back, chest thrust forward, hands in pockets, hips a cocky swagger; he's transformed into a hard man.

'You heard me,' I say, facing up to him, happy to fight,

angry enough for ten men. 'Now back off or I'll make sure you regret it.'

He raises his fists. The two little girls look scared. One is pulling at his jacket. 'Daddy, stop now.'

A crowd is gathering and I see a couple of men deliberating about whether or not they should step in. The rain is increasing and umbrellas are going up. As good a weapon as any, I go to grab one from a woman behind me when a voice says, 'Show over. Break it up.'

It's Mac. He flashes his ID and the hard man backs off, shouting, 'She needs to watch her mouth.'

Mac takes my arm. 'I think you could do with a lift home.' He marches me to the edge of the pavement.

'I was fine,' I say, trying to shake him off. 'I was dealing with him.'

'You and whose army?' His car is parked on a double yellow line and already there are cars sounding their horns. He opens the door for me, then goes round to the driver's side. 'It might have turned nasty.'

'He was all bluster and no substance.'

'Since when did you go around picking fights?' He starts the engine. 'Don't add to your troubles, Claire.'

'I just feel so angry. I feel so fucking angry. About Lisa. About Bea. About everything.'

'Put your seatbelt on,' he says. 'Remember, anger without focus isn't a strategy.'

'What are you doing here, anyway?' I glare at him. 'Why aren't you questioning Sezen? The two officers who came for her looked about twelve.' I pull the strap across my waist. 'I can't imagine they'll get anything out of her.'

'You'd be surprised. They're both better – and older – than they look.'

I ram the belt into the clip. 'Were you following me?'

'Julian told me you were jogging along the prom. I have some photos for you to look through. You still OK with that?'

'Of course.' My temper subsides to a simmer.

'Any cafés you know around here that we can go to?'

'There's one just up here on the left.'

He stops the car on a single yellow line, then stretches behind him to take a folder off the back seat. The café is dense with steam and chatter. Both the female waitresses smile and say hello as he walks us through to the back, where there's a free table.

'Are you hungry?' he asks, handing me a menu.

'You eat,' I tell him. 'I had a late breakfast.'

The waitress comes across. She is about my age, good figure, hair peroxide blonde and pulled back on top of her head in generous waves held stiff with hairspray. She's all eyes for Mac. 'Hello there! And what can I get you?'

'What do you recommend?'

Mac has a slow smile on his face as he listens to her run through the favourites. 'You've persuaded me. I'll go for the cooked breakfast. And a tea.' He looks across at me.

The waitress's eyes follow his. 'And for you, madam?'

I skim the menu. 'Just a tea. Thank you.'

'Not even a scone?' Mac says. The waitress has told him they're homemade.

'I'm OK.'

He looks regretful.

'Did you want one?' I say.

'I thought I might get half.'

I look up at the waitress. 'And a scone, please.'

'Coming right up.' She places a casual hand on Mac's shoulder, then walks back towards the counter.

'You've not lost your touch, then?'

'People skills. Part of a policeman's toolbox.'

'That's what they all say.' I point to the folder at his feet. 'Shall I look through it now, before the food comes?'

'Yup.' He places it on the table. 'Take your time. You know the drill. Don't focus on hair or clothes. Look at the shape of their eyes, their nose, bone structure.'

I open the folder. There are A4-size photographs of men, one after the other, about fifty of them. I take my time. Sezen's lover had a distinctive hooked nose and high cheekbones. Many of the photos I discount at once. They are of heavy, thickset men with small eyes and tattoos. The man I'm looking for is slight, and his features are Middle Eastern, not Eastern European. I get to the end of the folder without being able to pick him out.

'He's not there,' I say, disappointed, passing the folder back.

'Definitely not?'

'Definitely not,' I confirm. Our mugs of tea arrive. I lean away from the table so that the waitress can put them down. 'I had a clear view of him through the binoculars.'

'OK.' He thinks for a moment. 'Let's wait and see what Sezen has to say for herself. Then we'll take it from there.'

I take a drink of my tea and watch Mac put two spoons of sugar in his. He sees me watching him and pats his small but evident belly. 'I know. Donna's working on me. I have to use sweetener at home.'

'Andrew MacPherson tamed by a woman.' I take another drink of tea. 'Who would have thought it?'

He laughs. 'Marriage,' he says. 'The sharing and the caring.'

He gives me a look, one that could lead me into saying all sorts of things I should keep to myself.

'Are you and Julian managing to hold it together?'

I'm not about to answer that. Instead, I lean across the table until I am six inches from his face and say quietly, 'You are a crass, predatory ape who just so happens to be a good detective.'

He laughs so loud that several people look across at us. 'Those were the days,' he says. 'Margery Prendergast. Whatever happened to her?'

'She took herself off to Scotland. Last I heard she was living in an artists' commune on the Black Isle.'

Margery Prendergast was also a solicitor with the CPS. She'd gone to a girls' school, was unmarried, didn't have any brothers or male friends and found men 'surplus to requirements'. We all suspected that secretly she quite liked Mac, but in public she regularly tried to humiliate him. It never worked, of course, and we started a top ten of Prendergast putdowns that we repeated to Mac at opportune moments.

'She wasn't cut out for the law.'

'She wasn't cut out for you lot, more like,' I say. I scrape some spilled sugar into my hand. 'Do you know Megan Jennings? She works for the CPS. She's assigned to Georgiev's trial.'

He nods. 'Posh bird? Likes to think she's a bit superior?'

'That's her. Does she have a boyfriend?'

'Nobody seems to have shagged her, and a couple of good ones have tried.'

'It couldn't be that she just doesn't fancy any of you?'

He makes a point of considering this. 'Unlikely.'

'She was chatting up Faraway just now, but she has had designs on Julian.'

He shakes his head. 'Nothing's going on.' He waves his arm to attract the waitress's attention and mimes eating with a knife and fork. 'I would know about it.'

'Your cop's antennae?'

'Not just that. You know what a goldfish bowl that place is.' He takes a long drink of tea. 'Anyway, Julian would be a fool to take her over you, and he's no fool.'

I raise my mug up to his. 'Cheers for the vote of confidence.'

The food arrives. My scone is perfect; soft and sweet-smelling, it looks like it's been baked by everyone's favourite grandmother. 'Did DCI Grubb ever get himself on *Mastermind*?' I say, splitting it in half and spooning jam on to one side.

'Still trying to get through the selection process. He's changed his specialist subject twice since you were around. He's moved on from the Super Bowl, was stuck on the animals of Madagascar for a while, and now he's discovered Voltaire.'

'Voltaire?' I think. '"May God defend me from my friends; from my enemies I can defend myself."'

'Did Voltaire say that?'

'I believe so. I shared a flat with an arts graduate when I was in my third year at uni. He used to stick quotes up all over the walls.'

'Not a bad piece of advice.' He takes a forkful of food and finishes chewing it before saying, 'Dave and Barry are in training for the Berlin Marathon in September. You wouldn't recognise them.'

'No more doughnuts, then?'

'Rabbit food all the way.'

I laugh. 'You're going to make me miss you all in a minute. I'll forget the frustration, the wasted leads, the relentless round of paperwork.'

'When all this is over, you should come back, part-time even. I can't believe you get off on staying at home all day. There's only so much daytime TV you can watch.'

'I've never had the opportunity to get bored. First there was the moving down here, settling the kids into schools, having work done on the house, my dad dying, Bea arriving and, more recently, Lisa's illness.'

'And now this.'

'And now this.'

'Seriously, Claire.' He gives me a sympathetic smile. 'How are you holding up?'

'Well . . .' I almost laugh. 'It's not easy. I don't feel like I can trust anyone. I thought Sezen was genuine – she isn't. Mary Percival acts strangely around me. Turns out she's my half-sister.' I make a face. 'I haven't had time to think about that yet. And then there's Jem.' I throw my arms out. 'I knew she was a bit fidgety around the police, but GBH? That's a serious crime.' I take a bite of scone. 'And these are three people I previously trusted with my child.'

'I agree that they're all hiding something, but there are no direct connections to Pavel Georgiev or organised crime of any sort.'

'Even Sezen?'

'We'll see what turns up today, but thus far her life looks transparent enough. She lived in Paris for four years. She worked for the French Embassy as a chef. They were extremely sorry to see her go.'

'But it appears she was brought up in Bulgaria and Georgiev is Bulgarian, and, like you say, they have a tendency to keep it within the family or at least within their own culture. Is she still insisting she's Turkish?'

'Yeah.'

I think back to her meeting at the roundabout. 'Do you know who Lara's father is?'

'She was born here. No father's name is recorded on the birth certificate.'

'I wonder whether the mystery man is Lara's dad.'

'Could be.'

'Perhaps he's the one who knows Georgiev. Perhaps Sezen's only job was to open my front door. When the time came.' I swallow a mouthful of scone. 'In retrospect, all that business about her accommodation round the corner falling through – she knew I would offer a room in my house. I need to change the code for the burglar alarm. Just in case.' I finish the last of my tea. 'What was it Grubb used to say when he was in his American-football phase?'

'Linebacker mentality – read the game and then react.' He uses his fork to point at his plate. 'Want some?'

'What?'

'You're staring at my food.'

'Am I?' Somehow that mouthful of scone was my last and Mac's right – I'm now eyeing up the last of his breakfast. I use my fingers to break off a piece of his toast. 'Actually, I am quite hungry.' I take a bite. It's soggy but warm from melted butter and egg yolk. 'You drumming much?'

'Still doing the rounds of the clubs.'

'Is that how you met Donna?'

He nods. 'She's a yoga teacher, but she trained as a singer. Jazz mostly.'

'So are you in a band together?'

'Of sorts. We have a few gigs coming up at the end of June. I can email you details.' He sees my face. 'Or maybe not.'

'No offence, but I don't think I'll be allowed out of my safe house. Talking of which,' I say lightly, 'if you were to just give me the name and whereabouts of the witness, we could skip the safe house. Save all that taxpayers' money.'

He stares at me, trying to gauge whether my request is an idle one or whether I mean it. 'It's putting away a man like Georgiev that makes this job worth it. You know that. This trial is the culmination of years of investigation. For over fifteen years policemen have been gathering evidence against Georgiev and finally we have a rock-hard case that even the smartest defence won't be able to break. This is . . .' He searches for the right word.

'Exciting?' I say.

He looks uncomfortable.

'Well, pardon me for not sharing your excitement, but my daughter's safety is not a fair trade for a successful conviction.'

'No, it isn't,' he agrees. 'We will keep Bea safe. You know that. You know we'll do everything we can.'

'And if that isn't enough?'

'It will be enough.'

'I'm not so sure.' I stand up. 'I may have to persuade you to my way of thinking.' I look down at him. I hold his eyes. It's a warning shot across the bow. He feels it. I watch him pull his arms into his sides. 'Thank you for the scone.'

As I walk away, I'm aware of his eyes on my back. I don't turn round.

15

By the time I get home it's two o'clock. The first thing I do is change the four-digit code on the alarm. Then I go inside to check on Lara and Bea. They're in the kitchen. Wendy has delivered a gingerbread house covered in icing and jellied sweets. There are several indents in the icing where sweets have been taken off.

'It wasn't me,' Bea says. There's icing around her mouth. 'I had two.' She holds up four fingers.

'She'll never be a mathematician,' Charlie says. 'Do you need any shopping, Mum? I thought I'd go out for a bit.'

'Just some milk.'

Fortunately, he doesn't have to go further than the end of the road. I don't intend to tell him that I saw Amy kissing someone else. His feelings will take enough of a bashing as it is without me wading in.

'And you could do with some bread,' Wendy chips in, opening up the bread bin so that I can see there's very little inside.

'And bread.' I look at Charlie. 'Take some money from the jar.'

'Where's Sezen?' Wendy says.

'Yeah, where is Sezen?' Charlie echoes.

I look over at Lara. She's beside Bea. They are kneeling on chairs and have their elbows on the table, leaning into the gingerbread house, looking through the windows and discussing which part looks the best to eat.

'Well . . .' The truth will only lead to questions that can't be fully answered. I don't want to scare anyone and I don't want to have them crossing bridges that might not need to be crossed.

I am having enough trouble dealing with my own anxiety. 'She's gone out to meet up with someone and should be back later. I said we'd look after Lara until then.'

'Be good for her to get some time to herself,' Wendy says. 'Lara's a super little girl, but single parenting can't be easy. Now, here.' She passes me a tray with a pot of tea and spelt toast and honey. 'This is for Lisa.'

'She's awake?' I take the tray and balance it against my hip so that I can hold my glass of water with the other hand.

'Feeling very rested and just a little bit hungry.' She wipes down the breadboard. 'Why don't you take it through?'

I add bananas and cheese to Charlie's shopping list, then go along the hallway to Lisa's room, pushing the door open with my foot. 'Wakey, wakey.'

Lisa is sitting up in bed looking out of the window into the back garden. 'I could have got up for that.' She leans forward to take it from me. 'Wendy insisted. I gave in because I thought I might get in her way in the kitchen.'

'We like spoiling you,' I tell her. 'All these years you've been the one doing the looking after.' I perch on the end of her bed. 'Now it's time for us to give something back to you.' Her face is relaxed, no sign of the pain that often creases her forehead. Her skin is pale with a smattering of freckles over her cheekbones. Her eyes are grey, the colour of morning mist. 'You look rested.' I smile. 'You look beautiful, actually.'

She laughs. 'Must be because all morning I've been dreaming about Mum.' She takes a sip of tea. 'She was playing with us in the garden. Remember the one with the overgrown orchard at the bottom?'

I nod.

'When I woke up, I felt like I'd really been with her.' She puts a hand to her chest. 'I've been left with a warm glow.'

'Lucky.'

'Do you remember how she used to sit on our beds and read to us?'

I do have a vague memory, a mingled feeling of warmth and cosiness, but it's indistinct, mixed up with feelings for my own children. 'I don't know whether what I remember of Mum is true any more,' I say to Lisa. 'It's such a long time ago and I've piled imaginary moments one on top of another.'

'I remember that she loved to wear Je Reviens perfume.'

'Ironic, really.'

'I'm sure she didn't want to die, Claire.' She reaches over and takes my hand. 'I do remember how much she loved us. Don't you?'

'No.' I shake my head. 'I wish I did, but I don't. I think I was just too young.'

'I had two more years to get to know her.'

'I wish we'd talked about her more with Dad.'

'We did try.'

'You're right, we did. As far as he was concerned, he'd given us Wendy and that was an end to it. He never seemed to be able to respond to our feelings.' I'm frowning now and am conscious that I'm grumbling, but I don't stop. 'Two little girls and still he always put himself first.' And probably a third little girl. I think about Mary, approaching me, her sister, and getting nothing but grief for it. 'He was so bloody irresponsible.'

Lisa leans to one side and starts rummaging around in the top drawer of her bedside cabinet.

'What are you looking for?' I stand up. 'I'll get it for you.'

'I'm looking for a violin. Thought I could play you a tune.'

'Funny.' I make a face and then we both laugh. She pats the bed and I sit back down.

'So what have you been doing today?'

'Well . . .' I take a breath. 'Sezen is with the police.' I tell her about finding the passports. 'She didn't have an explanation, and she wasn't willing to come clean about this mysterious man she knows, so she's at the station being questioned.'

Lisa is chewing on her toast. 'Wow,' she says. 'Could this be it, do you think? Could we find out who's blackmailing Julian and then maybe the safe house won't even be necessary?'

'I'm hoping,' I say. 'I'm really hoping. Unfortunately, I couldn't identify Sezen's man as one of Georgiev's people, so nothing's conclusive yet.'

'You've looked through mug shots?'

'Mac met me this morning and we went to a café.' I tell her about seeing Amy with someone else.

'Oh, no! Poor Charlie.'

'And then I don't know what got into me. I came over all paranoid and angry and was ready to take on this stranger, in front of his children. Luckily, Mac got me out of it.'

'So how's it going?' She eats the final piece of her toast. 'With you and Mac?'

'Good.' I think about the way we parted just now: me angry that I was being kept in a position of impotence; Mac, just like Julian, trying to make me see that it's possible to both convict Georgiev and keep Bea safe. 'He's doing everything he can.'

'Nothing between you both?'

'Lisa, believe me, sex is the last thing on my mind.' *Except as a means to an end.* And that will be with Julian. I fully intend to seduce him this evening. It's the best way to have him relaxed and feeling close and willing to open up to me. And then I'll have the information I want.

'And Julian still doesn't know that you had an affair with Mac?'

'I didn't have an affair with him. It was a one-off, a mistake.'

'I know you, Claire. No matter how drunk or unhappy you were, you wouldn't have had sex with him if you didn't have feelings for him.'

'It's irrelevant.' She's right, but none of that matters any more. 'Here and now, with all this going on, it means nothing.'

'I know. I'm sorry.' She moves the tray to one side and hugs me. 'I'm not trying to be your conscience. I just know how much you and Julian love each other. You're great together and you have fantastic kids.' She looks around her. 'A beautiful house. You have it all.'

'I do, and I'm trying to hang on to that.' I don't say that at the moment life feels tougher than it has ever felt. That I'm terrified of something happening to Bea and that losing her is worse than unthinkable. It sets up an ache inside me that feels cataclysmic. I will never be able to forgive myself or Julian if she is taken. We have to act in her best interests. And if Julian won't, then I will.

By nine o'clock in the evening all I can think about is engineering some space where Julian and I can be on our own. Sezen still isn't back. Mac called to say they would be keeping her overnight. She isn't talking. She's being very polite but is refusing to say who the man is or how she knows him. She has said, however, that it has nothing to do with the Georgiev case. Whether this is true or not is anybody's guess. Megan left around teatime and Julian has been spending time with the children. We still have Lara. Bea has persuaded her to sleep in her bed with her and I settled them down about eight o'clock. Lara asked for Sezen and I told her that her mummy had to stay out for another evening but that she would be back tomorrow. She readily accepted this, nodding her small head so that her black curls bounced over her cheeks.

I know that Julian won't come to bed before midnight. Even though he has officially resigned from the case, he's still involved in making sure it all comes together smoothly for the pre-trial hearing tomorrow. That means I'm going to have to tempt him upstairs. I rummage in my underwear drawer looking for something special. Last year we had our twentieth wedding anniversary. It was just before Lisa was diagnosed with cancer and she offered to look after the children while we went to Paris for the weekend. We saw the city, but we also spent a lot of time in bed. After a trip to the Louvre, we strolled back to the hotel along the Rue Saint-Honoré and we shopped in the boutiques. He bought me expensive silk underwear, the sort that, although beautiful to feel and wear, is both flimsy and impractical. I haven't worn it since. I find it at the back of the drawer and put it on. A basque, it has upwards of thirty clips down the front. By the time I've attached the stockings to the suspenders, I'm almost puffing. I look at myself in the mirror: front, sides and back. I don't look bad, all things considered. Better if I had some height, though. I slip my feet into heels and automatically my legs grow longer. I cover up with a short silk robe, a swirly pattern of pale blues and pinks. Pleased with myself, I open the bedroom door and then close it again. The erotic and the domestic, they don't mix easily, and I'm forgetting that it's not a normal weekday; there are several other people in the house. Lisa is most likely asleep but Charlie and Jack will still be awake. They are in their rooms but might just go to the kitchen for a snack so I can hardly wander the hallway like this. I cover the whole lot up with the large towelling dressing gown that I've had for years. It looks incongruous with the heels, but it'll have to do.

I walk down the stairs, the basque riding up on the waist until I'm forced to pull it down. The heels are higher than I'm used to and I compensate by leaning forwards slightly and swinging my hips from side to side. Feeling faintly ridiculous, I go to Julian's study via the kitchen, have a slug of wine, then take two glasses and a chilled bottle of Sauvignon Blanc down the next flight of stairs. As I pass Jack's door, I hear him talking loudly on his mobile. He'll be busy for a while.

Just before I open the door, I have second thoughts. Do I really want to try to manipulate Julian's feelings this way? Bugger. I look down at myself and almost succumb to a feeling of self-loathing. Perhaps I should forget Plan A and move straight on to Plan B – the plan that involves Mac. I deliberate over this for a few moments, wrestling with the fact that forcing Mac to give me the details will involve even more deceit. Julian is my husband; Bea is his daughter. We should be drawing Bea away from danger together. It's right that he tells me.

I pull the towelling dressing gown together around me and go into his study. He's sitting behind his desk, papers laid out in front of him.

'Still busy with work?' I say.

He nods. 'Reading through some of the bundles again. I don't want any surprises at the pre-trial.'

I put the wine and glasses on his desk, pour us both some and stand behind his chair, leaning my elbows on his shoulders and resting my face against his neck.

He pats the side of my head absentmindedly. 'So what's on your mind?'

'Just thought I'd come down and see if you want to come to bed.'

'Is Bea in our bed?'

'No. We have a temporary reprieve. She's sharing a bed with Lara.'

He pulls me round on to his knees.

'Julian, I was thinking . . . you know when we met?' I've always liked his hair. It's soft and wavy and springs back under my hands. I run my fingers through it. 'Do you remember?'

He laughs. 'Of course I remember.'

'When we were stuck in the lift?'

'I bet I can tell you the whole conversation, word for word.'

'You can?'

'Try me.'

'OK. Let me think. I'll tell you where to start.'

I look up at the ceiling and cast my mind back. We met in the university library. I was a first-year law student; Julian was a third-year. The library building was huge and covered four floors. The first floor was not so much for studying as for eating and chatting. What books there were, were basic introductory texts. The higher up the building you climbed, the more serious it became. The airless fourth floor was dense with law books and heavy with disapproval should anyone make the mistake of so much as whispering. Single tables and chairs were set at intervals throughout the shelves of books. Julian and I had already noticed each other and were at the stage where we acknowledged one another with a smile. I was struggling with an end-of-year assignment and decided to ask him a question. As the atmosphere

discouraged loud breathing, never mind talking, I wrote him a
note. He answered me by walking over to a shelf, finding the
correct volume of *Halsbury's Statutes*, bringing it to me and
opening it up at the right page. He pointed out the act of
Parliament I needed. I mouthed a thank-you and he smiled, held
my eyes for a second or two and then went back to his seat.
Suddenly I couldn't concentrate. I stroked the page where his
fingers had been. My heart was racing. Somehow, not being able
to speak had made our interaction feel more intimate. My face
was hot. I needed air.

Leaving my papers behind, I headed for the lift. Just as the
doors closed, Julian stepped inside. 'Giving up?' he said.

I'm brought back to the present as Julian's hands find their
way inside my dressing gown. 'Well, well, well!' He smiles at me.
'Is this for my benefit?'

'Maybe. But first you have to prove you remember what we
said to each other when we met.'

'No problem. Are we going from when we were in the lift?'

I nod.

'I said, "Giving up?"'

'And I said, "No. I just need a drink."'

'I said, "I'll buy you a coffee."' He pulls the towelling dressing
gown off my shoulders, out from under me and throws it across
the room. 'That's better,' he says.

'And I said, "That would be great."'

'Actually, it was more of a stammer,' he reminds me. 'You were
tripping over your words. You were blushing.'

'I felt faint.'

'Overwhelmed by my charm?'

I'm not giving in that easily. 'It was hot up there. They never
opened any windows.'

'So that's what it was!' He pulls the silk robe to the edges of
my shoulders and kisses my throat. 'And there was I thinking
you'd fallen for me.'

His kisses are making me tingle. I hold him away from me.

'Then the lift started to make those grinding metal-on-metal noises,' I remind him. 'And you said—'

'"Doesn't sound very healthy."'

'And then the lift juddered to a stop.'

'I thought it was too good to be true. I'd been watching you for six months and here we were stuck in a lift together.'

I shrug my shoulders nonchalantly. 'I'd only just noticed you,' I tell him.

He laughs and leans forward to kiss me again.

'Not so fast,' I say. 'We haven't got to the best bit yet.'

'OK.' He leans back against the seat but keeps one hand on my thigh and the other round my waist. 'So we used the phone to call the janitor and he said—'

'"We'll have you out in a jiffy."'

'We sat down on the floor and then—'

'We asked each other where we were from,' I say. 'And we played a game of one-upmanship.'

'Family trumps.'

'That's right!' I manage a laugh. This would be fun if the reality of the emails wasn't lodged in my mind like a violent squatter who's taken up residence in my living room and is just waiting for the opportunity to wreak havoc. 'We compared our upbringings.'

'I didn't have a pair of shoes until I was eight,' Julian reminds me.

'Until Wendy came along, Lisa and I cooked our own food. We stood on chairs to make scrambled egg and beans. My father thought babysitters were a waste of time because we could look after ourselves.'

'When I was four, I was almost eaten by a crocodile.'

I laugh again, remember how he had told me this and then taken off his shoe to show me that the little toe on his right foot was missing. I marvelled at the absent toe and then said, 'Lucky it wasn't your whole foot. Was it only a baby croc?'

He was staring at my face and then he stroked my cheek. 'I can't lie to you. You're too honest.' He looked sheepish. 'Wasn't actually a croc. Nothing as exciting as that. I just caught it in a door.'

'Must have been sore, though.'

His fingers felt cool, persuasive. I let the side of my face rest in his hand. 'You're really lovely.' His voice was quiet. 'Will you go out with me?'

'When I was four, my mother died,' I blurted out.

'True?'

'True,' I said. 'I win.'

'I consider myself well and truly trumped.'

He was kissing me when the janitor prised open the door. We went down to the café in the basement. We drank coffee and we talked and then we collected our books from upstairs and I invited him back to my shared flat.

Julian's face is in my neck again. I look down at myself. The clips at the top of the basque are straining. I can see red marks beginning to form on my skin. 'You can undo the top two clips, if you want,' I say into his ear.

With the excitement of a little boy unwrapping a train set, he undoes them. 'My birthday has come early.'

'I remember when we went back to my flat, we made a promise to each other.'

'That we would always be honest.' He's kissing the tops of my breasts.

'Exactly.'

I lift his head so that I can see the expression in his eyes. 'We've come a long way, Jules. Haven't we?'

'We have.' He stands us both up. 'And now I'd like to go a bit further.' He drinks back his wine, keeps hold of the glass, puts the bottle under his arm and grabs my hand. 'Bring your glass. We're going upstairs.'

I hold him back long enough for me to lift the towelling dressing gown off the floor and cover myself up. 'Should we say goodnight to the boys?'

He looks from left to right, then gives me a quizzical frown. 'What boys?'

'You really are playing along.'

'I am.' He looks pleased with himself. 'And now I'm thinking ice cubes.'

'We don't need to go that far.'

He's not listening. We're off up the stairs so quickly I'm in danger of breaking my ankle. Part of me admires his ability to live in the moment. He is losing himself in the story as if . . . we are fine. No one is threatening us; no one is coming to take our daughter. We're just another married couple with twenty-odd years on the clock spicing up our sex lives on a Sunday night. But while I do my best to join in, I'm not feeling it. In fact the last thing I want is sex. I feel like shaking him, demanding why he isn't seeing this like I am. Why we're not sat down at the computer emailing the blackmailer the details so that we'll all be safe again. I want to tell him that I feel betrayed and lonely and desperate and I don't know why he can't see that.

When we get to the kitchen, I take off my shoes and stand next to him as he rummages in the freezer behind frozen loaves of bread and vegetables and Wendy's fruitcake.

'Doesn't look like we have any,' I say.

He continues to look. Once upon a time I had a thing for ice cubes. But that was when I was young and lived in an attic bedroom. The one small skylight window didn't open up very far and the room would heat up like an oven.

'Oh look!' Triumphant, he holds up the tray. 'They're shaped like elephants, but that won't matter.' He twists the tray and pops them out into a glass.

'Do we have to?'

'What's happened to your sense of fun?'

I pull the dressing gown around me. 'I just think it might be too cold.'

'We can generate some heat.'

My smile feels stiff. I'm not sure I can keep this up. I'm now going to have to pretend to enjoy elaborate foreplay when I just want to cut to the chase and get the information. He sees my face and thinks my look has more to do with trepidation than ulterior motives. He laughs.

'Come on.' He takes my hand and I run to keep up with him as he climbs the stairs two at a time. 'You're nineteen, remember.' He closes the bedroom door behind us, puts a chair against it – he's not completely forgetting about children, then – and undresses with the speed of a teenager. He sits on the bed and pulls me to him. 'Am I allowed unwrap you now?'

I manage a flirty smile and let the dressing gown and the silk robe fall behind me onto the carpet. 'Only if you take your time.'

He undoes the rest of the basque clips one by one, kissing his way down my breasts and then my belly as he goes. I shiver but not in a good way. This isn't me. I'm not someone who pretends or manipulates. I've never pretended to want him. I've never had to. I've never even faked an orgasm. But if I'm going to do it, I might as well attempt to enjoy it, so I shut my eyes and try to let go to the feeling rising inside me like a geyser. He lays me back on the bed. His hands and mouth are everywhere, hard and soft at the right time in the right places, but still it does nothing to bring me into the moment.

'Naked bodies are the best, aren't they?' he says.

'For a barrister you can be remarkably hedonistic.'

'You shouldn't judge us barristers quite so harshly.' He takes an ice cube and drops it between my breasts. It slides its way down my stomach. He catches it with his tongue. 'Anyway, I am first and foremost a man.'

'You don't say.'

'Feel like you're nineteen yet?'

'Sex wasn't this good at nineteen.' I pull him in for a kiss. 'There's something to be said for being grown-up.'

Fortunately, he's in the mood for doing all the work. Nothing is expected of me except that I moan in the right places and move my hips at the right times. When at last he's lying beside me sated, I give him a few minutes to enjoy the feeling as I work out exactly how to approach this. Julian is intelligent and rational.

He believes passionately in equality and fair treatment. He believes in empowering people and he believes in justice.

'Julian, we've never had any trouble being straight with one another, have we?'

He pretends to frown. 'This isn't going to get serious, is it?'

'I don't mean it to. It's just that we're coming up against the biggest problem we've ever faced and I need to know that we're being honest with each other.'

'I haven't lied to you.'

'I know.' I stroke his chest. 'It's more what you haven't said.'

He takes a moment to consider. 'You're not still thinking I might be having a scene with Megan?'

'No.' I kiss the soft spot behind his ear. 'But I wonder if she's the reason you didn't tell me about the emails before now.'

'She's not. The decision was entirely mine. I didn't ask for her opinion, but if I had, I expect she would have told me to tell you.'

'OK.' I believe him. 'Thank you.'

'Anything else?'

'Yes.' I keep my tone light. 'Will you please tell me what the witness is called and where he is?'

He gives me a questioning look.

'As a couple we're close, aren't we?'

'Claire—'

'Aren't we?'

'Yes.'

'We always said we would share everything.'

'I know, but this is a professional decision.'

'It's not, Julian. It's personal.'

'Claire—'

'I won't use the information. I won't.' I find I can look him straight in the eye and lie. 'But I'll have it if I need it. It's like giving me a life raft so that if the sea is choppy, I can bail our daughter out.'

'I can't give you the name.'

'Because you think I'll bail out before you?' He goes to answer me, but I think of something else and briefly put my fingers over his mouth. 'Do you think I'm a good mother?'

'I think you're an excellent mother. Our children couldn't do any better.'

'Do you trust me to know what's best for them. For Bea?'

'Claire—'

'I know how special this case is to you.' I hold his face squarely in my hands so that he's forced to maintain eye contact. 'I do, Jules. I've worked in that world. I remember the buzz, the adrenaline rush of being part of a team taking a case as important as this to trial. I can only imagine what it's like for you being the lead counsel. I know you've had to resign, but nevertheless the credit will be yours. Not only have you been working on it for months but you have had an interest in nailing Georgiev for fifteen years. This case is a career-maker and on a personal level incredibly satisfying for you when you win. Because you will win.'

'It's also important to those people who've been hurt by Georgiev.'

'I understand that. And I understand that you can't be the one to communicate with the blackmailer, but I can.'

He shakes his head.

'I'm not saying I'd do it now. But if for some reason we are separated or there is an emergency of some sort, I may be the only one who can help Bea. Our daughter, Julian. *Our child.* We made her. We made her on a night just like this one. You have information that could help me care for Bea – save her life even. You need to trust me.'

I'm getting through to him. I see the first shadow of doubt flicker across his eyes.

'Do you love me, Julian?'

'Yes, I love you. You're my wife. I love you more than I can say. You are my soul mate, my best friend and my lover all rolled up in one package.' He strokes the small of my back. 'One very lovely package.'

At another time such a declaration would have warmed my heart, but now I see it as the green light to take me right where I want to be.

'Then prove it. Please.' I bring my face close to his and whisper, 'Prove that you love me. Tell me who the witness is and where he's being kept.'

16

Seconds pass and in those seconds I watch tears form in his eyes. His lips are trembling. He looks more upset and conflicted than I have ever seen him and I draw back. Anxiety climbs into my throat and sits there, heavy as stone.

'What?' I say.

He gives a monumental sigh, not from boredom but from the weight of what he's about to say. 'I can't tell you, Claire,' he says quietly.

'You can't, or you won't?'

'I can't.' He looks regretful. 'I asked for the witness to be moved and that I shouldn't be told where. I emailed that to the blackmailer this morning.'

A noise comes out of my throat. I feel like I'm choking.

Julian puts a steadying hand on my shoulder. 'I had to, Claire.'

I move away from him.

'It's the best way to protect Bea.'

I am filled with complete and utter disbelief. All I can do is stare at him.

'If we have nothing she wants, then she has no reason to come after Bea.'

I move to the edge of the bed and stand up. My legs are jelly and I fall over, catching my head on the edge of the bedside table. A searing pain bites into my right temple and I let out an involuntary cry. Julian helps me up, sitting me back down on the bed. I touch the side of my head and feel the beginnings of a bump. The glass with the remaining ice cubes is on the other side of the bed. Julian gets it and gently presses the cold surface against my temple. I take it from him and hold it there myself. At first it makes the burning pain more acute than the injury itself and then there's an increasing numbness, spreading cold beneath my skin, around my eye and down on to my cheek.

'It was the best solution,' he says.

We're both still naked. He's squatting in front of me, looking up into my face. I don't meet his eyes.

'You do see that, don't you?'

The shock of his revelation is beginning to dissipate. Like dense, rolling mist it evaporates and leaves behind a clear view and with that there is heat.

I breathe in and feel anger mix with the air that fills my lungs. 'No, I don't see that.'

'I no long—'

I cut in, 'You still know his name.'

'The name alone isn't enough. It's more important to know where he is.'

'And she's going to believe that you don't?' I snap back. 'You're the lead counsel. He's your star witness.'

'I was the lead counsel.' He purses his lips. 'Claire, we had to do something.'

'We? *We?*' My hand starts to shake. I press the glass more firmly against my temple. 'This decision has nothing to do with me.'

'I know.' He nods. 'And I'm sorry you couldn't be included in the discussion.'

'What discussion?'

'I discussed it with Mac and with the profilers and with the criminal psycho—'

He stops talking when I hurl the glass at the wall. Water, ice and shards of broken glass fan out from the point of impact. 'Damn you, Julian!' I shout. 'If anything were to happen, it was the only bargaining chip we had.'

He looks at the wall and then back at me. 'Taking this step means that nothing will happen. That is the point.' He's talking slowly. He wants me to calm myself, but my pulse is racing and my heart is in my mouth. 'She's not going to attempt to take Bea unless there's a guarantee she'll get what she wants.'

'You think she'll just back off?'

'It's a calculated risk, but yes, we do.'

'Crossing the road is a risk. Swimming in the sea is a risk. But this? This is madness! It's asking for trouble.' I stand up and lift my nightdress off the low stool at the end of the bed. 'What has happened to you? Have you forgotten that we make decisions concerning our children together. *Together*, Julian.'

'I hoped that you would see the sense in this.'

'Sense? This is ludicrous! You think she's just going to shrug her shoulders and forget about it?' I stare him down. 'What if it makes her mad as hell? What then?'

'She won't jeopardise her ultimate goal.'

'So why didn't you do this a week ago? Why leave it until this morning?'

'Because we hoped we would either find her or that she would change tack when I resigned. You know that.'

'Damn you, Julian!' I bang my hand against the wall. 'Damn you for excluding me and damn you for treating this like some sort of game.'

'I am not treating this like a game.' He grabs my arm and swings me round to look at him. 'I love our daughter just as much as you do. This is exactly the sort of emotional, knee-jerk re-action that is unhelpful.'

'You think our daughter being kidnapped isn't something to get emotional about?'

'Claire, you of all people should understand that it's for this sort of intimidation that Georgiev is being brought to justice in the first place. The law can't buckle and fold in the face of threats, no matter how extreme. You have to see that.'

'I'll tell you what I see. I see that you want to do this on your own. You don't want to hear what I think and you're even less interested in what I feel.'

'That's not—'

'There's a mother in Italy who's living with the memory of a murdered son. I will not be her.' I move close to his face. 'I am not interested in rhetoric. I am not interested in what's right. I want our daughter safe, and if you have it in your power to keep her safe and you don't exercise that power, then I will not live with you any more.' I hold his eyes. 'I could not live with you.'

He doesn't have an answer to that and in his eyes there is an acute sadness. It doesn't make me retract my threat and it doesn't make me feel sympathy for him. I want to hurt him like he is hurting me. I want him to know what it feels like to be pushed away. I want him to see that he's putting his work before his family. I'm just about to reiterate this when our bedroom door is pushed. It moves only a couple of inches before it hits the back of the chair. I pull the nightdress on over my head and take the chair away from the door. The light in the hallway is on, the dimmer switch turned down low, just like it is in our bedroom. Bea is there. Her eyes are barely open. She doesn't look to the right or the left, doesn't see Julian and me watching her. She moves automatically towards the bed. She is holding one of Bertie's legs, the rest of him trailing on the carpet behind her.

She whispers loudly, 'I not wake Daddy. I just climb in velly velly quiet-y.' In seconds she is under the covers, her small head hardly denting the pillow.

The air is crackling with an overt significance. This little girl. She is what we're battling over. She is the one who is prized by both sides and yet she is completely oblivious to the danger that's swirling round her, drawing ever closer.

I point towards the bed. 'Bea trusts us to do what's best for her.' I pause. 'Can you honestly tell me that's what you're doing?' I wait a couple of seconds, watching him wrestle with an answer.

When none is forthcoming, I go downstairs and into the kitchen.

I pour myself a glass of wine, my hands shaking so much that some spills on to the work surface. I sit down at the table and drink the wine down quickly as if it's medicine. I hadn't expected this. At the back of my mind there was always the safety button, the if-push-came-to-shove option. Julian had the information the blackmailer wanted. We could give it to her and bugger the consequences. Our daughter would be safe. But now Julian has relinquished that power and fear is curling inside me, turning round in the centre of my chest like a corkscrew. I am the first to admit that I can't detach myself in the same way that Julian can. My daughter is four. She is hardly more than a baby and she is in danger. I believe that British law is more balanced, fairer and more sophisticated than any other country in the world. I believe in its power to bring justice and maintain order. But British justice comes second to my child's safety, and I'm both horrified and angry by Julian's decision.

Within five minutes he follows me into the kitchen. He's wearing pyjamas now, his expression cloudy with tension. He takes a dustpan and brush out of the cupboard. He's about to leave the room when he turns back and says, 'Was that what the sex was for, Claire? So you could find out about the witness?'

I flick my eyes towards his. 'Yes.'

Julian is rarely lost for words. 'The . . .' He clears his throat. 'Claire, I . . .' He thinks. 'While I . . .' He leans his back against the wall and sighs. Then he walks away.

I drink some more wine and remember that Mac was also involved in this decision. It doesn't surprise me. I know the way the police operate. They're not going to decide strategy with me, the child's mother. This is a matter of what's lawful. It's not about emotions. Parents can sacrifice the greater good for their child's safety, but the system can't do that. It has to stand firm. I accept that. What I can't accept is that Julian is more concerned with doing what's right on a grand scale than he is with doing what's right for his family. I can't reconcile that. I would never have predicted this reaction. Never.

Two glasses of wine later and I'm coming to terms with what I have to do next. Mac. He knows the witness's name and he'll also know where he's been moved to. OK, it didn't work with Julian, but that doesn't mean it won't work with Mac. I have to try to bring him on to my side. Mac is a rarity among policemen. He's not all about rules and payback, black and white crime and punishment. He is compassionate. I've seen that side of him and I'm sure I can make him understand my position. If not one way, then the other. Put simply, I have information that could ruin his career. A whisper in the right place and he'd be discredited. It's not what I want – the police service would be a lesser place without him – but my options are running out and I don't have the luxury of sentiment.

I'm not in the least bit tired, so I make way down the stairs, to the bottom of the house, and poke my head round the door to Jack's room. He has fallen asleep with the television on, the remote control still in his hand. I take the remote and turn off the TV. He doesn't stir. I kiss his forehead and look at him for a minute. When he's asleep, he looks so young, his face smooth and unlined. He's lucky not to have suffered from teenage acne and his skin is soft. He doesn't need to shave yet, and in spite of his assertion that he is almost a man, he still looks every bit sixteen.

I go up to the ground floor and into the sitting room, stand at the bay window and pull the curtain a little to one side. The police have stepped up their security. One of them is standing at the bottom of the steps. The porch light is on and he is alert, looking out into the darkness, his head moving from side to side as if waiting for someone to materialise. Feeling reassured, I slide the curtain back and go into the hallway. I hover outside Lisa's door, listening for the sound of her breathing. I push it open a crack and the hinges creak.

'Is that you, Claire?'

'I'm so sorry,' I whisper. 'I didn't mean to wake you.'

'I was already awake.' She switches on the bedside light. 'I spent too much time sleeping during the day. And you?'

'I'm not tired.'

I come into the room. She pats the space beside her. I climb into bed and lean back against the pillow.

'What on earth happened to your head?' She reaches to touch it and I stop her hand in mid-air.

'It's really sore. Even after two glasses of wine it hurts.'

'Have you taken painkillers?'

'Not yet.'

'Then you should. And use arnica cream. That will help with the bruising.' She adjusts herself and her pillow so that she can both rest her own head and see my face. 'How did you do it?'

'I hit it on the bedside cabinet. I was . . . shocked and I fell over. Julian and I were arguing. In fact . . .' I hesitate, then decide to go ahead and say it. 'I'm furious with him. And hurt. And appalled.'

'What's happened?'

'He's asked for the witness to be moved. He won't be informed as to where they're keeping him. He sent the blackmailer an email saying as much. So that's that.' Tears come into my eyes. I press my fingers into them until it hurts. Water spills out and I wipe it away with the edge of the duvet cover. 'We have no power,' I say. 'None.'

'But surely that means she won't come for Bea,' Lisa says, her tone tinged with urgency. 'There wouldn't be any reason to, would there?'

I recall the photos of the murdered priest and the little Italian boy. Both of them drained of blood. 'Georgiev is behind this, Lisa. He doesn't give up until he gets what he wants.'

'What are the police saying?' She hesitates. 'Mac – what's he saying?'

I shrug. I'm not going to tell Lisa about my plan to get the information from Mac. I don't think she'll approve and I'm not giving her the opportunity to dissuade me out of it. 'Julian and Mac are of like mind. I expect when he comes tomorrow, after the pre-trial hearing, he'll be pushing for the safe house.' I shiver. 'I can't trust either of them.'

'Claire?'

'I won't forgive Julian for this. Never.' I look into Lisa's eyes, misty with fear and empathy. 'I can't believe that he's doing this. He goes ahead and makes decisions without even considering my point of view.'

'That must be hard for you.' She takes my hand. 'But you have to remember that Julian is Bea's father. He's not putting her in danger by doing this. In fact, by making clear he doesn't know where the witness is, potentially he's putting her in less danger.'

'I don't buy that. There's no guarantee that she'll believe him. She's very certain she's going to get Bea, and her confidence is not misplaced.' I think again about the photos. 'Georgiev has engineered this kind of operation before.' I tell Lisa about the little Italian boy. 'The kidnapper was the family au pair. Her papers and her references were checked. The boy's parents and the police thought they had all their bases covered. Still he was taken.'

'But Bea won't leave the house.'

'No, she won't, but still.' I shake my head. 'Oh, Lisa . . .'

I don't know how to explain it: the emails, the words she uses, her surety, her knowingness. She is prepared. She is more than one step ahead of us. She is an expert at this. She enjoys it. This is her world, not ours.

I turn my head and focus on my sister's face. 'Some people have a gift for fooling others. I read an article once about a woman who managed to hide three pregnancies, each of them two years apart. After she gave birth to three full-term babies, she gave them up for adoption and carried on as normal. She was married and she had a loving extended family. I remember reading the article and thinking, Why didn't her husband comment on her growing bump? How could her family have missed it? What sort of family were they?'

'Perhaps her bump was really small.'

'She was a swimming instructress! Most of us could get away with baggy jumpers and leggings, but she was on display every day and yet she fooled dozens of people.'

'That's bizarre.'

'It is, and when I looked into the story, you know what she told her family?'

'What?'

'That she had irritable bowel syndrome and that she bloated out. You'd think her family were idiots to believe that, wouldn't you?'

Lisa nods.

'They weren't. They were switched-on people, and her husband was an intelligent man, well respected, well liked. They all believed her because she had authority. She was self-assured. She was convincing. She pre-empted any suspicion by offering explanations.'

'Weird.'

'Very. She fooled everyone, even those closest to her.'

Lisa thinks. 'You're saying this blackmailer is someone we know? Someone who is fooling all of us?'

'Yes.'

'But who?'

'I don't know!' I throw my arms out. 'I don't want it to be Sezen, but I hope that it is her because at least she's in custody at the moment. Mac's looked into the people it could be, including members of the police and the CPS. It's unlikely to be any of them, but' – I shrug – 'I just don't know.'

'Claire, listen.' She swings round in the bed to face me. 'If you want to go away with Bea, if you think that will be the easiest way to keep her safe, promise me you will do that.'

'I will.' I kiss her cheek. 'I promise.'

Her head falls back on the pillow. She looks drained and at once I feel guilty for using up what little energy she has with my troubles. I leave her to sleep, go upstairs and climb into bed. Bea is lying between Julian and me. I lay my hand on her back and gradually drift off. I fall asleep three times, but each time wake up within minutes to check that Bea is still there.

The bump on my head hurts so that I can't lie on my right side. I move around trying to get comfortable.

Julian's voice whispers into the almost darkness, 'Shall I get you some painkillers?'

'No.'

'Claire?'

I don't answer.

'This is going to work out,' he says softly. 'You know that, don't you?'

'No, I don't.'

'Claire.' He stretches across Bea to find a piece of me to touch: my hand, my arm, my side. I keep myself out of his reach. He stands up and walks round to my side of the bed. He sits down close to my middle. 'Claire, please talk to me.'

I leave a few seconds before I say, 'Can't you see that the decision you've made might be the wrong one?'

'I'm confident we can beat her.'

'Well, I don't share your confidence. I have a horrible, sinking feeling she's going to get Bea.'

'How, Claire? How?'

'I don't know *how*,' I say, my voice rising so that Bea stirs beside me. I take a second to compose myself and then say much more quietly, 'But I do know that she's smarter than us and that's why we should have given her what she wanted.'

'I can't agree with you.'

'Then we've nothing to say to each other.'

I shift over on to my right side, ignoring the pain in my temple, it being more important to turn my back on Julian. He rests his hand on my back and I shrink away from it. I hear him sigh, then stand up and return to his own side of the bed. I sense him lying awake in the dark, on the other side of Bea, our positions in the bed reflecting our separate approaches to this: Julian on one side, me on the other and

Bea in the middle. I can't think about what this rift will do to our marriage in the long run. I have to take one minute, one hour at a time.

Bertie's fur on my cheek, Bea's hair on my neck, I put my arm round her and lie there mulling everything over, trying to work out from which direction the threat will come. Rationally, of course I agree with Julian. I am the only person who knows the code for the burglar alarm. There are two policemen outside the house. CCTV cameras are focused on the front and back doors. How could she get inside? The simple answer is that she can't unless she comes with reinforcements and then the police will be able to arrest them all.

I spend what's left of the night drifting in and out of sleep. Come six o'clock, I decide to get up and face the day. It's Monday, the day of the pre-trial hearing. The judge will decide whether to grant the defence's request for full witness disclosure. Julian's already up and I know that he'll leave for work early. I get dressed. My head is still pounding, the lump on my temple the size of a quail's egg. Lisa and Julian are in the kitchen. They both look up when I walk in.

'I've made some porridge,' Lisa says, standing up.

I wave her down again. 'I'll get it.'

I see her look at Julian, waiting for him to say something: a good morning, ask me about my head, pour me a coffee. He doesn't speak. He doesn't acknowledge my presence. Fine by me. I ladle some porridge into a bowl and join them at the table. Lisa has poured me a coffee. She tops up the mug with milk. I thank her and take a drink.

'Of course there's a moral imperative, and as laws are drawn up, this is taken into account in the courtroom,' Julian is saying to Lisa. 'What has to be established are not so much the rights and wrongs of it, but whether the defendant has broken the law.' He takes a spoonful of porridge. 'It's about proof. In an ideal world justice would always prevail, but we don't live in an ideal world.'

'But with witness anonymity,' Lisa says, 'there must be some problems.'

'There are credibility issues. Does the witness have motive to lie? That's the main one. But in a case like this, with Georgiev as dangerous as we know he is, anonymity is the only way to stay alive.'

'Do you have forensic evidence?'

'Criminals like Georgiev can't be caught with direct evidence: fingerprints, DNA, blood, CCTV. Useless. He has other people doing his dirty work. We need a witness to testify. To give names, dates, times, details that tie in with minor witness statements and police intelligence.' He finishes his porridge and pushes the bowl across the table. 'Finally we have a chance to get him.'

'And your family is paying the price for that,' I say. And then compound it by adding, 'Or hadn't you noticed?'

He glances across at me. 'What's happening is inconvenient, Claire, I grant you, but in the grand scheme of things, having to live in a safe house for a month or so is hardly the greatest of hardships.'

'It's not just being shut in the house, though, is it? It's the incipient danger and the fear that it generates.' I bang my chest. 'I am afraid, Julian. *Me*. Your wife.'

'Claire, there are young girls being trafficked and murdered out there.'

'And you have brought your children, *our* children into that world.'

'Like it or not, this is the world we live in.'

'Well, I don't like it, and it isn't my world.' I stand up. 'And for me, my family comes first.'

'And it doesn't for me?'

'You're sacrificing your family's safety for your principles.'

'I am not.' He stands up and leans towards me. He is angry; it simmers in his eyes. 'I am not sacrificing their safety.'

'Claire?' Lisa stands up too. 'Sweetheart, why don't you finish your porridge?'

I don't answer her. My eyes are still on Julian.

'When did you lose your principles, Claire? What happened to the girl who went into law to make a difference?'

I recognise the look on his face. It's one that's shrunk many a witness in the past. It's a cross between contempt and surety, and something inside me snaps.

'She woke up!' I slam my bowl down on the table and it breaks into two halves; left over milk spills on to the wooden surface. 'I don't have the luxury of principles, not when my daughter's life is at stake.'

'I can't talk to you when you're like this.' He turns away from me. 'You need to calm down.'

'Fuck you, Julian. And fuck your principles.' My tone is even, but at once Lisa is beside me, gripping my elbow, urging me to sit. I shake her off and follow Julian across the kitchen. 'If something happens to our daughter, I will cry every day for the rest of my life. I won't be able to live; I won't be able to breathe.' I follow him into the hallway. 'It will never be bearable. We will never have peace. We will never be a family again. We will never be a couple again.' He's on his way downstairs to his study and I move quickly, stepping in front of him to block his path. 'I am not ready to lose my sister, I was not ready to lose my mother or my father, and I will never, *never* be ready to lose a child. Do you understand that?' His expression is stony. 'If we lose our child because of your principles, then God damn you to hell, Julian. I mean that.'

I move out of his way and he goes off down the stairs. I'm shaking from anger and from the realisation that I meant every word I said. And as each word sinks in, I am brought that bit closer to the nub of it. Julian and I are moving further apart. Our outlooks are irreconcilable. I am sacrificing my marriage to ensure my daughter's safety. That's the way it has to be.

The doorbell rings and I answer it straight away. Megan. I bring her into the porch but no further.

'Big day,' I say. 'Are you all ready for it?'

'I have butterflies.' She presses her stomach and gives me her busy-but-interested smile. 'We're well prepared.'

'I saw you yesterday making friends with the two policemen.'

'Well, they seem nice, you know.' Her eyes flick to the side, suddenly nervous. 'Claire, I haven't had the chance to tell you properly how sorry I am about what's happening.'

'It's shit,' I say. 'It's frightening and it's desperate.'

'Yes.' She shifts from one foot to the other.

'What do you know about the witness?'

'Sorry?' She looks around as if she thinks I might be talking to an invisible someone behind her.

'The witness,' I say. 'Do you know who he is and where he's being kept?'

'No, I . . .' She clears her throat. 'That's not the sort of information I'm given. This one's top secret. You know how it is.'

'Yes, I do.' I move a step closer. She keeps her gaze away from mine. 'Do you have aspirations to be a mother some day?'

'I would have to find a man first.' She looks up at me through her lashes. 'The young policeman – Alec Faraway. What do you think?'

'He seems very nice.' I hold her gaze. 'Are you sure you don't know the witness's name?'

'Claire . . .' She shuffles her feet again. 'I know that Julian . . .' She trails off.

'You know that Julian what?' I keep my tone light, unthreatening.

'He feels bad about this. He's worried. He knows he's walking a tightrope, but there are no other options.'

'He shares his thoughts with you?'

She draws back.

'Megan, at the moment, with the direction my life is taking' – I lean right into her face – 'I don't care how close you are to my husband. I don't care whether you've had sex with him. I have much bigger things to worry about.'

'You shouldn't be saying this to me.'

'Woman to woman, I am asking you whether you can help me.'

'I don't know anything, Claire.' She makes big eyes at me, then touches her heart. It's a sweet but theatrical gesture and I don't buy it. She knows more than she's letting on. 'Trust the police. Trust Julian.'

The inside door opens and Julian is standing there. Megan immediately straightens up and steps away from me. I open the outside door for them both and they start off down the steps. When they're almost at the bottom, Julian glances back at me. 'I'll be in touch after the pre-trial ruling.'

Why bother? I almost shout, but don't want the two policemen and Megan as an audience. I make do with pretending he hasn't spoken and close the door.

'Has Daddy gone?' Bea is on her way down the stairs. 'He didn't say goodbye.'

'He thought you were sleeping.' I swing her from the fourth stair on to my hip. 'Is Lara not up yet?'

'She needs her sleep,' Bea says, moulding herself into my body and putting her thumb in her mouth while her left hand keeps tight hold of Bertie. 'She needs to grow.'

I smile. 'I think Wendy might be right.' I tickle her feet as we walk into the kitchen. 'You spend too much time with adults, young lady.'

She giggles into my shoulder and wraps her legs further round me. 'Look!' I tip her forward so she can see into the pot. 'Auntie Lisa made some lovely porridge.'

'I like Coco Pops.'

'We don't have any Coco Pops,' I say, beginning the negotiations. 'But if you have just ten spoons of porridge, you can have some toast with chocolate spread on it.'

I set her down at the table while she considers this, her legs swinging backwards and forwards. I place a bowl of porridge in front of her and hand her a spoon. Holding the spoon vertical and with both hands, she stirs it round vigorously so that some milk spills over the edge. 'Oops.' She catches the milk with her finger and then licks it.

'It's just the right temperature,' I say. We've recently read Goldilocks. 'Try some. It's like Baby Bear's porridge.'

'Was Baby Bear Goldilocks's friend?'

'I expect they became friends.'

She squints up at me through her hair. 'You and Daddy are my special friends, and Bertie is my special friend.' She lifts Bertie from his seat beside her up on to the table. His head hangs down into the bowl. 'He's sniffing it.'

'Yes, he is,' I say. 'But don't let him fall in or he'll end up in the washing machine again.' She snatches him off the table at once and puts him on to her knee. I find some hairclips in the pocket of my jeans and pin up her hair. 'Shall I do aeroplanes?'

She pulls her chin in towards her neck. 'No, Mummy! I'm not a *baby*.' Then she notices the lump on my temple and gasps, 'What happened?'

'I bumped my head.'

She stands up on her chair and reaches across. 'It's sore?' She touches it so gently, so reverently that I can barely feel it. Then she draws her hand back and says, 'Did Daddy kiss it better?'

I smile. 'No.'

'I do it.' She leans across again and gives the quail's egg the merest of kisses. 'Is it better now?' she whispers.

I move my eyes right and left to show that I'm thinking. 'You know what, it is better!'

She claps her hands and jumps a couple of times so that the chair tips to one side and threatens to topple. I catch her arm to steady her and she sits back down again.

'Porridge time,' I say.

'And Lara.' She knocks all the porridge off the spoon, then brings it up to her mouth. 'She is *my* special friend too. She sleeps in my bed. She can stay for ever and ever, amen.'

'Well . . .'

'I ask Sezen.' She drops the spoon and is off out of the kitchen before I can remind her that Sezen spent the night elsewhere – in a police cell. Not something I'll tell Bea, but it is something that's constantly on my mind. I look at the clock. It's only just after seven. A bit too early to ring Mac. He won't have got to the station yet. I fill the sink with hot soapy water and start cleaning the kitchen surfaces. I've been at it for twenty minutes or so, trying to lose myself in the rhythmic motion, when Bea comes back with Lara, who has dressed herself and even managed to brush her hair and put a hairband across the front to keep the hair out of her eyes. She is as composed as ever and it makes me wonder how often Sezen has left her and with whom. When Lara sits at the table to have breakfast, Bea bobbing around on the floor behind her as she tries to master her hula-hoop, I ask her whether Mummy often has to leave her with a friend.

'Mummy has to work.' She nods into her bowl of porridge. 'She has to make money to help Jalal.'

'Of course.' I give her a reassuring smile. 'And does Jalal live in Brighton too?'

She pulls her sleeve back and shows me a multicoloured bracelet, the threads woven together like a plait and then tied to form a circle. 'He gave me this. It is for friendship.' She says the last word very deliberately as if she has been practising it.

'I see. And did you meet Jalal yesterday?'

'Yes, but he has to do work for the men. To make them leave him alone.'

'Right.' My pulse rate begins a steady climb. I stand up and lift my mobile from the dresser. 'I'm just going to make a phone call, girls. I'll be next door.'

I go through to the sitting room, select Mac's number and wait for it to connect. The two policemen outside see me at the window and I raise my hand by way of a hello.

'Mac.'

'It's me. Claire.'

'Morning.' He takes a big breath. 'We're still questioning Sezen. She's a tough nut. Whoever she's protecting, he either means a lot to her or she's afraid of reprisals.'

I tell him about the conversation I've just had with Lara. 'I think you could get more out of her. She's a bright little button. She might even be able to show you where he lives.'

'Well, if nothing else, the threat of questioning her daughter will be more power to our elbow with Sezen.' He stops talking and I hear the rustle of cellophane. 'Officers have questioned Jem Ravens but couldn't find anything suspicious.' He's speaking through a mouthful of something doughy. 'She was shocked and upset and appeared very genuine in her assertion that she knew nothing about this.'

'Well, that's always something, I suppose.'

'You don't sound very convinced.'

'Well . . . honestly, Mac, I never believed it would be Jem. And let's face it, we still don't have a lot to go on, do we?'

'No, but by the end of the morning we will have ruled Sezen either in or out and that's what police work is all about – finding the clues, following them to see where they might lead, fitting together the pieces.'

I think of those jigsaw puzzles where the picture is baked beans or jelly babies – almost impossible to put together. Especially when there's time pressure.

'Can we have a chat on our own today, Mac? Please.'

There's a split second of hesitation before he says, 'Of course. How does later this morning sound?'

'That's good for me.'

'I'll come to you. Around eleven?'

'Great. I'll see you then.'

I put my phone into the back pocket of my jeans and think about what I'll need to say, or do, for him to give me the witness's details. I'll promise. I'll plead. I'll beg. I'll flirt. Whatever it takes, I'll do it. While Julian seems to be happy with a David and Goliath scenario, I'm not.

I'll get the details and I'll give them to the blackmailer. And in the meantime, if Julian can email the blackmailer with his intentions, then I can surely do the same. I log on to my laptop and open my email. I click on 'New message' and type her address into the first box.

Subject: Witness Details

Please do not attempt to take my child. I will get you the details. I will have them to you by midnight tonight.

Claire Miller

17

I'm in a limbo of waiting. I've brought my laptop into the kitchen beside me. Every five minutes I press the refresh button. Nothing yet. While I wait for eleven o'clock to come round and Mac to arrive, I keep myself busy in the kitchen, dusting and polishing the Welsh dresser. The girls are under the table, playing house. They have draped two tablecloths over the surface so that they hang down almost to the floor and have dragged the small rug from the hallway for them to sit on. An assortment of pans and plates, wooden spoons and jars are under the table with them and they are deciding what to cook.

'. . . for when the men come back from the fields,' Bea says.

'. . . with two dead rabbits and a fish,' Lara says.

'No fish.' Bea is insistent about this because 'Fish have feelings,' she tells Lara. 'Like Nemo.'

When the doorbell rings, I expect the postman, but Jem is standing on the step. Her hands are in her pockets. Her clothes are grubby; her hair is unkempt.

'I spent the night in the van.' She moves from one foot to the other as if the step is hot. 'I hadn't told Pete about prison. I should have done.' Her face flushes and I see she's close to tears. 'I'm hoping he'll cool off.'

'It was quite a secret you were keeping, Jem.'

'I know. I was ashamed.' She purses her lips. 'Pete has always been too good for me.'

'Oh, come on! That simply isn't true.' For a moment I forget about the blackmailer and the threats and give her a hug. 'I'm sorry that my troubles brought this out, but Pete will forgive you.

You two are bigger than this. Give him time.' I'm about to offer
her a shower and a place to stay when I remember that, unlikely
as it is that Jem is involved, I can't risk it. I've seen unlikely. I've
seen people barefaced lying and I've seen people successfully fool
even the most experienced police officers.

'I'm sorry I can't offer you a place to stay,' I say, 'but I can
give you the money I owe you for painting Lisa's room.'

She shakes her head. 'So the cops were watching out for you?'

'Yeah. Who would have thought it, eh?' I hesitate. 'What
happened, though? Back then, I mean.'

'The assault?'

'Yeah.'

'Temper. Tiredness. Too many free drinks. I was saving up for
a deposit on a house and worked two jobs: daytime with a builder
and evenings in a pub. There was a bloke there who had been
lairing me off all evening. He was a regular bully and harassed
all the female members of staff. In fact, several of them were able
to testify that he'd been harassing me all evening and that I'd
asked him to back off.' She shrugs. 'Anyway, I went to change a
keg and he caught me in the cellar, hands everywhere, stinking
breath in my face. The golf club was handy and before I knew
it I'd thumped him over the head with it. Hard.' She shakes her
head. 'It was absolute bloody madness and I deserved every minute
of the five months I served.'

'I'm not so sure. It sounds like you were provoked,' I say. 'Did
you have a decent defence counsel?'

She gives me a small smile. 'I used unreasonable force. He
spent three weeks in intensive care. To be honest, I was just
grateful I hadn't killed him.'

'Sounds like he deserved it.'

'Maybe. But tell me, what's going on with you? The police
wouldn't give me any details. Just that someone was threatening
your family.'

'Yes . . . it's to do with Julian's case.' I think about Mac. He'll
be here in an hour. 'Hopefully, it will all be over soon.'

'Well.' She sees I'm not going to say any more and goes down a couple of steps. 'If I can do anything . . . help in any way . . . get in touch.'

'I will. Sure you don't need the money?'

'No. I'll get it some other time.'

I stand on the step and watch as she climbs into her van, then drives off. It's a bit late for me to hope our friendship hasn't suffered, but still I hope it hasn't been damaged beyond repair because she's my best friend in Brighton and I'd hate to be without her. With or without a criminal record, she's still the same Jem, and when this is over, I intend to make it up to her.

The postman's van has stopped close to the kerb. I'm expecting some of the macrobiotic ingredients Sezen and I ordered on the Internet, so I wait to see what he has for me. He comes up the steps with three parcels, which I sign for and take indoors. Charlie is beside the kettle making coffee. The girls are still under the table.

'You're not forgetting that later today we're having a family meeting, love, are you?' I say.

'Nope. Four o'clock, wasn't it?'

'About then. Whenever Dad gets back from the pre-trial hearing.'

'So is it some big bombshell?'

'Yes.' I pick up the smallest parcel. It's an oblong shape about six inches long and four inches high. There's no company logo on the box, and the postmark is local. I slice the packing tape with the end of a pair of scissors, being careful not to go too deeply into the box.

Charlie is staring at me, his arms wide. 'Well, what is it?'

Inside is a black plastic bag. I lift it out. It fits the shape of my palm and feels as if it weighs a couple of pounds. I frown. 'I'm not sure what this is.'

'Not *that*! The bombshell.'

'You'll find out later.' I look straight at him. 'I would tell you now. I have been tempted to tell you, but I think it's something your dad and I should tell you together.'

His lips tremble. 'You're getting divorced?'

'No! Heavens above!' Still holding the plastic bag, I walk across and give him a hug. Then I point with my free hand under the table and put my finger to my lips. I don't want Bea announcing to all and sundry that we're getting divorced. 'It's to do with Dad's trial.'

'Not that again. Dad told me he'd resigned. I thought the emails had stopped. I thought I'd be able to ask Amy back.'

'Not yet, darling.' I think of the sight of her with her tongue down some other boy's throat. 'I know it's hard, but we all need to be patient.'

'So what is it, then?' he whispers.

'Charlie, honestly, I can't say.'

'Fine, then.' He turns away, just a bit disgruntled, mumbling to himself.

I go back to the table and check the box for a delivery note. Nothing.

The bag is made of tough plastic and is secured at one end with tape. I put it on the table and pull off the tape. As soon as the seal is broken, I notice a smell: earthy, metallic, sharp. Something in my head says, *Stop now! Don't open it. Don't go any further*, but my hands keep unwrapping. I slide it out of the bag on to the table and stifle a scream. It's a piece of meat shaped like a fist. There are thick, rubbery, tube-like vessels coming out of the top. I know without anyone having to tell me that it's a heart. My jaw clenches tight against the nausea rising into my throat. I hold my hands away from me, staring at them and then staring at the bloody mass on the table.

Charlie takes control. He guides me to the sink, squirts liquid soap on my hands and runs the hot tap. He holds my hands under the flow of water and says, 'What the hell, Mum? I didn't know you were ordering body parts.'

'I didn't order it,' I say, my mind locking down on what this could mean.

He goes over to the table and peers at it. 'I'm not sure what animal it's from. We dissected hearts in biology once. Oh, look!' Inside the black plastic bag there is a cellophane envelope. He holds it at the edge so as not to get blood on his fingers, brings it to the sink and runs it under the tap. 'There should be a delivery note inside.' He dries it with a paper towel and slits the packet with a knife. Inside is a piece of paper folded down the centre. He hands it to me. I take a breath and then I read it. There are seven words printed in a regular font: *Next time it will be your daughter's.*

A scream resounds inside my head, insistent as a police siren. I clamp my mouth shut to stop the sound escaping.

'Mum?' Charlie looks panicked. 'What does it say?'

I slip the note into my pocket. 'Charlie, I need you to take Bea and Lara downstairs.' He goes to protest. 'Please. Please do this for me. Don't let them see what's on the table. Ask Jack to stay with them, and then when you come back, I will try to explain what's going on.'

'OK.'

I wait until he's crawled under the table to speak to the girls and then, without looking at the heart, I go to the front door and down the steps. I'm still holding my hands away from me. They're scrubbed clean, but the smell clings inside my nose. And I'm whimpering. I stagger towards the police car. They see me coming and are out of the car before I get that far. I don't trust myself to speak. I point towards the house and then turn so that they can follow me inside. I lead them into the kitchen and point at the table.

'What the . . .' Faraway, the younger of the two, visibly shivers when he sees the heart, a solid, bloody lump of muscle and sinew.

DS Baker looks at the heart, then back to me. 'This was delivered just now?'

I nod. My hands are shaking as I hand them the note. They both read it and then everything happens quickly. Faraway calls Mac and within ten minutes he arrives. Brisk and efficient, he takes a statement from me and from the policemen and then from Charlie. The forensic team arrive to deal with the heart. First of all, they take photographs and then they dust the packaging for prints, taking fingerprints from all of us to exclude us from the investigation.

The whole thing takes over three hours. In the middle of it all Wendy turns up. 'Claire, what on earth is going on?'

The kitchen out of bounds, we've all congregated in Jack's room. Lisa and I are on beanbags on the floor; Bea and Lara are lying on their fronts on the bed watching television; Charlie is pacing up and down. I've told him that this is the emailer taking the threat to the next level.

Jack, sitting cross-legged on his bed, has brought milk and cereal down from the kitchen. He is eating one bowl after the next, his noisy munching punctuated with questions: 'Why would someone send a heart to us?', 'How come that cop already knows you, Mum?' and 'What's this got to do with Dad's case?' To every question I say the same thing: 'When Dad gets back from London, we'll give you all the details.'

I answer Wendy's questions in the same way. She sits down on the chair at Jack's desk and looks around at us all. 'And where's Sezen?'

'She's . . . out.' I stand up. I know that Wendy will have questions lining up on her tongue, none of which I'll be able to answer to her satisfaction. 'I'm going upstairs to see how things are progressing.'

Charlie steps forward to come with me, but I shake my head. He sighs and throws himself down on the beanbag next to Lisa. I climb the stairs, my mind tormented with what I've just seen and read, the words 'Next time it will be your daughter's' flashing in neon letters in my mind – a headline that can't be ignored. All the more reason why I need to get the details from Mac.

He's at the top of the stairs finishing off a phone call. 'That was Julian. He's on his way back. The judge has upheld the anonymity order.'

It's what I expected but still it feels like another blow and I slump against the wall. 'Well, that's that, then,' I say.

'The trial date has been set for two weeks' time.'

Fourteen whole days. Unless I can put a stop to this we will be in a safe house, wondering at every footstep on the pavement or knock on the door. And then when the trial begins, how long will it be before the witness has given his testimony? One week? Two? Three?

'We finally got something out of Sezen.'

'Oh?'

'This bloke she's been protecting is called Jalal Khatib. He's an illegal immigrant and, what's worse, he owes money to a couple of heavies who live in North London.'

'But at the roundabout, he was the one who gave her money.'

'She puts a certain amount in a bank account. As well as paying off the heavies with cash, she sends money back to his parents in the Middle East.'

I raise my eyebrows at this.

'It's true,' Mac says. 'We've checked her bank statements.'

'What about the business of her having two passports?'

'She was born Sezen Serbest, Turkish but living in Bulgaria. In 1984 all Bulgarian nationals who were ethnically Turkish were ordered to exchange their names for Bulgarian ones or be forced to leave. Sezen translates to Sylvia and her father had to choose another surname. He chose Cyrilova.'

'Do you believe all this?'

'It's historically accurate.'

'So she was telling the truth when she told us she was Turkish?'

'In effect, yes.'

'It can't be legal to have two passports in two different names, surely?'

'No.' It's his turn to raise his eyebrows. 'But I'm in no mind to pursue it.'

'This business of the safe house . . .' I say.

'It'll be ready tomorrow.' He gives me a considered look. 'Is that what you wanted to talk to me about?'

'No.' I hold his eyes. 'I want to ask you for something.' I pause. 'I want you to help me.'

'I am helping you, aren't I?'

'Not enough.'

We're both leaning against the wall, sideways on to each other, our faces close. His eyes tell me that he gets my meaning. I feel the connection between us tighten a notch. 'I wondered whether we might get to that.'

One of the forensic team, dressed in a white boilersuit, comes out of the kitchen. Mac and I move apart.

'You almost done in there?' Mac asks him.

'Two minutes,' he says, and looks at me. 'Then we'll be out of your hair.'

'Thank you,' I say.

Mac moves off towards the kitchen, walking the first few steps backwards. 'Later?' he says.

I nod and go downstairs again.

Charlie is standing at the bottom. 'So Dad's on his way?'

'Yes.'

We go in to tell the others. More questions that I'm unable to answer, but I do reiterate that we'll be having the family meeting as soon as Julian is home.

'Should I be staying for that?' Wendy asks.

'I'd like you to.'

'Right . . . Well, in that case, with the kitchen clear, how about I make some sandwiches?'

'Great idea.'

We all troop upstairs again. I'm hanging back. Since the heart was delivered I've felt dizzy. I know I'm breathing too quickly, but I can't seem to stop. I stand outside on the step, holding on to the railings, and try to take slower, deeper breaths. I know my body is experiencing the flight-or-fight response, my blood pumped full of adrenaline and oxygen. But I have nowhere to run, and the person I'm fighting is still invisible to us.

The forensic team are now packing their equipment into their van. Baker and Faraway have been joined by another half a dozen policemen, all milling around on the pavement. Several passers-by look up at the house to try and work out what's going on. I don't acknowledge them. Instead, I turn my face up to the sky and watch two seagulls wrestle mid-flight over what looks like a crust of bread. The bigger, stronger one wins and flies off with the prize, while the smaller one squawks his defeat and glides down to the pavement, satisfied with pecking around in the gutter.

Another police car pulls up outside and Sezen climbs out. It's the first time I've ever seen her looking tired and unkempt. She comes up the steps, her face tight with an emotion that I take to be betrayal. I want to look away, but I don't. I don't believe that, under the circumstances, questioning her was unreasonable.

She stands in front of me. 'I have come for Lara and for our things.'

'Of course.' I take a breath. 'I'm sorry for what you've had to go through.'

'Are you?' Her expression is defiant.

'Yes, I am.' I hold my ground. If she hadn't been lying, she wouldn't have been under suspicion. 'Is your friend seeking asylum?'

'He spent eighteen months in a detention centre.'

'And then what?'

'He escaped.'

'Is he in danger if he goes home?'

She looks at me as if I'm stupid. 'Of course.'

'Why didn't you tell me this?' I take her arm. 'We're lawyers. If he needs asylum, we might be able to help you.'

'You expect me to trust you when it is clear you do not trust me?'

'It's not that simple. Bea is being threatened and you were hiding something. How was I to know that you're—'

'I am the foreigner, the one most likely to be involved.'

'I understand that you're angry.'

'You are not the one who has spent the night in a police cell.' Her tone is vicious and it makes me recoil. 'You know what, Sezen? Keep your pride; keep your anger.' I raise my hands and step out of her way. 'I simply don't have time for this.'

I stay at the front door while she marches inside. I count the seconds until Wendy appears.

'What's going on now? What's happening with Sezen? She seems very upset.'

'Wendy, please.' I fold my arms. 'It will all be explained soon.'

'Increased security,' Mac says, appearing at just the right time. He introduces himself, holding out a hand for Wendy to shake. 'And you must be the lovely Wendy. Claire tells me you're indispensible.'

'Well, I . . .'

He explains that the imminent trial has meant extra precautions. He manages to make it sound both serious and manageable. There's no question of Sezen and Lara being turned out, but not only is it better for them to go somewhere less hectic, it will keep things simple in this household too.

Wendy is visibly bowled over by his charm. She blushes and pats her hair at the point where the bob curls into her neck. 'Detective Inspector, would it help if I was to give Sezen a bed for the night?'

'That's very kind, but we have organised a quiet B and B for her.'

'I owe her money,' I say. 'I'll get my purse.'

Fortunately I have enough cash and I give it to Wendy. 'Would you mind passing it on to Sezen?'

I go back indoors. Bea is playing under the stairs. I give her a bowl of her favourite snack foods: a small bunch of grapes, slices of apple and cubes of cheese. She settles back on the cushions and switches on a talking book.

Mac introduces me to a female officer. She can't be more than twenty-five, dark hair, dark eyes. She's called Pam and she is to be our family liaison officer. I shake her hand. She is sincere, polite and sympathetic. She says all the right things about being there to support the family and understanding how hard this must be for us. She is trying hard to make a good first impression. I know the sort of briefing officers get when dealing with cases like this: eye contact is important, keep the family calm, explain everything slowly and carefully, only give information on a need-to-know basis.

Mac takes her through to the sitting room, where everyone is gathered: the boys, plus Lisa and Wendy. I hold back in the hallway, knowing that any second now Julian will walk through the front door. I start counting the seconds and only get as far as fifteen before his key is in the lock and he comes in.

'So no more emails today?' I blurt out straight away. Of course, he doesn't know that I've sent my own email, but I have been wondering whether the blackmailer would tell Julian I had written, just to further divide us.

He takes off his jacket and hangs it on one of the pegs inside the porch, his face turned away from me when he says, 'No.'

'Why do you think she hasn't replied to the one you sent her? The one that told her you no longer know where the witness is.'

'I don't know.' He throws me a look. 'Are you and the children OK?'

'A heart was delivered to the house today, Julian. *A heart.*'

'I heard.' He looks tired. Worse than that, he looks anxious, scared even.

Wendy comes out of the sitting room. 'Julian, you're home!' She kisses him on both cheeks. 'I'm going to bring through some tea and sandwiches. I've everything laid out on a tray. Won't take a moment.' She goes off to the kitchen.

'I don't suppose there was any need to send an email,' I say. 'The heart said it all. That was her reply.'

'According to the postmark, the heart was posted first thing yesterday morning. Before I sent the email.'

'So she was planning this all along?'

'Looks like it.'

'Daddy!' The curtain covering Bea's makeshift den moves aside and she hangs her head out. 'I'm in here!'

'So you are!' Julian bends down to kiss her.

'Lara's gone away now.'

'Has she?' He leans further into her den. 'And what are you up to in there?'

'Nothing for nosey folks,' she says, giggling, and abruptly pulls back the curtain.

Julian gives me a questioning look. 'Where did she learn that expression?'

'Jack. But listen.' I hold on to his lapels. 'The note she sent with the heart.' I give an involuntary shiver. 'She's not giving up, Julian.'

'It must have been a shock.'

'Truthfully? It's really shaken me up.'

He puts his arms round my waist and pulls me close. I see a glimmer of the old Julian, the one I can trust. It gives me hope that I won't have to go it alone, that he'll see how dangerous this is, act now and put the family first.

'It's the intent behind the note,' I say. 'Is this what happened to the Italian couple whose son was taken and murdered?'

'I don't know all the details.'

'Maybe not, but I think we both know that they had time to react, just like we have.' I lean into his chest. 'It's too much, Julian. This has gone far enough.'

'Mission accomplished!' Wendy is back with the tray. She gives us an appraising glance, then goes into the sitting room. I pull the door shut behind her.

'Julian, time is running out. We have to do something ourselves.'

'You're out of your depth with this, Claire.'

'I'm out of my depth?' I give a short laugh. 'We're all out of our depth! It's just that I'm the only one who can admit it.'

'I want Georgiev convicted.'

'I see.' I take a step back. 'Now we're getting to the nub of it.'

'Public office brings with it honour and responsibility. You know that!'

'You are Bea's *father*.'

'Will you stop this!' he hisses. 'You're making it black and white, as if we can't have Bea's safety without giving up on the witness.'

'Sometimes life *is* black and white.'

'Keeping Bea safe and winning the trial are not mutually exclusive. We can have both.'

'Not without risk.' I grind out the words. 'That's why we have to step back from this.'

'Are you two coming in?' Wendy appears again. She senses the atmosphere and looks uncertainly from me to Julian and back again. 'Everyone's waiting.'

Julian gives me a dismissive glare and we go into the sitting room. I sit down on the sofa next to Lisa. The mood is expectant. Nobody is talking apart from Wendy, who is passing around the plate of sandwiches. 'Your tea is on the table over there, Claire.'

I try to catch Julian's eye, but his elbow is on the mantelpiece, his chin is in his hand, and he is looking through the window. He is tapping his foot on the fire surround. I walk over for my tea and on the way back to my seat I place my hand on his back. No response. I sit down again.

'So.' Mac smiles around at us all. 'I'm going to kick off this meeting. At any time if anyone has a question, please feel free to ask it.'

Immediately Jack's hand goes up. 'I don't know why we're here.' He looks around the room. 'Does anybody?'

'That's what we're going to talk about,' Mac says. 'As you all know, Julian' – he looks at the boys – 'your dad, is working on an important case.'

'Pavel Georgiev?' Jack says. 'The Bulgarian Mafia guy?'

'Exactly,' Mac says. 'The prosecution has a watertight case,

but much of their evidence rests on a key witness. The identity
and whereabouts of this witness are being kept a secret.'

'Because Georgiev's men might get to him?' Jack says.

'That's right.' He glances across at Julian before he says, 'There's
no easy way to tell you all this. Georgiev's men have been sending
threatening emails and, as a precaution, you're going to be moving
to a safe house tomorrow.'

A second of silence and then several people speak at once.

'What sort of threats?'

'For how long?'

'Did you know about this, Claire?' Wendy says, her eyes wide
and fearful as if she's stumbled into something that's beyond her
comprehension.

'I haven't known for long,' I say.

Mac starts talking again. He explains about the emails. He says
they haven't been able to trace whoever is writing them, but their
suspicion is that she is a woman.

'So what's some woman going to do to us?' Jack says. 'There
are three men living here.'

Charlie gives him a sceptical look.

'I'm as strong as a man,' Jack says, and turns to Lisa for verifi-
cation.

'Absolutely,' she says.

'It's likely this woman is a professional,' Mac says, 'but if she
isn't, she will have help.'

'But what would she do?' Charlie says. 'If she was to get in, I
mean.'

Both boys are struggling to believe that a woman could pose
a real threat.

'Does she carry a gun?' Charlie says.

'More probably a knife,' I say. 'The emails indicate she carries
a knife and—'

'Claire!' It's the first time Julian has spoken. His voice is loud
and almost everyone jumps.

'What?' I challenge his stare. I know he thinks I'm about to give gory details from the Italian and Bulgarian cases. I'm not, but at the same time I think we need to be more direct. 'If we don't tell them the truth, they won't realise how serious it is,' I say. I look at both the boys. 'We know Georgiev has engineered at least two situations like this before where young women who were working for him infiltrated people's lives and committed murder.'

Wendy lets out a cry, her eyes wide and staring. Her lips move as she works it out and then her attention locks on to Mac. 'DI MacPherson, are the children, and Julian and Claire' – she takes a breath – 'are their lives in *danger*?'

Mac nods. 'Possibly.'

'How? Why?' Wendy's head jerks from side to side. 'What would someone gain from it?'

'The emailer wants information, Wendy. If she doesn't get it, she has threatened to kidnap Bea.' It's my voice again and this time Julian doesn't interrupt. 'Bea will be the easiest to take.'

'Little Bea?' Wendy's breathing is loud and fast as she struggles to take it in. 'She's just a baby.' She starts to cry and Pam, the family liaison officer, goes across to comfort her.

Julian gives me an are-you-happy-now look, which I don't feel I deserve. I stand up.

'Mum?' Charlie is pale, sober.

'I'm sorry, Charlie,' I say, 'but this is a very serious situation.'

'I could take on a woman!' Jack says. He jumps to his feet, his mouth trembling but his words full of bravado. 'Even if she does have a knife, I could still take her.'

'This is real life, Jack,' I say. 'Georgiev doesn't make mistakes. If he has sent her to do a job, she will be capable of it. It's extremely unlikely that anything you could come up with would stop her.'

'Dad? Don't you think we could take a woman?'

'Not in this case, no,' Julian says. 'It's important to Mum and me that it doesn't get that far.'

'So what can we do?' Lisa says, looking at Mac. 'In your experience how should we proceed from here?'

'As I mentioned, tomorrow we will be moving you to a safe house. This will mean that you won't be able to phone or see friends for a number of weeks.'

A great hullaballoo breaks out as Jack and, to a lesser extent, Charlie object to such stringency. Mac explains the reasons for this and I tune out, thinking instead about how soon I can be alone with Mac and put an end to all of this.

'The most important thing is for every one of us to be aware of safety,' Mac is saying. 'Keep the doors and the windows locked. Don't invite people home. Report anything unusual, anything at all, no matter how small or insignificant: a phone call, an email, somebody taking an unexpected interest in you.'

'But that means we're giving in,' Jack says. 'We shouldn't give in to intimidation.'

'Giving in would be handing her the witness,' Julian says. 'We're simply taking sensible precautions.'

Jack throws himself against the back of his seat. 'I still reckon I could take her.' He looks at his brother. 'Charlie? You and me, we could sort her out.'

Charlie, older and more realistic, turns to him. 'Just because she's a woman doesn't mean she won't be quick and strong.'

Wendy has stopped crying and says, 'I will cooperate in whatever way I can.'

Mac smiles at her. 'You won't be confined to barracks, but I would urge extreme caution.'

'The children won't be going out,' Julian says before I can voice the same thought.

Everyone looks at him.

'Non-negotiable.'

Jack says, 'Well, I was grounded anyway.' He sighs, then raises his mug of tea. 'Here's to a happy summer, everyone.'

'Any further questions?'

Silence as we all digest what we've just heard and then Bea comes into the room. '*Horrid Henry* is finished.' All eyes swivel to her. She's holding on to the front of her dress. 'And I need a wee,' she says, then, suddenly shy, runs to me and hides her face in my lap.

'I'll take you.' I stand up.

'Let me, Claire.' Wendy comes forward and takes Bea's hand. 'It'll let you get on with the packing.'

I take part in the charade of packing. We start in Jack's room. While I help Jack sort through his stuff, Bea sits on the bed watching *Finding Nemo*. A wire stretches from the television to a pair of earphones, which look enormous on her small head. They keep slipping down to her neck and she pushes them up again. Her lips are moving in time with the characters' speech. Every so often she waves her arm at Jack and points at the screen. He nods and gives her a thumbs-up and she goes back to watching.

'She can sleep in my bed, Mum,' Jack says. 'Charlie and I have decided that as long as she's with one of us, nothing can happen to her.' He puts a hand on her leg and she wriggles it off again. 'This woman, she'd have to have a whole frickin' army with her. There's no way anyone's getting my sister.' He stands in front of me, his expression sober. 'Seriously, though, Mum, maybe we should have a gun.'

'We don't know how to use a gun.' I hand him his boxers from the drawer. 'But the policewoman who's coming to live with us does, so she'll keep us safe.'

When Jack's organised, we go upstairs. I sit on Bea's bed and watch her fill a portable toy box. I've told her we're going off on holiday for a few weeks and she accepts this without question. Much time is taken up with deliberation. Bertie and the rest of her dogs are a must, and then we discuss the merits of taking her countryside scene, in which woollen sheep and lopsided shepherds are patrolling a green felt hillside, as opposed to her princess castle with the crenulated roof and drawbridge. She plumps for the shepherds because 'They'll get lonely.'

Then it's her turn to sit on the bed and I pack a suitcase of clothes for her. I hold up her tops and skirts and trousers and she mimics Jack by giving me a thumbs-up or -down. She has her shoes and socks off and is curling her toes under. Her feet are broad, her toes small and perfectly formed. At the moment her toenails are painted a vivid pink. Wendy did it for her. She rubs her heels on the cover and then touches her big toes together. Out of nowhere I get this sudden and overwhelming feeling that this woman will take her. No matter what precautions we come up with, this woman will get her. Dizziness creeps up from my feet and fills my head with flashing lights and sickness. I go into the landing and crouch down with my back against the wall.

'Are you OK, Mum?' Charlie sees me from his room and comes across.

I grit my teeth. 'I'm OK. I'm fine. Actually' – I reach for his hands and he pulls me upright – 'I'm going to go out for a bit. Dad's downstairs and Lisa's there and the police are outside.' I look out of the window to check that's true and see them walking backwards and forwards on the pavement. 'I need some air.'

'Mummy!' Bea shouts.

'Will you be OK?' he says. 'Do you want me to come?'

'I'll be fine.' I stroke his cheek. 'Would you put Bea to bed for me?'

'Yeah. No probs.'

We both go back into her room and I tell her I'm going out. 'But what about my packing?' She is standing on the bed and her head is almost level with ours.

'Charlie will help you.'

'He doesn't know about girls' clothes.' She brings her arm across her chest. They're not long enough to fold, but she makes a good job of trying.

'I do,' Charlie says. 'Amy taught me.'

She pulls her chin into her neck and frowns. 'Are you sure?'

'Yeah. I'm good.' He comes into her room and picks up her pink hooded sweatshirt. 'This is a key piece in any girl's wardrobe.' He holds it up to himself. 'Does it suit me?'

She starts to giggle. I kiss her cheeks, give Charlie a grateful smile and head down the stairs. It's after nine. Mac will be home by now. I stop in the hallway to put on my shoes.

'You're going out?'

I jump. 'Julian, you scared me.' I look up from tying my laces. 'Why are you standing in the shadows?'

'Lisa and I are chatting.'

He steps forward and I see Lisa's there too. At once I feel guilty. I haven't been looking after her the way I wanted to. She has dark shadows under her eyes. 'I'm sorry, Lisa.' I reach for her hands. They are cold to the touch and I rub them in mine. 'I want to look after you better and I will. I just need to pop out for a bit.'

'It's OK. I know how upsetting this is.' She clears her throat. 'Do you really think you should be going out? It's late and it's raining again.'

'I know, but I just need some time.'

'Julian and I both feel . . .' She glances at Julian before she says, 'You have a lot to cope with right now.'

'Yes, I do.'

'Claire, we all need to be on the same page here.'

'Whoa! Hold on a minute.' I look at Julian, then back to her. 'What is this? Some sort of ambush?'

'We're both worried about you.'

'Worried about *me*? Why? It's Bea you should be worried about.'

'You're talking to yourself. You're distracted. Your nails – look at them! You never normally chew your nails.'

'Well, thanks a bunch, Lisa,' I say. 'My daughter's in danger and you expect me to be looking good.'

'No, no, sweetheart, that isn't what I mean.' She strokes my hair. It feels comforting and I lean into her hand. 'It's just that Julian and I care for you and we want to help.'

I pull away. 'Is that right?' I look up at the ceiling and then straight at Julian. 'You keep this a secret for more than a week, you resign, and you make a critical decision about the witness details without talking to me first. That's caring, is it?' He doesn't speak. 'And now you've roped in my sister.'

'Claire!' Lisa steps forward. 'It's not like that. At times like this we can't risk not working as a team.'

'Which makes it a great pity that my husband couldn't be honest with me in the first place.'

'Honesty?' Julian says, temper simmering in his eyes. 'We stopped being honest with each other a long time before this.'

'Meaning?'

'Lisa, would you excuse us for a minute?' Julian says.

She nods her head and goes off into her room.

'Round about the time you decided to have sex with someone else,' he says.

'That was five years ago. Once.' I hold up my right index finger. 'One mistake. I know it was stupid and pathetic, and I know I hurt both of us, but I—'

'You think I could just forget about that?' He moves in close. 'You think it's easy to listen to your wife tell you she had sex with someone else? Good sex, I seem to recall.'

'I never said that.'

His look is scathing. 'You didn't have to.'

'You're bringing this up *now*?' I can't believe this. 'You're shutting me out because five years ago I had one misguided moment? Is that what you're saying?'

'The glue that keeps a relationship together is loyalty and trust. You broke that trust.'

'This is not the time to have this conversation.' I shake my head. 'I know the last few years have brought more than our fair share of stresses, but it's not as bad as you're making out, and if you were still hurt, then why didn't you say something?'

'What was there to say?' He looks up at the ceiling and ponders. 'I wish you hadn't done it? I wish I didn't have images of my wife with another man? I wish I'd been enough for you?'

'You are enough for me.' I sigh. 'You always have been.' I shrug my shoulders and give him a sorry smile. 'But this.' I wave my arms around. 'Our family's disintegrating. Our safety is under threat and *you can't see it.*'

He leans back against the wall and folds his arms. 'Where are you going, Claire?'

I consider storming off or simply fudging my answer, but this is the problem with being married to a barrister – he doesn't tolerate convenient misunderstandings. He gets to the nub of problems, terrier-like, and doesn't let go until he's satisfied with the answer. So just as I did last night in bed, I lie to him, barefaced and with conviction. 'I'm going out for a drive to clear my head. I plan to park at the seafront, sit in the car and listen to music.' I move in closer, still holding his eyes. 'I'm sorry that neither you nor Lisa has faith in me, but I'm dealing with this in the only way I know how and at the moment I need a couple of hours alone before I'm cooped up in a safe house.'

I take my car keys off the hook. 'I'm setting the alarm. The code, should you need to go out, is 2949. Charlie's putting Bea to bed.'

On the way down the steps, I speed-dial Mac's number. 'I need to see you.'

'I'm at home.'

I climb in the car. 'I can come to you.'

'OK.' He gives me his postcode. I key it into my sat nav.

'I'm setting off now,' I say, and start the engine.

18

The drive to Mac's house takes about fifty minutes. He lives halfway between London and Brighton, close to a small village on the edge of the Ashdown Forest. The road is a twisty, turny affair with hedgerows either side and farmed fields rolling off into the distance. Then all at once the scenery changes as I come up onto the forest and see signs for deer. I keep my speed within the limit. I know that deer roam freely and the last thing I need to do is have an accident.

The sun is setting, and the moon is hidden behind dirty great clouds that threaten more rain. I keep my car headlights on full beam and mull over my latest argument with Julian. They say a crisis shows up all the holes in a relationship and that's certainly happening to us. I thought I'd been forgiven. I knew he'd never forget what I'd done, but I thought we'd put it a long way behind us. We have a lot of miles on the clock, after all. Sex with Mac couldn't have lasted more than ten minutes and yet the repercussions have rippled into the last five years. With Julian, it seems, operating a 'one strike and you're out' policy. Never again to be trusted. Never again to be considered honest, and yet the reason he knows about it at all is because I was honest. I don't keep secrets. I've only ever told him two lies and both of those were in the last twenty-four hours. A week ago I would never have believed myself capable of such a thing, and under normal circumstances I would be saddened by this, but at the moment I don't have time to fix my marriage. It's just another problem stacking up behind the critical one: the threat of Bea's kidnap. I have no intention of leaving Mac's house tonight without the witness

details. I'll break all my own rules and more to put an end to
this.

I leave the main road and drive for almost a mile down a
bumpy track to his house. The outside lights are on, illuminating
a character cottage sympathetically extended to twice its original
size. It's set in what looks to be over an acre of ground and my
first thought is, You don't get this on a policeman's salary. My
second is that the money must come from his wife and it looks
like she's there to greet me as there's a woman standing at the
front door. She's wearing flat leather boots with jeans tucked in
below her knees, a white T-shirt and a camel-coloured suede
jacket. Her smile is wide, her teeth perfectly white and straight.
She looks like an advert for healthy living.

I climb out of my car and approach the front door just as Mac
appears alongside her.

'This is my wife, Donna,' he says. 'Donna, this is Claire.'

'Hi! How are ya?' She holds out her hand.

She is American. Blonde and leggy, almost six feet tall, she
oozes sunshine and blue skies even on a cold and cloudy night
when the wind is whipping through the trees.

'Pleased to meet you.' I shake her hand and admire the cottage,
with its slate roof and leaded windows, and then around at the
clutch of silver birches to the side of the parking area. 'This is a
lovely spot.'

'Even better in the daytime. You must come.' She widens clear
blue eyes. 'Mac tells me you two were colleagues once.'

'Yes.' I smile. The skin on my face feels dry, tight and salty
like it's about to crack.

'Well . . .' She kisses him. She takes her time. It's a hands-off-my-
man kiss. 'I'll leave you to it.' She strides towards her car and
starts the engine.

Mac ushers me into a hallway with exposed stone walls and
wooden beams. The floor is highly polished oak with an expensive-
looking rug leading to the large living room at the end. Just
before we reach it, he heads off at an angle into the kitchen.

Bespoke oak units, topped by marble work surfaces, hug the walls, which are tiled a deep blue, interspersed at intervals with friendly tiled depictions of the sun, moon and stars in a contrasting yellow shade. And there are small oil paintings dotted around, the images indistinct splashes of colour on canvas. It feels welcoming and homely.

'Tea? Coffee? Or something stronger?'

'Tea's fine,' I say. 'This is beautiful workmanship.' I run my hand along one of the cupboard doors.

'The carpenter was in and out for almost three months building it. Weekends as well. Almost drove me nuts.'

'Beats the bachelor flat in Islington.'

He smiles.

'It's late for Donna to be going out, isn't it?'

'She's doing an all-night yoga session. Breathing. Meditation.' He shrugs. 'It's all going on around here.'

'She's not how I imagined.'

'Isn't she?'

'She's perky. She's glamorous.' I pause before adding, 'She's American.'

'Now, now.' He pretends to look offended. 'Let's not be prejudiced.'

'I thought you'd have married someone . . .' I stop to think.

'Hard-bitten like myself?'

'No, but . . . you're all sardonic humour and irony, which Americans don't get. Or is that just a rumour?'

'Mm.' His head goes from side to side as if he's weighing it up. 'I'm working on her.' He hands me a mug of tea. 'She lives in a world where people are good and do good things.'

I narrow my eyes. 'And does she know what you do for a living?'

'She doesn't think career choice defines a person.'

'No, it doesn't, but after a while you become the company you keep.'

'Maybe.' He's staring at me as if figuring something out. The dishwasher hums quietly in the background. Seconds tick by. I find I can't hold his gaze and look away.

'Let's go through.' He sets off along the hallway, past the front door and into a blokeish den, decorated in cream, with a browny-grey speckled carpet, a battered leather couch against one wall and a huge antique pine table, close to ten feet long. There's a flat-screen monitor and keyboard at one end of the table and the rest of the surface is covered in books and papers. But it's the jazz memorabilia on the walls that makes it Mac's space. It's always been his passion, his escape from the dirt and grind of police work. With some cops, it's fishing; with others, football; for Mac, it's jazz: playing it, listening to it or travelling miles to see his favourites. My eyes are drawn to a poster of John Coltrane, signed with a flourish by the man himself.

'He died the year I was born,' Mac tells me. 'He worked with Elvin Jones, a jazz drumming legend.' He whistles through his teeth. 'But before I slip on my anorak' – he gestures towards the couch – 'take a seat. Tell me why you're here.'

I sit down and try to relax into the leather couch, worn soft and accommodating by years of bodies. I've thought about this: what I'll say first, what I'll say only if it becomes absolutely necessary, but now that I'm here, I find I can't remember my lines and so I say the first thing that comes into my head: 'Are you and Donna thinking of having children?'

'We've been trying.'

'It's fun trying, isn't it?'

'I think it's better fun without the trying.'

'The trying is trying.'

'Very.' He makes a face. 'Thermometers and timing and eating the right food.'

'But you want a baby. The miracle of your own child?'

He nods. 'I really do.'

'Do you remember the first case we worked on together?'

'Marcia Green, November 1995. You'd only just started at the CPS and I was cutting my teeth on my first murder.'

'Five years old and murdered by her neighbour. We went to the funeral and . . .' I pause and think about that day, sunshine and blue skies, everyone sweltering in black suits, a small white coffin covered in roses, her parents unable to stand, their backs bent as if they'd been whipped, and when they did look up, the expression in their eyes was of such stark desperation that no one could hold their gaze for long. '. . . and as we stood there under the blazing sun, I remember exactly what you said to me. You said, "There's nothing worse than losing a child."'

I see from his eyes that he hasn't forgotten this.

'Mac, I need you to give me the witness information because if something happens to Bea, I won't have a life any more.'

'Claire.' He lengthens my name, sounding out the letters. He's standing opposite me in front of the table. He folds his arms and looks up at the ceiling. When he looks back at me, it's with regret. 'You know that isn't possible. It would ruin the chances of bringing Georgiev to justice.'

'It doesn't have to. Think about it. At the moment she's coming after my daughter and you're spending time and money protecting us. What if she does know where the witness is? Protect him instead. Double his security. Lock him up in a cell, if need be. Surely that's fairer than what's happening now, an innocent child caught up in it because of her father's job.'

'The law doesn't look at it that way.'

'But you can,' I say quietly. 'I know you. Your belief in the system only goes so far and in that we're alike.' I pause. 'You know when to break it and when to keep it.'

He looks down at his feet and gives a half-smile. 'Have you tried to get the information out of Julian?'

'Yes. Last night he told me the witness had been moved. Is that true?'

He nods.

'And Julian doesn't know where he is.'

'Also true.'

'Was that your suggestion?'

'It was his.'

'Do you know where the witness is?'

'Yes.' He comes across and sits alongside me on the sofa, his body sideways, one leg pulled up. I mirror him, so that we're facing each other, our knees almost touching.

'Are you going to tell me?' I say quietly.

'This witness is key, Claire. Georgiev will walk free without him.'

'I know. I've thought it through. I've turned it every which way in my head. But Bea is a little girl. She deserves protection.'

'There are policemen front and back. They're carrying firearms. They're trained to react.' He rubs his eyes. 'And the safe house is ready. We can move you there tonight if you'd prefer.'

I change tack. 'Julian is an idealist. He believes in the system in a way that I never have. As a couple, we've never been tested like this before, but here we are in two separate camps – he's on the side of the justice system, while I stand up for our family. Rationally, of course, I understand his position, but in my heart . . .' I shake my head. 'What he's doing is wrong.'

'Good men like Julian are important to our justice system.'

'I know.' I nod. 'And I love that about him. But in this case . . .' I take a deep breath. 'Julian's background is very different from mine or yours. His dad was a diplomat in Africa so Julian and his siblings were ferried to and from boarding schools in England. In some ways it was a chaotic household but there was always lots of love and with that love came security. Nowadays, his brothers and sisters are all married and successful. Their families are thriving. Both his parents are alive and well, and after almost fifty years together they still hold hands. Julian is privileged, and not because he went to Eton, but because he's never suffered. He knows nothing about loss and about the finality of death.' I shrug. 'He's lucky. He has confidence in the world. He hasn't been hurt.' I take a drink of my tea, almost drain the cup. 'You and I, on the other hand, we're alike. We know life goes belly up for the best of people.' I raise my voice.

'I need the witness information and I won't leave until you give it to me.'

His eyebrows lift at this, the look on his face a warning for me not to overstep the mark. My confidence falters and then I think about a particular phrase from the emails – *Mostly I favour the knife . . . Sometimes I enjoy making it slow*. I won't let someone like that near my child. I sit up straighter and stare back at him. I feel sad for the state of my marriage, and I feel guilty that I am aiming to sabotage the trial, but both these feelings are dwarfed by the reality of the risk to Bea.

'I will owe you, big time. I know that. I won't tell anyone how I came by the information. I'll email it from my own laptop directly to her email address. I can't lose my child and I'm not convinced that we can adequately protect her. It's two weeks until the trial starts and longer than that before he's given his evidence. Four weeks, a month, thirty whole days without a slip-up? It's too risky.' I swallow the last of my tea. 'And if you need any more convincing, then you must know that I will report you for falsifying records that led to Abe Martin's conviction.'

I say all this in a flat tone because for the first time since I opened the parcel with the heart in it I feel completely calm. Mac is still eyeballing me. No facial expression. Nothing. Years of being a policeman gives most cops an unreadable expression that they can use at will, but with Mac I suspect he's always been this way. His Scottish ancestry has given him a tough exterior.

'We can play the game of you resisting and me pushing, if you like,' I say, 'but I'm not going to leave here until you tell me.'

More silence. I wait.

'Abe Martin murdered Kerry Smith,' he says slowly. 'He was guilty as fuck. You know it and I know it.'

'You're a policeman, an upholder of the law, and yet you broke it. You broke several laws, in fact. And those offences could not only have you sacked but also prosecuted. Maximum sentence five years in prison.' I blow out some air. 'It's a hard life for a policeman in prison.'

'You're threatening me?'

'Yes.'

'And here I was thinking you would offer yourself to me.'

'A repeat of what we did after Kerry's funeral?' I smile. 'Would you like that?'

He looks me up and down. 'Would you?'

'Yes.'

'But only if I give you the details?'

'I would like it anyway.'

He leans in close and kisses me lightly on the lips. 'I don't believe you.'

'You want me to prove it?' My lips are tingling and there's heat in my stomach.

'No, I don't want you to prove it.' He leans in again and this time he kisses me properly, his tongue persuading its way into my mouth. It's fiery and intense and I feel the effects of it in my toes.

'You have balls, Claire. I'll give you that.'

'Look me in the eye and tell me you wouldn't do the same.'

'For my child?' He leans back and thinks about it. 'By now I'd have you strung up by the heels. I'd torture it out of you if that's what it took.'

My heart stops. 'Then you'll give it to me?'

'Yes.' He's staring right into my eyes. 'But not because you threatened me. I'll give you the details because my gut feeling is that I should. And I learned a long time ago that I'm no policeman at all if I can't listen to that.' He stands up. 'You know that people will assume the leak came through Julian?'

'Yes.' I can barely breathe. I hover beside him as he writes a name and address down on a piece of paper. He holds it out to me. I read it and put it in the pocket of my jeans. 'Thank you.' I blink and tears run down my cheeks. 'Thank you so, so much.'

'You're welcome. Now go.' He turns me round. 'Do your worst.'

I walk ahead of him to the front door, and when I open it, there's a stag standing outside. Over six feet tall, he is silent and noble and completely unfazed by the sight of Mac and me.

'Gorgeous, isn't he?' Mac speaks quietly into my ear. 'People say they're pests because they eat everything in the garden, but I love seeing deer. They remind me that there is a world beyond the city and police work.'

'Beautiful.' I take deep breaths of the night air and let my lungs fill with not just oxygen but also the sense of peace and time-lessness that the forest and the deer embody. We move towards my car and the stag turns slowly towards the trees. I climb in and say one last thank-you to Mac before I begin the drive home. Now that I have what I need, I feel the tension begin to dissolve into my bones. I'm not home and dry yet, of course. I still have to send her the email. I'll have to do it behind Julian's back, and heaven knows what will happen if he finds out, but the main thing is that Bea will be safe. She comes first.

The journey home takes twice as long as it should. There's been an accident – a four-wheel drive has knocked someone off their bike and the ambulance is blocking the road – and the few of us who're travelling this late are sent the long way round. It gives me time to acknowledge the question that's lurking in the corner of my mind: is it my imagination or did Mac give over the information a bit too easily? Shouldn't I have had to wrestle it out of him? Has he given me a bogus name and address?

The very thought that he could be playing me for a fool sends freezing-cold shivers through my sternum. My mind conjures up a scenario in which Mac is now ringing Julian, telling him that I've been given false information to keep me busy. The little woman with her fears and mistrust has been dealt with.

As my heart races and anger bites, I quickly realise that I can't afford to entertain such doubt. It's distracting. I need all my energy to be directed towards Bea's safety. I can't afford to be too suspicious or too paranoid. It won't help. I have to take this tip-off at face value and act on it.

I drive home as quickly as I can, but still, I'm dismayed to find that time has run ahead of me and I've missed my midnight deadline. When I arrive back into our street, it's almost one in the morning. There's no movement apart from a dark blue Fiat that pulls away from the kerb. I automatically clock the registration. I even go so far as to write it down on a used parking ticket that's sitting in a hollow in the dashboard. Then I step out of the car and pull my cardigan around me. A freezing wind is blowing, spiteful as a witch, fingering my clothes and lifting my hair. I run up the steps and am at the top before I realise that Baker and Faraway are missing. They are working a double shift and were here when I left. And they're not supposed to leave their posts. I look down the street but can't see any sign of them. And then I hear the sound of footsteps and watch as the two policemen who were patrolling the back of the house run into the street. They have their firearms out and are using their radios.

Fear grips my throat. I step into the porch. The lights on the console are unlit because the alarm has been switched off. I push open the inside door and in the dim light see what looks like someone lying on the floor. I run towards it and slide on a wet patch, crashing down hard on my elbow.

Lights! Lights! I say to myself, get up on my knees and then my feet, grope along the wall and switch on the light. I blink. There are fingerprints in red paint on the wall and the light switch. And there's red paint on my hands. I stare at them. It's not paint. It's blood. Ruby red, crimson, scarlet. Human blood. There's a gurgling noise behind me. I turn round and see that the person lying on the floor is Julian. His hand is clutching at the side of his throat as blood escapes through his fingers. I drop to my knees beside him and place my hands where his are, feel his pulse, each beat sending a further spurt of blood out of his body and into my hands.

'Help!' I shout. 'Help us!'

Lisa's bedroom door opens and she comes out, gives a howl of disbelief.

'Call an ambulance,' I'm shrieking. 'Now. Quickly.'

She runs to the kitchen for the phone just as the light goes on at the top of the stairs and Charlie almost flies down.

'Get me a towel,' I shout.

He's staring. His mouth open, eyes like saucers.

'Now!' I scream. 'Do it.'

He gets one from the downstairs bathroom and I pull it tight round the cut, afraid that to pull it too tight will mean Julian won't be able to breathe but not tight enough and he will bleed to death. I press some more but still he bleeds. I watch the towel redden. 'No, no, no, no, no.'

Lisa appears at my side and sobs as she and Charlie cling to each other. 'I don't understand,' she says. 'I didn't hear a thing.'

Julian's eyes are still open but only just. His face and cheeks are now a blue-grey colour. He is losing too much blood. He tries to speak – no words, just more blood, coming from his mouth this time.

'Don't talk,' I say. 'The ambulance is coming. Don't be afraid. We have time. You're going to be OK.' And then I see what he's trying to tell me. It's written in his eyes. 'Sweet Jesus.' My hands start to shake, but I don't let go of the towel. 'Charlie, go upstairs and check that Bea's in her bed.'

'Mum.' His voice cracks.

'Do it.' I look back at my husband. 'Julian, you have to hang on.' His eyes are closing. I watch his tears run down into the blood. 'Don't you dare die. Do you hear me? Look at me. I will not lose you. I. Will. Not. Lose. You.' His eyes flutter open again. 'Good,' I say. 'You keep looking at me. You keep doing that.'

I am split in two. My eyes are with Julian; my ears are with Charlie. I hear him upstairs, turning on every light, going into every room. When he arrives back at my side, he cries out, 'She's not in the house, Mum. Bea's not here.'

I am pitched into a dark and dreadful place. My worst fear has been realised. Bea has been taken. I am too late. The black-mailer has moved quicker than I thought she would. I have let my daughter down.

Charlie is gulping back uncontrolled sobs, his body shaking so much he can barely stand, and Jack is with him, hanging on to the back of Charlie's T-shirt, looking terrified. I want to join them both and huddle together and let go to the despair inside me. But I can't.

'Boys, put on some warm clothes, then go into the sitting room and stay there.' I turn my head to shout to Lisa, 'Take my phone from my back pocket. Press number two and then the green key. It's Mac's number. Tell him what's happening.' I look down at Julian. His eyes are shut. I don't think he's breathing. 'No, Julian, please.' I put my face close to his. 'You can't leave me. Please, please. Fight. Fight hard.' I want to kiss him, shake him, bully him awake and alive, but I have to keep my hands on his neck.

Then I hear steps outside and I scream, 'In here!'

The paramedics push their way inside, urgency dictating their speech and their movements. I stand up. I stand back. I watch them. They move in synchrony. One cuts away Julian's clothes and shocks his heart as the other stems the flow of blood. Another two paramedics arrive and three of them work on Julian while the fourth calls back to base, 'Adult male. Serious knife wound to right side of throat. Lost a lot of blood. We're stabilising him now. ETA ten minutes.' He looks at me. 'Do you know his blood type?'

'He's O positive,' I say. 'He had his appendix out ten years ago. We found out then.'

'And you're his wife?'

I nod. 'His name is Julian Miller.' I'm watching the heart monitor. They shock him a third time and his heart starts to beat for itself. Relief washes through me. One second at a time, I tell myself. Take each second. Live it. Don't look ahead.

Lisa appears at my elbow dressed in jeans and a sweater. 'Are you going to the hospital with Julian?' she asks me.

I nod my head and then immediately shake it as I remember that I still have to send the email. It's not too late. I have the details the blackmailer wants. I can negotiate. I can get Bea back. I'm torn between going with Julian and staying here. I don't want to leave Julian's side, but at the same time I need to let the blackmailer know that I have the details.

Lisa sees my indecision and says, 'I can go to the hospital with Julian. If you want to stay here . . . with the boys . . . and in case Bea comes home.' She holds my wrist tight. 'Mac is on his way.' She tightens her grip. 'Claire—'

'Don't say it,' I whisper. 'Don't even think it.'

She kisses me on both cheeks and then goes to stand by the door. The paramedics lift Julian on to a stretcher. They've stuck patches to his chest attached to leads that connect to a heart monitor. There's an oxygen mask covering his face and IV lines with fluids going into either arm. I walk with the stretcher as far as the door and say into his ear, 'I love you, Julian. I'll get Bea back.' I kiss his waxen cheek. 'I'll find her.' I stand on the step as they slide the stretcher on to the ambulance. Lisa climbs into the back beside him and they close the door.

The police and ambulance services are arriving in force. They're out of their vehicles, their headlights left on, so that the street is flooded with light. My eyes scan the whole scene and then I look down the steps and to the side where there's a gate leading down to the basement level. Faraway is lying on the ground in a puddle of blood. He is surrounded by paramedics. It looks like he has also had his throat cut but help has come too late. The heart monitor is registering a continuous line and the paramedics are packing up their equipment. I hold on to the railings to steady myself. Such a waste of a young life. I daren't think about the anguish his family will have to endure, nor can I think about Julian's condition and what will happen if he deteriorates. I have to send the email. Right now.

I run inside and downstairs to Julian's study. I log myself on to my laptop. My hands and clothes are stained with Julian's blood. Some of it has already dried and flakes on to the keyboard. I want to wash it off. I hear myself moan. I catch hold of the hysteria building in my chest.

Not now. The voice inside my head is stern, like a schoolteacher. I'm grateful for that. I make the effort to listen. *Email first.*

I type in the blackmailer's address and write:

I have the witness's name and whereabouts. I will give you the details. Do not harm my daughter.

I add my mobile-phone number and then I press 'Send' and watch the screen change to 'Message sent'.

Right. OK. What now? I run back upstairs and, sidestepping the blood on the floor, up another flight to my bedroom. No time for a shower, I strip off my clothes as far as my underwear and go into the en suite. I catch a fleeting glimpse of someone in the mirror. Me. The sight makes me gasp. Putty for skin, startled eyebrows and huge, flickering eyes. And there's a bloodstain on my cheek, like a livid birthmark spreading from chin to eye socket. I look away, repeating like a mantra, Hold it together. You can do this. Just hold it together.

I run the tap. I use soap to scrub my hands and my face, and watch Julian's blood turn pink in the water as it rushes towards the plughole. I grab a towel and quickly dry myself, back into clean clothes and down the stairs. *Next. What's next?* I remember I gave my mobile phone to Lisa. I find it in her room, slip it into my pocket and go to Charlie and Jack. They're sitting next to each other on the sofa, dressed in jeans and hoodies. Jack is completely still, as if he's been placed in a trance. Charlie is agitating his legs up and down.

'Boys?'

They both look up at me, painfully, as if their eyes are sore.

'Dad is on his way to hospital. Bea has been kidnapped, but we will get her back.'

Charlie jumps to his feet. 'We could go out on our bikes,' he says. 'Cycle around. We might see something.'

'I want you both here,' I say. He goes to protest. 'I promise that if Mac says we need to go out on the streets looking for her, then that's what we'll do. In the meantime we're going to stay here. That's an order.'

Jack nods; Charlie paces.

'Charlie.' I remember the dark blue Fiat. 'Go outside to my

car.' I tell him where to find the used parking ticket. 'Bring it back to me.'

He runs off. I sit down next to Jack and hug him. He clings to me, his face buried in my neck, his arms squeezing me tight. I cup my hands around his face and look him in the eye. 'We'll get through this. We will.'

I leave him on the sofa and go back to the front door. The street is teeming with police and the immediate area in front of our house is now cordoned off with incident tape. Mac has arrived. He's nodding his head as two policemen give him details. He sees me and comes running up the steps.

'Claire.' His eyes are full of concern. He catches sight of the blood on the floor behind me. 'Fuck.' He leans forward to touch me and I step back from him.

'Are Baker and Faraway dead?' I say.

He nods. 'They had their throats cut.'

'Jesus.' I briefly drop my head, then look back at Mac. 'I hope I got to Julian in time. Lisa's gone to the hospital with him.' I say this quite calmly, as if it isn't a matter of life and death to me. I don't know where I'm finding the strength. 'I've sent the blackmailer an email telling her I have the information she wants.' I take the parking ticket from Charlie's hand as he comes inside. 'Here.' I give it to Mac and tell him what it is. 'It must have been her in the car, leaving as I arrived home, otherwise Julian would have been . . . gone.' I take a steadying breath. 'He must have let her in. He had to have put the alarm off. Apart from me, he was the only person who knew the code.' I think. 'Maybe she was holding a knife to the policeman's throat.'

Mac shakes his head. 'Julian wouldn't have opened the door.'

'So he must have known her.'

We both stare at each other, thinking. Sezen? Jem? In the park, pretending they were being attacked? Would he open the door if a woman were screaming for help?

'We'll find out. The CCTV at your front door is being checked,' Mac says. Then, 'Is that Julian's phone?'

I follow his eyes. Julian's BlackBerry is lying under the table in the hallway. I pick it up.

'See who called him last.'

I scroll through and find the name. 'Megan,' I say. 'At half past midnight.'

Mac's eyes narrow. He takes the phone from me and calls her. It goes straight to the answering service.

'Megan?' My mind tries to engage. 'Has someone taken her too?' A dizzy blindness settles behind my eyes. 'My God! Do you think she was forced to help the blackmailer?' My ears are ringing. 'Julian would open the door to Megan. He trusts her.' The hallway slumps to one side and I slump with it. Mac catches me before I hit the floor. He leans me up against the wall.

'Do you need to sit down?'

'No.' I hold myself as straight as I can. 'I'm just trying to keep up.' My brain is spooling through a scenario – Megan waking up to find someone in her bedroom, one of Georgiev's heavies holding a gun to her head so that she is forced to ring Julian. Then she's dragged out in the middle of the night. Julian opens the door, and the heavies push in behind her. Bea is taken.

I give a convulsive shiver. 'This just gets worse and worse.'

'I have the tape.' A policeman comes into the hallway. He's carrying the tape from the CCTV camera. 'We have clear views of the three people who came to the door.'

We watch it in Julian's study. At five minutes before one, the policeman on duty goes down the steps. Thirty seconds later Megan comes to the front door. The front door opens. I'm unable to see Julian's face as he is below the camera, but Megan's is in clear view. It's her. And she doesn't look as if she's been coerced. In fact she seems as relaxed and confident as ever. And then, as she comes inside, two men dressed in black take the steps two at a time and push their way into the house behind her. Two minutes pass and then all three come out. Megan is carrying a sleepy Bea, whose head is draped over her shoulder. I let out a cry and Mac throws me a worried glance. Another minute goes by and then I appear on the steps, looking first bewildered and then afraid.

'I need to go to the bathroom,' I say. I leave Julian's study and go back upstairs. I lock myself in the toilet. I start to shake. It begins in my hands and feet, and spreads up my limbs and into my torso. My legs buckle and I slide down the back of the door on to the floor tiles. I don't know how long I lie there, my limbs shaking as if in the throes of some dreadful neurological sickness, but when it finally subsides, I crawl on my hands and knees to the toilet and hang my head over it. I empty out the contents of my stomach, retching and retching until there's nothing left except a solid nugget of anger. I stand up and rinse my mouth out with water, then look at myself in the mirror. My face looks different from before. I still look pale, but I no longer look startled. I look determined.

Megan Jennings is more English than Julian. She outclassed several other ambitious solicitors to become part of his team. She has spent long days working for the Crown, for Queen and country.

Megan Jennings has sat at my dinner table and eaten my food.

And now it appears that Megan Jennings is the blackmailer. She was present while two policemen were murdered. She watched as Julian had his throat cut and was left for dead.

Megan Jennings has kidnapped my daughter.

19

Lisa calls me from the hospital. 'Julian's just gone into surgery. He's holding on, Claire. He's holding on.'

Thank God.

'Any word of Bea?'

Her voice wavers, tremulous as an old lady's. It prompts a strangling feeling in my throat and I pull my sweater away from round my neck. It doesn't help me breathe any easier. 'Nothing yet,' I say. 'I'm coming to the hospital. I'll be there within the hour.'

Mac has persuaded me that there's nothing I can do here. He promises to keep me updated. The boys are still in the living room. I suggest that they watch a video or play games, anything to help take their mind away from what's happening.

'I just want to *do* something, Mum,' Charlie says, still pacing. 'I just want to help. Anything. It doesn't matter how small.'

I understand. I feel the same way. I ask Mac whether he has anything for Charlie to do. He tells him to go through Julian's emails and papers to see if there's a clue to suggest where Megan has alternative accommodation. The police have been to her flat round the corner and it's empty – completely empty. It looks like she knew her cover would be blown after tonight and has taken all her possessions. And up in Hertfordshire, her parents have been pulled from their beds and brought in for questioning.

Every couple of minutes my hand strays to my back pocket to feel for my phone. It's still there. No call yet. And in my other pocket is Julian's BlackBerry. I'll be able to check for emails on that. But will she even read, never mind reply to, the one I've sent her? I'm not sure. So I leave her a phone message as well. Let her know that I have the witness's identity and whereabouts. Although Mac's already established she's not answering it, she might be picking up messages. I can only hope. I can only hope that she'll try to negotiate her way out of this. She wants the details. I want my daughter. Straight swap.

Each second is a battle. The effort required to stop my mind tormenting me with thoughts of Bea being harmed is colossal. Sometimes I'm caught off guard and a split second later I slide into the reality of the fact that *she has been taken.* The map of my life has Bea at its centre. She is my daughter, my baby girl, and she's in extreme and mortal danger. My stomach shrinks and tightens into a fist, a hard knot that makes each breath a hardship, as I pull against the pain that's dragging me down to the floor. Deep, heavy, hell, embedded in my stomach like concrete, like stone, like headstones, like graves.

I stop the slide by digging my nails into the flesh of my forearms, forcing myself to feel the very real and present physical pain. Like resetting a timer, I'm back in the present and the battle begins again. *Don't think ahead. Just hold it together. Breathe.*

A policeman drives me to the hospital. Julian is in theatre and then he'll be brought to the high-dependency unit. I meet Lisa walking up and down the corridor. It's after three in the morning. The corridors are deserted apart from a few lone members of staff moving between wards. She runs to hug me and I let her, but only for a second.

'Please look after the boys for me,' I say.

'Of course.'

'They're with each other in the sitting room. Charlie is looking through Julian's emails and papers. Jack is on the PlayStation.'

'I'll go straight home.'

'Thank you, Lisa.'

I walk on to the ward, remembering that it was only three days ago I collected Lisa from another part of the hospital. Lisa, who is sick, and is now having to cope with this. I should have let her hug me for longer. I should have been kinder. I shouldn't have fought with them both before I went off to Mac's. What was the last thing I said to Julian?

I think and then I remember. I told him a lie. I said I was going to the seafront to sit quietly. A big, fat lie. If I hadn't gone, I would have been home when Megan came. I could have stopped her.

'Mrs Miller?'

'Yes?' I swing round sharply. There's a nurse behind me.

'Would you like to wait in our relatives' room? The doctor will come and speak to you as soon as he can.'

I follow her into a small room, painted magnolia. Bland water-colours take up space on the walls. Three of them are hanging squint, as if somebody fell against them and didn't bother to set them right afterwards. Four padded bottle-green chairs face each other. There's a coffee table in the middle with a box of tissues and a pile of magazines on it.

'There's a vending machine back along the corridor if you want a drink. I'm sorry we don't have any facilities to make you something ourselves.'

'That's OK.' I sit down. She closes the door on her way out and I'm left alone. There's a clock facing me. It sits high up on the bare magnolia wall. Loud and malevolent as a playground bully, it marks the seconds.

Tick . . . Julian is in a critical condition.

Tock . . . I slid on his blood. It's on the floor, on the walls, on the light switch, on my clothes, on the keyboard of my laptop.

Tick . . . He could die.

Tock . . . My daughter has been kidnapped.

Tick . . . She is in grave danger.

Tock . . . I don't know whether she has Bertie with her.

I should have checked. Why didn't I check? I start to moan. At first it's a low, monotonous sound and then it rises in pitch and I snap my back up straight.

Enough.

I want to cry, wail, tear my hair, seize the chair and hurl it at the clock. I want to scream the place down, demand that we wind back time. I want to be held by Julian. I want to see my daughter's face.

The clock keeps up its relentless ticking and I know that I can't stay in this room. Herein lies the way to madness. And madness is not an option. I haul myself up and walk out of the room and along the corridor. I'll do something normal. I'll get a drink. That's what I'll do.

The drinks machine has a range of choices. I drop some coins in the slot and choose hot chocolate. I wait. Nothing happens. I press the return button but still nothing happens. No money, no hot chocolate. I knock my head against the front of the machine, then give it a swift, angry kick. A cup drops down, wobbles on the plinth and is caught by two metal arms. Boiling milk trickles down into the cup, then a shot of chocolate and some more milk.

'Claire!' Jem is jogging along the corridor towards me. She stops just short of me, doesn't speak, just holds my eyes and then says, 'Christ. Oh Christ! He's not, is he?'

I shake my head. 'He's in the operating theatre.'

Her face crumples like she's going to cry. She puts her elbows and forearms against the wall and rests her head between them. When she's composed herself, she looks back at me. 'Tell me what I can do to help.'

'The boys,' I say immediately. 'Will you look after the boys for me?' I offer her the drink. She shakes her head. 'And Lisa,' I say. 'I'm worried that she'll do too much.' I take a drink of the hot chocolate. It tastes powdery and overly sweet. 'And someone needs to tell Wendy.'

'Will do.' She reaches out a hand and lightly touches my shoulder. 'Julian's strong. He'll get through this.'

I nod. Neither of us mentions Bea, but I feel her presence and I'm sure Jem does too. I visualise her skipping ahead of us along the corridor, Bertie under her arm. I feel her so strongly that I don't understand why she doesn't materialise in front of me.

'I'll walk with you to the door,' I say. 'I want to use my mobile.'

I haven't turned it off just in case a text comes through from Megan, but I know that using it in the hospital is frowned upon.

We make our way back to the main entrance. It's a long walk, two hundred metres or more, and when we get there, I take Jem's hand and say, 'Thank you for coming out like this.'

'It's the least—'

'After . . . you know. Being accused of something you hadn't done.' I give her a half-smile. 'No hard feelings?'

'None.' There are tears in her eyes again and I look away, not wanting to see what's written there. She feels sorry for me. She feels sorry for me because my husband is closer to death than he is to life and my daughter has been taken by people who have killed, and shown themselves willing to kill again.

We say our goodbyes, Jem promising to look after the family, me promising to 'keep my hopes up'. As soon as she's a few steps away, I check my emails – nothing. I call Mac for an update. There's no news yet on finding Megan, but her parents have been shedding light on how Megan could have met Georgiev.

'She worked in Europe during her gap year, in one of the mountain ski resorts in the Alps,' Mac tells me.

'I know about that,' I say. 'She was only telling me about it the other day.'

When she returned, she had changed, her parents said. She was more secretive. They thought it was all part of her growing up. She seemed more mature, had a clear sense of direction. Having been disillusioned with life and unsure about what she wanted to study at university, she announced she wanted to be a solicitor. Naturally, they were delighted.

'He was setting her up that long ago?' I say, astonished.

'Seems so,' Mac affirms. 'Georgiev knew that at some point the law would catch up with him. There had already been attempts to build a case against him, but the evidence hadn't been strong enough to support a prosecution. He wanted someone on the inside. The Italian Mafia are past masters at this.'

'Any other updates?'

'The two men with her on the CCTV are known associates of Georgiev, and we've traced the dark blue Fiat. It was bought for cash from a woman in Worthing last week. She said the man who bought it was foreign – Polish, she thought.'

'It'll be dumped somewhere.'

'Most likely,' he agrees.

'Thanks, Mac. I'm going back inside now. See whether Julian's out of surgery yet.'

'We'll speak soon.'

'Find her, Mac,' I say quietly. 'Please just find her.'

I end the call and go back into the hospital. The night cleaners are mopping the corridors, the smell of strong disinfectant wafting around them. I make my apologies as I tiptoe my way along the edges of their clean floor and arrive back in the HDU. The duty doctor is waiting for me. He introduces himself. His name is Dr Sam Kitto. He is wearing small, round Harry Potter glasses. His eyes behind them are bloodshot as if he has either drunk too much or not slept in weeks. Or maybe he's a swimmer and the chlorine affects his eyes. Or maybe he's had an allergic reaction to contact lenses. These thoughts go through my head, one after the other, like horses on a carousel. They take care of the time between him introducing himself and ushering me into the room with the ticking clock.

He takes my elbow and sits me down, then sighs as he lowers himself into the seat opposite me. I think of all the television programmes I've seen about the National Health Service. The state it's in. How doctors are working up to a hundred hours a week. The mistakes that are made.

'We have private health insurance,' I blurt out.

He shakes his head as if this is an irrelevance not worth considering. 'Mrs Miller, your husband is in a critical condition.' He pauses. I think he expects me to acknowledge his words, so I nod. 'He has lost large volumes of blood. Mr Murray is repairing the knife wound to his throat, but' – he takes a big breath and I do the same – 'he may have suffered brain damage.'

'I see,' I say, choosing not to believe it. Brain damage? Julian? Not possible. I can't imagine him like that. I won't imagine him like that.

'We are replacing blood and fluids to raise his blood pressure.' His accent is soft, a gentle Irish brogue. I tune into the melody that almost makes a lie of the words. 'His condition will remain critical for a number of hours. Mr Murray will be out of theatre presently and will be able to tell you more.'

'In your experience' – I clear my throat – 'is Julian's case very bad? What I mean is that . . . people recover from this sort of injury, don't they?'

'We need to get your husband through the next twenty-four hours.' He's looking at me with a heartfelt yet measured empathy. 'Then the next twenty-four hours after that.'

'Do you come from Dublin?'

'Yes.' He gives me a half-smile. 'My father was a general practitioner in the city centre, before it became as fashionable as it is now.'

'We went there for our honeymoon. We stayed in a bed and breakfast close to the river. It rained almost constantly.' I can feel tears running down my cheeks and realise that I'm crying. 'But it didn't spoil its beauty.'

He takes several tissues from the box on the table and hands them to me. 'We must take one hour at a time,' he says. 'I've seen people recover from the most devastating injuries. Your husband is not lost to you, Mrs Miller.'

I'm grateful for this because I can't countenance the idea that I might lose Julian. I try to smile my thanks, but the tension in my face won't let me.

Dr Kitto goes back to the ward and for a second, when the door is open, I look beyond him to where two nurses are standing either side of a bed, a blood-stained sheet, blinking monitor lights and a bag of fluid suspended from a drip-stand with a tube attached leading down to the body in the bed. Not Julian, but someone else who's fighting for life. I think about the two policemen, Baker and Faraway, on their first shift of night duty, their throats cut, and Megan, just two days before, standing on the pavement, flirting with them, her behaviour so callous, so calculating that it's difficult to count her as a human being. I think about the policemen's families as they were given the news. The shock and the horror of it. The reality taking a lifetime to sink in.

I don't know how much longer Julian will be in theatre. Dr Kitto said I should rest, but resting is impossible. I'm wide awake. The feeling inside is too big for me to contain. I want to lift a car, scale a building, die if that's what it takes. But there's nothing I can do except walk up and down and hope and pray. I feel like a beggar. I want to drop to my knees in front of God and explain why my husband and my daughter can't die. I know that every minute of every hour of every day someone loses a loved one, but please not me, not my husband, not my child.

It's after seven o'clock in the morning now and I risk using both phones in the relatives' room. No emails have arrived, and Mac has nothing else to tell me. Bea has been gone for more than six hours and we have no idea where she is. She could be anywhere. She could be in London or Manchester or Birmingham, and the more minutes that tick by, the harder she'll be to find. We have no leads. No clear direction.

I start to cry. I try to hold the tears back, I make great, loud gulping sounds, but there's no catching them. I ache with everything that I am for this to be over and for both Julian and Bea to be safe. I will never again take my life for granted. I will never complain. I will live each day in the knowledge that I am blessed beyond words.

There's a knock at the door – Julian is out of theatre. It's a relief to get the message and I hope that this might be it. Lowest point reached, we will now begin the slow climb back to normality. I straighten my clothes, smooth my hair and blow my nose. I look at the clock, remembering that when my mother died, I would hold my breath, convinced that if I held it for long enough, I could stop time and maybe even reverse it and then my mum would come back to us. But now I know different. I know that time has its own engine, fuelled as much by death as by life. It won't stop. It won't even wait. Not for any of us.

I walk out of the room and a tall man with grey hair and large feet approaches me. He's called Mr Murray and he's the surgeon who's just sewn my husband's throat back together. He's still wearing green theatre garb. He takes me aside and asks me about the attack. I tell him what little I know.

'Your husband was lucky,' he says. 'He must have turned his head just as the knife was used. The aim was slightly off and missed completely severing his carotid artery, otherwise he would have bled to death before anyone could help him. As it is, we've managed to repair the damage.' He takes my elbow. 'Come through and see him now.'

He leads me to a bed. I don't recognise the man lying there as Julian. He's not breathing for himself. He has a tube down his throat. The ventilator is pushing air into his lungs. There's a constant beeping noise from all the machinery registering his blood pressure, temperature, oxygen saturation levels and heartbeat. Areas of the mattress blow up and then down to relieve his pressure points. Fluid is going in through one arm and blood through the other. One side of his head has been partly shaved. Matted black hair is pushed back under a bandage that stretches round his head and down over his throat. His face is bruised, his eyelids swollen. And then I recognise his left hand. This is Julian. These are his long, slender, pianist's fingers, his freckled skin, blue veins and paler skin where his watch normally is. This is my husband's hand. I bring it up to my cheek, then bend down to kiss the motionless face.

'My darling,' I say, 'the operation was a success. You're going to be OK.'

'Talking is good.'

I look up. A nurse is reading results from one of the machines and jotting it down on a chart. She finishes writing and brings a chair around behind me. 'Hearing is the last sense to go and the first sense to return. Talk to him as much as you can.'

'Right.' I sit down and I start to talk. At first I feel self-conscious and then I forget all that and just talk about anything and everything: memories from university, Charlie's love of eco-politics, Jack's love of rugby, what we'll do with the summerhouse, whether we'll go to France this year or submit to pressure from the boys and fly to New York. What I don't talk about is the trial or Megan. And I don't mention Bea because I can't tell him she's still missing and I'm too afraid that if he can hear me, he'll grow agitated and upset.

The nurse caring for him is called Teresa and she doesn't look much older than a teenager. She explains everything to me and whenever I ask a question she answers me slowly, looking into my eyes as she does so. Every fifteen minutes she tries to rouse Julian. I stay out of the way so that she can make her observations. She asks Julian to open his eyes and she tests his motor response. Then she gives him a score: 7 out of 20.

'That's not good?'

'No.' She looks regretful. 'But his heart is strong and Mr Murray is an excellent surgeon. Let's give him time.'

I stay with him until ten o'clock and then I take a taxi back home. I want to make sure the boys are OK. I want to have a shower. But mostly I want to stand in Bea's bedroom and feel her presence. I want to see whether Bertie's there. I don't know whether him being there or not being there will make me feel worse or better. I just need to know.

The police tape is still cordoning off the area in front of my house. No through traffic is allowed into the street. 'Something happening along there this morning,' the driver says, craning his neck to see better. 'You'll have to climb out here.'

I pay him and step out on to the pavement. It's thirty yards or so to my house and I'm about halfway along when a figure rushes into my peripheral vision. I jerk round quickly, not so much afraid of what's coming, more to get myself in a good position if I need to fight back.

'I'm sorry. I'm not— Oh God.' It's Mary Percival. She puts her hand over her mouth. Her face twists. 'I heard about Julian and about Bea.' She takes a tearful breath. 'I'm so very, very sorry.'

'Thank you.' I feel the weight of her sincerity, but just like with Lisa and with Jem, I can't take it on board. I don't want to see what they see. My husband is *alive*, only just, but he is alive. And Bea is alive. She is. If she wasn't, my heart would stop. I put my hand to my chest, reassured to feel it beat through my sweater. 'And I'm sorry to have been rude to you. It was Megan we should have been watching out for. Not you.' I continue walking. After a few seconds she follows me.

'Megan?'

'She worked with Julian. It seems she fooled us all.' My phone beeps twice. It's the sound of a text arriving. I take it out of my pocket and read the message: *Come to the playing fields on the London Road. Alone.*

My heart starts to pound. I look along the street. I need to get to my car. It's in the cordoned-off area.

'Mary,' I say, 'will you do something for me?'

'Of course.'

'I want to get my car out. The police will ask me where I'm going. I need to have a reason. I'm dropping you at the vet. Douglas isn't well, so I'm taking you there.'

Mary looks down at Douglas and then at me. 'OK,' she says. 'But he looks well. Shall we say it's for his vaccinations?'

'Fine.' I walk quickly and Mary follows me. I go into the house. The first thing I notice is that someone has washed Julian's blood off the floor. Mac is in the hallway making a phone call and stops as soon as he sees me.

'How's Julian?' he says.

'He's out of theatre.' I walk past him and lift my keys off the hall table. 'We'll know more later.'

'Are you driving somewhere?'

'I'm dropping Mary at the vet. Douglas is due injections.'

He starts back in surprise. 'What?'

'I need to stay busy.' I go back outside and run down the steps.

'Claire?'

I ignore him. Mary and I climb into the car. The policeman on patrol moves the barrier and I drive off while Mac stands on the kerb and watches.

20

'I'll drop you round the corner,' I tell Mary. 'Thank you for covering for me.'

She sits beside me with Douglas on her knee, his tail wagging as he sniffs the air, then stares straight ahead through the window. Mary is completely upright, the tension in her body palpable as I overtake on the bend, then have to brake abruptly when an old lady steps off the pavement. 'Come on, come on.' I'm tapping the steering wheel. My mobile rings.

'Do you want me to get that?' Mary asks.

'No,' I say. I know it'll be Mac. I don't want him along. I don't want him taking charge and doing it his way. I don't have much of a plan, but what I do know is that if Megan comes to meet me, then I'll offer myself and the information as a trade for my daughter.

'How is Julian?' Mary asks.

'He's . . . holding his own.' I think of him lying in the bed plugged into machinery looking both strange and vulnerable. My heart aches. I try to breathe. 'We don't know yet whether there'll be any permanent damage.'

'I'm sorry.' She brushes Douglas's fur out of his eyes. 'I'm so sorry. This is a horrible time for you.'

I stop by the kerb. 'Is this OK?'

'Thank you.' As she's climbing out, she turns back and says, 'If you need any more help, please ask.'

'I will. And, Mary?'

'Yes?'

'About Dad. About you. We'll talk soon. I promise.'

She gives me a grateful smile and I set off for the playing fields. I drive too fast. I watch one speed camera flash and then another. I talk myself through what I need to do. Park the car. Go into the playing fields and wait, and when I see her coming, I'll give her the piece of paper Mac gave me and— 'Shit.' I bang the heel of my hand on my forehead. I've left the paper in the pocket of my blood-stained jeans and they're lying on the floor in my bedroom. I don't have time to go back for the paper and anyway Mac would start questioning me. I rack my brains and find that I can remember the witness's name – Kaloyan Batchev – and he's being held in a safe house in East London, but was it Gordon Place or Gordon Avenue? Number fifteen or number thirteen?

Think, Claire, *think*.

I could call Charlie or Jack and ask him to find my jeans and read me the address, but I don't want to involve either of them. I can't expect them to keep it a secret. It's too much responsibility and if something were to go wrong, they would blame themselves. I could call Mac, but there's no way he'll let me handle this my way. He might decide to bring a tactical unit and Bea could get caught up in the crossfire. I know I have to be realistic. Megan Jennings is more than just the solicitor I'm familiar with; she is with the two men who killed Baker and Faraway last night and left Julian for dead – Julian, whom she's worked with for the last nine months. If she's capable of that, then what chance do I have of coming out alive?

The answer is probably zero, but that's not my main concern. It may look like blind recklessness, but to me it feels like the last few days have been leading up to this and I'm not going to let the police or anyone else take this chance away from me. With me in charge, Bea is put first, if necessary at the expense of my own safety. And that's the way it has to be. That's not to say I'm fearless – I am, in fact, so afraid that my skin feels tight from the terror that's been growing inside me since Bea first disappeared – but I'm not afraid for myself. I'm only afraid for Bea. My sanity has been walking a tightrope and I have to stare straight ahead or else I see what's pressing in around me: images of my daughter lying cold and dead on a mortuary slab. And the only sure way to prevent this is for Megan to get the information she wants. The police won't give it to her. But I will. I rack my brains some more and decide the house number was fifteen. If it was thirteen, I'm sure a thought along the lines of unlucky-for-some would have gone through my head. So was it avenue or place? I think hard. I try to visualise the piece of paper. It doesn't work. I have no idea which one it is. All I can do is choose one and hope I can secure Bea's release before Georgiev's men arrive at the address.

It takes me ten minutes to get to the playing fields. On one side are the fields, their perimeters dotted with trees. On the other is a row of 1930s semi-detached houses. Several boys are kicking a football into the goal in the far field, and there's a man walking his dog along the street, but otherwise it's quiet. I walk on to the field and send a text back: *I'm here.*

I hold my phone in my hand and wait. I look around me. There's no one in sight. I stand there for a quarter of an hour, each minute feeling longer than the last. When my phone finally rings, I get such a shock that I drop it. I scrabble around in the grass for it and press the green button.

'Hello,' I say.

'Walk diagonally across the field.' It's Megan's voice. 'Cross the road and come in the front door of number thirty-nine. If I get so much as an inkling that you're being followed, you won't see Bea again.'

'I'm not. I—' She ends the call.

I start walking. I know she'll be watching me. This is an open spot, the perfect place for her to see whether or not I've brought anyone along with me. I walk at a normal pace, being careful not to break into a run. I feel remarkably calm. Somewhere inside there is the terrified me, but she's behind triple-glazed glass and although she's bashing her fists against it, the sounds are muffled. I can ignore her.

The sun is shining and my eyes are watering, but I daren't raise my hand to shield them in case Megan thinks I'm signalling to someone. I walk up the path to number thirty-nine, my shoes scrunching noisily on the gravel. The door is slightly ajar. I push it open and walk inside. As I turn to close it, the back of my right knee is kicked. It buckles and I topple backwards. In one flowing movement Megan's left hand yanks my arm up my back and her right hand comes to the front and round my throat, where I feel a blade settle against my skin. She moves with such speed and precision that I am disabled before I even register the kick.

'You wouldn't lie to me, Claire, would you?'

I can't speak. Her hold is too tight. I have to fight hard to stave off a feeling of panic because I know that when I try to breathe, I won't be able to. She twists round and throws me ahead of her into the front room, where I land on the floor with a thud. I automatically rub my throat and then look up at her. 'Where's Bea?'

She's dressed completely in black – trainers, T-shirt and trousers. Her hair is tied back and she isn't wearing make-up. The Megan I know is never without her mascara and her lip gloss and her perfectly pressed white shirts. Gone is the accommodating tilt to the head, the work-focused, slightly shy, slightly breathless air. In its place there is a deliberate lack of expression. She slides the knife back in the sheath attached to a belt round her waist.

'Where's Bea?' I say again.

'Get up.' The room is about twelve feet square and dingy. The décor doesn't look as if it's been refreshed for forty or more years. The fitted carpet is a mottled greeny-brown nylon, the curtains the same. There is a mirror above a disused fireplace, but otherwise the walls are bare apart from yellowed wallpaper, which is curling at the corners. The only items of furniture are two hard-back chairs facing each other in the centre of the room. She points to one of them. 'Sit.'

I do it. I'm not about to argue. I just want to see Bea.

In another part of the house, I hear a phone ring, followed by a man speaking in short, staccato sentences. Then two men appear at the entrance to the room. They could be twins. They are stocky; their faces are pockmarked and scarred. They each have a diamond stud in one ear and a chunky gold bracelet on their right wrist. I recognise them from the CCTV footage. I don't know which one of the three of them cut Julian's throat, but my gut feeling tells me it wasn't Megan. Despite the fact that she's carrying a knife, I don't believe she could swing so radically from solicitor to murderer. I think it far more likely that her job was to get the information, and when that was not forthcoming, these men were called in to provide the muscle. One or both of these men murdered Baker and Faraway, and seriously injured Julian.

They repulse me. My eyes burn as I stare at them. I would like to make them pay for what they've done, slowly and painfully, so that they never find peace again. I know my feelings are showing on my face, but fortunately neither of them is looking at me. It's as if I don't exist and it gives me the chance to observe Megan's interaction with them. One stays silent, while the other talks to her. His tone is irritable and short-tempered. Megan replies in Bulgarian, her voice rising and falling with annoyance and then agreement. She is different from her 'English' self. Not only is her tone of voice more forceful, more masculine, but so too is her body language, which is pushy and dominant.

Abruptly, the men turn and leave the room. They go out through the front door, closing it behind them. I feel like I've just been given a gift. Without the men here, I have more chance of persuading Megan to set Bea free.

She comes towards me, stopping inches from my feet. 'Tell me who the witness is,' she says.

'Where's Bea?'

She cuffs me across the face with the back of her hand. I don't see it coming. My lower jaw takes the brunt of it and is pushed to one side so that an intense pain, worse than any toothache, shoots up the side of my face. I feel my cheekbone gingerly. It's still in one piece, but the ache grinds through my facial bones from my chin to the backs of my eyes.

'Tell me who the witness is.'

'Where's Bea?'

She cuffs me again. This time, my vision jumps and then blurs. I blink several times until finally it clears and I'm left with ringing ears and a battered cheek.

'How long do you think you can keep this up?' She pulls the chair in close and sits down. She taps my knee. 'Three or four minutes?'

'As long as it takes.' I make a point of holding my back straight. 'Where's Bea?'

She looks up at the ceiling and sighs. I brace myself, but this time she doesn't hit me. She stands up, grabs me by my hair and pulls me along behind her. We go through to a room at the back, where the curtains are closed. 'If you wake her,' Megan says into my ear, 'I'll knock her out. Is that clear?'

I nod and walk towards a single bed under the window, where I can see the outline of a child's body. I have to hold my hand over my mouth to suppress a cry of bittersweet joy and anguish. Joy because it's Bea. So precious, my fingers itch to reach out to her. She's lying on her side fast asleep, her breathing deep and regular. And in her arms she has Bertie, his soft head resting against her cheek just as he does at home. Anguish because I want to take her in my arms and hold her, run out on to the pavement and back to my car, but I know I won't get as far as the front door. For the moment, I have to be satisfied with the fact that Bea is alive and safe.

'That's it,' Megan says, and pushes me ahead of her back to the front room and on to the chair. She sits down opposite me again and says, 'Now tell me.'

'Will you please let Bea go free?'

'When we have the witness, I'll let you both go free.' Her expression is one part restraint, two parts impatience. She leans towards me. 'Now tell me what I want to know.'

'Kaloyan Batchev.'

'Batchev?' she snaps back and for one heart-stopping moment

I think Mac has given me false information. And then she says, 'Pavel thought he was dead.' She nods like this explains a lot and then she laughs and talks under her breath. She muses for a bit, looking up at the corner of the room, seeming to find conversation among the cobwebs and peeling wallpaper.

When she stares back at me, it's with flat eyes. 'And where is he?'

'Fifteen Gordon Avenue,' I say, making a sudden decision that avenue or place, the important thing is that I buy some time and get Bea out of here before the men return. 'It's in the East End.'

'You're not playing a game with me, Claire?' Her voice is gentle. 'Are you?'

'What do you mean?'

'Making up an address to buy you time?'

'No.' She's so close to my thinking that I wonder whether it will show on my face. I make a point of holding her stare. 'I wouldn't do that.'

'So how did you get the details?'

'I have my contacts,' I say.

'Well, I know Julian didn't tell you. He's far too principled for that.' She moves in close. 'Was it our trusty copper?'

I look down.

'So it was.' She thinks about this. 'Why did he tell you?'

'I have something on him.'

'What?'

'We used to work together.'

'And?'

I hesitate. While I don't want to give Megan any power over Mac, the choice between keeping his secret and ensuring Bea's safety is an easy one. Still, I won't give Megan more information than I have to. 'Some years ago he made a procedural mistake,' I say. 'I could make sure it comes back to haunt him.'

'I see.' She stares into my face for a few seconds more, seems satisfied and stands up. She pulls her phone from her pocket and makes a call. She talks curtly in Bulgarian, apart from the address, which she repeats in English. When she finishes, she lights up a cigarette and goes to the window. She stands with her back to me, and with each inhalation of nicotine, her shoulders relax. There are net curtains across the glass so that no one can see in. She moves the curtain slightly to one side and looks along the street in both directions. Then she rests the cigarette on the edge of the windowsill and raises binoculars to her eyes. She checks across the park in a wide, slow, panoramic sweep. I have the brief and foolish idea to rush her, try to get her down on the ground before she knows what hit her, grab the knife from her belt and threaten her with it. I'm contemplating doing it – it may be our best and only shot at escape – when she tunes into my thoughts and says casually, 'Don't even think about it. I won't hesitate to kill you.'

I don't believe her. Despite the blackmailer's assertion that she'd killed before, I'm not convinced Megan is a cold-blooded murderer. But nevertheless she does have a knife and I don't want to find myself on the wrong end of it. I decide that the best thing to do is to get her talking. See whether I can reach the Megan who is familiar to me. She has to be in there somewhere.

'Will you let Bea go now?' I ask.

'Not until we have Batchev.'

'Why didn't you wait?'

'Wait for what?'

'I got you the information. I told you I would. There was an accident on the road and that's why I was late.'

'You were the one who'd set the midnight deadline.' She turns to face me. 'We didn't want you moving to a safe house. It would have complicated things.'

'And were you following us?' I think about walking back from the deli and then Bea being watched as she played in the sandpit. 'Did you go to the nursery?'

'If you'd had the sense to check,' she says smugly. 'You'd have discovered I was working from home on both those days.'

How well she fooled us all. Not once did it even cross my

mind that the blackmailer could be Megan. In spite of the fact that she regularly came to my house, I never once suspected her. I was blinded by her ambition and her professionalism and her all English background.

'And how did you know about what happened at Bea's party?' I say.

'That was Julian.' False regret puckers her eyebrows. 'I spoke to him when he was in the taxi going to the airport and he told me all about it.'

I look down at my feet, feeling sick to my stomach. When Julian wakes up, he will be devastated to remember that he has unwittingly helped Megan, and that opening the door to her led to Bea being taken. But he's not the only one who'll suffer from feelings of guilt. I'm already beginning to question my own involvement. If I hadn't set the deadline, would Megan still have come for Bea? If I had been at home, would Julian have opened the door? If I had acted differently, could all this have been prevented?

'And the magazine at your front door?' Megan says. 'Did you find that?'

I nod. The one I blamed Mary for. 'You left it?'

'I slipped in without anyone hearing me.' She shrugs. 'And still you were several steps away from realising it was me.'

'I have to hand it to you, Megan,' I say, wondering whether I will reach her through flattery, 'you managed to stay successfully under the radar. There was no suggestion that you had any links with Georgiev.'

'We have always been extra careful.'

'You met him when you were on your gap year?'

That surprises her. 'How do you know that?'

'Your parents.' She's thrown for a moment. Her eyes narrow and slide away from mine. It's fleeting, but it's there and it gives me hope. 'They're being questioned by the police.'

She raises a lazy eyebrow. 'Goodness knows how they'll explain that at the country club.'

I lift my hand up to my face to bite my nails and notice traces of Julian's blood trapped in the cuticles. I shudder and slide my hands under my thighs. I don't want to think about the moment when I found him, helpless and dying, and we were both swallowed into a facsimile of hell. I rock myself backwards and forwards.

'How could you do that to Julian?' I blurt out. 'He's lying in hospital hovering between life and death.'

'He's still alive?'

'Yes.' I nod my head emphatically.

'Well, good for him,' she says, as if he's won a tennis tournament or run a marathon.

'You left him for dead, Megan.' My eyes sting. 'How could you do that?'

'He was in the wrong place at the wrong time.' She pauses for thought. 'A couple of months ago I tried to get him into bed, you know? But he was having none of it.' She gives a short laugh. 'Just think, if he had been willing to commit adultery, I could have found out what I needed to know and none of you would be going through this. It's a case of too much virtue.'

This is so unfair. Her view of what's happening is so twisted that bitterness fills my mouth and hardens my spine to steel. 'So when you sat in my house five days ago and said you admired and respected Julian, that was a lie?'

'It wasn't a lie. I've learned a lot from him. He's an excellent barrister.'

'And yet you allowed someone to slit his throat?'

She has no answer to this. I feel a power shift and I move to capitalise on it.

'Georgiev is worth that? He's worth you becoming a woman without a heart? *Is he?*'

She stares at me blankly.

'And what will happen now your cover's blown?'

'I'm more than just a solicitor to Pavel.'

'But surely he values you in proportion to your usefulness?'

As I say this, I realise it might be a mistake to push her to examine her relationship with Georgiev, but instead of making her angry, it has the opposite effect.

'Poor Claire.' She laughs. It's silent. Her shoulders shake but no sound comes out of her mouth. 'I really thought you were smarter than this.'

'Then help me understand,' I say, keen to draw her physically closer because I'm not going to put up with this for much longer and if it's her against me, then I reckon I can handle myself. Yes, I'm smaller and lighter and not trained to fight, but my daughter is lying unprotected in the next room and that's powering me with a strength that makes me believe I could lift a small car. 'Explain it to me.'

She takes the last drag of her cigarette and sits down opposite me again. 'Pavel has made me everything I am.'

'He's a criminal.'

'Yes.' The edges of her face soften. 'But I see past that.' There is not even a spark of self-doubt in her expression. 'I love him.'

'And your elaborate charade? Working for the CPS when you're in bed with a criminal? That's love, is it?'

'Have you ever been in love, Claire?'

'You know how much I love Julian.'

'Then you have to understand that for me, love doesn't have any limits.'

'And *you* have to understand,' I say quietly, 'that there's more than just a touch of craziness about that.'

She throws out her hands. 'Do I appear crazy to you?'

I have to admit that she doesn't. She seems remarkably poised, considering.

'So this is all about love?' I say.

'Yes.'

'Two policemen are dead, Megan.' I look down at my feet and shake my head. 'Faraway and Baker – my God! You were making friends with them just the other day. They didn't have to die.'

'If it was up to me, I would have left them alive.' She shrugs. 'But that's not the way it's done.'

I want to end this. I feel my heart's yearning for Bea, fast asleep, not thirty feet away. 'Did you give Bea a sedative of some sort?'

'It won't cause her any long-term damage.'

Another chink. Another toe in the door that leads to the Megan I know. I have the sure and sudden knowledge that there's no need to physically fight with her. The vestiges of the Megan who has been to my house, sat Bea on her knee, chatted to us all – I think I can talk her round. 'You have to let Bea go before the men get back. You know you do.'

'I've told you. I'll let you both go when we have the witness.'

'When the trial collapses, are you and Georgiev going to go off together? Happy ever after?'

She can't help but smile. 'Something like that.'

'Do you want a child's death on your conscience?'

'Nothing will happen to Bea.'

'You sure about that? You sure that when the men get back, they won't just kill me and Bea? I mean, why not? We're loose ends. And like you say, it's the way it's done.'

'I won't allow it.' Doubt flickers at the corners of her eyes. She looks at her watch. 'It won't be long now.'

I lean forward in my seat. 'You really think you can stop those two?' I take a gamble. I don't believe that Georgiev is even halfway decent – how can he be when he traffics teenage girls for sex? – but my hunch is that Megan considers him an 'honourable' criminal, however much evidence points to the contrary. 'Georgiev is sophisticated. He's cultured. He keeps his hands clean,' I say. 'But by necessity, some of the men who work for him are not. Granted, Georgiev is a criminal, but he has old-fashioned values. Like for like is acceptable. The policemen, Julian – they were pitting themselves against him. They're fair game. But a child? A little girl? Would he be happy with that?'

Doubt holds her in the chair. I watch her lips tremble and know that she is conflicted.

'I'm going to the bedroom.' Energy and determination thunder through me. 'I'm taking Bea.' I stand up. 'I'm not going to look back. I'm not going to tell anyone about what happened here. I just want my child.'

I don't wait for her reply. I turn. I walk fast. I hold my breath. I reach the bedroom. I gather Bea into my arms. She doesn't stir. I walk back along the hallway. One, two, three . . . ten, eleven, twelve steps. I reach the front door. I balance Bea on my right arm and open the door with my left hand. I step on to the gravel. The sunlight bathes my face. I feel a moment of pure joy and then there's a loud crash, my ears buzz and I'm falling back against the wall of the house. A rough edge of brick scratches along my neck.

'Steady.' A policeman wearing a flak jacket takes Bea out of my arms. 'Come with me, Mrs Miller.' He walks off to one side, but before I follow him, I glance behind me, bewildered. There are half a dozen men, dressed like him, filling the hallway. I can hear Mac's voice shouting, 'On the ground! Face down!'

I blink. Another policeman lays a jacket on the grass. The one carrying Bea lowers her down gently. The garden has been left to its own devices; the grass is long and straggly. I fall down on my knees in front of Bea. She's lying exactly as she was in the bed: on her right side, her legs drawn up, Bertie close to her cheek. I stroke her hair and shake her gently. 'Wake up, Bea. We need to go home.' She snuggles further into herself, feeling for Bertie.

There's a commotion behind me. I look round. My eyes focus on Mac. He's on the driveway, pushing Megan ahead of him, her hands cuffed behind her back. She is staring at the ground, her expression hidden. But her body language says it all: hair tangled, slumped shoulders, feet dragging two or three seconds behind her body, which sways as if drunk.

I don't want any more of this. 'Bea.' A sob catches in my throat. 'Please open your eyes.' I shake her more forcefully. 'Wake up, sweetheart.'

And she does. She opens her eyes very slowly and sits up. 'I don't like Megan, Mummy.' She frowns at me. 'She gave me pink milk and it tasted funny.'

Without warning, tears spring from my eyes. They are huge, hot and quick, Olympic tears running at the sound of the starter's gun. They course down my cheeks and make a soggy puddle on my T-shirt.

'Mummy.' She yawns. 'Why are you crying?'

'I'm just so happy.' I bring her on to my knee and hug her tight. She looks at me closely then yawns again, her eyes drooping.

'You have blood.' She forces her eyes open wide and looks at me closer still, leaning right in so that I can feel her breath on my throat. 'You cut yourself.' She sits back a bit and nods. 'You need a plaster.'

'Let's go and find one, shall we?' I stand up and lift her into my arms. Her head settles against my neck.

'I need my *Nemo* boots,' she says, her voice still drowsy with sleep. 'And can I have Coco Pops?'

'Yes.' I wipe the tears from my cheeks. 'Let's go home.'

21

'Comas like this normally last between two and four weeks.'

'And then what?'

'And then he may wake up . . .' Teresa leaves the sentence hanging.

'Or?'

'He may slip into a persistent vegetative state.' She looks apologetic. 'But his observations are encouraging and he *is* triggering the ventilator now, which means he's almost ready to breathe for himself, so let's stay with that.'

One week has passed and Julian is no longer critically ill. He is now just seriously ill. His last scan shows that his brain is swollen. I learn a whole new vocabulary. I know what 'raised intracranial pressure' means. I know what the brain stem does. I write words down in my notebook – Glasgow coma scale, dexamethasone, peritoneal dialysis – and when I get home, I look them up on the Internet so that when the doctors do their rounds every morning, I'm able to ask relevant questions.

'How are his bloods this morning?' I ask Teresa.

'Potassium levels are low. We're correcting that.'

I watch as she inserts a bolus of potassium into the bag of saline that runs into his central line. 'That's bad for the heart,' I say. 'Fluctuating potassium levels.'

'Don't worry, Mrs Miller. We'll have that sorted directly.'

She teaches me how to care for him. His lips crack as the tube pulls at the edges of his mouth. I rub Vaseline into them. His right eye is still swollen shut and I rub ointment over it.

The physiotherapist visits every morning. 'Passive limb

movements are important,' she tells me. She cycles his legs through the air like he's riding an imaginary bicycle. 'Otherwise the ligaments shorten and the muscles waste away and he'll have all sorts of problems when he starts to walk again.'

Several times a day I whisper in his ear, 'We found her, Jules. She's safe. Not at all traumatised. Her normal self.' I don't tell him about Megan being in the prison hospital or the delay to the trial. I don't know what's going on inside his head, so I try to keep it simple. For hours at a time I sit beside his bed, hold his hand and talk to him about the little things that Bea's doing and how much we're looking forward to him coming home. Other times I just sit and stare. I don't know how long I sit there. I think of nothing. Nothing at all. I'm not asleep and I'm not awake. I exist in a kind of nowhere land, awaiting my next trigger.

The children come to visit him every day. Charlie is worried about Julian but manages to act fairly normally around him, chatting about university and politics as he always has. Jack struggles to stay any longer than ten minutes. His hands hover over the covers; then he bends to kiss Julian but stops an inch from his cheek. His fists clench and unclench. His face flushes; then he rocks backwards and forwards on his trainers. 'I'll get you some coffee from the machine, Mum,' he tells me, and leaves the room, blinking back tears.

After the initial rush of questions from Bea – 'Why is that tube in Daddy's mouth?', 'Why doesn't he open his eyes?', 'Why can't he talk?' – she sits on the edge of the bed and strokes his hair and chats to him. 'And when you're finished your long, long sleep, Daddy,' she says, 'you can see my new puppy because he'll be born soon.'

With my permission, Mary has promised Bea one of the puppies Douglas has fathered. Mary is becoming a regular visitor to our house. Julian had been in hospital a week when I knew I could no longer keep Mary's revelation a secret. During the long hours next to his bed, I thought about her finding out that the man who raised her wasn't her biological father, meeting my dad and then him dying before she had a chance to get to know him. I thought about how lucky I was having my father's love for as long as I did. And about how lucky I still am to have those I love around me. I decided to tell Lisa first. I tried to break it to her slowly, but in the end there was no easy way to say it.

'Dad had another daughter,' I told her, as I sat with her at breakfast. 'It's Mary Percival, Bea's nursery teacher.'

I counted the beats before she could lift her chin off the table and speak. Five long seconds and then a slew of questions – 'What the hell?', 'When did it happen?', 'Does Wendy know?'

Lisa took a couple of hours to get used to the idea and then we told Wendy, mindful that this would be a reminder of our dad's infidelity, something that had cost her many a sleepless night. She listened to the news without interruption and then, as ever, she humbled us both with her generosity when she said, 'She's part of our family? Girls! What news! We must invite her round.'

With whole lives to catch up on, there's no end to the talking and soon I realise that, when she sheds her shyness, this new sister of mine is fun. The boys and Bea think so too, but Bea refuses to believe she's her auntie. 'She's my teacher, Mummy. You've made a mistake.'

'It'll take time,' I tell Mary.

'Of course,' she says. 'I'm just so happy that I've told you at last.'

After ten days Julian is taken off the ventilator and he breathes for himself. He's still unconscious, but it's progress and so I'm thankful. He's moved out of the HDU into a side room on an adjacent ward. He no longer has a nurse by his side at all times. He looks peaceful. His wound is healing, and his hair is growing back. The scans show that his brain is settling down. His pupils are equal and reacting to light. He responds to painful stimuli. These are very encouraging signs that he doesn't have permanent damage. We just need him to wake up.

I lurch between emotional states. I feel immensely grateful. My daughter is alive, blessedly, miraculously alive. I'm transfixed by the smallest things that she does. I watch her drinking juice. Her fingers don't make it all the way round the cup, so she holds it with both hands. I am lost in the tilt of her eyelashes and the unflinching gaze she turns on me. I see God in her.

Then abruptly, as if on dodgems in the fairground, my direction changes and my heart twists until I gasp. My husband is unconscious. The MRI scan shows that his cerebrum was damaged by the lack of oxygen. There were complications. He had raised intracranial pressure. The surgeon had to drill through his skull to release the pressure on his brain. If it were a cartoon, steam would escape.

Home and hospital are two separate worlds. I leave Julian for the night and come home to the family. In my absence Wendy, Lisa and Jem have rallied round and my house is running better than it normally does.

Lisa's cancer is in remission. 'Too much else going on,' she says. She's gaining weight, her pain medication is working, and the wound on her hip has healed. It's unclear how long this phase will last, but I'm not counting days. I'm thankful that today, now, she's well.

Jem comes round every day. Pete has forgiven her for keeping her prison time a secret and she tells me she's never felt better. She was always worried that it was going to come out and now that it has, she feels a weight has lifted. She's working hard in the garden and has started what she's calling Project Summerhouse. The boys told her that Julian was talking about doing it up and so she's drawn up plans, shopped for the materials and is in the garden full-time, roping the boys in to help and bringing laughter and industry into their lives, the perfect antidote while we wait anxiously for Julian's recovery.

Wendy runs the kitchen. She turns out meals that manage to please everyone. She's even taken to macrobiotics and, in Sezen's absence, is working her way through the cookery book, sourcing the ingredients online and preparing foods with seaweed and soya that taste delicious.

No one mentions Sezen, but that doesn't mean she isn't on my mind. I think about her often and wonder what's become of her and Lara and Jalal. I make up my mind to try to find her. Not yet. When the dust has settled, I'll ask Mac to trace her and see whether I can help her with Jalal's situation. While I know very little about immigration law, I have contacts who do.

Charlie spends a couple of weeks with a broken heart when he realises that, in spite of his attempts to win Amy back, she's already moved on. I don't mention meeting her on the pier, or the fact they had sex in Julian's study; I'm simply there for him, as best I can be, as he wrestles with feelings of loss and betrayal before managing to file them away somewhere in his heart, what's going on with Julian taking precedence over everything else.

Mac calls me most days. Communication between us is strained since I found out he'd not only followed me to where Bea was being kept, but the information he had given me was not accurate. The witness's name was indeed Batchev, but he was being kept somewhere in North London. Four of Georgiev's men turned up to the Gordon Avenue address - so I guessed right after all - and were met by a dozen armed officers. After several shots were fired, two of them ended up dead and the other two were taken into custody.

'And what if one of them had had the time to phone Megan?' I say to Mac. 'And Bea was still in the house? What then?'

'It couldn't have happened that way.' He gives a confident shake of his head, flying high on the adrenaline of success. 'We knew we'd have you out before the fight kicked off. Anyway' – he looks at me with grudging respect – 'you had everything under control.'

'Yes, I did.'

I walk away from him then, but the next day he calls me to let me know how the case is progressing. The trial has only been delayed by three weeks. Batchev is still in a safe house, all ready to testify. Megan was remanded in prison, charged with several offences that would see her serving upwards of twenty years. On the tenth day she slit her own throat. How she acquired the razor blade was never established and led to a *Question Time* discussion on the 'overcrowding in prisons causing stress and increased suicides'. Mac visited Belmarsh Prison himself to tell Georgiev that Megan had taken her own life. He told me Georgiev cried like a baby. It seems that their love for each other, however warped, was genuine.

I'm offered counselling and at first I refuse, but after two weeks with precious little sleep I decide to go along. The therapist is a woman in her fifties. She dresses in layers of cotton and cashmere, and is relaxed and kind. I tell her that all day long fear is my stalker. It taunts me from the sidelines, and as soon as I relax into sleep, it jumps on me and I'm awake again, my heart pounding as I gulp in air, the panic inside me even more intense than it was for those twelve hours Bea was missing. She listens to this. She holds my hands and looks me in the eye. 'The first thing to remember is that you survived a major, life-threatening event. You *all* survived: you, your husband and your children. The resonance of this trauma needs time to leave your body.'

That makes sense and it's a relief to know that my reaction is normal. I won't be this way for the rest of my life. She holds me as I cry. She listens as I talk about my fears for Julian and losing my mother and father and now my sister. It helps to talk and I find myself beginning to see my life differently. I don't want to be defined by loss. I want to be defined by what I am and what I have.

And then the momentous day comes: Julian wakes up. I'm sticking the latest card Bea has made for him on the pinboard at the side of his hospital bed.

'Thirsty.'

I stand stock-still.

'Claire, thirsty.'

I look down at the bed. His eyes are open. I scream with delight and then I laugh and then I jump up and down. 'Julian!' I kiss his face. 'You're awake!'

The nurses come running. We give him some water and almost at once he falls back to sleep again. We're all grinning like mad. I run to phone the family and word spreads. He recognised me. He's still in there. After four long weeks he's come back to us.

His recovery begins in earnest. Sometimes it's one step forward and two steps back, but for the most part it's forward motion. He has two main areas to work on: a left-sided weakness in his limbs and a difficulty with language. He begins an intensive course of physiotherapy. Walking is tough. His left leg drags behind him and the therapists urge him to concentrate on lifting it up and then forwards. He grows tired and cross. The nurse tells me it's common with brain injury, but still, it's hard for me to watch. I'm used to the strong Julian, the patient Julian, not someone who cries and loses his temper, and I feel for him, wish I could save him from the pain and frustration of relearning what was once so familiar.

Speech therapy is even more frustrating for him. He understands what's being said to him, but has difficulty finding the right words when he replies. Nouns are especially hard to pinpoint. The therapist shows him cards and he has to say what the object is. Sometimes he's close. He'll say 'shed' for 'house' or 'dog' for 'cat'. Other times his choice is completely random.

Bea helps him. 'You have to unscramble your head, Daddy,' she tells him. She's sitting cross-legged on his hospital bed. She takes her time choosing and then holds up a card with a banana on it. 'What's this?'

'Tortoise,' he says.

She giggles so much she slides off his bed and I have to lift her back on again. Unlike Charlie and Jack, who've realised that Julian will probably never work as a barrister again, Bea thinks his problem with language is funny and this helps Julian. Her laughter becomes his laughter and soon she's calling the window a chair and he says the water jug is a pillow.

When he's seven weeks into his recovery, Mac comes to visit. He gives Julian the news we've all been hoping for – Pavel Georgiev has been convicted of people-trafficking, drug-dealing and several counts of murder. He's given four consecutive life sentences. He'll never walk free again. 'And they wouldn't have got there without all the hard work that you put in,' Mac says.

Julian smiles and I take his hand. 'It's finally over,' I say.

'Just need to dot the i's and cross the t's and the case can be put to bed,' Mac says, and asks Julian what he remembers about that night.

Julian thinks hard. 'She called me on the . . .'

He looks at me. I've been told by the speech therapist to avoid prompting him unless I absolutely have to. I figure this is one of those times. 'Phone,' I say.

'Phone,' he says. 'On the phone. She said she had important cooking . . . recipes.'

'Information?'

He nods gratefully.

'So you opened the door?' Mac says. His tone is not accusing, but Julian flinches.

'Yes,' he says. 'And then . . .' He looks away so that Mac can't see the shame in his eyes. 'I don't remember anything else.'

Mac thanks Julian and I walk with him along the corridor. 'He hates not being the man he was,' I say.

'He'll get there.' He gives me a sympathetic smile. 'And with you fighting his corner he'll get there in double-quick time.'

I stop at the top of the stairs. 'Goodbye, then,' I say.

'It was good to see you again, Claire.'

'Under those circumstances?' I give a short laugh. 'I could have done without it.'

'You coped brilliantly.'

'It's the hardest, loneliest road I've ever walked and I never want to go there again.' There's a crack in my voice and he steps forward to give me a hug. I hold out my hand to keep him away from me. 'See you around.'

He briefly clasps my hand, then lets it go and shifts from one foot to the other. 'Don't be a stranger.' He starts off down the stairs and glances back up at me, our eyes meeting for a few brief seconds, confirming that what was there between us is still there. And I suppose it always will be, but I am happy to bury it underneath the layers of love and commitment that I want to give to my family.

I walk back along the corridor and into Julian's side room. I see at once that he's in a black mood. Unlike the old Julian, he now has fits of temper when he throws his walking stick or a book across the room, not to hit me, but to make a point. And then glares at me as if he hates me, as if it's my fault that he's in this hospital bed. I don't retaliate, but still it hurts me to be the butt of his anger.

He's sitting on a chair at the side of his bed and I sit down opposite him. A wounded silence separates us. 'Julian' – I lean my elbows on my knees and look up into his face – 'I love you. I'm so glad that you're alive. I can only imagine how hard this is for you.'

'Do you blame me?' he blurts out.

I take his hand. 'For what?'

'For Bea. For Megan.'

'No!' I almost laugh. 'I thought you blamed me!'

'I should have listened to you.' There's a sadness in his eyes that makes my breath catch in my throat. He looks defeated, beaten down by force of circumstance.

'I didn't see that coming, Julian.' I stroke the side of his face. 'I didn't clock Megan. Nobody did.'

I tell him then about my own feelings of guilt. I tell him the whole story of those intense few days: how I took matters into my own hands, went behind his back, went to see Mac. He holds my hands and listens and I can see that he doesn't blame me.

'The responsibility was mine,' he says. 'I don't trust myself. I don't trust my . . .' He gropes for the word. ' . . . law . . . article . . .'

'Judgement?'

He nods. 'I'm no good.'

'Never say that.' I put my arms round him. 'It isn't true. You must never, never say that.'

We both cry. We hug each other, and for the first time in weeks I know I'm going to get him back. Maybe he'll never be able to walk long distances and there will always be occasions when he can't find the right word, but the essence of him, the man that I love, is coming back and I thank everyone – the angels, the gods, the sun, moon and stars – for this blessing.

He's been in the hospital for ten weeks and finally the day arrives when he's well enough to come home.

'I have to warn you that the children have organised a small party,' I say, as we pull up outside the front door.

I'm about to get out when he stops me. 'Claire?'

'Yes?' I twist round in my seat to face him.

'About Mac.' He pauses. 'I always wondered whether he might have been the one.'

For a moment I can't speak. Of course. Of course he knew that it was Mac I slept with. He knew and he said nothing, because to acknowledge the possibility might have jeopardised the smooth running of the case. While I was spewing out every doubt, every suspicion about him and Megan, he kept this to himself, focusing instead on what was important. It makes me feel humbled. 'You, Julian.' I take his hand and look deep into his eyes, hoping he can read the sincerity in mine. 'You're the one.'

'Are you sure?'

'A hundred and ten per cent.' I smile slowly and then kiss him. 'Now, come on. They're waiting.'

He uses his stick to help him up the steps and we go inside. Bea is waiting just inside the door, carrying her new puppy. 'This is Puppy.' She passes the ball of white fluff to Julian. Small enough to sit on the palm of his hand, the puppy's tail wags round in circles like the propeller on an aeroplane.

Julian laughs. 'So what are you calling him, Bea?'

'Puppy.'

'Doesn't he need a proper name?'

'Miss Percival says I can take a few weeks to decide.'

'He's lively as a bag of eels, I know that much,' Jem says, walking through from the kitchen. She puts her hand on Julian's back. 'Great to have you home.' And then she gives me a surreptitious thumbs-up.

'Let's go and sit down in the garden,' I say.

Bea claps her hand over her mouth and makes wide eyes at me. I put my finger over my lips and we follow Julian through to the back. He sees it from the kitchen window.

'What on earth?' He turns to look at me, his eyes shining. A cloth banner – 'Welcome home, Daddy!' painted in red and gold - is hanging in front of a brand-new purpose-built wooden summerhouse, equipped with running water and electricity and with a comfy chair for Julian to rest on.

'They've been working hard,' I say. 'Go and have a look.'

Jem on one side and Bea on the other, he goes down the back steps into the garden. Lisa, Mary and the boys are standing outside, smiling widely, and I watch them take Julian by the arm and show him around.

I've waited a long time for this moment, ten weeks of hope and hard work, and my chest swells with love and with relief that we're all back together again. But nothing in life is certain and I feel like from now on I'll always be on my guard. So that next time I'll see the danger coming.

I'll see it and I'll be prepared.

JULIE CORBIN

Tell Me No Secrets

They say that everybody has a secret. Mine lies underground. Her name was Rose and she was nine years old when she died . . .

Grace lives in a quiet, Scottish fishing village – the perfect place for bringing up her twin girls with her loving husband Paul. Life is good.

Until a phone call from her old best-friend, a woman Grace hasn't seen since her teens – and for good reason – threatens to destroy everything. Caught up in a manipulative and spiteful game that turns into an obsession, Grace is about to realise that some secrets can't stay buried forever.

For if Orla reveals what happened on that camping trip twenty-four years ago, she will take away all that Grace holds dear . . .

'This is Corbin's first novel and it's an absolute corker. She weaves this tale of tragedy and secrecy with flair and pulls you into Grace's distress with deft strokes. This book will creep under your skin and have you thinking about it in the small hours. You won't want to put it down.' – *News of the World*

HODDER